THE EDEN SEED

(Book 1 of the Seraphim Series)

DAMIAN PECK

Published by Gallus Press
www.olidapublishing.com

First printing: July 2014
Copyright (c) 2007 and 2014 - Damian Peck
All rights reserved.

Printed in the United Kingdom

Cover Design: Jeremy Robinson and Joe Murdoch

Trade Paperback – format - ISBN: 978-1-907354-45-8

To Tiny

ACKNOWLEDGEMENTS

For their input at the early stages: John and Katrina who proffered their thoughts, unhindered by any sense of diplomacy. To Allyson, for being my virgin tester and offering her encouragement.

To Sara and Billy - who gave it a once over.

To the nuns, monks, priests and priestesses who got me interested in the tapestry of the unknown.

To my family - for their tolerance.

To Traci, somewhere in deepest Arizona - for your patience.

To Kirsty Noble - for her edits in 2013.

BEFORE HE BEGAN, Matt Malcolm glanced up at the people that lined the plush boardroom table. The European Chief Justice sat opposite three of the most powerful company Chief Executive Officers in the world. Hemmed in by a mixture of statisticians, economists and high-power lawyers, her elbows had slipped off the arm rests of her chair.

Matt stood up and took a sip of water. As Product Manager for the world's first cancer vaccine, he was centre stage. What he was about to say, and how he said it, would decide his fate in more ways than one.

He noticed his reflection in the glass door to the rear of the meeting room and slackened his tie. Still convinced he looked like a dishevelled schoolboy, he adjusted his black-rimmed glasses and pressed F7 on his laptop.

The data projector sprang to life and he read out the following quote: "Lamech had lived a hundred and eighty-two years. He became the father of a son, and called him Noah, saying - Out of the ground which the LORD has cursed this one shall bring us relief from our work and from the toil of our hands."

Matt stopped and studied the faces that stared incredulously at the screen. Enjoying every second of their confusion, he smiled and continued, "Lamech lived after the birth of Noah five hundred and ninety five years, and had other sons and daughters. Thus, all the days of Lamech were seven hundred and seventy-seven years, and he died."

Matt walked down one side of the table and stood behind Jessica Baron, the European Chief Justice. He produced a small laser pointer and circled the number seven hundred and seventy-seven. As the murmurs began to build, he walked back to his seat and clicked to the next slide. "After Noah was five hundred years old, he became the father of Shem, Ham and Japheth... and then went on to live another four hundred and fifty years." Matt looked along the table towards the statistician. "That's a lifespan of nine hundred and fifty years. Admittedly, the average fell two or three hundred years after the flood, but they lived a great deal longer than the seventy-five year average of today."

Ted Burrows, the man from Milwaukee and CEO of Meldan Industries, the number one company in heart management, tapped his fingers on the table. "Genesis, Chapter 5, verses 28 - 32. Probably written around 600 B.C."

Next to him, Shoji Ueshima gave a curt nod and sniffed. "I hope I've not come half way round the world for a bible class, Mr. Malcolm." He ran Gaijin

Pacific, by far the biggest producer of antibiotics in the world. "I thought we were here to listen to the merits of your new cancer vaccine."

"I'm afraid not," said Matt.

There was a long, awkward pause before Matt continued in a more sinister tone. "As you know, the company we represent, Vectan-Brosman, is the world leader in vaccines, so between us we would have a lot to lose if, for example, death and disease were suddenly not as big a problem as they used to be."

Chief Justice Baron looked up, her blonde hair electric in the dim beam of the solitary halogen. "What's this all about, Mr. Malcolm?"

"Your Honour, this is all about confidence. It's all about balance." Matt smiled at the Chief Justice then turned to address Ueshima and Burrows. "This meeting is all about the very existence of both your companies."

Matt sensed the tension building and checked the Vectan-Brosman contingent for any reaction. The majority were either staring blankly at the ceiling or fiddling needlessly with their notes. Sir John, alone, remained unmoved.

In the momentary silence he saw Miss Baron drop some ice into her water. He heard it snap.

Burrows thumped the table. He ignored Matt and addressed Sir John James. "John, are you trying to stage-manage some kind of takeover, or what? You'd better come out with it!"

Sir John tapped the polished table with the rubber end of his pencil. His skin was like parchment and he had the cold, marble eyes of an executioner. He took on the tone of a father chastising a child, and said, "Let Mr. Malcolm finish, Ted."

Taking his cue, Matt moved round the table until he stood behind a tall, shy-looking man sporting a thick, silver moustache. "I'm sure you all know Dr. Lucius Schlesinger. Well, while he was working on his usual variety of material he found something that had an incredible effect on our laboratory animals. The substance boosted the immune systems of the animals to such a level that, so far, we have been unable to infect them with bacteria, viruses or cancer cells." Matt edged round and looked down at the professor. "Lucius?"

Lucius gave a curt nod before refocusing.

Ted Burrows took a quick sip of water and watched as the professor opened his mouth to speak. He had a thick Swiss-German accent. "So far, we have only been able to measure the lifespan of fruit flies and mice, but both have lived more than ten times longer than the controls."

Matt toyed with the bristles on his chin as the old man cleared his throat and removed two folders from his briefcase. "Matt is correct. We cannot make these specimens ill, no matter how we introduce the pathogens: orally, by injection-"

"They will be able to read the data for themselves later, Lucius," said Matt, interrupting the doctor after receiving a particularly deadly glare from his line manager, Barclay.

"Yes, of course." Oblivious to the fact that he'd said a little too much, Lucius smiled demurely and sat down.

Matt addressed Burrows and Ueshima. "Rather than launch, let's call it Product X, and take you both out of the industry forever," Matt watched the company lawyers bristle, "we thought we'd invite you to join us in maintaining the status quo. The consequences of launching such a product to the general public would be..." Matt stretched out the moment by taking another sip of his water, "...extremely disruptive."

The room had become stuffy. The air was thin. Matt moved over to the small dial that controlled the temperature. He turned it up a notch.

"What is this Product X?" hissed Ueshima.

Sir John spoke. "It would be unprofessional to divulge its composition at this point, but Matt will explain how we intended to advertise."

Matt watched as his audience loosened their ties and unbuttoned their expensive suits. He felt a particular satisfaction with his positioning of Justice Baron. Bathed in the warmth of the soft halogen, she sighed impatiently and unfastened her tight-fitting jacket.

With renewed excitement, Matt feigned an American accent and slipped into the role of cinematic narrator. "The elixir of life, Manna, Star Fire, a substance thought so precious it was carried inside the Ark of the Covenant, is now available at your local pharmacy. Your grandchildren, your great-great grandchildren; all will see you in the prime of your life. Live for a thousand years, disease free!" Matt bellowed the last part, revelling in the theatrics of the marketeer.

Ueshima feigned indifference. "That wasn't very scientific, Mr. Malcolm."

Sir John interjected. "I agree. We've always thought Matt much more suited to the commodity market. This new discovery, however, could be sold in such a way if that's what we really wanted."

Matt saw Sir John glance over at Barclay, the calculating American he'd just promoted to Business Head of Vaccines. He was Matt's immediate boss but completely different in his approach to business. Barclay was the ultimate analyst, calculating, overcautious, whereas Matt liked to think he was the archetypal expressive: a flamboyant and refreshing risk-taker who challenged the stiff wheels of the pharmaceutical machine. Barclay and Matt constantly clashed over ethics and advertising. Matt knew that Sir John had put them together on purpose. The old man liked to mix it up.

Jessica Baron, looking very uncomfortable, addressed the Vectan-Brosman contingent. "Why haven't you just released the product to the marketplace? If it's as good as you say, you have a moral duty-"

She was interrupted mid-flow as the projector hummed into life again.

"Sorry, your Honour, but I'd like our economist to say a few words at this point." Matt invited the smug-looking man with the underdeveloped goatee to comment on the graph that now filled the screen.

"Good-day. Professor Rod Millar. Economics, Harvard." He spoke with a southern drawl and used the word 'Harvard' as a kind of trump card, expecting immediate respect. "Apart from the demise of the pharmaceutical industry, which accounts for more than eight percent of the global economy, there would be knock-on effects for the medical professions, pension companies, insurance firms... the world's financial systems, as we know them, would simply collapse."

Next to him, a thin, chinless statistician with the dented posture of a weasel, joined in. "The global population would rise exponentially and..." he pointed to the graph and continued in his high voice, "with food and fuel soon becoming limiting factors, the only options would be conflict or rationing of the Vectan-Brosman product." He cleared his throat. "Which, in turn, could also lead to further mass aggression."

Matt examined Jessica Baron for a reaction. "Nature is self-limiting, Miss Baron. It would be immoral to release Product X to the marketplace at this point in time. However," he returned his gaze to Burrows and Ueshima, "as the patent holders, we have decided to restrain ourselves for a nominal contribution."

Burrows shook his head and thumped the table even harder this time. "I knew it, you son-of-a-bitch..."

Sensing litigation, the company lawyers opened their briefcases.

Her face flushing, Jessica Barron traced a slightly shaky finger over her right eyebrow.

Matt raised his voice over the growing din and said, "We will sit on this wonder-product for another ten years until we work out the finer details of roll-out. It will only cost you one hundred million U.S. dollars per month... each." The word 'each' ricocheted round the room like a lose bullet. This was followed by an awkward silence. A stifling, unbearable, silence that almost dripped with tension.

Matt knew it was time to keep his mouth shut. The longer the silence, the greater the pressure.

Unable to hold his position, it was the Vectan-Brosman lawyer who made the first move. He handed out the prepared agreements, one to the puce-faced man from Milwaukee and another to Mr. Ueshima who was still frozen in a state of apoplexy.

Matt had never seen a face as red as the one Ted Burrows had at that moment. "How... how dare you think that we would listen to such a heap of crap!"

Solemn-faced, Matt held his ground.

"One," continued Burrows, "there is no proof that you even have such a product, and two; even if you have, this is nothing short of blackmail!" He pointed across the table at Jessica Baron. "And you have the audacity to pull this stunt in front of the European Chief Justice."

Ted Burrows stood up to leave but Barclay, Sir John and their lawyer sat tight. Lucius Schlesinger, sweating and shifting nervously, also made to stand up.

Matt cupped his shoulder and gently pushed him back down into his seat.

As they gathered up their things, the Vectan-Brosman lawyer addressed Ueshima and Burrows in the most boring of monotone voices. "We have already sent copies of the agreements and some of the trial data to your respective head offices..."

But the two CEOs and their lawyers were already marching out of the room.

Ueshima spat out a parting volley. "I will see you in court! Good-day!"

The glass doors of the boardroom swung shut and the Vectan-Brosman lawyer, suddenly superfluous, fell silent.

Matt turned to face Jessica Baron. She was flustering in an effort to close her bag. She stopped struggling and looked straight into his eyes. "How dare you! How dare you bring me here under false pretences, Mr. Malcolm. 'The European Pharmaceutical Overview', that's what you said!"

"I think you've caught your skirt in the strap," said Matt, peering over the table.

In the rush to escape her predicament, Jessica had snagged her skirt, revealing a good six inches of her nylon-covered thigh.

Matt moved round and made to unhitch the material.

"Don't touch me!" Her full lips quivered.

He backed off and raised his hands in surrender, but it was too late. He'd felt the warmth of her body, tasted her flowery perfume.

She jerked her skirt free, almost ripping the pressed cotton hem before striding out through the doors into the bright corridor beyond.

Matt could still hear still the moans and curses of disgruntled executives in the distance. He sighed and then turned to face his mentors. "We expected that, didn't we?"

"We did," said Sir John.

Three weeks later, two hundred million U.S. dollars was deposited into a special Vectan-Brosman account.

2

SIX MONTHS LATER, on the top floor of the Brosman Building, Matt and Barclay eyed each other for the first time that day. Matt, the younger of the two, positioned himself behind his dark, veneered desk and stared down at the wedge of printed e-mails clutched in his manager's left hand.

Having an idea of what was coming next, he slunk down into his chair and flashed a nervous smile. He swung his computer screen into position, as a barrier between himself and the big American.

Barclay immediately swung the screen out of his way and moved in.

Wide-eyed, Matt nodded towards the print outs. "Shareholders?"

"For once, you're right on the fuckin' money," growled Barclay. Four hundred and twenty, and still counting... They want my head on a platter, although a good number of them say I hired the wrong Product Manager."

Matt, unnerved by the early morning coverage they'd received on breakfast TV, had made a special effort to get in early. He'd had a stressful day, waiting for the moment when his boss would return from the executive leadership meeting on the top floor.

Barclay repeated the news flash he'd heard earlier on the T.V. "Vectan-Brosman's Leukivec – the world's first cancer vaccine has been withdrawn over safety concerns."

Matt took his glasses off and began wiping them with a small lens cloth.

Barclay continued, "You may have pulled off your little stunt in Munich with Burrows and Ueshima, got yourself a little 'money in the bank' with Sir John, but the shareholders don't know about that one."

"Of course they don't. Product X, the Seed, is top secret." Matt felt a stab of paranoia. Had he been set up?

"Product X isn't the issue, it's Leukivec that's on the world radar."

"But all that extra money coming in since Munich must mean something," said Matt.

"It means fuck all, zilch. Finance have got it wrapped up in so much shit that it's going to stay buried for years."

"All I'm trying to say is that Product X must act as some kind of buffer in times like these," protested Matt.

"You're not listening," said Barclay. "Right now we need our legitimate products to perform. I've just been in to see Sir John, and he says the share price is down fifteen percent!" Barclay formed a sardonic smile before spilling the pile of e-mails onto Matt's desk.

"How is this my fault?" said Matt.

Barclay turned away and strolled over to the large window that framed the city below.

Tapping his chubby fingers on the triple glazing, Barclay began mumbling to himself. "Sir John had to insist on a fucking marketeer this time."

"It's a marketing job," said Matt, "you've been through four product managers in two years, each one a highly qualified doctor or pharmacist, but none of them pushy enough.

"Any one of them would have checked the field data better than you."

"What?" blurted Matt, "that's a regulatory problem! Go and shout at one of them. If the FDA spotted a problem with the cancer vaccine it's not my fault."

"Your accountability is shit, son."

Matt's mind flickered back to the long list of company values and behaviours.

"I was raised in Sol, Massachusetts," drawled Burrows, still facing the window. "I studied Chemistry in Boston and then worked my way around the world for twenty-four years before getting this job. I've grafted for it." He spun round to face Matt, pointing. "You, on the other hand, have been fast-tracked."

Matt opened his hands in placation.

"I hate it when kids like you are given the big short cut. I mean, a sales rep for three years, a stint at marketing, then Global Product Manager. Lady Luck gave you the cancer vaccine and now you've managed to fuck it up."

Matt knew that Barclay considered him arrogant and rash. He watched the big man's cold eyes narrow as he moved closer.

"There's a good chance that the Federal Drug Administration are going to completely pull Leukivec for good."

"But that's got nothing to do with me."

"Really? Don't you think it might have something to do with the makeup of the board of the FDA these days?"

Matt knew that Ted Burrows had been voted on. "Look, you told me to make that pitch in Munich. You…"

"I knew it was a mistake to make enemies like Burrows and Ueshima," whispered Barclay.

"Have they stopped the payments?" Matt hoped they hadn't.

"Not yet, but Sir John's just informed me that things have become a little more complicated."

Matt couldn't see how anything could be worse than the demise of his vaccine and a potential suspension of the payments he'd arranged in Munich.

"There's a problem with The Seed Project," said Barclay.

Matt knew they were at a key stage. "The crop?" he asked.

"It's been destroyed, along with the reserves and the gene bank," snapped Barclay.

"You mean you kept all the sources in one place? But no one knew where the crop was being cultivated!" Matt couldn't believe anyone in Vectan-Brosman would have leaked the information. "There was top security on the Seed project. Only four people knew the production timelines."

"It was supposed to be four," said Barclay. "Sir John, Dr. Schlesinger, you and myself."

"Are you saying someone else knew?" asked Matt,, "What about the people in Spain?"

"The farmers at the site didn't even know they were growing the stuff. They were told it was genetically modified linseed." Barclay lifted something from his in-tray and walked back over to Matt's desk. "Listen Matt, I've had a long chat with Sir John and we've come up with a proposal."

Sweat caused Matt's glasses to slip down his nose. He pushed them back into place.

Barclay's voice deepened, "We need time to investigate the situation and..." pausing, he peered distractedly behind Matt into the marketing department, "...the shareholders will need a sacrifice for this Leukivec business."

Matt didn't like the sound of this.

Barclay placed a headed sheet of paper on Matt's desk and spun it round. "We'd like you to sign this."

"Sign what?" Matt caught the smell of garlic on Barclay's breath. A hint of cheap vodka and stale cigars infused the stench as his boss moved in closer. "It's time to take a trip, Matt."

"What kind of trip?" said Matt.

"A trip where nothing can be traced back to Vectan-Brosman. You will be completely on your own," said Barclay.

"You're losing me here," complained Matt.

"You're suspended on full pay, but as far as the rest of the planet is concerned, you're fired. Clear?"

Matt stood up and looked down at the headed paper. "What the..?"

Barclay pushed on without allowing Matt to re-join the conversation. "Sacking a high profile executive like you might just salvage five or ten percent of the share price, boost confidence a little while we step up the pressure on the FDA." Barclay produced a heavy gold pen from the inside pocket of his Armani jacket. "Sign it, Matt."

Matt's mouth went dry. "I don't think-"

"That's right. Don't think; just do it," interrupted Barclay. "We need a fall guy, Matt." He produced a tight-lipped smile.

Matt felt the back of his neck flush hot.

"You see, Mr. fast-track, failure to sign this piece of paper is not an option."

"Are you out of your mind?" gasped Matt.

Barclay slipped into a conspiratorial whisper, "You're getting it all wrong. Don't let the fact that I'm enjoying this cloud the main issue. You see, we need someone within the four, someone who knows all the players, the product, and, of course, the dire consequences, should some other party acquire any remaining information on The Seed Project. In short, we need you to investigate this whole fuckin' fiasco."

Matt knew Barclay was keeping something else back. "What else is going on, Barclay?"

Barclay heaved a reluctant sigh before he said, "Schlesinger has disappeared."

"I want to see Sir John," said Matt, dreading to think what Barclay might have meant by the word 'disappeared'.

Barclay ignored the request. "Yeah, that's right Matt; your buddy, Dr. Lucius Schlesinger, PhD, has done a runner, no doubt with a few samples of the Seed and all the paperwork that goes with it. Who'd have thought that the doctor would have been the first of us to get greedy?"

Matt knew Lucius Schlesinger would never knowingly betray them. "That's crazy; besides, some of the crop must have survived."

"The people who destroyed the crop used sulphuric acid," snapped Barclay, "The same spray they use to burn back diseased potato crops."

"I used to work in the agri-"

"-chemical business," interrupted Barclay. "I know you did. So, you'll understand that there will be no trace of the crop. Nothing we can use."

A vein above Matt's temple started to flick and pulse at random. "What do you expect me to do? I'm not an investigator. Besides, there must be other Seeds we can cultivate."

"We'd like to think so, but by the looks of things, our invisible man, Schlesinger, has been extremely thorough."

Barclay's mobile vibrated. He glanced down at the screen before turning it off.

"Look Matt, you can always walk away from the whole situation, regard this as your final payment." Barclay slipped a manila envelope across the desk. "Take this small amount as official severance pay. We won't emphasize your lack of attention to detail too much. And we know you would never spill on The Seed

Project, as your pension would definitely suffer." Barclay smiled, enjoying the threat.

"My pension?" said Matt, a black wave of paranoia washing over him.

"On the other hand, you can use this money to cover any initial expenses. As I've said already, there can be no transactions traceable to the company." Barclay slid the envelope to the side, once more revealing the company annulment decree.

"I'm sorry, but there's no way on Earth I'm signing that." Matt slipped back into a stronger version of Glaswegian that was normally reserved for close friends and family.

"You called the meeting in Munich, Matt," said Barclay, impatiently. "Admittedly, you may have pissed off Burrows, caused him to highlight problems to the FDA, but without the Seed we have no bargaining chips. The Seed is much more important than any cancer drug."

Matt was still annoyed by his boss's previous threats.

Barclay looked him straight in the eye. "You discovered the original sample of the Seed."

"But it was a mistake and..." Matt hesitated.

"You jeopardised six years of analysis with your schoolboy prank, but I guess you still found it. That's why you were one of the 'four'".

Matt flushed. "Lucius was the one that really found it."

"Look Matt...!" Barclay glanced through the glass dividing wall at the heads turning round to see what was going on. He lightened his tone. "Either you take this fifty thousand and sign this annulment or I'll make sure that you leave in disgrace. You won't just be sacked; I'll make sure you do some time in prison like your father."

The tension he felt knotted in his stomach suddenly spread up over his chest and down his arms. His wrists burned. "Don't you dare bring my father into this."

"I'm simply trying to let you see where this could go. I'm sure I could dig out a few receipts, a few forged documents..."

"Documents that you told me to pre-date and sign off," Matt hissed. He clenched his fists beneath his desk, but he knew he was beaten.

Barclay tapped the manila envelope containing the money. "Take it and sign."

The money only represented a third of Matt's annual salary. "So, it's only a suspension? You'll take me back when everything dies down?"

"Look, the old man doesn't want to lose you. He knows you and Schlesinger spent a lot of time together in Zurich, became good friends, so just find Schlesinger. More importantly, you need to get another sample of the original Seed before Burrows and Ueshima find out we've nothing to threaten them with. For all we know they might both be behind this whole fuckin' thing. They might already have the Seed for themselves. They might even have Lucius. You didn't tell Lucius where you got the original sample from, did you?"

"No, never, but..."

"You never really told us either Matt, did you?" And again, without waiting for him to reply, Barclay turned away. "The fact that Burrows even dared to cause us a problem with the FDA worries me," he said, distractedly.

Matt felt the weight of Barclay's gold pen and, still in a daze, he scribbled his signature on the company annulment decree. He said no more; instead he picked up the picture of his wife and son and picked up his security pass. He'd suddenly lost the will to fight.

"Leave your pass and corporate card with Linda. She'll give you the flight tickets." Barclay pointed to their secretary outside the inner sanctum of the office.

"Tickets to where?" asked Matt, slipping the silver credit card from his wallet.

Turning away, Barclay began to gaze out at the snow-laden sky. "Go dig. Call me when you think you're onto something." said Barclay. "You're going back to Zurich to find your old friend, the one that helped you find the Seed in the first place... Get Schlesinger, and get The Seed Project back on track before it's too late!"

Matt saw Barclay turn to face the window again. His boss inadvertently tapped the mobile bulging in his pocket.

He suddenly imagined some weather-beaten cowboy testing his six-gun. And, as he stood facing the broad expanse of checked Armani jacket that covered Barclay's back, he had an overpowering urge to plunge something sharp and jagged between his boss's shoulder blades. In his mind's eye he saw the American's thick neck tense, his legs buckle... A warm stream of urine spattered his patent leather shoes as he slumped, still twitching, on the stain-resistant, nylon carpet.

Loudly, a printer clicked into life, snapping Matt out of his daydream. Then, suppressing the urge to say any more, he made for the glass door he'd come through earlier.

Forcing a smile, he paused at Linda's desk, revelling in her familiar flowery scent.

Probably in her late fifties by now, she gave him that look, the one that told him she was very tasty but not on the menu.

She always smelt so beautiful, like some virginal aunt who burned with inner lust and, in his daydreams, he had imagined, many times, what she might 'be like'.

His eyes drifted over her heavy breasts then down to the garnished rings that adorned her fingers. He'd convinced himself that each one was a reward from her lucky husband, a little thank you for years of unblemished loyalty and unrivalled sexual satisfaction. The same rings, however, also acted as a force-field, rebuffing the weak-willed and draining licentious desire from pathetic men like him.

Multi-tasking, Linda continued to type with one hand while she opened a small metal drawer with the other. "Remember and bring me back some of that nice Swiss chocolate." Her voice was husky and conspiratorial.

Matt tried to maintain his smile, but his head was still pounding. Well short of his usual bravado, he added, "with or without nuts?"

"'With, of course," she answered. Linda drew her words out and then waved him to the side. She peered at Barclay's silhouette against the weather outside. "Matt, you're not in the bad books again, are you?"

"You know I am, Linda."

She took his card and handed him his tickets before issuing two small tut-tuts.

3

EVEN IN THE SAFETY of his car Matt's mind was still a jumble of anger and regret. He'd been ill-prepared, cornered into signing his job away. He'd let himself be bullied by a brash Boston arsehole. What 'old friend' was Barclay talking about? He tried to remember what he'd said to Sir John and Barclay after the Zurich incident. And then, slowly, like treacle running out if a tin, it began to come back to him.

It wasn't always easy to remember lies. In fact, that was the main problem with them: they always seemed incredibly ingenious at the time but were usually just a random train of thought that best fitted that one given situation. It was usually a situation that needed elaboration, or an injection of excitement, but in this particular case, the one involving the museum, the incident in Zurich, the situation had called for a serious amount of untangling.

What had really happened back then was just too embarrassing. More to the point, the truth would have got Matt sacked there and then. So, he'd untangled the actual memory and tailor-made a new one instead. His new version of the truth had, he remembered, included a non-existent friend.

As he drove along the M25, he relived the lie as best he could. He'd told Barclay that a friend of his, at Zurich University, had been on a North African dig; and how, after a few drinks, the friend had shown him some artefacts: pots, urns, jars, and other bits and pieces he'd collected. All Matt had done was to borrow a sample of dried grass from the inside of one of his friend's pots and then drop this into the Vectan-Brosman lab examination tray. It had just been meant as a joke.

Thankfully, he'd never named the friend, mainly because he couldn't think of a plausible name at the time, and now Barclay was sending him back to Zurich to make contact with someone who had never existed in the first place. Actually, the real truth wasn't that far removed from the lie, so he would take the flight to Zurich and do some digging of his own.

After the destruction of the crop site in Almeria, he was probably Vectan-Brosman's only hope. He would need to examine his Munich presentation notes one more time. He'd have to check all the names of the lawyers and experts who'd attended and, now that the office was closed to him, he would have to find the file on his home computer or, perhaps, in the one other place he kept any kind of records.

On the way to his London home, he made the familiar twenty-mile detour to the village of Alescorth; to the one woman who knew the real Matt Malcolm. That is to say, she knew the vibrant, optimistic, sexy Matt, not the dull, over-tired, moody one.

As he drove, he decided that his personality probably split into three: the adventurer; the husband; and the businessman.

He had a chameleon-like trait he just couldn't control. He acted differently depending on the situation and who he was with. He changed the way he spoke and, if he had the time, even the way he dressed. If someone talked loudly, he would match his or her tone accordingly. If someone was more laid back or softly spoken, he would lower his voice to match. He did this without the person involved having the slightest clue they were being copied. The transition was flawless.

Only Jenny, his wife, saw how he slipped under other people's skin, and she mistrusted him because of it.

Sometimes Matt didn't even realise it was happening. It was probably the one biggest factor in his success. People felt comfortable when he spoke to them because he reacted in exactly the way they would have done themselves. It was only Jenny who hated this facet of his personality. She suspected a deeper kind of deceit. But there was none. That is to say, there was no dishonesty in this particular chameleon-like trait. It just happened naturally. The affair, on the other hand, was a more difficult matter.

As he pulled into the quartz-chipped drive of Brin Cottage, it was the survival of his career rather than deceit that plagued his thoughts. His work files were in the living room, but more importantly, at a time like this, there was the comfortable sanctuary of Sylvie's easy embrace to look forward to. He often wondered if all men were as pathetic as him. Most men he'd ever known had strayed at some time or other.

Long ago, he'd decided that only a saintly few could stifle their instincts and train themselves to stay monogamous. The stats around adultery, which had the Danes down as the worst nation on earth, around thirty percent, were the tip of the iceberg. He used these kinds of statistics as an excuse for his own behaviour and often thought back to the words of his father. "Always remember the eleventh commandment, son. Thou shalt not get caught!" His father was in fact referring to company embezzlement at the time, which had, unfortunately, resulted in Matt Malcolm Senior serving a three-year prison sentence in Belmarsh.

Matt clicked off the ignition and stretched out in his seat. Sylvie was so different from Jenny. She was undemanding and uncomplicated. She knew about his various affairs through the years, every nuance, every fantasy. She was his confessor and he needed her now more than ever.

Closing the door of his BMW, he pressed the 'lock' button and crunched up the drive. He could taste the frost in the air, and looking up, he glanced at the stars as they blinked through a deep, cobalt sky. Sylvie had always yearned for immortality. It was weird, but she wanted Matt to name a star after her. He'd looked into it, but it was not in the cosmos that Sylvie would find everlasting fame, it was in the microcosm. Matt had found the perfect opportunity to grant her wish.

It had turned out that in amongst the material he'd acquired from the Zurich University there were a few strangely shaped seeds. Thought to be an ancient species of linseed, they contained a small amount of bacteria in their husks. This bacterium, a type of Lanthobacter, had been completely new to modern science and Matt, because of his close friendship with Lucius Schlesinger, had possessed the necessary clout to name this new species at the very point of its discovery. He had suggested the name Lanthobacter Sylvie Imunitass. Lucius Schlesinger had asked him what the Sylvie part had referred to, so Matt had, as usual, lied exquisitely. "Sylvie was the Sumerian god of healing," he'd said. "She could bestow immortality on her followers, and as no other species of bacteria on the planet has been, or probably ever will be as miraculous at preventing disease and death as this one, it's only fitting that it should contain the goddess's name."

As his thoughts drifted back to Lucius's puzzled expression, he could suddenly smell the freshness of the frost-glazed snow. There was also a faint hint of wood-smoke filtering through the trees behind the cottage. However, as he turned to look up at Sylvie's bedroom window, he was overcome by a real sense of foreboding. He was puzzled by the lack of movement in the house. Billie-boy, her crazy Red Setter, would normally have heard his car by now and gone berserk.

Perhaps she's gone out, he thought.

Matt stepped back and peered round the side of the cottage, but the nose of Sylvie's red mini coupe still poked out from the carport. She must have taken Billie-boy for a walk, he decided. It was a beautiful evening and she'd probably gone down to the river. Matt walked up to the front door and fingered the ornate brass dragonhead. His skin stuck to the cold metal as he tapped twice. He jerked back, however, as the door swung inward.

Cautiously, he called into the stillness of the house. "Sylvie?" Stepping into the hall, he noticed a small pile of unopened mail but, as he lifted his head, he saw Billie-boy's auburn tail twitching at the end of the hallway. "Bill... Billie?" Twice, the feathered tail brushed against the kitchen floor before it stopped. Matt knew this was all wrong.

Rushing up the narrow hall, he turned into the kitchen. "What's wrong, son? Where's Sylvie?" Matt slipped on something sticky and black. A dark pool had spread out round Billie-boy. It covered the granite-tiled floor. Matt knelt down in the mess and patted the dog's smooth head. The Setter whined and tried to turn. It panted uncontrollably.

"Steady, boy. Steady."

Frantically, he scanned the rest of the kitchen for any clue as to what might have happened. Blood continued to spread round his shoes. Breathing heavily, he moved out of the gore and edged towards the living-room door. It was slightly ajar and a small table lamp threw some light onto the goatskin rug that lay at the fireplace. Matt pushed the door open another few inches and stepped inside. There, on the coffee table, he saw Sylvie's keys and Billie-boy's lead. An unfamiliar musty smell filled the house, a mixture of old books, singed hair and something else that smelt like herbs or perhaps perfume. He couldn't decide. He racked his brains for a logical explanation: an accident? A mistake of some kind? Sylvie was probably out looking for help. But then why had she left her house keys on the coffee table?

Something creaked upstairs.

Matt froze. He looked up at the old oak beams above his head and tried to remember if the cottage had creaked like this before.

He moved back towards the kitchen and saw that Billie-boy had stopped moving. Panic flooded over him and snuffed out any trace of rational thought. Again, he heard the same creaking noise as before. Someone was definitely upstairs. His own breathing sounded like an express train; every step he took sounded like some crazed giant clumping about.

It could, of course, be Sylvie moving round upstairs, and there he was, too petrified to rush up and comfort her. Reaching the bottom of the stairs, he imagined all kinds of terrors as his fingers clawed at the cold handrail. Her bedroom door was shut, but lamplight winked through the crack between the bottom of the door and the floor. It definitely winked, off then on, as if someone had moved across the light.

It flickered again.

He hesitated for an instant then, glancing about for something he might use as a weapon, he spied the old metal-tipped walking stick. It lay in its usual place, against the wall of the top landing. He snatched it up and tested its weight. It would be next to useless against a gun or more than one assailant. Besides, he wasn't really sure what he would do if he had to confront anyone. The light under the door seemed more constant. It was now or never.

His walking stick raised, Matt pushed against the bedroom door and fell inside. A heap of clothes lay strewn across the bed's candlewick cover. There were bloodstains and muddy footprints on the carpet. A delicate lace bra lay beside a solitary shoe and a pair of Sylvie's jeans. The discarded clothes glistened in the pale light.

"SYLVIE!"

Recklessly, he searched the room for any sign of her, all thoughts of an intruder or his own personal safety gone. Deep red droplets had sprayed up the wall behind the pink headrest of the bed, and more blood lay in lumpy pools on the floor.

It was then that he noticed the half-open door of the en-suite bathroom. Edging towards it, he felt his stomach tighten, and suddenly he threw up a trail of yellow bile that added to the mess on the pink Wilton carpet. Shaking uncontrollably, Matt dropped the walking stick and steadied himself on the wall. He'd just glimpsed one of her ankles. Crimson splashes laced her shins and the neighbour of the cream-coloured shoe that he'd seen on the bed hung inelegantly from her left foot. The heel had snapped off.

There was no sign of life, and as he moved closer to the door of the bathroom, his heart quickened.

As more of her body came into view, he noticed that her hands had been tied and that a towel had been thrown over her naked body in a pathetic attempt to cover her modesty.

Under the blood drenched towel there was deformity and stiffness. An eerie stillness ebbed over him and, increasingly, a darkening void filled his thoughts and pulled him towards her. No movement, no signs. Matt eased the towel from her legs. Her soft thighs were cut and bruised, and the stench of faeces and urine was overpowering. He threw the towel back down and drew away.

"Sylvie!"

He knew she was past saving, and as he staggered back, he threw up a second time. Edging out of the bedroom he half slipped, half fell down the stairs until he stumbled against the front door. Stunned, he ran out into the driveway, his breath freezing instantly in the icy air.

Matt looked round, suddenly alert to the fact that the murderer could still be close by. His heart rate quickened as he remembered the flickering light in Sylvie's bedroom. He tried, in vain, to convince himself that he'd imagined everything. His forearm ached from his collision with the front door and, as he rummaged in his pockets for his car keys, he felt another unwelcome wave of nausea. He searched again, each pocket of his coat and trousers, at least twice, but they weren't there. He must have left his keys in the house. Tears began to roll down his cheeks as he banged his fist on the car door in frustration.

A sudden rustle of paper startled him.

The bitter breeze had flicked a few unopened letters against the bottom of the stairs. The flapping of redwings and fieldfares as they danced above the cottage mirrored the random movement in the doorway. Like leaves caught in the wind, the birds fluttered erratically in the winter sky.

A car roared past the driveway and shocked him into action. He had to find his keys and get away from this place, now.

With renewed determination, he marched back in through the front door and tried not to look as he passed the still body of Billie-boy. There in the living room, to his utter relief, he saw the familiar yellow loop of his plastic key ring on the coffee table.

As he knelt down to pick them up, his gaze fell on the desk beside the window. There was no sign of his laptop, and there was a space where his two black company folders had once been, but there was one other folder he'd kept safe, even from Sylvie. He groped beneath the desk until he felt its cold, smooth cover touch his fingers. Without opening it, he tucked it under his arm and stumbled back through the living room and hall. Out in the cold night air, he took a deep breath before unlocking his car and jumping inside. He felt pathetic, hiding like a coward in his car, but it was too late. Sylvie was dead. There was nothing he could do.

Still fumbling with the ignition he thought he saw someone move upstairs.

"Shit, c'mon, come ON!" Adrenalin flooded into his cardio vascular system as he struggled with his keys.

"YES!" Matt revved the engine and slammed into reverse. Skidding recklessly out of the driveway, he spun round on the empty road and put his foot down. He felt the acceleration force him further back into the cold leather seat. Sweat ran down his neck, soaking his shirt and making him shiver. He had to call the office. He had to report this somehow. But he couldn't. There was Jenny, his wife, to consider.

Maybe it was best to leave it. Someone else could call the police. Then they would find his bloody footprints all over the place.

"Shit!" He was so damn feckless. Matt held down the number two on his mobile and waited for the ring-tone to come through the car speakers.

"Hello. It's Matt Malcolm here. Can you put me through to Linda in marketing?"

"Sorry, who?" The voice was unfamiliar.

Matt repeated the question.

"Sorry sir, I think you have the wrong number." This time the girl's voice sounded more abrupt, as if she were trying to get him off the line.

Matt glanced down at his mobile, "This is Vectan-Brosman Pharmaceuticals?" Matt spoke clearer this time, affecting his best Southeast accent. "This is Matt Malcolm. Could you please find someone...?"

The phone went dead.

4

JENNY MALCOLM STIRRED her homemade spaghetti Bolognese, cursing when the mixture bubbled red spots up her white tiles and splattered the hob.

"Peter! Your dinner's ready!" She could see him across the hall, staring at the TV, stuffing his face with spicy, chicken-tikka-flavoured crisps.

"I'm not hungry, Mum," he moaned.

She tapped her wooden spoon on the edge of the pot as she watched him force another fistful of fragments into his mouth. His eyes were glazed and his shirt was littered with crumbs. Peter was twelve, and already thirteen stone. She'd let it happen. For the last eleven years, TV had been his babysitter and his only true friend. It was more than addiction. By now, it was complete and utter dependency. He rarely strayed far from his comfortable leather chair and as a result, he was very easy to manage.

Jenny stepped through into the living room with his yellow cushion tray and placed it on his lap. She slotted a fresh can of fizzy orange into the clip that Matt had fixed to the chair and backed off.

Peter smelt the Bolognese sauce. "Thanks Mum, but I'm not hungry; not for that."

"Look!" Jenny interrupted. "Don't you make my life any harder than it already is! Just leave it there until you're ready for it."

"Okay, mum," said Peter, not once taking his eyes off the screen.

As the Bolognese congealed on his knee, Jenny Malcolm pulled a green Tupperware bowl from the top shelf of a tall kitchen unit and began preparing Matt's favourite salad. Olive oil, lime juice and soya sauce were drizzled over a pile of thinly sliced carrot and cucumber squares. But as she kneaded the mixture in a trance-like state, a tear dripped from her eye into the bowl.

She knew everything now; Matt's other life had revealed itself to her. As if by magic, his affair had suddenly appeared in front of her very eyes.

Jenny knew that the morning news and call from his boss had unnerved Matt. He'd disappeared, without saying goodbye, around 7.30 that morning.

There was no such thing as a decent good bye from Matt, no real love in the marriage. She'd thought as much for years, and now she had inadvertently stumbled upon the evidence that confirmed it.

Not long after lunch, she'd picked up the polish and worked her way round the living room, along the hall, and finally into Matt's office. She'd hardly noticed the computer in the corner, but as she'd polished his desk, her cloth had brushed against the mouse. It was only then that the screen had come alive. Jenny had flinched back, but then she'd been drawn, like a moth to a flame, closer to the words that now burned so brightly before her eyes: 'See you as soon as I possibly can. Love, Matt. xx.'

It was addressed to someone called Sylvie. This was no office e-mail, it was written in a completely different style, not the usual Vectan-Brosman crap. It was light-hearted and sensual. Matt was telling someone called Sylvie how much he wanted her and, worse than that, how much he'd enjoyed her.

"God!" Jenny sniffed and then banged her hand down onto the worktop. The pain brought her a few moments of relief from the waking nightmare. But then the rage and hate and sorrow and emptiness gripped her again. Her life had changed for good and nothing could bring her old, safe, boring one back again.

As she wallowed in self-pity, she began to remember something from her childhood. Seven or eight at the time, she'd met a little boy who'd lost his sight. She recalled the sadness she'd felt when he'd told her about his dreams. The colours, the people, the trees, everything just as it had been before his accident. But then, every morning, as he opened his eyes, he had to deal with the reality of perpetual darkness.

She sniffed back another tear, suddenly longing for blissful ignorance. She couldn't bear the thought of waking up every morning, day after day, knowing Matt's affair was real, that her life was a sham.

She tried to put her predicament into perspective but it proved impossible. She yelled out, "Why?"

Peter's voice filtered through into the kitchen. "Mum, are you okay?"

"Fine son. Fine." Jenny stabbed the knife into the wooden chopping board and emptied the salad into the bin. Her mind was cluttered with his sensual phrases and warm, tender promises. The kind of words she'd dreamed of getting from Matt all her dreary life, but never did.

She shook as resentment grew inside her, gripping the worktop until her knuckles turned white, she yelled out even louder this time, "Bastard!"

"Mum?" Jenny thought she'd heard Peter's voice, but a strange darkness was closing in on her. It bit into her and spread outwards from her heart. The sensation made her feel weak and confused, but she was determined, determined to push on with normality as long as she could.

One of the lines from the last e-mail she'd read still rattled round in her head: Only when I'm with you, Sylvie, do I feel totally complete, totally free and fulfilled...

How can he be so passionate and romantic with her?

That one line annoyed her more than any other.

She'd become the drudge, the steady, boring constant that let Matt experiment elsewhere. Only her own hunger for pain had made her read every single word. Two years of e-mails all saved in cyberspace forever. Distracted by his bloody 'Leukivec' yet again, the selfish bastard had rushed out of the house without realising he'd left his other life there for her to see.

The lid of the stainless steel bin clattered against the old kitchen tiles as she picked several chunks of cucumber and carrot from the edge of the plastic bin-liner and, once more, arranged them neatly on a green-edged china plate. Jenny did this, not out of revenge or any kind of malice; she'd simply switched over to automatic pilot.

She placed the plate on the pine kitchen table and set the knife and fork neatly on either side. She opened the fridge, lifted out a bottle of Premier Cru Chablis and found the chorizo sausage she'd bought especially for Matt the day before. But as she turned back towards the kitchen table, her legs gave way and she flopped down onto the floor, sobbing uncontrollably. The light thrown from the fridge washed over her as her tears splashed onto the linoleum. She felt completely helpless.

"Mum?" Peter's voice drifted in from the TV lounge, but it was immediately drowned out by a barrage of yells and gunfire.

The phone rang.

"Mum, it's the phone!"

She hoped it would stop.

"Mum, I said it's the phone..."

"I know it's the bloody phone." Jenny could barely lift her head.

"Mum?" Peter was standing in the kitchen doorway.

Sighing heavily, she squinted up at him.

"Mum, what's wrong?"

The phone continued to ring.

Peter pointed over to the phone on the wall. "Are you sure you don't want me to answer it?"

"I don't bloody care," snapped Jenny, wiping her eyes with the hem of her skirt.

Peter stopped halfway across the kitchen his face full of concern.

She reached for his hand. "I'm sorry, son. It's just that..." She hesitated. "It's just that it's not been a good day. Not the best day I've ever had." She tried to pull herself together; to get back into the role of mother and protector.

"I'll stop watching so much TV. I'm sorry for not helping you and..." Peter babbled.

"It's not that. Well, not just that." Jenny sniffed. "It's..."

She didn't know if she should tell him about Matt. It would be selfish but...

Still, the phone burred loudly.

Jenny let go of her son's hand and the moment passed. They had never been so close. Nervously, she itched at her scalp and lifted the receiver, "Yes?"

She hoped it wasn't him, not Matt, not just yet. She wasn't prepared for his voice.

"Inspector Wills speaking, madam."

Jenny felt like a little child as she listened. It was almost surreal. She felt detached, as if she was watching someone else in a movie.

"Is Mr. Malcolm there at the moment, madam?" "N... no." Jenny's voice wavered.

"I take it you're Mrs. Malcolm?" The voice was serious and yet sympathetic.

"That's correct." Jenny involuntary fixed her hair.

"Well, Mr. Malcolm's car has been found abandoned on the verge of the A547, near to the village of Alescorth. It's hit a tree but there's no sign of your husband. I don't suppose he's contacted you?"

"Hit a tree, you said?" A sudden feeling of exhilaration made her feel ashamed. Jenny's head reeled as she tried to put two and two together. He'd been with Sylvie again, she thought. Why else would he have taken that particular road? The sordid accounts of Matt's philandering in Alescorth and Brin Cottage were now etched into her mind forever.

Inspector Wills continued. "We assume he's unhurt, but if he's left the scene of an accident... well, it's quite a serious offence. And there is the matter of the car..." Inspector Wills changed tack. "Has he been acting strangely or...?"

"Very!" Jenny was transfixed. Her gaze had settled on a little holiday snap she'd pinned to the fridge a few months before. It showed Peter as a baby, his face covered in ice cream, and there, holding him in his arms, was Matt, beaming out of the picture at her. The snap had been taken in Spain almost ten years ago and, as she moved closer, she screwed up her face in an attempt to look into Matt's eyes. Had he been with someone else back then too? Was this and every other family memory a lie?

"He has?" the inspector's voice made her jump and a fresh flush of tears blurred the seaside snap until it turned into a series of Monet-like splashes. Pent-up anger boiled somewhere deep in her chest.

"Look, why don't you try Brin Cottage? He seems to prefer it there!" Jenny slammed the phone down and slumped back onto the floor.

She could see that Peter was struggling to make sense of the situation; his chubby, freckled arms gathered her in once more. She shuddered with grief, oblivious to the little crunching noises caused by the countless fragments of chicken tikka crisps that littered the folds of his shirt.

5

MATT WAS STARING down at his mobile in disbelief when the rear wheels of his BMW spun recklessly on the black ice. Trees and sky alternated for a few seconds before he heard the crunch of steel and felt the jolt of the airbag. He lay sprawled between the two front seats, pushed to his left by the thick trunk of a dead elm. The A547 was deserted and the only disruption other than the crash itself was the incessant racket caused by a large flock of rooks that now flapped and circled back towards their roost.

Matt groped for his mobile then eased himself out of the passenger door. Panting with exertion, he felt the icy evening air on his face and saw his breath trace skyward.

In the same moment, his mind flashed back to the vision of Sylvie's bruised and bloodied legs. He remembered the way they'd appeared to him, twisted and broken, as if some creature had picked her up and then smashed her, callously, to the floor. He also felt a tinge of guilt, the same guilt he'd felt when his courage had failed him so badly in her bedroom. Too scared to look at her face, he'd left the blood-stained towel where it had lain.

Stepping out onto the hardening grass verge, he reached back into the car for the clear folder and checked his left inside pocket. It was still there, bulging and reassuring, the manila envelope that Barclay had given him. His manager's final blast of rage still rattled round in his head, "Find Schlesinger, and get The Seed Project back on track before it's too late!"

Had one of their rivals already found out about The Seed Project? Was Sylvie killed because of it? Matt's head was pounding. Whoever had taken his laptop and folders had known what they'd been looking for. Confused, he began to wander down the road in the opposite direction to Brin Cottage.

A few hundred yards from what was left of his car, he pulled his jacket collar up against the cold and turned to look ahead towards the busy A1 in the distance. Then, less than a mile away, he saw the headlights of a car flashing round the cambers and corners of the distant stretch of road that lead to his position. He glanced back at his abandoned car. Again, not particularly sure why, he endured another wave of dread. It mirrored the trepidation he'd felt back at Brin Cottage. A rush of adrenalin sharpened his senses as he slipped through a half-opened farm gate. He hunkered down behind a hawthorn hedge and waited.

Passing his hiding place at high speed, the car slowed as it reached the buckled wreck of his BMW. It screeched to a halt. A tall man stepped out of a dark-coloured Audi TT and peered inside his car. A second man arrived on the scene. Matt wasn't sure whether he'd come out of the car or the woods. The two men seemed to be arguing.

Although they were over two hundred yards away, he could see that one of them, the taller of the two, had long dark hair; while the other, a good deal thinner and smaller, wore a padded, green jacket that looked too big for him.

He has a gun. Jesus! Matt crouched down further, holding his breath lest any tell-tale blast of warm air escaped from his lips.

He chanced another look. The smaller man wore a black, woollen balaclava. With his gun pointed at Matt's driver-side window, the younger man opened the door and peered into the car. Turning to face the man with the long hair, he cursed and then thumped his gun down hard on the roof of Matt's BMW. They seemed to argue for a few seconds before the older man pointed to the grass verge that ran along the roadside. Matt shrank back. The taller man pointed straight at him.

Matt realised that his footprints would be easily visible in the frosted grass. He had to move fast. Had they murdered Sylvie? There was no time to dwell on the various possibilities. He had to hide.

Unable to escape over the road, he would have to go across the field behind him. Newly ploughed and solid with frost, it was edged by a rank of tall beeches that loomed over him as he ran.

Already wheezing, he soon realised how unfit he'd become. Years of dining on the rich cuisine of Michelin star restaurants had taken its toll.

He was almost at the line of beeches when he tripped and sprawled headlong over the rough ground. His elbows shuddered on the unforgiving earth as he rolled into one of the shallow furrows. Just at the same moment, he spied the younger of the two pursuers step into the field. Pain searing through his arms and chest, Matt flattened against the cold earth and drew his legs into his stomach in a foetal position. He hoped that he'd covered enough ground to stay hidden, masked by the early dusk. He lay still for a moment and then chanced a look over the shallow bank of earth.

At the gate, the long-haired man stooped down and examined the patch of ground directly behind the hedge where Matt had taken cover. The smaller one scanned the field until his gaze eventually fixed on the tall beeches behind Matt.

In a slow and purposeful movement, the older man stood up, pointing over the ploughed ground. He nodded, and yelled out, "There!"

His finger wavered in the direction of a small cottage at the far end of the field where a wisp of smoke seeped skyward and a small light signalled some life.

"I'll drive round," said the taller man, "you walk through the field and check for any signs."

Matt couldn't hear the smaller man too well, but it was obvious by his gestures that he was complaining about something.

The older man ruffled his hair and then waved his younger accomplice away.

Matt lay incredibly still and prayed to God that some cloud would cover the ever-brightening moon. He'd made about seventy yards before his tumble, but the spot where he lay dipped a good foot below his pursuers' line of sight.

If the smaller man walked through the field there was every chance that Matt would be seen. He watched in horror as the man raised his gun and screwed on the silencer.

Matt ducked back down and flattened himself even further into the cold earth. He heard the crunch of boots on the flaky soil a few yards away and held his breath. The outline of the smaller man appeared above him.

A cock pheasant screeched in alarm, its cry echoing out towards the darkening trees.

The man spun round and pointed the gun towards the sound. He was only six feet away from Matt's position. He wavered for a long moment and then lowered his gun. The growing darkness and a scattering of wispy clouds had kept him out of sight.

Before long, the footsteps grew quieter and Matt dared to lift his head higher. The man was staggering over the remainder of the field in the direction of the keeper's cottage. Matt knew that Shawn Green, a retired French teacher, lived there.

The TT pulled into the driveway.

With his jacket wet through and pins and needles still tingling in his left leg, Matt limped closer to the cottage. He could see the two men outside Shawn's front door.

Back at his car, a blue flashing light winked through the hedgerow. He could hear distant voices and the unremitting cackle of a short-wave radio. Afraid of drawing the psychos' attention, however, he held his position and continued to watch.

He'd met Shawn Green many times over the years. A small, demure man with a ruddy complexion, Matt had often seen him walking in the woods or fishing the river.

At that very moment the right thing to do would be run straight for the police car. But what if the police didn't believe him? What if the police had already been to Brin cottage and found the body? How would that look for him; bedraggled, emerging surreptitiously from the middle of a field less than a mile away from the murder scene? His prints would be all over the place. He needed more time to think this through.

Shawn's doorbell clattered and eventually issued a small ding.

Thankfully, Shawn didn't open the door. "Yes. Can I help you?" he said through his letterbox. Shawn's voice sounded strange from Matt's position. Muffled, yet frightened and slightly slurred.

The taller man moved closer. "It's okay sir, just a routine call." He pushed a small white card up against the frosted glass pane of the front door and, in an accent Matt decided might be Welsh, said "C.I.D."

Matt listened as Shawn clanked the letterbox shut and fumbled with the door chain.

No! Don't open it, thought Matt. He wanted to shout out, warn him.

"Inspector," said Shawn, his voice suddenly much chirpier.

Matt felt his heart thump harder as he saw what was in taller man's left hand. It was the old hickory walking stick that he'd had dropped in Sylvie's bedroom.

The tall man smiled sadistically.

Shawn's expectant expression became quizzical. He looked down.

The walking stick jabbed upward and dug into Shawn's face.

The retired teacher yelped like a child who'd simply had a fright, and fell back, his body thumping hard onto the lobby carpet.

The taller man pulled him out onto the front step as Shawn clawed blindly at the hickory spear that now protruded from his left eye.

He motioned to his smaller accomplice, "Finish him!"

Callously, the smaller man stepped into the light, aimed, and then emptied two bullets into Shawn's twitching body; the first thudded into his chest, the second caused Shawn's forehead to explode like a melon, his brains fanning out across the front step.

As Matt covered his mouth with the back of his hand and ducked down, he heard them overturning furniture and banging doors.

They're looking for me, he decided.

In moments the assailants stepped back out into the night air. The taller man cursed, "Travoshki!"

"I've let you down, Stiller."

The smaller man's voice sounded familiar. Stiller... was that the taller man's name?

"The car crash was unforeseen but it should have been considered," he replied. "Still, he has his precious file and will soon receive his orders."

They know I have the file, thought Matt. He fingered the folder still clutched tight under his jacket. What orders are they talking about?

"I'll drop you off at his house and then check with my contacts. He should be easy enough to track down," said Stiller. He turned and stepped back into the house. He fussed over his long black hair in a slightly effeminate way before digging his heel into what remained of Shawn's face. He gripped the handle of the walking stick with a gloved hand and pulled it free with a sickening squelch before stepping through the door. He glanced over at Matt's position, towards the flashing blue light at the other end of the field and then threw the stick into the back seat of the Audi TT.

6

FEELING HIS HANDS beginning to shake, Matt ducked down even further and waited until he heard the Audi TT pull away. He moved, still crouched, in the direction of the A1 in the distance. He had to get away from these people and he had to stay clear of the police until he could think this through. The walking stick would have his prints all over it.

Stumbling over the ground, he kept moving away from the cottage. There was no need to kill Shawn, he kept thinking. As soon as Matt leapt out onto the noisy verge of the northbound A1, a succession of diesel-laden backdrafts slammed into him and ruffled his hair. Picking his way through the litter and muck, he shielded his eyes and made for the lay-by ahead.

He edged past an overfilled bin and looked up at the sign on a truck that read: 'Jimmy Coil's Removals and Logistics - From here to there and much, much *mair*.' Matt was surprised by the use of the Irish-Glaswegian spelling of the word 'more'. A dim light illuminated the cabin of the twenty-ton truck. Matt could see the driver.

Shivering, he edged forward and knocked on the passenger door.

The driver almost choked on his snack as he spun round in his seat. He brushed some pieces of blueberry muffin from his chin and looked down at Matt. "Where the fuck did you come from? Fuckin' prick." He'd mumbled the last part as he shimmied across his seat and looked out of the passenger window.

Matt wondered if this was Jimmy, in person, and apologised for giving the driver such a fright. Making it up as he went along, he said, "I'm a bit stuck mate, and I just wondered if you could give me a lift. Car's let me down and I need to get north in a hurry."

The driver gave Matt a particularly harsh stare.

Matt waited in the darkness, shivering uncomfortably.

"And yer car is where?" said the driver, suspiciously. Matt pointed at the hedge. "It's over that field, but..."

"But you want to abandon it and get north quick-style? Doesn't quite add up, does it?"

This was not going well and time was not on his side. The two psychos were bound to be closing in. This distrustful Scotsman was his only chance. "Look, I can pay you if..."

"Pay me? Well you could buy me another fuckin' blueberry muffin for a start." The driver paused and then said, "Jump up."

He helped Matt into the cabin and shuffled back to his seat. Turning ignition, he revved the engine and smiled as the hydraulic brakes hissed free. The lorry lurched forward.

Matt eased himself back into the big seat and checked the wing mirror for anything that looked remotely like an Audi TT.

The driver piped up. "How far north are you going: Grantham, Newcastle, Glesga?" He paused, glanced over at Matt and added, "Timbuktu?" a cheeky grin forming on his thin lips.

Matt's mind was still cluttered. He gave an involuntary shrug.

"Ah... Timbuktu it is then. Name's Jimmy, by the way." He continued to probe. "So you're in trouble? Let me guess..."

Matt opened his mouth to speak.

"Naw, naw, let me guess..." He stretched out the word 'guess' and then barked out, "Women trouble?"

Matt coughed, steam rising from his wet clothes. "I don't suppose I could borrow your mobile for a second? Mine needs recharging." Matt had tried several times to switch his on, but it was completely dead.

"Cheeky bastard!" yelled Jimmy, suddenly distracted by another motorist. He rolled down his window and shouted, "you need pulled over and beaten with a big fuckin' stick, pal! Fuckin' cut me up..."

Matt edged back in his seat.

"Did you see that?" said Jimmy.

Matt struggled to concentrate. He was too busy wondering if it was Burrows or Ueshima that had caused the complete collapse of his life. His family was the only stable thing he had left. He had to call Jenny.

"Here, take it." Jimmy slid his mobile across the seat towards Matt.

"Thanks," said Matt, already dialling home. The phone rang six times then clicked onto the answer machine. "Sorry. No one can get to the phone just now. Please leave your message after the tone."

"Jenny? Hello?" He waited. "Peter, it's dad. Are you there?" Matt hated it when they didn't pick up. Peter usually had the TV up far too loud and Jenny just couldn't be bothered half the time. She wasn't very good on the phone.

"Jenny it's me. I have to go on a business trip. It's to do with the news this morning. The vaccine." he lied. "You know how it is. I've no clothes or anything." He paused hoping she would pick up, but there was nothing. "Anyway, I'll call you later." Matt killed the call and offered the mobile back to Jimmy.

Jimmy continued to stare at the road ahead. "And you are?"

"Pardon?" said Matt.

Jimmy sniffed. "Your name, man?"

"Oh right, I'm Matt." Matt instantly regretted blurting out his name. How bloody stupid was that? Also, he'd begun to panic about the call he'd just made. All the police would have to do was dial 1471 and they would be straight on the line to the delightful Jimmy.

"Is it you then?" said Matt, trying to pull himself free from his growing paranoia, "on the side of the lorry?"

"Naw! Nae chance. That's Jimmy Coil, the one hundred and sixth richest man in Scotland. Removals, buses, taxis, drugs..."

"Right..." Matt was miles away again.

"And of course there's the contracts, the prostitution and his porn empire."

Matt gave Jimmy a sideways glance.

Jimmy winked. "Made up the last bit, eh..."

Matt was trying to ignore him so he could figure things out, but Jimmy wasn't for giving up. "So, what's the real reason you're on the run then? Mass murder, kidnapping, robbery?"

Matt was growing tired of Jimmy. He saw him eye the clear folder and edged it under his leg.

Jimmy steadied the steering wheel with his elbow and began to roll a cigarette.

"Nothing as exciting as that," said Matt.

Jimmy gripped the roll-up in his lips and smiled. He began drumming rhythms on the steering wheel. "Used to be a drummer you know. Even did a stint with the Bay City Rollers." Jimmy looked expectantly, as if he was waiting for a gasp of amazement. He sighed and refocused on the road. "It was only for two weeks, mind. Not that impressive, I suppose."

Matt slipped the clear folder from under his leg.

"Well, that's enough about me," continued Jimmy, "Matt's short for Matthew, isn't it?"

"Yes, that's right." Matt's eyes settled on Jimmy's shirt collar. It was black with grime and his fingers were yellowed with the nicotine from a lifetime of rollups. He reckoned Jimmy was a similar age to himself, perhaps a bit older. He was also about the same height and build. Matt couldn't help noticing the stains on Jimmy's clothes - long, oily streaks and great, greasy blotches. There were burn marks on Jimmy's baggy blue pants too where hot ash had settled on his lap.

Matt slipped his hand into the folder. He glanced across at Jimmy. He'd smelt 'the smell' from the moment he'd climbed into the cabin, a stale towel, 'old man' kind of smell, which permeated the upholstery of the cabin and was probably ingrained in Jimmy's skin.

"Full of cash, is it?" asked Jimmy, performing a little side-ways squint at the folder.

Matt looked down at the folder and smiled. "I wish. No, it's just business reports, expenses, that kind of stuff."

"Was that the missus you were trying to get on the phone?" Jimmy pressed.

Matt felt like telling him to mind his own bloody business, but being at Jimmy's mercy and already considerably in debt to the little tramp, he bit his tongue and nodded. Why hadn't Jenny answered? Was she safe? Had she found out about his suspension? He felt a rush of panic. His files on the Munich meeting were missing from the folder. There was only one piece of paper in there. He fingered it gingerly and then pulled it free. He waited until Jimmy began ranting at another car before glancing down to read it. It said: 'You have six days to produce another sample of the Seed. Your girlfriend was expendable; your wife and kid, we presume, are not. Your deadline is Sunday, 4 P.M.'

Anxiously checking the folder for any other pieces of paper, he read the note again. Matt felt sick. A cold sweat caused the piece of paper to slip from his hands. It floated into the foot-well. He scrambled to retrieve it.

"Everything okay, pal?" said Jimmy.

"Yeah, just dropped my expenses sheet," Matt lied, pinching the edge of the paper. He whisked it up, folded it in half, and placed it in his jacket beside the manila envelope.

It was Monday. He had six days, tops. Who had written the note? Had they killed Sylvie merely to set him an example? His mind raced with every aspect of The Seed Project. Who else knew about the Seed? As far as he knew there were only the four: Barclay, Sir John, Lucius and himself. Surely it was unlikely that a multinational company would issue instructions to kill someone, or was it? Barclay and Sir John had already told him to go dig; so it was unlikely to be them. Lucius, on the other hand, had disappeared.

Matt tried to remember if he'd told Sylvie about the Seed. He'd only mentioned it in passing. It was when he'd told her about her name being part of a new discovery. Had they tortured her before she was killed, extracted the phrase from her or...? His mind racing, he began to panic about Jenny and Peter. He needed to know if they were alright.

Unsure what to do next, Matt watched Jimmy crush out his roll-up and pop it into his shirt pocket. I have to pull myself together and get that flight to Zurich, he decided. He would fly from Edinburgh and get another sample of the Seed; it should be reasonably easy to find. He felt some keys jingle in his pocket and pulled them free. Fingering each key one at a time, he was relieved to find out that he still had the key to Lucius's flat in Zurich.

Snow spiralled towards the windscreen like an endless barrage of Second World War strafing. It was surreal, just like this whole nightmare of a day.

Jimmy stopped tapping the steering wheel. "It's time you bought me that muffin," he grumbled.

"Already?" Matt was now desperate to get to Edinburgh as fast as he could. "I'll make it a full meal if you get me right up to Edinburgh."

"Edinburgh?" balked Jimmy, "I'm fuckin' starving mate. A man needs to eat, you know."

Matt was about to protest when Jimmy sniffed and explained, "Look, we'll just stop for a few minutes then I'll get us up the road, pronto. What do ye say?"

"Fine, okay, if you're really hungry." Matt thought about the possibility of changing rides. "Can I borrow your phone again?"

"Sure, keep it," said Jimmy, with more than a hint of sarcasm.

Nervously, Matt dialled home again. This time the stakes were much higher. He had to know if they were safe. He waited as it rang, willing Peter to pick it up. Why doesn't Jenny ever answer the bloody phone?

7

JENNY HEARD Matt's voice on the answer machine, but the last thing she needed was another bunch of lies and excuses. Peter tried to lift the receiver but she waved her finger at him. "Leave it."

"But Mum," said Peter.

"I'm not talking to him just now." Jenny had to use all her strength to keep calm. What she really wanted to say was: "I'm leaving him and I have no intention of ever talking to him for the rest of my life," but she had decided, sensibly, she thought, to keep this little nugget for another day. It was almost seven and she was completely drained.

It was dark and she caught her reflection in the kitchen window. Her auburn hair had been tied back from her face and her deep blue eyes had black shadows that made her seem much older than she really was. The day had taken its toll on her.

She scraped Matt's chorizo into the bin followed by the plate of spaghetti bolognaise she'd kept warm for herself. I'll change the locks, she decided. Then, I'll send him a letter with my demands: half his income, the house, and a reminder that he'll owe me half of his pension for all those years I've stayed at home to look after his son. Besides, they aren't demands; they are my rights. I'd better make an appointment with my solicitor, Jones and Jones, she thought. Then again, perhaps she would be better off changing to another firm. Just as she pondered on the various pros and cons of changing solicitors, there was a knock at the front door.

Peter, still visibly concerned, made another effort to cheer her up by offering to answer it.

Jenny wondered who it was. It wasn't Matt, he was off on one of his jollies, and it wasn't her mother; she'd taken a last minute cruise with her 'new man'. Perhaps it was the police with Matt's car.

As they both moved towards the front door, Jenny saw the silhouettes of two men through the semi-circular window of stained glass. The taller of the two looked as if he had long black hair.

* * *

INSPECTOR WILLS HAD decided to pay a visit to Brin Cottage. He knew it well. He passed it every day on his way to the station in Alescorth. He'd always admired it, even envied it. It would have suited Mrs. Wills and him perfectly, with its clean, whitewashed walls and its quaint rust-coloured tiles. But it was the location that really suited him. Just a few yards from the River Ells there was a path that ran a full mile through the beech woods towards the keeper's cottage and then back gain along the opposite bank. Retirement was only three more years away and he'd already begun counting the months, weeks and days. It would be perfect for fishing and walking his dogs.

His short-wave radio fizzled and then sprung to life. "Inspector, we've put the tape round the vehicle and stuck the Police Aware sign in the back window. It's off the road enough for now."

"Fine," he replied, "I'm going to take a look at Brin Cottage." Mrs. Malcolm had given him the perfect excuse to have a nosy inside. He fingered his notebook until he found the entry: "Look, why don't you try Brin Cottage? He seems to prefer it there!" she'd said. That was good enough for him.

According to his notes, a Miss Sylvie Bern lived there with her dog. However, the lads on the beat said she had a regular man-friend. About five feet-six, he wore glasses and had silver BMW. It seemed pretty obvious to him that Matt Malcolm was going to turn out to be the regular man-friend. Surprisingly, Jenny Malcolm seemed to know all about it.

As he walked up the quartz-stone path, he wondered how long Jenny Malcolm had tolerated the affair. Had she confronted her husband or had she played it quietly for the sake of the children, allowed the late nights and missing days to go unchallenged? As a Police Inspector, a man who must be trusted by the public, he'd never risked anything like an affair. His life was complicated enough.

As he reached Brin Cottage he saw that wheel spin had rutted the small quartz stones in the driveway, and that the frost had now moulded these into deep, solid furrows. Moonlight bathed Brin's whitewashed walls and the amber glow from an upstairs window made the cottage look even more perfect than he'd imagined. He would change the modern blinds to lush velvet curtains and he would mono-block the drive. Brin Cottage deserved better.

* * *

IT WAS PETER who reached the door first. He turned the lock as quickly as he could.

Jenny, angry at her son's rashness, tried to shout out but stopped as the door opened.

"Mrs. Malcolm?" A tall man with a mop of thick, black hair and unusually pale skin asked the question in stilted English.

"Eh... Yes. And you are?" replied Jenny.

The taller man covered her mouth and knocked her to the ground. The second one, wearing a black balaclava, stuffed a silk hanky into Peter's mouth and slapped him hard.

"Sssto..." She couldn't speak. Above the calloused hand that covered her mouth and pushed her head against the floor, she eyes strained to her left. Her gaze was fixed on Peter's attacker. She knew in that instant that this was a woman. A mother's instinct told her to analyse and assess. Despite her own pain, she scanned the hall for possible weapons and some method of raising the alarm.

A long strand of blonde hair slipped from the black balaclava of the woman who held Peter.

Her assailant smiled and then picked her up like a rag doll. He whisked her into the living room and threw her against the wall. The pictures rattled and several small ornaments toppled from the wooden mantelpiece.

It was then that Jenny noticed the stick in her attacker's right hand. He removed his left hand from her mouth and brought the gory tip of the stick up to her face. She froze, the blurred metal tip wavering an inch from her eye. "What do you want?" she whispered. She was desperate to move, look behind her attacker for Peter, but she had the feeling that this man wanted her to try.

Her attacker spoke slowly. "I want every piece of you." He moved his face in close until it blurred. A greasy strand of his jet-black hair fell across her eyes. She felt it sting.

"But first I want to know where your cheating husband has gone."

"He's not here," she panted, "the police said..." She hesitated.

"We know about his car," he whispered.

Jenny felt him rip a piece of cloth from her skirt. He forced her to her knees and then began to tie her to the radiator pipes.

The woman walked into the room behind him.

"Search every inch of the place for any mention of the Seed," he snapped. "Where's the boy?"

Jenny's heart almost stopped.

The girl removed her balaclava. "He's in the kitchen."

Jenny started to cry. "What do you mean? What have you done to him?"

The point of the walking stick slid under her chin. "Nothing yet," said the man. He brought the stick down at a slight angle. It traced the heaving curve of her breasts and then moved down over her stomach until it reached the ripped hem of her skirt. Her attacker smiled and then lifted her skirt. He eyed her carefully.

He's older than he seems... His hair is dyed... He's about six four... Jenny braced.

The cold tip of the walking stick slid up her inner thigh before thrusting forwards.

"Argh!" screamed Jenny.

It pierced the thin plaster wall an inch below her groin.

The blonde woman laughed. "She's going to scream like a bitch when you get started on her."

"Keep them both here," he snapped. "Search the house and phone me if you find anything of interest. Malcolm must have hitched north."

"But he took the file. He'll know by now what he has to do," the girl protested.

"Just keep them secure until I return. Kill the boy if she tries anything stupid." He jerked the stick free of the wall and pressed it against her.

Jenny studied every line in the man's face. Every pore and hair was etched into her mind as she boiled with a rage that was impossible to conceal. His knuckles whitened as he pressed the stick even harder. Her legs shook. He stank of cheap herbal cologne and cigars; his strange black eyes were dead and completely without emotion. He wore a grey trench coat with a blue scarf tucked inside the collar. He drew back and she exhaled. His boots were wet. They dripped dirty puddles over her new carpet as he turned to go. He had to stoop to leave the room.

The young girl moved closer as the door slammed shut. Jenny straightened herself and tested the knots that held her.

"They will be very tight, I can assure you," hissed the woman.

Jenny's back was hard against the ridges of the radiator.

The woman, though attractive, had a malevolent tone to her voice that somehow frightened her even more than the man. "I will kill your son if you try anything stupid. So don't even think about it. By the end of this week you have every chance of returning to your pathetic little life, albeit slightly abused, so don't risk it. Behave and live."

Jenny didn't believe her. As the girl walked over to the bookshelf and began rummaging through a pile of magazines and paperbacks Jenny decided that she was probably one of the most beautiful women she had ever seen, about five-five, and in her early twenties she moved like a cat.

"Why are you doing this?" Jenny croaked.

"Money, of course," said the girl. "You just happen to be useful for the time being."

Jenny pushed her shoulder against the radiator. She felt the temperature beginning to build. The central heating was timed to switch on at seven fifteen. She shouted out, "Peter?"

"Shut up!" said the woman, "He's fine. Just keep quiet and don't move."

Jenny knew the heating would be at full pelt in about ten minutes. The radiator would start to burn her. "Please, the radiator's getting hotter. Couldn't you loosen me a little?"

The girl ignored Jenny and continued searching the shelves.

"I'm not joking, I'll get scalded." One of Jenny's bare arms was pinned to the hot feed pipe. She strained and felt the material that bound her give a little.

While the girl hunted, Jenny slowly arched her back and twisted her arm down, over the curve of the feed pipe until it touched the carpet beside her foot. She began to cramp but as her fingers searched the thick pile of the carpet until she felt something cold. Very carefully, Jenny managed to move her foot just enough to scrape the object into her hand.

The girl spun round.

Jenny froze and sniffed in an effort to look pathetic.

"Where does your husband keep his porn?" she asked.

"What?" Jenny fingered the ridged handle of a screwdriver.

"All guys keep a stash somewhere and most wives and girlfriends know where. So where is Matt's?" The girl smiled coyly. "Come on... under a floorboard? In an old paint pot in the garage? Where?"

"Look, I'm burning here. I can't think..." Jenny winced.

"Tell me where he keeps his stuff and I'll try and keep my boss at bay." The girl eyed Jenny's long legs before turning back to the bookshelf.

Jenny worked at the material of her torn dress as she answered. "There is one place."

"Tell me, quickly!" barked the girl.

She tried to think of some plausible place in the house, far enough away to give her the time she needed. "The loft," she whimpered. "In the loft there's a black bin-bag with old photos and stuff. I found some videos there once." This was actually true, but the videos turned out to be old Cary Grant movies, not exactly porn.

The girl walked over to Jenny and looked down.

Jenny froze.

"Any attempt to escape will be very bad news for your kid. Understand?"

Jenny nodded. "I understand." Inside, she was petrified and beginning to panic about the lack of noise from Peter. She sensed it was now or never. Her intuition told her that this pair would kill them both as soon as their usefulness was over.

As the girl left the room, Jenny worked feverishly at the material, her arm shaking as the radiator burned her skin.

"Ah..." Jenny gasped with relief, as her arm broke free of the scalding pipe. She twisted round and used the screwdriver to loosen the rest of the knots. Its star-shaped tip had a sharp enough point but it wasn't big enough to do any real damage. She wanted to check on Peter but she knew she had to find a decent weapon first. Then, to the left of the living-room door, she saw the walking stick. Her attacker had left it behind.

She heard the girl coming back down the stairs. She lifted the walking stick and stood, poised at the side of the door. The angle she'd chosen would let her strike the girl as she stepped into the room. She held it with two hands. The point would do the most damage.

The girl was only feet away. "There's nothing in the bin-bags except some videos and..."

Jenny braced, but the girl's voice trailed off. She heard her complaining about the contents of the bin-bag. "Did Matt ever mention something called The Seed Project?"

Jenny heard the girl swear. She was in the kitchen. "For fuck's sake... Wake up, son."

Panicking, Jenny realised that Peter must have lost consciousness.

No, she had to wait. Her exact spot would deliver the most surprise and the maximum damage.

The girl's voice had lost the slight echo of the kitchen. It was growing louder, "Your son's not asthmatic or..."

Jenny jumped out and forced the walking stick, as hard as she could, into the girl's face. "UUH!" She grunted with the effort.

The thud was sickening and Jenny felt the wood bend as it pushed home. Shaking uncontrollably, she stepped back and braced.

The metal tip of the walking stick had punctured the back of the girl's mouth and now protruded six inches, or so, out of the back of her neck.

Jenny spat out the word, 'bitch', but her knees weakened as she edged past the girl.

Still very much alive, the girl gagged and choked, clawing at Jenny and then the stick. Blood was pouring over the hall rug.

Jenny forced herself on and into the kitchen. Peter was slumped against the fridge, his mouth and hands taped.

A numbness spread over her as she ripped off the thick, silver tape. "Son! Peter, wake up!" She began blowing short blasts of air into Peter's mouth. He coughed then began to cry. Jenny banged her head on an open drawer as she scrambled to her feet. She rummaged about for his inhaler, found it. She placed it to his lips. "Breathe in. It's okay, son. It's okay now."

But Peter had stopped crying. His eyes were fixed on the kitchen door behind her.

Jenny saw a shadow cover his face.

There was a hissing sound and a series of gargled splutters as the girl pulled herself up. She had a gun in her right hand. It shook in their direction. The blonde girl was on the verge of losing consciousness.

Jenny flicked open the cupboard nearest to her and felt for the flex of the iron. She pulled Peter to the side just as the gun fired. The bullet ricocheted off the concrete floor and buried itself in the wall behind them. The stick still wavered hideously from the girl's mouth, like some obscene reptilian tongue.

She dropped the gun.

Peter screamed as his mother grasped the handle of the stick, drawing the girl down before swinging the heavy iron up, point first, into the girl's chest. There was a crack and the girl crumpled.

Jenny leapt up and pulled the girl into the hall by the handle of the walking stick. Closing the door over on Peter, she lifted the iron by the flex and felt its weight. It swung like a pendulum as she mustered every bit of hatred inside her.

Then she closed her eyes and brought it down hard, again and again and again and again.

Jenny fell to her knees and crawled like an animal back into the kitchen. She kicked the kitchen door shut on the corpse and cuddled into Peter.

He stared, wide-eyed at the kitchen door. Trembling, she reached up for the phone and pressed the calls-received button.

8

AS THE TWENTY-TON truck screeched to a halt, the whole cabin jolted forward and then eased back on its hydraulics.

Jimmy pulled on the brakes, turned off the ignition and then slid down, snakelike, from the driver's door.

Matt hesitated. Still shaken, he scanned the car park for any sign of a blue Audi TT. It had stopped snowing and the service station was full of truckers and reps trying to get home. They'd all crammed into the far end of the car park nearest to the all-night café. Steam was sailing up into the night air above the flat tar roof of the kitchen. The smell of burgers and hot dogs wafted across the tarmac as crows and gulls squabbled for the leftovers that spilled from the bins and verges.

"Are you comin', or what?" pressed Jimmy.

Matt climbed down and instantly felt the chill through his damp clothes. He was shaking.

Jimmy looked concerned. "Look, give me a fiver for a bite and I'm happy. You should get yourself a shower and freshen up if you're set on going north after this," said Jimmy.

Matt produced a crumpled five pound from his trouser pocket and handed it over.

"Ta," said Jimmy. He pointed towards a portacabin on the other side of the car park. "The showers are for the truckers, but just use them. No bugger will be any the wiser. Here..." Jimmy tossed Matt a plastic bag. "There's an old jacket of mine and a jumper in there."

Matt must have looked as horrified as he felt because Jimmy shook his head and muttered, "ungrateful bastard."

Shivering even more now, he shuddered to think what Jimmy's cast-offs would look like, but he was freezing and anything dry would be an improvement.

Checking for the manila envelope and his note, Matt strolled over to the cabin and stepped inside. The showers stank of diesel, cigarettes and carbolic soap, but he was bitterly cold and he needed to get himself warm and comfortable. He opened Jimmy's bag and got a strong whiff of shit. "No way!" He couldn't change into these rags. He'd rather fucking freeze.

He closed the door of the portacabin behind him and gazed across the car park at the bright green neon above the shop entrance, but as he stared and shivered something spun round the corner of the last parked lorry to his left.

An Audi TT, blue, and obviously in a hurry, screeched to a stop outside the cafe.

Matt flattened himself against the wall of the portacabin.

To his horror, a tall man with pallid skin and long greasy hair stepped out of the car and looked round.

Matt didn't know whether to head back to Jimmy's lorry or to hide. He waited until the man disappeared inside the cafe and then edged along the portacabin. He'd almost moved out of sight when he heard Jimmy's voice resonate across the car park. "Matt! Got you a burger! Onions, mustard and..."

Matt couldn't believe it. "Shhhh!" He put his forefinger to his lips and signalled Jimmy to be quiet.

"What?" said Jimmy, a disgruntled expression forming on his dirty face.

Matt saw Jimmy look to his left and eye the tall stranger. The man quickly followed Jimmy's gaze and broke into a run.

"Fuck!" Matt cursed. Gulls and crows flapped skyward as Jimmy rushed through their midst in the opposite direction towards his truck. What is that little shit doing now? Matt ducked down and rolled under the portacabin. As he scrambled and kicked his way through the debris and mud that lay beneath he heard the tall pursuer's footsteps.

Matt emerged in a car park on the other side of the showers and spied a white van amongst a cluster of parked cars. It was within reach. Sprinting over, he quickly tested the passenger door and jumped inside. He threw Jimmy's plastic bag inside, pushed himself into the foot-well and held his breath.

His tall pursuer couldn't be far. He might have seen him. Matt might be trapped.

"Mr. Malcolm!" The heavily accented voice echoed over the car park.

Matt tensed.

"You have your instructions! Do not involve anyone else."

Matt wanted to step out into the open, confront him, yell at him, but he was too scared.

"Show yourself, so I can be certain you understand!"

No, thought Matt, that's what he wants me to do.

The footsteps grew louder and he instantly began to regret hiding in such a stupid place. He imagined the door of the van being pulled open and the thud of the bullets. To die like a rat in such a confined space would be his worst nightmare. Claustrophobia gripped him and he thought about bolting.

Suddenly, Matt could see the black-haired pursuer in the rear view mirror above him. He'd clipped it as he'd jumped inside the van door and the angle was just right. The tall psychopath was checking every vehicle, searching for the slightest indication of movement, something out of the ordinary: a protruding snib that meant a door was unlocked, or the gentle rocking caused by someone attempting to adjust their hiding position.

Matt held his breath as the killer fixed his gaze on the mirror Matt was watching him through. He'd drawn his gun. How stupid had he been! He'd jumped inside the most conspicuous vehicle, and yes... the snib on the passenger door was up. Matt felt his mouth become dry as he watched the man twist a silencer onto the barrel of his gun. He smiled and aimed directly at the white van. Still, Matt didn't move. Now very close, he saw the man's finger slide into position behind the trigger. A thin smile teased his lips as he narrowed his strange black eyes.

Crack!

The gunman staggered back.

"Stand back from the gun, pal, or I'll smack you again." It was Jimmy. He raised the baseball bat higher and gave two small jerks to indicate he was serious.

Matt reached for the door handle and eased it down slowly. Then, he literally let himself spill onto the ground.

He noticed the gun. It was lying on the ground about five yards from the white van.

Mustering all the courage he could, he scampered round the side of the van just in time to see Jimmy swing the bat down a second time.

The killer moved unbelievably fast, twisting away from the blow and using the momentum of the swing to pull Jimmy towards him. As Jimmy teetered, the taller man stepped sideways and caught hold of Jimmy's hair. Then, in a movement that surprised Matt even more, he kicked Jimmy's feet away and threw him flat on his back. The air was forced from Jimmy's lungs and the bat clattered across the ground.

Matt crouched and watched in the wing mirror of the white van as the taller man placed his knee in the small of Jimmy's back. Resembling some deranged rock star, the psycho smiled to himself, flicked his long black hair, and then simply cracked the Scotsman's neck with one swift, sickening wrench.

By the time Jimmy's head hit the ground, his eyes were already glazed and lifeless.

Matt felt a rush of nausea; then, pulling himself to his feet, he ran as fast as he possibly could, slipping on patches of newly formed ice and banging noisily into parked cars before reaching the blackness of the surrounding fields. Panting and wheezing in the cold air, he turned to look back at the shower block. There was no one there. Tentatively, Matt edged round the perimeter of the service area until he arrived back at the lorry park. It was then, to his absolute relief, that he saw the TT move off and disappear onto the southbound lane of the A1. Matt scanned for another TT but found none. Shivering with a mixture of shock, relief, and bitter cold, he staggered out of the darkness towards Jimmy's truck. He saw the sign that read, 'Jimmy's Removals' on the side curtain and noticed that the driver's door had been left open. Jimmy must have left it unlocked in his hurry to help him. Again, another pang of nausea hit him hard. This time it was laced with a big dose of guilt. It all happened so quickly.

Matt pulled himself up into Jimmy's cabin and slumped down into the big leatherette seat. Still nervous but at least a little warmer now, he noticed some of Jimmy's things behind the seat. A small holdall and several tins of tobacco lay under an old tartan blanket. Matt checked one more time for any sign of the long-haired psycho but he was gone.

Reaching inside Jimmy's holdall, Matt found fifty pounds in cash, a passport and, surprisingly, a pile of very neatly pressed, clean clothes. He thought for a moment about the stinking plastic bag Jimmy had given him earlier and then picked up the passport. It might come in handy, especially if the police were on his tail. He couldn't afford any delays. He had to get another sample of the Seed as soon as he could.

Matt opened the passport and studied the picture. Jimmy looked surprisingly smart, and Matt calculated that by removing his glasses and darkening his hair a little he could pass for the picture in the passport without too much problem. In the dim light of the cabin, he read the name: James Serge Kaminski. The passport was British all right, but why had Jimmy lied about his name? Embarrassed? Possibly. Jimmy looked completely different in his passport picture. He wore a shirt and tie. He looked neat and respectable. The passport picture looked nothing like the little tramp Matt had known briefly. Tramp or not, Jimmy had given his life to save him.

Still terrified that the killer had doubled back in some elaborate effort to flush him out, Matt slipped down from the truck and made his way back to the shower block. He ran over the icy car park and edged round the cabin for one last look, but Jimmy was gone. There wasn't even the slightest hint of a struggle.

Matt's heart quickened as his thoughts became distorted. Everything rational was muted while everything irrational was amplified. Matt wondered if the killer was in the employ of Burrows or Ueshima, but then why had Vectan-Brosman refused to take his call? Where was the smaller man? Touching his temples, Matt made small circles with his forefinger as a piercing migraine kicked in. He entered the shower room, half expecting to hear Jimmy's voice: 'Got you' or 'Fell for it, didn't yeh!' But there were no such jibes, only the dripping of leaky taps and the hum of the blue strip lights. Junkies, thought Matt. The blue light was there to stop them shooting up; it made it almost impossible to find the veins.

He was losing his strength now, both physically and mentally. Where are Jenny and Peter? Is the smaller man with them?

He wondered if the smaller man been in the TT all along. Had he dragged Jimmy's body away? Matt would soon have to stop running and sleep.

His heart still pounding, Matt changed into Jimmy's clean clothes and wondered again why the little tramp had preferred to wear his old, stinking rags. As Matt unfolded a neatly pressed pair of trousers, something dropped to the floor. It was a metal pendant of some kind. He picked it up and more closely. It was in the shape of an angel. Not your usual two wings and a halo type of angel... it was more elaborate than that. Matt counted six wings: two regular ones protruding from the back, two that covered the angel's feet, and two more that covered the angel's eyes. Not really sure why, Matt popped the trinket into his jacket pocket and stepped out into the night. He was almost halfway across the car park when he suddenly remembered to check for the psycho. Holding his breath, he scanned the tarmac but, to his relief, there was no sign of the TT or his pursuer. Matt wandered into the shop and bought some henna hair dye, a pile of shirts and a bar of chocolate before making his way back to the A1 via the garage forecourt.

A bus pulled into the diesel pumps. He saw that it was an Intercity, bound for Edinburgh. Matt waited for the bus door to hiss open and then moved towards the driver. "Any room for one more passenger?" he enquired.

The driver gave Matt an irritable stare. "These passengers are straight through, non-stop ticket holders, mate, and..."

"But you have some spare seats," said Matt, trying not to let the driver's abrasive manner effect the steady tone of his voice.

The driver moved toward the pumps.

Matt waved a fifty-pound note and winked. "Look, I really need to get up the road tonight."

Without even looking at Matt directly, the driver snatched the red-coloured note and nodded toward the open door of the bus.

"Thanks mate," said Matt, hopping up the stairs. He quickly settled himself into a red and black chequered, nylon seat and thought, What a pathetic little prick. He hated the small people in life who took what little power they had and abused it. He'd seen traffic wardens and doctor's secretaries use this special power. He'd seen them shake their heads while the puny mortals squirmed and pleaded. Matt took a deep breath and then let his head settle on the cold window. It soothed his pounding head and allowed him to think. He had to end this nightmare, get to Zurich. He had to go back to the museum as quickly as he could before something terrible happened to Jenny or Peter. He had very little time to retrace the drunken steps he'd taken over a year ago and find the Seed. Why hadn't the psychopath just asked him to tell him where he'd first discovered the Seed? Why hadn't Barclay asked him to do the same? Why was he suddenly on some fucking goose chase?

The flakes of snow were bigger now and as the bus pulled away he toyed with the strange metal pendant that had fallen from Jimmy's jeans. He would never forget the look of disappointment on Jimmy's face. The way his dead eyes seemed to burn into him...

Never.

9

STILLER HAD THE whole procedure imprinted in his mind. Every twenty minutes he expected the vibration in his pocket that told him everything was all right. It told him he was still in control and that nothing had veered off course. But having dispensed with the lorry driver he felt uneasy, like something was missing. The text from Sylvie was late, and that wasn't like her. She'd shown potential from an early age. By thirteen, she'd already completed two highly sensitive missions of entrapment that had earned her the respect of her peers and a chance to train in the KGB's First Chief Directorate (Foreign Operations). Stiller had been her mentor. Her adaptability and acumen had proved extremely useful and her stunning western looks meant that Stiller had put her forward for transposition. She was fostered and trained by a sympathetic family in England who, with KGB money, had arranged a year of elocution lessons before enrolling her at one of the most prestigious schools in the South East.

However, by the time Vectan-Brosman began work on their first leukaemia vaccine, the KGB had fractured. It was now the Foreign Intelligence Service or the SVR that decided she should entrap one of Vectan-Brosman's young executives. Sylvie was, by this time, a seductive twenty-five years of age and Matt Malcolm was influential and malleable. He also had a family at stake should they ever need him to engineer events.

With the radical downsizing of the SVR, however, Stiller and Sylvie were suddenly surplus to requirements and, more importantly, budget. Sylvie had already gathered the vaccine information, so was dropped along with her operator, Stiller.

But then, out of the blue, an anonymous player had made contact with Stiller through a mutual friend. The instruction was clear: "Keep your agent in place and get as much information as you can on Vectan-Brosman's Seed Project." The money so far had been more than generous. Stiller had been promised $250,000 for the complete dossier and $500,000 for an actual sample of the product itself. But, after six months, Sylvie had gained nothing of any great value. Becoming impatient with the slow, subtle approach, Stiller had arranged a flushing tactic.

The announcement of Matt Malcolm's public sacking was the key. It was perfect. Double the pressure, double the chance he'd make a mistake and reveal the whereabouts of the Seed. He'd been instructed not to use torture. This, while frustrating, often meant that the subject was unreliable. He knew Malcolm was a nothing more than a jumped-up salesman, but tonight's events had already proved that he could be resourceful under pressure.

As Stiller drove past Matt Malcolm's house he punched the steering wheel of the TT and swore. Police lights danced on the sandstone facing of the detached house and two young officers were already cordoning off the driveway with blue and white tape. Stiller parked the TT a safe distance from the house, then made his way to the rear elevation. He used a small pair of Zeiss binoculars to look into each room. Methodically, he counted seven uniformed constables inside and an older, plain-clothes officer. The officer had just stepped outside into the back garden to make a phone call. There was no sign of Sylvie or the Malcolms.

As a torch beam traced the branches above his head, he fell back into the shadows. Reluctantly, he dialled the emergency number he'd been given. "It's Stiller, sir."

The voice on the line was, as it had been on all previous calls, disguised. "Has Malcolm revealed the original location of the Seed yet?"

"No sir, and we have complications. My agent is either captured or down."

"I thought you were the best!" snapped the voice.

Stiller cupped the mobile and spat. "If you'd just let me interrogate Malcolm, I-"

"I call the shots, Stiller," said the voice.

Stiller crouched down as another torch beam traced the branches above him. "In that case, I need to call on some old friends. Are you sure you want him followed?"

"Do it! And be aware that I am not the only interested party. Their Head of Research, Schlesinger, is missing. I need you to find out who's behind that. Remember, Malcolm and Schlesinger are crucial. Find them!"

"That will mean even more people, more money," said Stiller, a hint of reticence in his voice.

"Just do it. Money is not a concern. Remember, follow Malcolm, eliminate any other interested parties, and make sure his family is watched. He has five days, twenty hours and thirty-two minutes to succeed, or they die. Is he aware of his predicament?"

"Yes, he took the file," said Stiller.

"Are you sure he's read and understood it?"

"Yes," Stiller lied.

The phone went dead before Stiller could explain that he hadn't actually confirmed this last point for certain. As he ran back towards the TT, he felt an unfamiliar heaviness bare down upon him. Alive or dead, Sylvie had failed.

10

THE CARVINGS ON the ancient wooden sarcophagus puzzled Dr. Lucius Schlesinger. The striations definitely formed the shape of a bird's wing, but the physiology was flawed. He'd noticed it the moment he'd opened his eyes. There were the normal primary, secondary and tertiary feathers, as one might expect, but there were three sets of coverts, not the usual two. Obsessed by detail, Lucius wondered why someone had taken such a long time engraving this amazing representation only to get it wrong. He had estimated that each of the wings was approximately eight feet in length and that the, sarcophagus on whose sides these wings had been so exquisitely carved, was a good six feet high.

The carved sarcophagus dominated his dim prison, the only source of light coming from a bracketed torch that burned erratically on the opposite wall. The flickering light gave the beautifully carved wings the illusion of movement.

His eyes had become accustomed to the gloom but his mind had begun to torment him. The last thing he remembered before oblivion was going into Weiss's Tavern for his usual drink; the rest was just a blur.

He calculated he'd been held for two days, as he'd used the toilet twice and had received two meals, both of which consisted of unleavened bread and some kind of yellow dip. He suspected this was a kind of garbanzo. A mixture of chickpea and yoghurt, he hadn't tasted it since his time as a student in the Middle East, so he wasn't absolutely sure.

Approaching footsteps made him straighten. He watched carefully as a small man walked round the sarcophagus towards him. Sallow skinned, he spoke with a distinctly upper class English accent. "I do apologise for your discomfort, Professor. We would have held you somewhere else, but this is one of the few places that are truly unknown to the inhabitants of Zurich. There is also a certain history attached to your current location." A smile grew steadily beneath his lacquered moustache.

The Professor adjusted his spectacles and nervously traced his own moustache with his thumb and index finger. "Why have you taken me?"

"I think you know why, Professor. What you would really like to ask me is how you might be released and perhaps, who has taken you. Is that not so, Lucius?"

The Professor felt threatened by the little man's familiarity. "Please explain," said Lucius.

His captor put a finger to his lips to signal silence and then clapped his hands twice. Two more figures appeared from behind the carved sarcophagus.

The Professor began to pull at the rope that bound his legs to the wall but the knot was so complicated and tight that his efforts proved useless. So, instead, he pushed himself further back into the darkness of the cave.

Three shadows wavered over him as the small, dark-skinned man spoke once more. "Be still, my friend. You are merely the bait. You have proved yourself to be a man who has great intelligence but... no offence Professor, it is the actual provider of the Seed we seek."

"Matt...?" Lucius, tired and anxious, cursed himself for blurting out the name.

"Yes Professor, Matt Malcolm is the key to resolving our situation. We need to find out exactly how he understood the significance of his find."

"Significance?" The Professor almost smiled, longing to tell them that Matt was a likeable, loud-mouthed show-off who'd only chanced on the Seed as part of a practical joke, but something told him it might be safer for him and Matt if he kept quiet for the moment.

The three men began talking in a language Lucius recognised as Aramaic. As they chatted, he remembered how Matt had acquired the Seed in the first place.

Matt and Lucius had become drinking partners after two years of meetings and conferences. One night, after a particularly gruelling product roll-out session, Matt had taken Lucius to a local bar and proceeded to get drunk. He'd already told Lucius about his many exploits as a student, but that night Matt had recounted the time a fellow student had helped him break into the Glasgow University Zoological Museum. They'd had a project to complete, a collection of sorts that they should have handed in more than a week before. Matt had been three specimens short but, knowing dead insects were plentiful in the Zoological Museum, he'd decided to borrow a few specimens from their extensive collection rather than traipse around on the moors hunting for some real ones. Matt had told him how he'd marvelled at the teak-faced trays, each one brimming with pinned specimens. All he had to do was simply remove the insects he required.

Having done the deed, Matt mixed them in with his own collection, meticulously re-pinning and re-labelling the University insects before handing in his project. Two months later, however, when the final year results were displayed outside the Student's Union, Matt's results were missing. Worse still, on challenging Dr. Hopkins, Head of Entomology, Matt had received short shrift. "Matt, are you really trying to tell me that you collected your example of the 'Scarce Copper' here in the U.K.?" Matt had felt a knot tighten in his stomach, but his

Professor simply shook his head reprovingly. "Lycaena virgaureae has been extinct since 1850."

Matt had been forced to admit the prank and the Professor instantly downgraded him to a 2:2 BSc (Honours) degree. This put an end to any further advancement up the academic ladder within the realm of Entomology and, somewhat fortuitously, forced Matt Malcolm into sales and marketing.

After his fifth pint of Hellbier with Lucius that night, he'd decided to pay a visit to the Zurich University Museum on a kind of 're-enactment of the crime'. Matt was due to tour the Analysis Department of Vectan-Brosman the following day and had decided to collect something a bit more interesting than the usual crap that had adorned Lucius's laboratory on his last visit.

Lucius thought back to Matt's drunken confession. "I'll never admit this to anyone else, but you deserve the truth, Lucius. I got as far as the Antiquities Department when I saw an arrangement of clay pots. The display was labelled: The Etruscan Ware Collection, and, as the pot nearest to me contained some bits and pieces that looked vaguely interesting, I simply took a handful of dry vegetation and made my exit. I dropped the material into analysis bay ninety-nine the next morning. I was going to tell you soon enough, but I forgot until you said you'd discovered something remarkable in bay number ninety-nine.

The number rang a bell and when you showed me the Seeds, I vaguely remembered them from the museum: deep crimson and angular with those strange, little purple hooks." From that point on, Lucius knew the rest of the story. It was he who had separated the strange decagonal Seeds from the tangle of stems and begun the analysis that resulted in the discovery of Lanthobacter Sylvie Imunitass.

"Doctor Schlesinger?"

Lucius snapped out of his daydream and blinked in an effort to focus on his captors.

The small man continued, "Matt Malcolm is, as far as we can ascertain, already on his way to Zurich, but there are other interested parties in pursuit."

Lucius tugged on his ropes. "What other interested parties?"

"I'll come to that," said the small man. "Needless to say, we have agents in place to guide Mr. Malcolm here safely, should the need arise. But be sure of this: these 'other interested parties' are prepared to murder to obtain the results they require."

Lucius sat up and tried to speak in a more assertive tone. "And you are prepared to kidnap an old man. Who are you?" Lucius waited for the reply but his question hung unanswered in the gloom.

The small man placed a hand on one of the ornately carved wings and mumbled a prayer. The exquisitely carved sarcophagus behind him shone amber and gold in the flickering torchlight. "Have you ever heard of the Seraphim, Doctor?'

Lucius, being extremely well read, teased his white moustache before answering. "They are said to be God's own protecting angels." He glanced at the huge carved wings and smiled. "But I don't see any wings on your shoulders, shading your feet or covering your eyes. Three pairs of wings; is that not correct?"

"Very good, Dr. Schlesinger," said the small man. "But I fear you may be taking the highly edited biblical text available to you far too literally." The small man sniffed sharply before taking a pace towards Lucius. He bent down to look him in the eye. "We need to find out what more Mr. Malcolm knows about the origins of the Seed and," the little man's tone sharpened, "we are determined that all work on your project be terminated."

Lucius gave a sigh of exasperation. "But this discovery should be shared. The executives who've stifled the powers of this bacterium were wrong. Matt is just as bad as the rest of them."

"I must beg to differ," the small man snapped. "Chaos will ensue, as it did before, unless we remove the temptation completely."

"Chaos?" pressed Lucius. "I am in a state of chaos right now." Lucius felt a flush of anger rise in his cheeks.

"I need to ask you a question, Doctor," pressed the little man.

Exasperated, Lucius slumped back against the cold wall. "Ask away."

"What other examples of the bacterium remain, either in the raw form of the Seed or perhaps in the form of your pure substrate?"

Lucius sighed and wondered what he should say.

"You see," continued his captor, "I'm afraid we've already destroyed your laboratory samples, and the test crop in Almeria has been burned."

Lucius Schlesinger shook his head in frustration. "How do you know about Almeria? I mean, how can you be sure the test crop has totally killed off?

"You have not answered the question," snapped the little man.

"No, I don't suppose I have," said Lucius, drawing his legs in beneath him. Lucius knew there and then that his captors were completely unaware of the Seeds in the Zurich University Museum. "Vectan-Brosman has no other specimens other than the ones you have just mentioned."

"I'm still not sure you've answered my question, or that you fully understand the seriousness of your predicament." said the small sallow skinned man, "Where did Matt Malcolm get his initial sample of the Eden Seed?"

"What did you call it?" asked Lucius, dully.

"It is known by many names, but we call it that because it is the most accurate."

Lucius couldn't believe his bad luck: to be kidnapped by a rival pharmaceutical company would have been bad enough, but to be kidnapped by a group of self-deluded, religious fanatics was plainly dangerous. Lucius changed tack. "You said that you'd destroyed the crop in Almeria?"

The small man closed his eyes in an effort to hide his anger. "I said no such thing."

"Only four people knew where we grew those seeds," said Lucius. Before he could speculate any further, however, a fourth figure walked out from behind the sarcophagus. She was dressed more casually than the last time he'd seen her, but he recognised her instantly.

11

BY THE MORNING Matt Malcolm had reached Edinburgh Airport. Wandering into the Terminal around eight, he found a toilet, washed, and then rang home. Jenny should have been up by now, preparing Peter's packed lunch, but it clicked onto the answer machine again.

Fingering the piece of paper in his pocket, his 'instructions', he toyed with the idea of calling the police but then decided not to. He had to fight off this particular urge. He might be implicated in Sylvie's murder and could, at the very least, be delayed, he decided. He checked his watch. According to the note he had until four in the afternoon on Sunday to collect another sample of the Seed. It was Tuesday, so that meant he only had five days and eight hours left.

Should he tell Vectan-Brosman? How could he warn his bloody wife if she wouldn't pick up the phone? Then an ominous thought dropped, unbidden, into his mind. What if she couldn't answer the phone?

He stood to lose his family one way or another. With all this mess, Jenny was bound to find out about Sylvie eventually. The police would have no interest in protecting his wife from his various sexual misdemeanours once the shit hit the fan. Sweating profusely he dialled 118500 and asked to be connected to Vectan-Brosman. He waited a few seconds before, to his relief, the usual receptionist answered.

"Mary, it's Matt," he said.

There was a slight pause, as Mary seemed to gather her thoughts. She spoke in a stilted manner that made him wonder if she was reading out her response verbatim. "Sorry Mr. Malcolm, but we've been instructed to refer you to the police if you contact us."

"Mr. Malcolm? You're taking the piss, Mary, right? Put me through to Linda."

"I..."

For the second time in twenty-four hours, the line went dead.

"For Christ's sake!" He just managed to stop himself from smacking Jimmy's mobile off a glass counter encasing a rack of stylish laptops. Deciding to buy a ticket as Jimmy in case the Police were already onto him, he shuffled up to the Jenair sales desk. The girl hardly looked at the passport, which was just as well, as he'd forgotten to remove his glasses or dye his hair. Heart-burn and reflux caused him to rub his stomach as he wandered past the bookshops on his way to international departures. His lack of sleep on the bus meant that he felt giddy and over-anxious.

This anxiety grew as he approached the departure gate and thought about Jimmy Kaminski's passport photo again. He flushed.

He couldn't afford the slightest hitch or delay. He couldn't afford to risk his family, not now that he'd witnessed the hippy-haired psycho committing cold-blooded murder, twice. A lump in his throat made it hard to swallow. Now, more than ever, he had to look after number one. No one else seemed to give a damn. His wife wouldn't answer the bloody phone, his work had disowned him, and he still had the psycho on his trail. He had to get on that plane.

Soon, he was being ushered through the metal detectors and waved on to the departure gate. Only one out of the three people who'd glanced at his passport hesitated, but, distractedly, they'd ushered him onward after a child had thrown a tantrum in the queue behind him.

On the Jenair 737 Matt flopped, exhausted, next to a young, balding executive who wore a set of in-flight headphones that rattled with high frequency excerpts of AC/DC and Rush. Closing his eyes, his thoughts drifted back to Brin Cottage, and to Peter and Jenny. Still exhausted, he passed on the plastic breakfast and closed his eyes.

It was a good hour later before a jolt brought Matt back to the land of the living. Turbulence over Paris was the reason given by the captain, explaining, in his plumy accent, that cumulus clouds and a high pressure front from the east had resulted in uneven pockets of air. Matt was uninterested in the science, deciding that a simple apology tinged with some reassuring statement would have been fine.

The young executive beside him had slumped against his left shoulder. His earplugs ceased their incessant tinny rhythms and Matt tried to ease away. Unfortunately, however, the more he inched away, the more young man gripped his arm and snuggled in. Matt sighed and reached over to retrieve the in-flight magazine, but it was held tightly by the black elasticated netting of the seat in front and he couldn't quite reach it. About to try once more, he recoiled as a brown uniformed stewardess smiled and pulled it free.

"Em, thanks. I'm a bit stuck," he said, awkwardly.

"I can see that, sir. Let me help." As she leaned over Matt to wake the young executive, her ample nylon-covered breasts brushed against Matt's unshaven cheek. Feeling a sudden surge of mid-morning testosterone, he tried to distract himself by keeping his eyes fixed on the executive's head as it wavered in mid-air. Faltering on the edge of consciousness, the young man babbled incoherently, sucked some droll back into his mouth, and then resumed his snoring.

"Eh, thanks," said Matt, issuing a little 'Stan Laurel' grin that he instantly regretted.

The stewardess giggled and continued on down the aisle.

He felt his face flush as he followed the sway of her hips. Aroused, he hunkered back down into his seat and flicked through the in-flight magazine in an effort to find the most boring picture possible before his early morning urge became too visible.

Remembering to remove his glasses this time, he passed effortlessly through Swiss Passport Control, as James Serge Kaminski. He changed a little of the cash from his manila envelope into Swiss Francs, then stepped outside the terminal building to hail a taxi. His nostrils tingled as he sniffed in the cold, dry air of Zurich. Above him, a grey-white patch of sky looked heavy with snow. To his left, a busy tunnel opened out onto the main highway that led down to the centre of Zurich, already thick with morning traffic. Carbon monoxide stung the back of his throat.

"Where to?" A taxi driver was already stooping down to pick up Jimmy's holdall.

"It's okay, I'll get that," said Matt. He didn't want to go straight to the University, not yet. "The Wendell Strasse, please. Just drop me at the Café Zusse."

Matt decided that he could do with some strong coffee. A busy piano bar by night, the Café' Zusse was more neo-art deco during the day. There were plenty of little alcoves and snugs where he could panic in private.

He handed the taxi driver twenty-four Swiss francs and stepped out onto the busy pavement. A blond-haired policeman, dressed in an off-grey uniform, took note of the taxi's licence number. He looked Matt straight in the eye then began muttering into his intercom.

Stifling another wave of anxiety, Matt picked up his holdall and pushed open the heavy brass door of the Café Zusse.

The languorous odour of freshly crushed Columbian coffee washed over him. It gave him a pleasant feeling of contentment. Warm and welcoming as ever, the Café, with its red and yellow impressionist paintings, looked and felt as comforting as it always had. Being this exhausted, paranoia would always play tricks with his mind, he decided. He did, however, begin to worry about Jenny and Peter once more. He waited for Jimmy's mobile to find a good signal before dialling the house. As the phone in his house clicked over to the answer machine, he remembered that Peter had his own mobile. Jenny, he recalled, was completely anti-mobile. She just couldn't be persuaded to use one, no matter what he did to try and convince her. He knew it lay, unused, and already outdated, in her underwear drawer.

* * *

A DOCTOR HAD examined Peter before his mum had taken to him to his Nana's house. It was Tuesday, one o'clock, and he'd sunk back into the familiar red, crinoline sofa that marked all twelve of his childhood Christmases. Its red nylon bobbles smelt of home cooking and cigarette smoke. Already immersed in the reassuring blandness of the TV, Peter hid from the horrors of the last twenty-four hours amongst a non-stop selection of soaps and cartoons. His mum had gone out with the inspector and he'd been left with his Nana's next-door neighbour, Mrs. Leslie. Several police constables chattered in the kitchen.

Embedded amongst the snowdrops and crocus patches of his Nana's wide street, Peter had experienced a feeling of relief when he'd been told that he wouldn't have to go to school that day.

He could see the police car parked outside the front window and was just about to change the channel when the mobile buzzed in his pocket.

He fumbled with the small buttons. "Hello?"

12

MATT HEARD HIS son's voice and felt a rush of relief. "Are you okay, son?"

"Dad!" Peter sounded excited. "Dad, where are you? Mum's killed a woman burglar!"

Matt was totally unprepared for anything other than a few polite exchanges and perhaps a rundown of the previous day's activities at school. "Your... your Mum did what?"

"They pushed their way in last night. A big man with long black hair like that singer in Death Drone, and a woman..."

He heard a female voice in the background. "Where are you?" Matt had broken into a sweat at the thought of the long-haired psycho being anywhere near his family but the note, his instructions, had warned that his family would be in trouble.

"That's the policewoman. We're at Nana's house and Mum's gone with the police inspector," said Peter.

Matt heard the other voice more clearly now. "Peter, tell the Police to stay with you until I come back."

"When are you coming home?" said Peter.

"Soon, son, soon. But you're both okay?"

"Yeah."

He heard Peter sniff.

"Where did you say mum has gone?" asked Matt, anxiously.

"Some place. I heard the inspector telling Mum the name. Brim, Brine..."

The line crackled with interference. "Peter, are you still there?"

"Mr. Malcolm; this is the police. We need to talk to you. Where are..."

Matt clicked Jimmy's mobile off and flopped back into his cold, leather chair.

"Sir?" A dark-haired waitress was hovering beside his table.

Matt's eyes were glazed, his mind racing to make sense of the situation. The waitress smiled enquiringly. "Cappuccino, espresso, latte?"

"Just plain coffee," he snapped. He nodded and watched the waitress walk away. Brin Cottage. It had to be, he decided. "Shit!"

Confused, the waitress glanced back at him, shrugged, and then continued towards the bar.

The psycho's threat had been real. But is it still real? Would the police be able to protect his family? Should he go back now? An overwhelming feeling of helplessness washed over him as he fought the urge to bolt out of the café and get the first flight home. Who is the psycho working for? Why is Vectan-Brosman ignoring him? He remembered Barclay's instructions: "Get Schlesinger and get The Seed Project back on track before Burrows and Ueshima find out…" He then re-read the note he'd found in his folder the night before. 'You have six days to produce another sample of the Seed. Your girlfriend was expendable; your wife and kid, we presume, are not. Your deadline is Sunday, 4 P.M..'

He looked at the clock on the wall; the minute hand jerked to 12:31 P.M. He had to assume that the psycho's threat was completely real. Peter hadn't said what had happened to the man he'd seen the night before. It had to be the same, long-haired psycho, but Peter said something about Jenny killing a burglar… And he'd mentioned a woman. Who was the woman? "Fuck!"

On hearing Matt's expletive, several people rustled their morning papers.

He had five days, three hours and twenty-nine minutes to get that bloody Seed. The psycho must have left the other man he'd seen in the field back at his house, to guard Jenny and Peter. The psycho must have got a call to say things had gone wrong back at Matt's house. That's why he'd left the service station in such a hurry. But Peter had said that it was a woman. Jenny had killed a woman burglar… Jenny? Jenny wouldn't even crush a spider in the bath. And now she was on her way to Brin Cottage.

He thought about Sylvie's mutilated body upstairs. His spare clothes, still neatly folded in her tallboy. His car had been abandoned yards away from the cottage and… Oh God! There are pictures on the mantelpiece. Pictures of Sylvie, Billy-boy and me walking in the woods, smiling… having Christmas dinner. "Shit!" Jenny would find everything. How could anything possibly get worse than this? He'd lost his job and now he was sure to lose his family. But, most of all, he felt ashamed; he felt terribly ashamed that Jenny should find out like this.

The waitress gave Matt a puzzled stare as she placed the coffee on his table.

"Everything okay, sir?"

He looked up at her, watery eyed and said, "Yep." He shrugged. "Just having a bad day… shares and stuff… you know." He sipped the warm coffee and closed his eyes hoping that the girl would go away. He heard her footsteps. She was walking off to another table.

How on Earth could Jenny have killed anyone? What had they been through? But Peter sounded okay. Matt had heard the TV and there were police in the house watching out for him.

As he sipped his coffee, an inescapable feeling of dread built inside him. His eyes flicked over the people in the Café Zusse. Two businessmen chattered over an opened laptop in the corner. They spilled oily flakes of croissant over their black suits as they jostled for control of the keyboard. Oblivious to the mess they were making, they alternated between pointing at the screen and munching on their breakfast. Their simple excitement made Matt jealous.

He studied the waitress as she walked between the other tables; her sleek black hair shone on her shoulders. She was probably only eighteen or nineteen, most likely working off her student loan between lectures.

There were only two other people in the bar besides the businessmen, the waitress and himself: an older gent with a copy of Nueu Zurcher Zeitung, who hummed and hawed at the various articles, and a women of about sixty with shoulder-length, white hair. Dressed in lynx and leather, she fidgeted with a heavy, gold pen as she sipped her latte. Her lips were garish red and her skin was like polished paper, almost translucent, fragile but flawless. Her sad eyes were focused outside on the snowy street where trams rattled past and a little vehicle buzzed in-between the pedestrians.

Mainly white, with splashes of blue and green, the vehicle had a rotating brush that protruded from its bubble cabin like some giant proboscis. It licked all traces of filth from the Swiss gutters before moving on.

The distractions of Zurich momentarily eased the pain of his inevitable domestic destruction. Nothing would ever be the same again, and nothing he could do now was going to stop Jenny from seeing what she would see. He could, however, still protect her. That was the least he could do. He had to find the Seed.

He suddenly thought about Lucius and wondered if anyone had checked Lucius's flat, which was only yards from the University.

His coffee had grown a little patch of cold, milky skin and Matt had begun to scoop it to one side when the café's heavy brass door swung inward. Two tanned youths wearing short jerkins stepped inside and shook the snow from their shoulders. Behind them, bigger flakes had begun to tumble from an invisible sky, and the tall bank buildings on the opposite side of the street were becoming difficult to make out.

The first of the youths pointed to a seat in the corner beneath a large mirror. They murmured to each other in what sounded like Arabic, but Matt was too far away to say for sure. As they lit their cigarettes, the taller of the two tapped into a pencil-thin mobile. Then, looking directly at Matt, he began to scribble on a piece of paper. Matt suddenly felt uncomfortable. He glanced round for the waitress but she'd disappeared. They always did when you wanted to pay the bill. The smaller of the two youths wore a yellow v-neck sweater and had a gold tooth, which glinted every time he chattered to his friend. The taller youth seemed more nervous and had a pronounced hooked nose. He rubbed his left eyebrow in between each puff of his cigarette.

Matt stood up to leave, placing twenty Swiss francs on the glass-topped coffee table. It was snowing even heavier now, and he doubted that his tweed jacket and well-worn cords would stand up to the cold. He checked the manila envelope. He would need more Swiss currency.

Beside the envelope he found his own heavy, company Nokia. It had knocked against his ribs for the last time. Completely drained of power and the number dangerously recognisable, it was useless. Matt fingered Jimmy's phone. Lighter and fully charged, he still worried about his last call being traced by the police. Pretending to check his laces he shoved both phones under the cushion of his leather seat before making for the heavy brass door. He could see the reflection of the two youths in the glass that covered a large, black and red painting. Thankfully, neither moved nor even seemed to be remotely interested as he walked out into the blizzard.

Across the street he saw that the bank was now open, its austere entranceway barely discernible through the flurry of wet flakes. Its tall, black gates stood open, and a warm, yellow glow emanated from within, drawing him closer. As he stepped inside, a concierge approached him and smiled demurely. In heavily accented English, he asked, "Can I help, sir?"

Matt knew, by his tone, that what he really meant was: 'A tramp like you can't possibly think that I'm going to let you into a place like this.'

Matt smiled, nodded an assertive, "Good day," and asked for the currency desk.

"Eh... over to your left, sir." The concierge still eyed him suspiciously, and Matt noticed him signal to a colleague on the other side of the hall.

Matt tried to pull himself together, walk with some sense of purpose and pride. On approaching the ornate brass grill that separated him from the young teller, he wondered what kind of people had accounts in this place, so deep in the financial hub of Zurich. There were six such grills to his left and a further four to his right. The ceiling was vaulted and adorned with beautiful Michelangelo-like paintings that gave its otherwise pastel plastered walls a splash of opulence.

Matt knew the history of this part of the town; he'd been told the story of Zurich by Lucius Schlesinger many times. Once a Roman custom port known as Turicum, the trading of textiles sparked its growth and allowed it to become a free city of the Holy Roman Empire. Lucius had suggested that the ensuing merchant guilds that had forged the banking sector back then still pulled the strings in Zurich. This canton of Switzerland had always been the most affluent and the most secretive.

"Do you have an account, sir?" the smiling teller enquired.

Matt sighed as he handed over one thousand pounds, "No, but I would like to change this into Swiss Francs, please."

"A moment, sir." The teller pressed a small brass button on his desk.

Matt didn't like the look of this, and he became even more disconcerted when the teller beckoned a clerk from the foremost rank of desks behind him. They mumbled for a few seconds before the teller spoke to Matt. "I will need your passport, sir."

"Fine." Matt rummaged in Jimmy's holdall until he found the dimpled, burgundy passport and handed it over.

The teller held it up to the light and checked the franc marks. He then counted the fifty-pound notes before pressing a second button that made someone else behind him jump up. This person then slipped the teller a clear pouch. Matt couldn't believe how antiquated, overly complicated, and strangely traditional the whole business seemed. It was like, he decided, the Changing of the Guard, or the piping in of the haggis at a Burns Supper - tradition for tradition's sake, all for show. All part of the Swiss Banking experience, he presumed.

The pillar of the brass grill, polished as smooth as any mirror, suddenly revealed some familiar reflections. To Matt's horror, he recognised the two dark-skinned youths he'd seen in the Café Zusse. They were standing directly behind him. It was the yellow v-neck sweater that had caught his attention first. Jimmy's passport was still lying open in front of him. He could smell cheap tobacco as the taller youth leaned over in an effort to look at Jimmy's picture.

Matt snapped the passport shut. "Do you mind?" he said, sharply, eyeing the teller for some moral support.

The teller signalled the concierge. But before the uniformed concierge could cross the polished marble floor, the taller youth spoke, "You've changed a little, Mr. Kaminski."

"Pardon?" Matt was shaken.

The teller gave the tall youth a withering glance then smiled at Matt. "Do you know this man, Mr. Kaminski?"

"For years," the tall youth interjected. "But he's gained a few pounds, haven't you, James?"

Matt laughed nervously and moved closer to the grill, gathering in his money and pocketing the passport. He smiled at the teller and nervously attempted some humour. "He's right, of course. I blame all the wonderful restaurants you have here."

Matt saw the look of bewilderment fall, like a curtain, over the young teller's face. 'Removed at birth', he thought. This was the phrase Sir John always used to describe the Swiss sense of humour. In the lull that followed, Matt turned to face the tall, dark-skinned youth, but he was gone. Both of them had gone.

He nodded his thanks to the slightly disgruntled teller, and stuffed the cash, unceremoniously, into his trouser pockets. He strolled back towards the two concierges at the main doorway and then stepped outside. But just as he braced himself for the snow he felt a hand on his shoulder. The smell of cheap tobacco washed over him once more.

13

THE FINGERS ON his shoulder were stained yellow with nicotine. "Actually, I did not think the picture in the passport looked very much like you at all."

Slowly, Matt turned his head until he came face to face with the tall Arab youth. He didn't know what to say.

The smaller one with the v-necked sweater spoke up. "In fact it looked rather like an old friend of ours."

Matt jerked himself free and raced out into the blizzard. Without looking back, he slipped and skidded his way up the street in the direction of the University. He knew that if he got as far as the Funicular he could probably lose them in the busy Polybahn station.

The two dark-skinned youths had almost caught up with him when he saw the entrance to the Zeiss-Shtick Department Store on his left. Diving inside, he pushed past an older gentleman who fell in front of the youths and tripped the taller of the two. Matt then bolted up the downward elevator and made for the first floor.

Fur coats, hats, mole-skins and insulated gloves toppled over onto the polished wooden walkway as Matt pulled over the chrome stands. Running as far as the lifts, he pushed all the buttons and snatched a leather coat from the nearest display. Slipping it on, he backed into the gathering onlookers who'd by now focused their attention on the two dark-skinned youths who were scrambling awkwardly over the fallen coat stands.

Having temporarily lost sight of Matt, the taller of the two Arabs peered inside the first lift but the smaller of the two, with the yellow v-neck, jerked round and pointed Matt out in the crowd behind them. As the Arab youths ran toward the crowd of gawping shoppers, however, a huge security guard caught the taller youth's arm and twisted it painfully up his back.

Matt shuffled further back into the crowd.

The smaller youth, now realising their predicament, tried to placate the security guard who'd brought tears to the eyes of his taller companion, but by now a second security guard had rounded on him too. He drew a black cosh from the inside pocket of his smart black uniform.

The onlookers began to applaud and, not wishing to stand out, Matt joined them. "Bravo, well done!" The sound of alarm bells filled the store, adding to the excitement of the shoppers and the general pandemonium.

Matt, about to leave the scene, suddenly stopped short. There, around the neck of the smaller youth, no doubt loosened by the arm-twisting antics of the Arian guard, swung something that made Matt's heart jump. He pulled out the little metal object from his trouser pocket and opened his fingers. Looking down, he examined the silver statuette. Six silver wings: two protruding from its back, two over its eyes, and two over its feet. He looked up to see the youths being led away. The medallion he'd just seen round the Arab youth's neck had been exactly the same as Jimmy's.

In the cacophony of alarms and yells caused by the chase, he marched straight through the bank of screeching electronic detectors and out onto the street, still wearing his newly acquired leather coat.

His adrenaline levels still high, he decided, there and then, to make the slight detour to Lucius Schlesinger's flat. He still had the spare key Lucius had given him a year ago, so he could see for himself if there was any sign of the Professor. Matt hoped there might be some clue as to Lucius's whereabouts. He further hoped that the Professor could be found in time to help him identify the seeds he'd taken so long ago. He'd only held them for a few drunken moments. Lucius had worked with them for months on end. He couldn't afford to make a mistake and pick up the wrong ones.

Stepping onto the Kunsthaus, he followed the Ramistrasse uphill until he came to the University quarter. Just along from the Archaeological Collection, about half way up the Ramistrasse, Matt wound his way round the rear of the grey granite museum building that housed the fateful Etruscan Ware Collection. He passed the students'   accommodation and eventually reached a small lane that bisected the gardens to the rear of the lecturers' residency.

The sky was beginning to clear and Matt looked down the hill into the old town of Zurich. His gaze settled on the slate-grey lake that stretched out behind the city. Peppered, as usual, with cabin cruisers, rowing boats, swans and coots, it looked cold and unwelcoming.

He fingered his yellow looped key ring and spun it out of Jimmy's holdall. A bit of a loner, Lucius had grown fond of the brassy young marketeer who had dropped the biggest find of his career into sample tray ninety-nine, almost eighteen months earlier. As the key turned in the lock, Matt felt a tinge of sadness, not so much for the missing Dr. Schlesinger, but for his own wife, Jenny. He felt sad that she, like him, would probably be stepping into another house that held secrets, secrets best left undiscovered. He wanted to run, right now, all the way back to Brin cottage before she got there. He wanted to hide the pictures, burn his clothes and dust away any traces of his deceit before—

"Hello?"

The voice had caught Matt by surprise. It was familiar but he couldn't place it. Not in Zurich. Lucius's door swung inward and a strong, sickly-sweet perfume washed over him.

14

MATT HESITATED. "Linda?"

Linda beamed as she ruffled her snow-white hair. They both stood motionless in the doorway for a few moments before she pulled him in and shut the door. She was obviously relieved to see him, but Matt was still in a state of shock.

He began to mumble. "When...? I mean...?"

"How did I get here? Well, I put two and two together and decided you might need some help. I thought Barclay had just slipped into one of his bad moods, sent you off on some errand out of spite, but when they circulated the memo about you being fired I..." Linda paused, clearly amused by the look on Matt's face. "I hope you don't mind."

"No, no, of course not, but..." His mind was working overtime.

"Ah, so there's a 'but'?" said Linda, her eyes flashing with sheer mischief.

He gave her an awkward, little hug in the doorway. "No, I'm really pleased to see you, but I don't understand how you knew where I was going to go. You knew about Zurich but, I mean..." Matt saw her blush, "if you figured out where I would go, God knows who else might show up."

"When you didn't appear off the flight from Stansted, I didn't know what to do," said Linda, "I had some leave to take. In fact, I have three months." she laughed nervously. "Bit of a workaholic." She resumed the hug.

Matt tensed. "Linda, what else can you tell me?" He flushed with embarrassment.

She stepped back and looked into his eyes. "Your glasses are filthy."

It felt strange when she fussed over him. "Linda, all hell has broken loose and I need to know how you knew I'd come here." He looked out of the window, down into the snow filled streets. The sun was shining brightly now, and he was dazzled by the intensity of the glare. "We could both be in real danger here. Why would you want to get involved in my mess?"

She stopped him from saying any more with a small tut-tut. "I'm very fond of you, Matt, and I knew something was wrong when Lucius hadn't phoned."

"Lucius?" Matt had a sudden thought. "You and Lucius..."

"Have been seeing each other, on and off, for over twenty years now," Linda finished, a little 'mum knows best' smile forming on her lips.

"You and Lucius?" Matt repeated, churlishly. "I'd never have guessed."

"Guessed what, that a couple of old wrinklies like us would ever get up to anything exciting?"

"No, no, I didn't..."

Closing the door behind them, Linda wandered into the small kitchen and poured out a large mug of coffee.

Matt watched Linda closely. She seemed different out-with the confines of the office, more vibrant and even more alluring than usual. She was wearing a pair of tight-fitting jeans and a snug, purple polo-neck sweater that accentuated her Rubenesque curves.

Linda giggled to herself as she opened one of the kitchen units. She rummaged around for a moment and then produced a biscuit tin. "I told Lucius to hide these from you."

"You did, did you?" said Matt, still amazed at the Professor. He felt an unexpected wave of jealously grip him as he imagined Lucius and Linda upstairs.

She straightened her clinging top before sitting back. "I decided to come here for myself and see where Lucius had got to, especially when Barclay and Sir John couldn't, or should I say, wouldn't tell me what was really going on."

Matt sipped his coffee and placed it on Lucius's mantelpiece. "Linda, there are people after me. The kind of money involved in this...this situation, means that there are no holds barred. I don't know who's behind it, not for sure, but they've killed at least two people so far and, from what I can gather, Jenny's been attacked and..." Matt's voice tailed off as he saw Linda's eyes narrow.

She stood up and walked back towards the front door. "Look!" Linda held up a pile of letters. "Look at all this mail. He never goes anywhere without opening his mail. He's not been here for..." She checked the postmarks, "two, maybe three days."

Matt nodded, "You're right, of course but..."

"Matt, has this anything to do with the Seed Project?" Linda's tone was matter of fact.

"For God's sake, what don't you know?" He looked at her suspiciously.

"Secretaries are privy to all sorts of secrets that you, in middle management, would never even imagine. We should be paid hush money." Her voice deepened. "I'm sorry. Is Jenny okay?"

Matt, thrown by the question, answered cautiously, "Well, she is at the moment, but..."

"There's that 'but' thing again," said Linda. "What else is going on?" She walked over to the window and stood beside him.

He felt the warmth of her body and was drawn in by her syrupy perfume. "It's complicated, Linda."

She winked at him in a way that made him stir. "Try me."

Matt felt an overwhelming urge to tell her everything. He needed to share this with someone. "I... I was having an affair." He hesitated then said, "And now my wife is going to find out exactly where I've been when I was supposed to be working from home, flexitime."

She turned her head to look into Matt's eyes. "You mean Brin Cottage and the girl called Sylvie?"

Matt took a step back and slumped down into the green velvet sofa.

"Jesus." His mouth suddenly dry, he took another sip of his coffee and burnt his lip.

"Sir John wants to know every flexitime location; he wants to know where every minute of every mobile call is generated, and where every minute of every e-mail connection comes from. You've been stupid, Matt. Everything's traced, right down to the last dot, dash and whore."

He tensed then stood up, suddenly angry. "It would seem so, but Sylvie was no whore."

Unmoved by his anger, she continued to stare out blankly across the city below. The little red carriages of the Polybahn funicular slid down the forty-yard incline towards the city below. Crammed with students and tourists, they trundled up and down the two minutes' worth of track as they had for over a hundred years. Linda touched Matt's hand and spoke softly. "She was a Ukrainian agent, Matt. Whether she could be classed as a whore or not... Well, you'd be the best judge of that. You see, Sir John is no fool. He always made sure that any formulas or contra-indications discovered, for any of our new drugs, were slightly altered. He let you continue because the misinformation you were able to pass on was invaluable."

Matt's tongue re-stuck itself to the roof of his mouth. "I need a proper drink," he gasped.

"Here." Linda put her coffee down next to Matt's and lifted a small, silver flask from her handbag. She poured a few drops into each cup. "Schnapps. And don't feel too bad. You won't be the first or the last to be caught in a honey trap."

He turned to her and looked into her misty grey eyes. "What about you? What about your husband?"

"I've never been married." Linda smiled back at him and wiggled her fingers inches from His face. "But these rings have always proved useful in letting people think I was." She giggled, impishly.

Linda's ring-encrusted fingers became a blur of pink and gold as his eyes settled on her clinging purple sweater.

Smiling mischievously, she continued. "I prefer to do my own thing. The freedom to say 'yes' or 'no' has always been too precious for me to give up. I decided, a long time ago, to be honest with myself." She took his hand and placed it on her breast. "When was the last time you were honest with yourself, Matt?"

He was totally unprepared for this, and stood there feeling stupid for a moment until, very gently, his fingers began to tease her softness. Placing his other hand round her back he pulled her in close until her warmth pressed gently against his hard body. His muscles tensing, his heart pounding with years of unrequited lust, he placed his lips against hers and kissed her deeply. Slowly, he kneaded her breasts through the purple sweater until he felt her nipples harden. As he kissed her neck he tasted her bittersweet perfume and felt her hand move between his legs.

She gripped him tightly. "C'mon Matt, you can do better than that," she whispered.

Matt lifted her sweater up and unclipped her bra. He sighed with amazement as her breasts tumbled free. Large, brown nipples brushed against his face and he felt the warmth of her silky skin against his roughness. He teased her nipples, nipping then sucking before slowly and methodically working his way up past her collar bone and shoulder until he found her soft, willing neck. He revelled in her gasps and groans, biting her softly below her ear.

Linda suddenly gripped his hand.

He stopped, thinking he'd gone too far. But instead she guided him, slowly and surely, downwards until his fingers touched the warmth of her jeans. She placed his hand between her legs and smiled, her eyes still closed.

Unbuttoning the straining metal studs one by one, he held his breath as she kissed and bit his neck now. Then, as her jeans slipped free, she pushed him back onto the green sofa and turned away, bending over to pick up her fallen clothes. Matt marvelled at the fullness of her white cheeks and pulled his clothes off as quickly as he could, kicking his trousers away before reaching up to touch her.

She giggled and bent over even further, revealing herself to him. She was unkempt and wild. Unable to resist, he reached out and cupped her in both hands.

She placed her legs a little further apart and reached round, catching his hand. Matt was trembling as she guided his fingers into position. Then, with a long breath, she began to ease herself back onto him. Matt reached round with his other hand and cupped her breast.

Fully aroused, he withdrew his fingers and pushed himself into her. He felt her grip him, and then she began to rock backwards and forwards until they were both grinding hard against each other. Long and slow, then fast and furious, they reeled with a burning lust that possessed them both completely.

After a few moments Linda eased away from him. She turned and knelt down at Matt's feet. She used her long nails to trace his thighs and then grip his tight buttocks. She stared up at him and smiled before moving her mouth over him.

He tried to pull away but she wouldn't allow it. She gripped him even more tightly than before and guided him back. The more Matt tried to pull away, stretch out this ultimate fantasy for as long as he could, the more eagerly she gripped his buttocks and held him. She refused to set him free. Relentlessly, she persisted until his legs weakened and his thoughts turned into the most base of animal cravings. With a yell of release, every ounce of his existence was forced into one almighty push.

Linda waited until Matt was completely spent before setting him free. Then stood up and kissed him deeply.

Still shaking, Matt drew back. Linda reached for him but far too sensitive to endure another second this close to her he staggered further back.

Linda moaned before pulling him back towards her. "Don't move," she whispered.

He saw her reach between her legs. She held his arm tightly as her mouth fell open as she bucked and quivered. Caught in her own fantasy, she screamed out into some long-imagined dream then stopped with a shudder.

Matt stood completely still, his arm now marked and throbbing.

Tears welled up in her beautiful grey eyes.

Ignoring the trickle of blood that ran down his arm, he knelt down to face her, teasing her soft hair, pulling her close as she sobbed into his shoulder. "Are you alright?"

"I'm fine." She giggled, in between deep sobs, as they both stood up and held each other. His muscles tensed against her moist skin. Beads of sweat, now cold, made him shiver.

They moved over to the soft goatskin rug and lay down. Matt could feel the winter sun streaming in through the window. It bathed them in its warmth. Matt stared down at Linda and realised, there and then, that she was probably the most beautiful woman he had ever seen. Refined, sexual perfection lay before him. Honed by some long forgotten god, she was resplendent in the dappled light that traced her perfect curves.

15

IMUR DIRECTED HIS question at the youth in the yellow sweater. "I don't want a repeat of the mess in Almeria. I've still not discovered who got there first and who killed off the workers. What else can you tell me?"

The youth looked up at his taller companion before answering in the ancient tongue. "We were released an hour ago after we explained that it was just a student's prank. They searched us, of course, but found nothing to keep us there." The taller youth shuffled nervously then explained, "Matt Malcolm has Kaminski's passport; he used it to get some currency in the Grand Bank, but he began to run when we approached him."

"You should have approached him in a more subtle way," said Imur.

The two youths stared down at their feet.

Imur continued. "We've also spotted the long-haired assassin, Stiller. He obviously knows where Mr. Malcolm has alighted. But then I would expect nothing less from him." He reached over and gripped the silver pendant resting on the smaller youth's yellow sweater. "You don't deserve to wear this, do you?"

"We are sorry, sir. You're right, we should have been more careful." Imur toyed with the heavy pendant for a few seconds before letting it fall back against the youth's chest. "I have sent our newfound friend to fetch Mr. Malcolm. The marketeer appears to be in the doctor's apartment already."

He pointed across at Lucius Schlesinger, who lay asleep in the far corner of the room. The old man twitched and mumbled beneath the blanket they'd given him, obviously caught in some unwanted dream. "We were right to take him," Imur continued. "Mr. Malcolm will have no choice other than to come and help his old friend."

The two youths skirted the huge casket that lay in the centre of the chamber and then followed Imur up a set of stairs. When they reached the top landing, they pushed open a heavy door and shielded their eyes against the light. Turning round, Imur locked the door and checked the handle before proceeding. They were in a small cupboard full of buckets and brooms and had to climb a further set of stairs before emerging into the main hall of the museum. They passed a row of impressive Egyptian Fayoum portraits from the first century B.C., and then continued on towards a set of wall-sized steles once stolen from what used to be Nimrud, but is now better known as modern Iraq. They walked out, unnoticed by the group of noisy students who stood sketching one of the ancient Egyptian deities that lined the marbled hallway.

"Imur?" said the smaller of the two youths.

Imur stopped beside the Hellenic display and put his fore-finger to his lips. "Be careful not to let my name fall on unwanted ears." He scanned the hall and led the youths further away from a group of first year students, busy dismantling one of the displays. "Now, could you please go to the doctor's apartment and make sure that Miss Baron comes to no harm. Keep out of sight, and be sure to check for any signs of Stiller." Imur produced a small print from his brown corduroy jacket. The picture showed Stiller walking out of the airport arrivals terminal. "This was taken thirty minutes ago. He's the one who killed Serge."

The two youths shook their heads and sighed.

"You spent time training with James Serge Kaminski in Glasgow, didn't you?" said Imur.

They nodded, studying the pale features of a tall man with a mop of raven-black hair. Surreptitiously, Imur passed each of them a small silver pistol. "You know not to use these unless there is no other choice?"

"We do."

"Now listen," continued Imur, "Jessica Baron has been told what to do and where to go, but I fear that she is having second thoughts. The whole situation frightens her, and this may be the first time she could be directly threatened, so watch her."

The taller youth nodded. "Imur, are you sure she understands?"

"She supports our intrinsic values but she's more than a little uncomfortable with our methods. She's argued against the kidnap of the doctor from the start. I've had to persuade her that it will be safer for the old man and that it will cause the necessary ripples at Vectan-Brosman."

"What if she informs on us, tells the world about us?" said the smaller youth.

Imur pondered this for a moment then said, "I'm confident she will not. She understands how the Seraphim sect stretches back through time to the very beginning of mankind. She knows that we are doing God's work."

"But does she know how many of us there are?"

"I also explained that the sect has members everywhere: within governments, global companies, intelligence services; in fact, inside any decent sized bureaucracy where we feel it is necessary to listen." Imur made sure they could not be overheard. "I contacted Miss Baron three weeks after the Munich meeting. I received a copy of her report, even though she'd deleted it from her computer."

The youths checked their weapons and continued to listen. "Although she didn't want to see me at first, and actually denied that the meeting in Munich even took place, I told her that it would be a good idea to discuss the content of the meeting with us: a non-profit making organisation, yet still very interested in the best outcome. She is a clever lady but still very naive. Watch her carefully and make sure she stays safe."

As they left the museum, Imur wondered if the boys were really up to the job.

* * *

IN HER HOTEL room Jessica Baron remembered how, three weeks after the Munich meeting, she'd been impressed by Imur's breadth of knowledge of the pharmaceutical industry and the workings of the European Justice Department. Thrown at first, she'd listened in silence as he told her about the Vectan-Brosman crop that grew in Almeria and about their head of R&D, Dr. Lucius Schlesinger. Imur had reiterated the importance of denying any one company or government control of the wonder drug before she had finally asked him whom he represented. She remembered how he had gently stroked his black, waxed moustache and said, quite simply: "God."

Normally annoyed by such stupid claims she felt instead drawn to the little man. He had an air of calmness and a complete understanding of the situation that unnerved her. It made her hesitate just enough for Imur Falseth to flatter her. He'd told her how her position had merited respect and how he felt it necessary to inform her of his plan. Imur had produced a photograph of Matt Malcolm. "This man is crucial to our cause, and I have been informed that you could help us gain his confidence."

Jessica felt her pulse quicken. She had been attracted to Matt Malcolm's impudence and lack of respect, yet had been repulsed by his blatant attempt to manipulate her. He had specifically invited her to his meeting to give his terms some kind of stamp of approval. Her repeal of the European Parliament's generics mandate, two months before, meant that no copycat drugs could subsequently piggyback the original R&D work needed to bring a new drug to the marketplace. Lifelong patents were introduced and, as a result, all the main drug companies held Jessica Barron in the highest esteem. Imur had then explained how he in- tended to destroy the only live crop at the Vectan-Brosman research site in Almeria and then kidnap Dr. Schlesinger. He managed to convince her that by keeping this particular product from the marketplace he could achieve the best result for her and mankind. Imur had explained that the last time this wonder drug, the Eden Seed, as he called it, had been available to mankind it had caused the complete ruination of society. She remembered his soft, high-pitched voice: "Mankind is not sufficiently intelligent to use such gifts in moderation." He had further impressed her by calculating, correctly, that Matt Malcolm would be publicly sacked as a result of inter-company politics. He had also said something else that made her fear for her own safety: "Miss Baron, people will soon start to die as mankind's inevitable greed gathers momentum."

Her term as Chief Justice finished, as planned, on the fifteenth of February and she had, eventually, agreed to help Imur meet up with Matt Malcolm; the only man in the last three thousand years, other than Lucius Schlesinger, who could positively identify the small seed known to Imur and his sect as the Eden Seed.

The 'inevitable greed' Imur had predicted had already shown its ugly face in the form of Vlan Stiller. Imur had explained how this ex-KGB assassin was determined to either kill or capture Matt Malcolm and how she, nothing more than a law student who'd worked her way up through the legal ranks in Brussels, had to extract Matt Malcolm from Lucius Schlesinger's apartment before Stiller got there.

She slipped on her black, synthetic fur coat and looked out of her hotel window across the Lake. The sun had cut a wedge through the bleak sky and the water glinted and sparkled below the dark, shadowed hills.

A grey Mercedes taxi pulled up outside the marbled foyer of the Lakeside Hotel. She waved to attract the driver's attention. "Ramistrasse, please, the University Residence."

The taxi driver turned round and smiled at her. "No problem, Madam."

In minutes, Jessica found the doctor's front door and wondered if she would recognise Matt Malcolm. It had, after all, been more than eighteen months since he'd tried to unhitch her skirt from her handbag in Munich. She remembered that he was about five-seven, or so, with a slight frame. He had a cheeky, but handsome face and his mousy hair looked unkempt and out of control. She remembered his confident manner and the way he'd looked at her from behind his ridiculous black-rimmed glasses.

"I'll wait," said the pale-skinned driver.

Jessica took a deep breath and opened the taxi door. The cold air shocked her lungs into a coughing fit. Watery-eyed, she climbed the last remaining steps and knocked on the front door.

16

INSIDE THE APARTMENT Matt crouched down below the worktops in the kitchen. He pulled Linda down beside him. The freshly-made coffee steamed above their heads.

"Who the hell can that be?" said Matt.

Linda, struggling with the top button of her jeans, whispered, anxiously, "Maybe it's Lucius."

Matt peered down the hallway and instantly recognized the shape of a woman behind the frosted glass pane. "It's not Lucius, and it's not the psycho." He stood up and tucked in his shirt.

"Matt, what are you doing?" Linda's voice was laced with panic, but he had already begun to turn the door handle.

As the door opened, he leaned forward. "Can I help you"

"Mr. Malcolm?"

Matt's mind raced for a second or two as he tried to find her name, but he couldn't; he only managed her official title, "Chief Justice?"

"I know this is confusing but I need you to come with me right now. It's for your own good, believe me. I know where Lucius is and..."

"What do you mean you know where Lucius is?" Linda's voice was strong and assertive as she emerged from the kitchen. "What have you done with him?"

The Chief Justice seemed totally shocked to see Linda. Matt sensed her suspicion. Still clipping her bra, Linda ruffled her hair and adjusted her clinging purple jumper.

Matt moved himself between the ladies and suddenly found the name he'd been searching for, "Jessica... Jessica Baron?" Strangely, he felt ashamed and unbearably awkward.

"Take us to Lucius," snapped Linda.

"I didn't expect you to have company," said Jessica.

"Oh, it's not what it..." began Matt, instantly regretting opening his mouth.

"I don't want to know." Jessica glowered at Linda. "None of my business, but we have to go."

Linda pulled the front door fully open. "Where is Lucius?" She drew Jessica a hateful stare and tossed Matt his leather jacket.

Jessica glanced over her shoulder at her taxi driver. "I suppose you'd both better come. Quickly!"

Safely in the warmth of the taxi, Matt tried to explain, "This is Linda. She works for Vectan-Brosman. She's a good friend of Lucius. We've been-"

Jessica interrupted, "As I said, I don't need to know the sordid details, thank you." She eyed them both in the rear-view mirror. "You've been followed to Zurich by someone who'll think nothing of killing you both to get what he wants."

Matt sighed in disbelief as he thought of the tall psychopath he'd encountered the night before. His mind was still racing, remembering the killer's long, dank hair hanging like a pair of dreary curtains at the side of his face. "I think he's just checking on my progress. I'm not sure he'll know where I am just now."

"I knew you were here, and so did your elderly friend."

Linda's eyes narrowed.

Jessica ignored her. "His name is Stiller and, according to my sources, he is a trained killer who once worked for the KGB."

Matt glanced at Linda. "You know about this 'Stiller' too?" he asked, his heart pounding.

"Not exactly." She glanced at Jessica, "and I don't appreciate being referred to as an 'elderly friend'."

Matt knew that Linda had picked up on his embarrassment. He felt like a little boy who'd been caught out. Suddenly, every woman on the planet hated him.

"You'll meet my sources soon enough," said Jessica. "They've arranged to meet us on the lake. We're not sure if Stiller has any old contacts in Zurich but there's less chance of a positive interception on the water."

"Jessica, when exactly did you stop being a stuffy Chief Justice and turn into a secret agent?" Matt could feel his frustration building. Everyone seemed to know much more than him.

Jessica ignored him and tapped the driver on the shoulder. "Stop here, please."

The driver applied the brakes and brought the car to a halt with a jerk. "Wait there a moment," he said.

Matt saw the look of surprise on Jessica's face and immediately felt apprehensive when the driver clicked open his door.

The driver stepped from the car and opened the rear door nearest to the river. He unbuttoned his coat and tapped the handle of a small gun.

"What's going on, Jessica?" Matt whispered.

"My name is Muller," said the driver. "Imur asked me to look after you."

Jessica stepped onto the moorings. "Why didn't you say so earlier?" she snapped.

Matt noticed the now-familiar six-winged pendant around Muller's neck. He ducked out of the car and looked at the cold river below, then turned to help

Linda down the shaky wooden steps that led to the moorings. But he saw the anger in her eyes and backed off.

The River Limmat was packed with the pleasure boats of the Swiss elite. Cruisers, sailing boats, and small yachts were all jammed tight against the pristine wooden jetties that lined its banks. Matt's sense of rejection and fear was momentarily suspended as he watched a cluster of slate-coloured coots weave between the polished hulls. Squabbling for mates, the males nipped and pecked at each other while the females languished mid-stream.

Muller, the taxi driver, also turned out to be the pilot of their boat; a smart, single-hulled cruiser named Lavantina. They sat down on the plush leather seats while Muller climbed up to the raised internal driving seat and turned on the ignition. After a small splutter, the powerful twin engines roared and churned the water below. Muller spun the walnut wheel several revolutions to the left until the cruiser reversed out from the bank. He moved a similarly carved gear stick forward and the boat purred ahead, past a small island on their left, then under the busy A17.

Once free of the river, Muller opened up the throttle and the front of the boat lifted out of the water. Swans splashed out of the way as the cruiser built up speed and Linda steadied herself. She looks like she's going to be sick, thought Matt.

"Not too good on boats," she remarked.

But Muller just laughed and banked hard to the right. Ahead, the sun shone on a small whitewashed chapel, its fragile black spire perched on top of a red-tiled tower. The bleached walls intersected by long, arched windows winked through a row of upright poplars lining the bank.

"We stop here," said Muller, laughing once more when he saw the expression on Linda's face. "Don't worry, nice lady, it's very calm today. You should see it when the wind blows down from the Eiger. It's like the Atlantic Ocean!" He laughed again and opened the back door of the cabin.

Linda wasn't laughing back.

About half a mile behind the Lavantina a smaller speedboat cut a white scar across the murky surface of the lake. A blue stripe on a white hull was just visible through the spray and, as it got closer, they could see three figures sitting tight.

Matt looked into Jessica's amber eyes. "I presume these are your sources."

Jessica shrugged her shoulders.

"You mean you're not sure?" Matt stood up and studied the smaller craft. He felt sure he'd seen a very tall man at the helm, but it was difficult to be sure. "Jessica, if you're not convinced it's them, we should go now. Stiller is completely ruthless. We're sitting ducks here. He needs me, but if he sees that you're involved..."

"Don't worry," said Muller, "the Lavantina is one of the fastest cruisers on the lake. It can easily outrun anything else that might show up."

But as the speedboat closed in, Linda leapt to her feet. "Lucius! It's Lucius." She opened the back door of the cabin and balanced precariously on the varnished footboard. As they all shuffled in beside her, Matt saw that Linda was beaming like a little girl.

Jessica caught Matt's arm and whispered, "She seems to be madly in love with the doctor." She raised her eyebrows a little and added, "Don't worry, I won't tell."

Matt pulled away.

"I did not-" protested Matt.

"Rubbish. When I opened that door you looked like a rabbit in the head lights. If that's what you do to your friends, I wouldn't like to see what you do to your enemies." Jessica gave him a derisory snort before turning her attention back to the approaching speedboat.

His friend, Lucius, waved over to them. Beside him, a demure Middle Eastern gentleman steered the blue-striped speedboat alongside and signalled Muller to cut the engine of the Lavantina. The man on Lucius's right was bald and clean-shaven. He looked to be in his early twenties and his skin was the darkest ebony. He seemed uncomfortable in the smaller boat, far too tall for it, but he eventually stood up and gripped the side. Matt recognised the same height and power that marked the doctors and surgeons he'd spoken to at the North African launch of the cancer vaccine, Leukivec. This man could easily have been from Sudan, Eritrea, Djibouti, or even Ethiopia. Matt remembered the muted response to the cancer vaccine from the poorer African countries who barely managed to feed themselves and stave off the scourge of HIV.

Lucius beamed. "Matt, Linda, and... good to see you again, Miss Baron. I'm so pleased to see you all." He opened his big hands and waved at them like some deranged black and white minstrel, his gawky stance almost matching the North African's ungainly gait on the rippling waters of the lake.

Matt eyed the small, dark-skinned man with the waxed moustache. Matt liked to put people in boxes, categorise them before blending in as closely as he could. He thought the diminutive little man might be Syrian or Lebanese, but he knew one thing: this man was in charge. He saw the way Muller and even Jessica fussed around him.

They treated him with the same kind of reverence that would be bestowed upon a man of the cloth. So he was especially keen to find out who this man was, what he did and whom he represented.

17

JESSICA ASSUMED THE role of host, carrying out the introductions. "This is Imur Falsath."

"Charmed, I'm sure," said Linda, narrowing her eyes.

"Imur, this is Matt Malcolm and..." she looked to Linda for a prompt.

Linda smiled sweetly. "Linda Parfait, the doctor's mistress. Why have you kept Lucius against his will, Mr. Falsath?"

Ignoring Linda's question, Imur bowed and then climbed inside the cabin of the cruiser followed by Lucius and the North African. Once settled, he smiled at Linda. "I apologise for any discomfort the doctor may have experienced, madam."

Avoiding eye contact with Imur, Linda unbuttoned her jacket and threw her arms around Lucius's neck. She kissed him passionately, pulling him against her. Matt thought her display of affection out of place and unsettling.

"Eh, well, we should probably begin." Jessica looked to Imur.

"Yes, we should," said Imur, "but first, let me introduce Kalef Mandula. He is my equivalent on the African continent."

Matt nodded at the huge African and, still nervous, checked the surrounding lake for any other boats. It was empty, so he sat down beside Lucius. "Are you okay?"

Lucius patted Matt's hand affectionately. "I'm fine."

Matt could tell he wanted to say more.

Imur began, "Kalef and I are chief guardians of certain artefacts and secrets that have been deemed too dangerous for the stability of mankind."

Matt interrupted, "Deemed by whom?"

Imur gave a small bow. "God."

Matt fell silent but Linda, still holding Lucius's hand tightly, asked, "When did you last check?" She looked straight into Imur's onyx-coloured eyes.

This will be interesting, thought Matt.

Linda persisted in a school-marmish tone. "When did you last check with God that it was okay to kidnap people on his behalf?"

Imur cleared his throat and turned to Matt. "You, Mr. Malcolm, are the key to our present predicament."

Matt's incredulous stare caused Jessica to tap his hand. "Just listen for a moment," she whispered.

Imur continued, "You have stumbled upon one of these secrets, and this interests us on several levels. Firstly, where exactly did you find your initial sample of the Seed? Secondly, are there any more? And, finally, would you be able to identify a specimen of the Seed if we were to show it to you?"

Matt adjusted his glasses and rubbed his forehead. The cruiser bobbed on the surface of the lake. He could hear the lapping of water against its hull. "So it was you who destroyed the crop in Spain?"

Imur nodded.

"And you knew I would come, or should I say, be sent to Zurich to look for Lucius."

"We thought so," said Imur.

"I would like to speak to Lucius alone, please." Matt didn't think this request would be granted but he needed time to think this through.

As Imur and Kalef whispered to each other, Lucius turned to Matt and said, "It's Aramaic."

Typical Lucius, thought Matt. Instead of telling me exactly what these nutters know, he's identified their bloody language.

Jessica was now talking to Imur. "They're not exactly going to run off," she advised. "It's at least five hundred yards to the shore."

"You may have five minutes with your old friend, Mr. Malcolm." Imur signalled Muller to open the door that led out to the wooden footboard at the stern.

Surprised, Matt took hold of Lucius's arm, stepped out, and closed the door behind them. The speedboat was still attached to the cruiser. Lucius shook his head. "Don't even think about it, Matt."

"Don't worry," said Matt, "I'm not that brave." A tinge of guilt distracted him for a moment before he asked, "What do these nutters know about The Seed Project?"

Lucius pushed his long fingers through his wiry hair. "They obviously knew where our trial crop was being cultivated and they knew I was in charge of its development."

Matt's voice assumed a frantic tone. "How the hell did they know it was me who gave you the initial sample?" He bit his lip and checked himself.

Lucius sighed. "Sorry, Matt. I was frightened."

"Great. And the museum; did you tell them where I got it from?"

"No, but they know that you were in charge of the launch." Lucius hesitated. "Why is Miss Baron here?"

Matt took the cold air into his lungs, then sighed. "Yeah, I can't really work that one out yet either."

"Look Matt, just tell them where you found the Seeds and let's get out of this mess."

"Wait a minute; you don't know the half of it. I think one of the other companies who were at Munich has hired some KGB psycho called Stiller. He wants me to get hold of the Seed first. He's killed two people so far, and if I don't get a sample of the Seed to him by this Sunday, he's threatened to kill Jenny and Peter." Matt adjusted his glasses and gazed out over the lake, his heart sinking again as he thought of Jenny and where she might be now. "This guy, Stiller, would kill us all if I were to give the Seed to someone else first." Matt jerked his thumb in the direction of Imur and the others.

"What do you suggest?" pressed Lucius.

Matt closed his eyes.

Lucius spoke quickly, "Look Matt, last night, after Miss Baron made her entrance, I'm sure I overheard Imur chatting to a couple of his henchmen."

Matt steadied himself as a small wave lapped the hull. "Was one of them wearing a yellow v-neck sweater?"

"Yes, the smaller one. Well, from what I could gather, they didn't actually destroy the crop in Almeria. Someone else got there first."

There was movement behind the cabin door.

Matt whispered in Lucius's ear. "That fits in with the last part of the question from Imur. You see, they asked me if I could identify a specimen of the seed if they were to show it to me. They don't know what their secret seed looks like. They're bluffing."

Lucius nodded sternly. "I also heard them say that the farmers in Almeria had been killed."

The cabin door opened and Imur invited them back inside. "Well, have you decided to let us know where you obtained the original Seed?" Imur's accent is very upper class, thought Matt, perhaps Etonian. It was then, as his mind raced, that he noticed Linda wink at him, the way she had a thousand times before in the office. Then she slowly shook her head. It was a kind of code they'd used when she was trying to tell Matt to shut up. More often than not, it happened when he was about to blurt out where he had actually been instead of where his reports had indicated. She shook her head again.

"Mr. Malcolm." Kalef's jet black skin shimmered in the winter sun.

Matt glanced up and watched Kalef ease his overly-long fingers down his neck until they closed round an object. Kalef slipped a silver chain over his bald head and opened his hand. He held the object up to the light. It was one of the silver winged pendants. "This symbol is a sign of our allegiance to the Lord." His voice was surprisingly high and the 'i' in his 'this' and 'is' sounded more like the 'ee' sound in 'cheese'.

Matt reached into his jacket and felt the cold manila envelope touch the back of his hand. He lifted out the matching silver pendant he recovered from Jimmy's bag.

Imur and Muller both gasped in surprise.

"This was in Jimmy's holdall," said Matt. "I'm guessing he was a member of your club." He handed it over to Imur.

Lucius stared hard at the pendant. "May I?" he said.

Imur handed the little silver object over to the analytical Dr. Schlesinger.

"It's a seraphim," said Schlesinger. He showed Linda. "They have six wings: one pair over their eyes, one pair over their feet and another pair that protrude from their shoulders. They are supposed to be the highest ranking of all the Angels; God's personal attendants." He nodded towards Imur. "That is what you call yourselves, isn't it? The Seraphim?"

"It is," said Imur.

"Ridiculous," muttered Linda.

Kalef produced a tight-lipped smile and then said, "Thank you for retrieving our sacred symbol, Mr. Malcolm. We are the keepers. It is our job to guard the most holy of God's secrets."

Linda bristled. "Quite a bold statement, but please carry on, Kalef..."

Matt could tell that she was interested in Kalef. He recognised the lust in her grey eyes.

Kalef turned to Matt. "We need you to help us, Mr. Malcolm, not only here but elsewhere." Kalef was about to continue when Imur interjected, "We don't expect you to understand, or even believe us, but for the sake of your own safety please tell us what you know."

Matt wasn't sure if it had been Kalef's strange voice or just the complete sincerity that emanated from these people, but they exuded a kind of peaceful aura. Here, in the middle of the worst living nightmare he'd ever experienced, he got a strong sensation of relief. There was even a slight lifting of the anxiety he felt about Jenny. Kalef's voice was bordering on hypnotic.

If Jenny now knew about his other life there was a small chance that, for once in his life, he could be completely honest with her. "If you take me to the museum, Lucius and I will show you what we can."

Lucius gave him a look of utter disbelief. "What?"

Imur smiled and bowed once more. "Which museum, Mr. Malcolm?"

"The Zurich University Museum."

Imur's mouth fell open.

Linda grabbed Matt by the arm. "Are you sure you know what you're doing."

"Yes," said Matt.

Lucius was still confused, "But you just said..."

Unnoticed by Imur and Kalef, who were now busy giving instructions to Muller, Matt put his finger to his lips and hushed the doctor before he said anything else.

Jessica turned Matt to face her. "That's the first decent thing I've ever seen you do. These people might be a bit eccentric but they're right. We need to stop the chaos right now before anyone else gets hurt."

Matt drew back. "What do you mean, it's the first decent thing I've ever done?"

"Oh, I know your type, Mr. Malcolm," she continued.

He knew that this was a front. She liked him. He'd known from the first time he'd laid eyes on her in Munich. He'd known by the way she'd been unnerved when he'd tried to unhitch her skirt at the meeting.

She caught hold of his arm as the boat lurched forward.

"Wow!" Lucius fell back on top of Kalef. "Sorry..."

"Everyone get down low!" said Imur. "Muller has spotted something."

18

ABOUT FIVE HUNDRED yards behind them, Matt picked out a red and yellow speedboat powering towards them.

"It might be harmless enough," shouted Muller. "But it's better to be sure!"

Imur steadied himself on the built-in drinks cabinet and peered out over the stern. His white speedboat was adrift, bobbing about in their wake.

"Don't worry about the boat," said Muller. "It would just slow us down."

As the front of the cruiser lifted, the horizon disappeared. High in his seat, Muller banked hard to his left and headed back towards Zurich. At over five hundred horsepower, the Lavantina cut through the lake with ease, arching back in a huge loop round the oncoming speed-boat. "It's turning towards us!" he shouted down over the noise of the engines.

The first thing Matt saw was falling glass.

Imur reached up and tugged on Muller's sleeve. "Faster!"

A second bullet thumped into the starboard side and ripped past Linda's left ear.

"I said, get down!" Imur pulled her onto the floor and screamed out at Matt and Lucius, "Lie flat against the floor!" Muller drew his gun and let loose at the approaching speedboat.

Kalef was screwing a barrel onto a customised Beretta while squinting out of a porthole. "There are three of them in the boat."

"Aim for the one with the long black hair," screamed Matt.

A third bullet ripped through the side of the boat.

"Argh!" It was Muller, he was struggling to hold his gun and steer at the same time. Blood was seeping through his trousers and a sticky pool grew beneath his seat. "Take the wheel Imur," he gasped, "I can't..." His voice trembled as he tried to stay conscious.

Imur jumped up and pulled Muller down to the floor. He spun the wheel in the opposite direction, jerking the Lavantina hard to port. "Matt, help Kalef. Take this!" Imur threw him Muller's gun.

"But I haven't got a clue," wailed Matt.

"Just point it at the bad guys and pull the trigger!" screamed Linda.

Two more bullets whistled past Matt's head as he stood up to fire.

Only yards away, the unmistakable outline of Stiller took aim.

Matt pulled the trigger of his gun and felt the kick. He aimed lower and pulled the trigger again, this time ready for the recoil.

"Uhh!" A blond-haired man fell back on top of Stiller, a neat hole in the middle of his forehead.

The red and yellow speed-boat was veering across their path.

Matt felt sick as he ducked down low.

The boat lurched forward again as Imur pushed both throttles all the way. There was an almighty crunch.

"You went right over them," shouted Jessica.

"We've taken their outboard off," said Imur.

Kalef punched the air.

Matt winced. Jessica had dug her nails into his arm.

The roar of the twin engines meant that they soon gained enough water between themselves and the red and yellow speedboat to feel a little safer. The bullets stopped and the smack of small waves against the hull replaced the screams and gunfire. Imur eased back the throttles and jumped down to see to Muller. Matt found the first aid box and wrapped a tight tourniquet round the top of Muller's wounded leg while Linda stuffed a pad over the bullet-hole and reeled more bandages from the roll.

"I'm okay. I'm fine." Muller's voice was faint and when Matt saw the amount of blood on the floor, he stood up in horror.

Imur pushed the boat as hard as he could, through the mêlée of buoys and yachts that littered the north end of the lake. Instead of following the Uto Quai to the River Limmat, he banked west, past the Arboretum and under the A3 into the narrow canal that bisects Zurich's financial sector and links to the River Sihl. He knew Zurich well, but the Lavantina barely managed to squeeze through the narrow channel. Clipping the granite walls of the canal and shearing off several chrome facings, she eventually wedged tight on the sharp bend near Stockenstrasse.

Imur cursed as the Lavantina shuddered to a stop.

Slightly surprised by the holy man's language, Matt helped them pull Muller free of the trapped cruiser. They sat him down against the trunk of a huge weeping willow, but Muller had lost consciousness. His pulse was weak and his breathing shallow.

"God speed my friend." Imur kissed the big man's cheek and then let him slump down against the tree.

"You'd better put that away." Linda was squinting across at Matt. He was still holding Muller's gun.

Imur took the gun from Matt's hand and ushered them all towards the River Sihl, which sparkled and shimmered to their right. "One hundred yards ahead there's a Café called The Zimmerman. We'll get shelter there and time to think."

"Are you just going to leave him there?" asked Linda.

Imur scanned the concrete facing of the car park that overshadowed the willow tree. "Yes, Miss Parfait, I am. We need to move quickly. My friends at the café will retrieve Muller, if there is an opportunity."

Matt could still picture Stiller clinging to his sinking speedboat. He had a deep feeling of regret at not finishing him off and wondered if there would be any consequences for Jenny and Peter.

Imur seemed to read his mind. "If Stiller has enlisted ex-KGB help in Zurich, they're going to know the city just as well as us." He paused to examine Matt's expression. "You worry about something else, my friend."

A host of sirens howled through the tight, grey streets as they made their way to the café. Linda seemed to be as strong and resolute as ever, but Matt could tell that Jessica was still in a state of shock.

At The Zimmerman, the owner led them all through a heavy oak door into a dingy, unused restaurant behind the main counter.

Imur addressed the portly café owner. "You know Kalef, of course, but these are four more friends who need our protection."

The portly gentleman scanned Matt, Linda, Jessica and Lucius before embracing Imur. "Nothing is too much trouble." Matt observed the same kind of reverence that had been shown to Imur on the boat. "Should I call a meeting, Imur?"

Imur muttered in Aramaic to Kalef before answering. "Yes, but quickly, Muller has already passed before the Lord."

The café owner bowed again and backed out of the room.

Matt whispered into Jessica's ear, "Who exactly is Imur? I mean why do they scrape and bow to him like that?"

"In their sect, he's like a priest or a cleric of some kind. I've known Kalef for a long time, but never knew, until recently, that he held a similar position. He's from Ethiopia. I thought he was a Coptic Christian but-"

"Fuck!" Matt spat the word under his breath.

Jessica leaned back. "Pardon?"

"I've left my jacket on the boat." Matt punched the table.

Imur broke off his conversation with Kalef. "What's wrong, Mr. Malcolm?"

"My coat, I left it on the cruiser. My money, my passport..."

Imur saw the concern on Kalef's face but then turned back to face Matt. He closed his eyes and smiled, as if trying to calm himself. "We shall get you another coat, Mr. Malcolm, a better one than before. None of the things you've lost were ever truly yours in the first place, were they now?"

Matt gave Imur a quizzical stare then slumped back into his seat. "I'm sorry, Jessica. It's just that I can't wait here much longer. I'm running out of time. Besides..." He turned to face Imur once more. "The money was quite a substantial sum and..."

"And you are still alive, Mr. Malcolm, not a scratch." Imur pulled over a wooden chair and sat before the four Europeans. "Who else do you think might be involved in this hunt for the Seed?"

"You mean apart from a psychopathic and a bunch of religious nutters?" said Linda.

Lucius tapped Linda's arm in an attempt to check her, but she flicked his hand away.

Jessica turned to Matt. "Imur only wants to stop the chaos unlike-"

"Unlike who, Jessica?" said Matt, becoming more irritated by the second.

Jessica narrowed her eyes and pointed at the table. "As far as I can see there are two main suspects." She used some beer mats to map out her thoughts. "Both Ueshima and Ted Burrows stand to save one hundred million dollars a month each, if they find everything and destroy it."

Matt saw Imur give Kalef a quick glance.

Jessica continued, "They have the same goal as you Imur, but their motives are completely different." Jessica slid a third beer mat across the table to join the first two. "There is also the third suspect."

"And who the hell is that?" said Matt staring into Jessica's deep brown eyes.

"Vectan-Brosman," said Jessica.

"What?" Matt picked up the third beer mat but Linda lifted it from his fingers.

"Let her finish," said Linda, "they knew about your mistress."

"Yes, and now so does my wife." Matt's stomach sank and his immediate troubles faded away for a few seconds.

Linda's voice grew ominous, "They've used you before, Matt. Just remember, without the crop and Lucius, you may have been their last chance. You said yourself that you kept the original source of the Seed secret, and you've certainly flushed out all the main players: assassins, religious nuts..." Linda looked across at Imur and gave him a sarcastic smile. "No offence."

Matt's patience was wearing thin. "So I'm just a pathetic pawn in your opinion. Bait for the big sharks, eh? Are you saying that the company's murdered my mistress and threatened to kill my family just to flush out him?" Matt pointed at Imur but felt an incredible tiredness clog his thoughts. "I'm pleased Stiller's here. At least he isn't holding a gun to my wife's head anymore."

Imur's eyes brightened. "Ah, your other troubles, Mr. Malcolm."

Again, Matt was annoyed at himself for blurting too much out.

Lucius continued stroking Linda's arm. "Linda's just theorising, Matt. After the last few days, I feel anything is possible; but we should look to the moment."

"I couldn't agree more, Doctor." Imur shook his head as the sounds of ambulances and police cars filled the streets outside. "I have asked for a meeting to be held at the usual place which, as it happens, is the same place Mr. Malcolm says he found the original Seed." Imur laughed, "Imagine. The Eden Seed, under our noses all this time?"

A growing feeling of frustration burned inside Matt's chest. He'd said too much on the boat. "I didn't say I found it anywhere. I just said we should go to the University Museum first, that's all."

Kalef's eyes burned into him. "We should go now." His high-pitched voice cut through the tension and Linda threw the third beer coaster back at Matt. It bounced off his forehead and she laughed.

19

LINDA'S RINGS SPARKLED in the dimly-lit room as they followed Imur out through a low door onto the noisy back street behind the Café Zimmerman. Bins and empty kegs lay heaped against the opposite wall, and the smell of cooking and malt washed over them.

Wafts of warm air ruffled Matt's hair causing him to wince as they made his way along the alleyway.

Hidden fans propelled hot air across their path as they passed a series of grimy black mesh covers, designed to repel rats and mice. In this way, they meandered unnoticed through the tradesmen's lanes and culverts, back across to the River Limmat and then up to the Ramistrasse. The snow had begun to fall again. The flakes, heavier and wetter than before, stuck to their clothes and melted a chilling dampness into the fabric. Matt was shivering by the time they entered the museum. His less than adequate, tweed jacket was sodden and his wet shirt collar had rubbed a rash into his neck.

Matt hadn't set foot inside the museum since the night of his drunken sortie. It looked different to him now, brighter, and somehow more modern than he remembered. But he supposed that the five pints of Swiss beer he'd had with Lucius that night could have clouded his memory.

He recognised the Egyptian stele and marvelled at the ornate ceiling, with its huge beams and painted figurines. He remembered the animal display in the entrance hall but the rest looked very unfamiliar. He tugged at Lucius's sleeve. "Where's the Greek stuff, you know the pots and jewellery? It's all been changed round."

"What's been changed, Mr. Malcolm?" Imur pressed.

"The displays," he mumbled.

"Ah, yes. The students sometimes set up new displays for the spring. They are judged on their content and originality."

Lucius nodded and asked, "Why have I never seen you here in the museum before, Imur? You seem to know your way around."

"I only come here in the evenings, after hours. My family has funded this establishment for more than one hundred years, but we keep a low profile with the students and the University authorities."

The group of six soon reached the far end of the main hall. Imur had brought them to a small door labelled 'Private'. Continually looking round to check that no one was watching, he produced a small, brass key from his trouser pocket, clicked open the lock and quickly ushered them down a flight of stone steps until they reached a cramped storage cupboard. Imur pulled a tin bucket from the middle shelf and pushed the same brass key into what looked like a crack in the plasterwork. He turned it to the right and, with a shake, the whole wall in front of them moved to the left and revealed a further set of stairs going down into the gloom.

Linda steadied herself by placing her hand on a stone rail that curved down into the darkness. Lights had been set into the walls. They enlarged their shadows and gave the stairway an eerie ambience.

Eventually another door opened into a room that was completely familiar to Lucius. He saw the small bed in the corner where he'd been held. "My prison cell!" he exclaimed.

Linda whispered, "Nutters," behind him, but Matt could only stare, open-mouthed, at the huge wooden structure in the centre of the chamber. The intricately carved wings that adorned the sides caused him to gasp in genuine disbelief.

"Amazing, isn't it?" said Lucius.

"It's better than anything up there, that's for sure." Matt's eyes were wide and child-like. "Why is this thing kept down here? This should be your main exhibit, Imur."

"This is more than a trinket for display," he replied.

Lucius traced the winged relief with his long fingers. "You never fully explained what it is."

"Do not!" Imur grabbed Lucius's wrist. "It is forbidden to touch the tomb."

"Tomb?" Lucius shook his wrist free and held Linda at bay. "Whose tomb is it, Imur? I've never seen anything like it before. It's not Egyptian, Greek or Roman or-"

"It is Sumerian." Imur produced his own winged pendant. "It has the six wings of the seraphim carved on its sides. They protect the one within."

"And who might that be then?" pressed Lucius.

Imur's voice lowered. "I can only say that it was rescued from the Huns in Greater Bulgaria many, many years ago. My ancestors carried it north and west until they reached the cooler climes of this land and it has remained here ever since."

Linda sniffed and flicked the dust from her silver hair. "It all seems a bit far-fetched."

Imur threw her a withering stare.

Matt saw Jessica eye the tomb and beam. "What do you think, Matt?"

"Me?" Matt was surprised by the question. "I don't really know. It's wonderful but there are more pressing things to think about." He saw Kalef open the door of the chamber.

"We have more guests," said Kalef. He ushered another two men into the room, then another four, and, finally, the portly café owner. The café owner looked very agitated. Beads of sweat dripped from his chin onto his shirt. He wiped his face with the sleeve of his fleecy coat and bowed towards Imur. "There has been another problem."

Imur waved him in and asked him a question in another language.

Lucius mouthed the word 'Aramaic' to Matt and listened in.

"No!" Imur smacked his fist against the wall.

That's the second time in so many minutes Imur's rage has cut through his well-practised formality, thought Matt.

The café owner bowed quickly and stepped back into the shadows. "They've lost another two sect members to the back-haired assassin," whispered Lucius.

Imur turned round to address his small group of followers. "Ali and Abraham are dead. We have underestimated the speed and effectiveness of our opposition."

"You should have finished him off in the lake when you had the chance," murmured Matt.

Jessica glanced across at Matt and then concentrated on Imur. "This is getting out of hand, Imur. I'm not sure I can be involved if-"

"We are all involved Jessica, whether we like it or not. We have to ask Matt to identify the Seed now before any more lives are lost."

Lucius spoke quietly, out of the side of his mouth. "Matt, you need to tell them what the Seed looks like."

"If I do, they'll destroy them and that will be it for Jenny and Peter," he whispered, "I have to stall them until I can think of something."

Imur moved closer.

Matt paused and then asked, "Why do I need to identify the Seed if it was you've who destroyed the crop in Spain?" Matt checked for Imur's reaction. "You must have known what you were looking for, or at least brought a sample back with you."

Imur moved forward. "Unfortunately, it was not the Seraphim who destroyed the crop."

Matt saw the other men close round him.

"So you lied," said Linda. "A man of God, a defender of the ancient secrets..."

Imur took a deep breath and continued to address Matt, "If I've guessed correctly, you stole the Seed from my museum."

Matt's stomach turned. He didn't want to give away his last bargaining chip. "You could check for the Seed yourself if you're so convinced it's up there."

"I suppose I could examine all ninety-three thousand Coptic jars that might contain the one true Seed and then do all the screening and testing that's required to eliminate the innocuous grains, but we don't have the time, do we?" Imur's eyes burned. The other men closed round the small man and opened their jackets to reveal an array of knives and guns. "We are a peaceful brotherhood," continued Imur. "Don't force me to bend our own rules."

"Imur!" snapped Jessica, a look of revulsion on her face.

Matt struggled for the right words. "I will need Lucius. I'll struggle to pick out the right seed myself after all this time." Imur eyed Matt and Lucius suspiciously.

Lucius let go of Linda's hand and made for the stairs. "I hate to tell you all this, but my main responsibility was the fermentation of the substrate. I can barely remember what the actual Seeds look like."

"You'll do fine," said Matt, "it will come back to you." They stepped out into the main hall of the museum, followed by Imur and two of his heavily armed seraphim. Matt shielded his eyes against the glare of the strip lights. He struggled to remember where he'd gone on that infamous night. "Down there, I think; past the Hellenic display and through that archway."

Lucius shrugged.

After twenty or thirty yards they arrived at the Etruscan section. Lines of pots, bowls, jars and vases were encased behind the newly improved safety glass. Grasses and stones had been placed strategically in the sand to give the viewer the effect of a desert. Rustic red clays were interspersed with burnt umber urns, but none of the displays looked very familiar. In fact, there were several displays under construction on the very site where Matt thought he may have taken the original Seeds.

20

"IT'S ALL CHANGED since I was here, but I'm pretty sure that this is the display case I opened. It's probably a few feet away from its original position." Matt moved over to the case nearest the window and the fire escape. After a quick glance in the exhibit case, he took in a deep breath and then slumped his shoulders in disappointment. "Lucius, the pot was right there." He pointed to a pair of ancient sandals set on a piece of camel hide with a Swiss-German explanation of the presumed manufacturing process.

Imur's bodyguards scanned the museum's visitors, their fingers flicking over the hidden triggers beneath their jackets. Imur waved over a museum attendant. "Where is the previous material from this case?"

"What?" barked the attendant.

Matt tried to explain. "There were three red pots with seeds and grass, all laid out as if they were still in a field, right there." He pointed at the sandals again.

"The pots will have been put back into storage," said the attendant. "What about the grass and seeds used for decoration?" said Matt.

The attendant gave a nonplussed shrug. "Most probably binned, I would think. That stuff goes off and looks shabby after a while."

"Binned! Binned!" Imur was almost apoplectic.

"I'm sorry, but the curator nearly always prefers fresh material."

Matt realised that people had begun to look across the hall at them. He peered under the case at the polished floor. "Is the curator here today?"

Matt felt the attendant's eyes burn into him as he knelt down with Lucius. They eased themselves under the legs of the display case.

"Eh, no sir, he's on holiday but I could get the student who did this section."

Imur tried to stay calm. "Please do that."

Underneath the case Matt whispered to Lucius, "I remember now, the Seeds hung down like the single seeding head of an oat, but they were multisided."

Lucius nodded. "The Seeds were decagonal. They had purple hooks that brought me out in a rash."

Matt nipped the back of Lucius's hand and whispered, "I remember now too, but we should keep the exact description vague."

"Owch!" Lucius flinched, banging his head on the underside of the case. "Of course."

"I can't believe that Imur owns the very place I stole them from in the first place," said Matt.

Lucius reached for a small pile of dust and scraped it towards him. "My guess is that the Seeds you took came with the pot that's in storage."

Above them Imur was giving a young female student the third degree. "What do you mean he was fired?"

The girl was trying to explain. "The student who changed the display was let go for several irregularities."

Matt emerged with Lucius from below the case.

"I'm sorry sir," whimpered the girl, "but I don't think I can say. I mean I'm not really sure who you are."

Imur bristled, "I am the main sponsor of the museum. I pay your wages."

"I see," said the girl, a trace of scepticism in her voice. "Well I don't suppose it matters that much. You could say that he was over-fond of his wine. He left the museum unlocked on several occasions."

"Ah, yes. I remember now," agreed the attendant, waving the student away.

Imur turned to Matt and Lucius. "Did you find anything down there?"

Lucius opened his hand and let the fluff and dust fall back to the polished grey floor. "Nothing of any consequence."

One of the Seraphim pushed a hand inside his jacket. "Sir, there are two men approaching rather too quickly for my liking!" His eyes were fixed on two blond men walking through the archway that led to the Hall of Antiquities.

Matt could see that they were more interested in people's faces than the displays.

Imur spat out his instructions. "Split up and look as if you're interested in the cases."

The attendant and the young female student seemed confused by the group's sudden action.

The first blond stranger reached the female student and asked, "Have you seen an Englishman - short, black rimmed glasses and mousy hair?"

The student turned to where Matt and Lucius had been standing, but they were gone. "Well, I think he went..."

The strangers followed the student's gaze to the entrance of the next display area. Then, without stopping to ask any more, they both rushed on towards the Hall of the Dead.

Tucked back under the row of cases beside the fire escape, Matt and Lucius watched the strangers' shoes squeak across the polished floor away from them. They held their breath as the student and the attendant followed the two men.

"We could make a run for it," said Matt.

Lucius shook his head. "No, Matt. Linda is still down in that basement and we might run into that psychopath we saw on the lake."

Matt squinted out from beneath the case. "At least we could explain-"

"I get the impression that this Stiller character is not a particularly good listener," interrupted Lucius, his eyes still focused on the progress of the two strangers.

"You could be right." Matt sighed.

They heard a dull thud emanate from the Hall of the Dead, ahead. "Shit. What was that?" said Matt.

They shuffled out from the case and eased across to the Hall of the Dead. Ahead of them, dark shadows crisscrossed the marble floor.

"There," said Matt, drawing Lucius against the wall.

Amongst an incredible array of mummies and caskets, they saw one of the blond strangers lying on the floor. He moaned as blood trickled from his knee. His partner had ducked down behind a figurine a few yards further on.

Matt was just about to call out when he heard a second thud. His stomach tensed as the wounded man's scalp exploded across the polished floor.

The second blond stranger threw himself to the ground beside the twitching body of his partner and waved his arms. "STOP!"

Thud!

The second stranger slumped down beside his partner and lay still.

The female student bumped into Matt as she staggered out of the hall, an expanding pool of blood already seeping towards her as she backed away. She screamed at the attendant, who was standing, frozen to the spot. "GET HELP! We need to get help!"

They both ran off.

Matt stepped forwards. There was no sign of Imur or anyone else, just the two strangers lying on the floor.

The female student's cries faded as he moved over bits of bone and fleshy pink lumps. He slipped and cursed as his fingers touched the warm liquid.

The seraphim who fired the final shot stood up at the side of an onyx coffin cover and shouted out, "Imur?"

Imur appeared from behind an ornate third dynasty pillar and walked over to the bodies. He knelt down beside the stranger whose scalp had shattered and checked the blood-stained pockets of his black jacket. To Matt's horror, the stranger twitched twice before he stiffened.

Imur stepped back and examined a small laminated identity card before reading out, "Inspector Jan Hess. Police Department, Zurich."

Imur's expression hardened as he stared at the seraphim shooter. "Well done," he said, sarcastically.

"Sorry sir, but if you had seen what the one called Stiller did to Ali and... I thought..."

"Enough! We leave, now!"

Matt turned to see Lucius trying, in vain, to hold back a small crowd. The crowd seemed determined to see what had caused the female student and the attendant to bolt past them screaming at the tops of their voices.

Matt pushed in beside Lucius and addressed the crowd. "You all better back off."

Imur appeared between them and turned Matt round to face him. "Such immaturity will not be tolerated!"

The crowd watched as Matt got a dressing down. "To terrify that girl like that is just not acceptable. This is a serious institution, not a children's playground!"

"What the...," said Matt, his mind assessing the situation and already beginning to process a believable answer, "I'm sorry, Professor, but we always get the new students with something or other."

While Imur continued to give him the third degree the two seraphim heaved the policemen's bodies away from the middle of the floor. They kicked the various gory lumps under the glass cases.

The crowd weren't so easily convinced and at last Imur had to raise his voice. "Everyone, please fall back into the Hellenic Section! We will have to close this part of the museum while you," he pointed to Matt, "clean up the mess you made with your childish prank. You could have damaged the casket!" He turned to the remaining group of onlookers. "My apologies."

One or two of them wanted to ask more questions but Imur persisted, "Due to a display of immaturity on the part of a member of staff, who should know better, this part of the museum is temporarily closed. So, I'm sorry. Move away."

As soon as the stragglers had disappeared, they roped off the Hall behind them and walked swiftly across the floor to the door marked 'Private'.

Before inserting the key, Imur rounded on his own men. "Fantastic. Now we have at least a dozen witnesses who can put us all at the scene of a double police homicide!"

21

ONCE INSIDE, THEY passed through the fake storage cupboard and on to the hidden stairs that curved down toward the lower chamber. Imur continued to berate the taller of his two henchmen. "Steph, that was completely unprofessional." The one Imur referred to as Steph stood next to Matt. He was Slavic in appearance with thick brown hair and a smart suit that still bulged with weapons. Matt guessed that it was this man who had fired the first shot.

"But Imur," Steph protested, "it could have been us lying dead in the hall if it had been some of Stiller's men. They cut off Ali's head, skinned Abraham and then cut his throat."

"Enough." Imur took a deep breath and looked directly into Steph's light blue eyes. He tapped the bulge under Steph's jacket. "You let emotion dictate your actions rather than logic. They were police officers."

"Yes, but they were in plain clothes," protested Steph.

Linda and Jessica stood up as soon they saw Matt.

"Did you find it?" asked Jessica.

Matt shook his head, "No. As far as we know the remaining Seeds have been destroyed, but there were other complications." He eyed the large Slav, Steph.

Imur sat everyone down and resumed an air of serenity. "Two more men have died, and I'm sorry to say that it was our mistake." Matt noticed Steph flinch. "Jessica," continued Imur, "we will have to use a safe house and wait until things calm down."

Matt stepped forward, about to tell them all that he couldn't wait until things calmed down, and that his family had about four days left, unless he delivered a sample of the Eden Seed to Stiller, but he caught Lucius's eye and wavered. The old doctor slowly shook his head in warning.

Linda stepped forward with the air of headmistress who needed answers. "Now what?" She had a determined look on her face that threw Matt completely; he'd never seen her look so serious and so in control. "There is no reason for you or anyone else to perpetuate this madness. There are no Seeds left."

The chamber fell silent.

Kalef's high-pitched voice cut through the tension. "There are two other sites we could try."

Jessica Baron nodded her head and looked to Imur.

Imur stood in the shadow of the ancient Sumerian tomb. "Kalef, let Jessica explain why you are both here, how you came to meet...everything."

They stood in anticipation as Jessica adopted a more official tone. Pacing the floor, in the shadow of the tomb, Matt decided she was on familiar ground, comfortable in situations of summation and rhetoric. She reminded him of his boss, Barclay; in the know and on show. "I have always had an interest in early cultures," she began, "and I have written several pieces of work on the subject over the years."

As she paused, Matt marvelled at her beauty.

"Although my temporary role as European Chief Justice curtailed my hobby, it also gave me the opportunity to glean information that would normally have been out of reach." She walked over to Matt and looked up at the intricately carved tomb. "Matt, I liked your biblical introduction in Munich, and felt there was a real chance that you'd stumbled on something long forgotten. The child in me became excited at the thought of ancient treasures being rediscovered, but I was genuinely shocked when you said that you were going to hold back the discovery. I was even more disappointed when you resorted to extortion."

Matt shrugged. "Sorry to disappoint you."

Jessica continued, "I was beyond anger when I realised that you were using me as a silent witness, and that by being there I could have been seen as complicit."

"We asked nothing of you," said Matt.

"No, you didn't have to. It was a 'fait accompli'. They paid up, and I shut up." Jessica pushed her fingers through her hair and walked back over to Kalef. "Kalef and I met at a United Nations conference in The Hague. He's a Human Rights lawyer who also happens to be an expert on the Coptic religion of Egypt and Ethiopia. He mentioned that he'd read some of my articles from my student days, and we talked for hours until I felt I could ask him about some of the sites that had fascinated me over the years and, more importantly, confide in him about the Munich meeting."

Matt gave Jessica a sardonic smile. "You told him about the Seed?"

"Not at first, but eventually I decided to, yes." Jessica's eyes drifted away from Matt's disapproving frown. "Kalef became very animated and told me about the various legends and myths that surrounded what he called the Eden Seed, and indeed, how there had been mention of a Seed of Life in the Coptic texts. He also, unbeknown to me, informed Imur and the Seraphim about your find. It was then that Imur contacted me and asked me to help."

"Why would they ask you for help?" Linda interjected.

Matt was beginning to see a much stronger side to Linda. This facet of her nature, however, only added to her appeal. She wasn't afraid to say what she thought and, undoubtedly, wasn't afraid to ask for what she wanted.

Jessica addressed Lucius and Matt. "The Seraphim had a problem that, at last, could be solved. After explaining who was involved in the development of the Vectan-Brosman wonder-product, Imur had said he intended approaching Lucius and questioning you, Matt. He said no harm would come to either of you." Jessica glanced, reproachfully, at Imur.

"There's a big difference between approaching someone and kidnapping," snapped Linda.

"I objected to the whole thing but, as it turns out, I think Imur was right. It kept Lucius safe and it kept Matt viable."

"Viable?" snapped Linda.

"What was the problem you couldn't solve?", asked Matt.

Jessica answered, "Kalef and Imur know of two other archaeological sites that may contain samples of the Seed. I'm sure that they are now wondering if Matt or the Doctor can identify them.

Imur sighed deeply and nodded.

Jessica eyed Matt. "What Imur is about to suggest would not have been necessary if you'd been able to identify the Seeds here in Zurich."

"We must press on, and hope that our enemies have not already gained access to the Eden Seed," said Imur.

Jessica stepped forward. "Now I get to see two of the most interesting sites in the world, and Imur and Kalef get the knowledge they need to protect the Eden Seed from those who want to misuse it."

"And what do I get, Miss Baron?" Matt's head was reeling at the thought of how long it would take all of them to visit two other sites, God knows where.

Jessica smiled at him. "You get the peace of mind-"

"Not good enough," interrupted Matt. Again, he caught Lucius's gaze and just managed to stop himself from telling them everything.

"Are you sure that there's nothing left from the test site?" pressed Matt.

"Imur, how did you know about the test site location?" said Lucius. "It's pretty obvious that the people in Munich knew of our product, but the test site details were highly classified."

Matt could see that Lucius was still frustrated by the destruction of his work.

"An executive at Vectan-Brosman, a Mr. Barclay, e-mailed using an unprotected server," said Imur.

"Barclay!" Matt couldn't believe it.

Kalef addressed Matt. "Please, Matt, will you come with us to the other sites and help us identify the Eden Seed once and for all? Through the millennia we have lost the description." His sharp voice cut through the gloom. "We need this to keep its secret safe. It is God's will."

"I still need to know what I get out of this," said Matt.

Jessica threw Matt a disdainful look. "Typical!"

"I mean, Jessica, you get your tour of rare archaeological sites, Imur and Kalef get a multibillion dollar secret handed over to them, for free, and God gets his angels up to speed. I, on the other hand, still have no job, a psycho after me, and a wife who is no doubt in the process of contacting a damn good lawyer!"

"Well," said Jessica, "your morals are pretty non-existent as far as I can see." Her eyes flicked between Matt and Linda. "This will be a chance to put things right. Balance up some of that bad Karma."

22

JENNY MALCOLM THOUGHT back to the previous night, when she'd sat in the backseat of the police car with Inspector Watt and listened, incomprehensibly, as he grew more and more excited by the prospect of visiting Brin Cottage.

"Why do I have to go to Brin Cottage, Inspector?" she'd asked. "I thought we were going straight to the station." Jenny had been hoarse and her clothes were still covered in blood.

"Well, the cottage is on the way and-"

"And I'm still covered in blood," she'd interrupted.

The young constable at the wheel looked in his rear-view mirror and caught Jenny's eye. "Is there not a danger that Mrs. Malcolm could contaminate the crime scene, sir?"

The inspector had grunted reproachfully.

As the police car had pulled up to the cottage, Jenny wondered what horrendous secrets the place held for her. She hadn't been ready for that.

"Look, I'm freezing cold and I don't think this is right."

"She's got a point, Gov," the young constable had muttered.

"Fine, fine. Drive past. We'll take you to the station first and get you cleaned up." The old Inspector had sighed. "Hurry up, son! I want to get in there before the C.I.D begins crawling over the place. Phone ahead and get a team ready to take Mrs. Malcolm's clothes and get her organised with some new ones." Watt had turned to face her. "I won't take long. It looks pretty cut and dried; self-defence on your part, but we have to do the reports correctly."

She'd seen him glance down at her bare legs. Wrapped in a police blanket and with her hair all messed up and covered in blood, she'd felt a mixture of repulsion and flattery. She'd pretended to look out of the car window but actually focused in on his reflection.

She'd sen him glance down again and, this time, hold his stare. As soon as she'd turned to face him, however, Watt had become flustered. He'd adjusted his thinning grey hair. "It won't be long now until we're at the station. I'd still like you to come to Brin Cottage later."

"If you think it will help," she'd said, still relieved that she hadn't had to deal with Matt's betrayal straight away.

Four hours later, Jenny had washed, changed and given the police a full statement. Having insisted that Peter be exempt from any questioning at this point, she'd been informed that her son was safe at her mother's house with Mrs. Leslie, her mother's next-door neighbour. She phoned Mrs. Leslie to talk to Peter but had soon found out that he was fast asleep and had decided to wait until the morning. Completely exhausted, and unsure how she was going to cope mentally after the incident, she'd agreed to spend the rest of the night at a local hotel.

Inspector Watt had been compassionate during his questioning and had avoided over-emphasising Matt's affair with the girl at Brin Cottage. He'd explained that he would probably stay at the hotel too, as there was a remote chance that the incident at her house was more than just a break-in. He'd been polite and made sure she'd had everything she needed: toiletries, clothes and a phone.

Before she'd checked in to the hotel, Inspector Watt had tried calling Matt's mobile, but it just went straight onto the answer machine. *He's probably turned it off by now,* she'd decided. She'd been convinced that Watt suspected a connection between Matt's abandoned car and the incident at their house, especially since his car had been found so near to his mistress's cottage. She'd given Watt Matt's office number, but when security had put him through to Barclay, he'd told Watt that Matt had been sacked that very day. It was more than a coincidence. It had to be.

She'd been unable to sleep in the overheated hotel room and had regretted not going to her mother's to be with Peter. There'd been too much adrenaline pumping through her veins to relax enough for sleep, too many things racing through her mind

* * *

STILLER TOOK ANOTHER call from his paymaster. "Have you found a suitable person?" the voice asked.

He was still smarting from the encounter on the lake. "Yes, one of my operatives in the U.K. has the man under observation."

"Remember, I want no traceable characteristics." The voice, as usual, was disguised.

"Yes, yes. We know how to make identification more difficult. No prints and no head." Stiller sighed and stared across at the remaining Swiss operative he'd activated that morning. He cupped the phone and whispered, "Any sign of Matt Malcolm and his new-found friends yet?"

Stein, an ex-KGB Swiss operative nodded. "It might just be a coincidence, but there's been a disturbance at the University Museum, two policemen dead."

He spoke into the mobile, "I think we're onto them again. It won't be long."

"Good. Don't lose them this time," said the voice, "and remind Malcolm of the consequences if someone else gets hold of a sample of the Seed first."

The line went dead. Stiller snapped his phone shut before screwing the silencer back onto his Heckler. "What about Karl's body?"

Stein was busy tapping into his laptop. Without looking up he said, "He's at the bottom of the lake. I tied the anchor to his legs. He might never be found."

"Fine. I need to make another call. Get hold of Landenberg and Schmitt; activate them both."

"No problem, sir. The same fee?" asked Stein.

"Yes." Stiller dialled 0044 then the local number. "Kennedy?"

The voice on the other line sounded slurred. "Ah, yes. Is that Stiller, the main man?"

"Mr. Stiller, to you," he snapped.

Stiller knew Kennedy was an alcoholic, who spent most of his time chain-smoking and endlessly doodling, but his methods were faultless, and he always did exactly what he was told, no more, no less. There was no creativity but you always got the job you asked for. "You've still got our man under surveillance?"

"Stiller the killer, eh?"

Stiller heard him draw on a cigarette.

"Yes, the man is under surveillance."

Kennedy had never shown him any respect.

"I'm looking at my tools right now," said Kennedy. "In fact, I've just added a few extra utensils to my box of delights. When do you want the job done?"

"Do it tonight," snapped Stiller.

"Understood. Over and-"

Stiller cut him off, annoyed by his lack of discipline and obvious state of inebriation. When it came to fingers, toes, and heads, Kennedy was very thorough; sadistic, but very thorough. Stiller's long black hair fell over his leather collar and lay neatly across his broad shoulders. He caught a glimpse of himself in the car mirror. His widow's peak was becoming more pronounced, but he liked that. It accentuated the sharpness of his features, added to his mystique. He hated working in daylight. He preferred the easy light of dusk or dawn. The night, however, was his true friend. His line of work depended on him being sharp when others were tired and worn out. It made things so much easier.

He had killed three hundred and six men, four women and two children in his time. He could still recount every moment of their agony. At night, he sometimes played back these devilish scenes in his head, digging his nails into his pillow whenever he recalled a kill that fell short of his own punishing standards.

Although he had gleaned little from the two Arabs that afternoon, he was pleased with the way he'd got them to talk. He'd partially skinned the most belligerent one before removing his head. His operative, Stein, had twitched nervously during the second execution. He always liked to surpass his own people's expectations. He wanted people like Stein to think that they stood as much chance of dying at his hand as at the hand of any possible foe. This kept them focussed.

"Sir?" Stein was typing furiously. "Landenberg and Schmitt have accepted the offer."

"Excellent. Tell them to meet us at the University Museum at 6 P.M.." Stiller was becoming irritated by Stein's laptop fixation. "And Stein..?"

"Sir?"

"Make sure they're properly armed. I want to take this bunch of fanatics out of the picture."

Stiller had learned that a Syrian called Imur Falsath had become involved in the hunt for the Vectan-Brosman information. He'd seen him on the lake that afternoon; a small man, about five foot four, with a waxed moustache. Besides Malcolm and the Doctor, he'd also seen two women and an African. The pilot of their boat, one Martin Muller, had now been confirmed dead. As yet, he had no idea who the two women were or who the African was, but he had the old department working on their descriptions. He could only believe that the two Arabs genuinely didn't know either, as the pain they endured was more than adequate to loosen tongues.

His revised instructions from his paymaster had been relayed during their 3 P.M. discussion. He'd checked in after the interrogation of the two Arabs. He was to kill them all except Dr. Lucius Schlesinger and Matt Malcolm. It was only once he'd been given a genuine sample of the Vectan-Brosman Seed that he would be allowed to dispatch them too. His paymaster had reminded him that time was of the essence, and that the Syrian was probably behind the burning of the test crop in Spain.

It was now 5:45 P.M., and Stiller had spotted Stein pretending to look into a nearby shop window on the Ramistrasse. Two others joined him at the window. He'd never met Landenberg or Schmitt but they looked the part. Both had served in Afghanistan and Somalia.

He wondered how he could get into the museum. The place was swarming with Police and there was a helicopter circling above.

There was no certainty that the Syrian was even there. Indeed, it would be more logical for them to be holed up nearer to the part of town where their boat, the Lavantina, had been found.

As soon as Stein had told him of the incident, however, his skin bristled and his mind began to turn over the various possibilities.

He had a feeling that the two murdered police officers had been mistaken for his own men. It was almost certain that the two Arabs he'd dispatched earlier had been found and that the police had been searching the nearby museum when they'd been intercepted. It was all too much of a coincidence. Someone must have got trigger happy.

Stiller signalled the three men at the shop window to meet him in the narrow lane opposite. The pavement glistened with frost and his breath seeped up into the darkening sky as he spoke, "I have to get inside the museum. They must be hiding somewhere pretty secure if the police haven't found them by now. Which one of you is Schmitt?"

A thin weasel-faced man with jet-black hair nodded.

"Get me a uniform. There are plenty of policemen milling about outside. One of them must be my build."

Stiller turned to Stein and Landenberg. "Find a position up there." He pointed to the rooftop that overlooked the museum on the opposite side of the street. "Just watch out for that helicopter. Schmitt can remain here when he comes back, cover the rear exit. I'm going in alone."

23

SCHMITT ARRIVED BACK with a uniform to fit Stiller, a small speck of blood on the hat hinting at the previous owner's demise. Stiller tucked his hair into the hat and placed the policeman's dark glasses over his eyes.

"It's a good fit. Your mother wouldn't even recognise you," said Schmitt.

"It's not my mother I'm worried about. We've lost one operative to these fanatics already, so don't underestimate them."

Schmitt smiled, revealing a set of nicotine-stained teeth. "Of course," he said.

Stiller walked out onto the Ramistrasse and approached the main entrance of the museum. A riotous mixture of blue and red police lights helped him get past the two officers at the door. Well-disguised in his Swiss police uniform, all it took was a swift, confident nod and he was in. He soon passed the natural history display at the reception area and read the sign that said: The Hellenic Exhibition. He stepped inside and immediately saw that blue and white tape that sealed off the next hall. He could just make out the sign above the arched entrance. This one read: The Hall of the Dead.

"Where should you be?" said a voice.

The Swiss-German accent broke Stiller's concentration for a second, but he simply shrugged at the plain-clothes inspector.

"Get up to the second floor and search the library."

Stiller nodded, turned, and proceeded up the spiral metal stairway to his left.

The library occupied almost half of the upper level. It was mainly a storage area, but there were six or seven policemen searching there already. No, he had a feeling that Imur Falsath and Matt Malcolm were somewhere below ground. He'd seen several windows to the rear of the building, well below ground level of the museum's ground floor.

On reaching the Hellenic Hall once more, he avoided the plain-clothes policeman and counted the doors around the hall. There were three. The first was marked as a staff toilet, the other two were labelled, 'Private' and 'Computer Room' respectively. He nipped into the toilet, but there was nothing in there. Next he tried the door marked 'Private'.

"We've looked in all those already," said the young officer. "Besides, I thought I told you to get upstairs?" The young, plain-clothes policeman moved closer.

"Sorry sir. There was nothing to see upstairs. Besides, we have plenty of colleagues..."

"Where are you from? Your accent is..."

Stiller tapped the door marked 'Private'. "I'm sure I can hear something in there." He placed his ear against the door and turned the handle.

"Wait! There's nothing there except a set of stairs that lead to a store cupboard." The officer held up a key. "You haven't answered my question."

"No sir, I definitely heard it again." The door swung inward and Stiller slipped inside.

"Are you listening to me?" The young officer barged into the stairway behind Stiller. "Come back here right now!"

The young policeman's voice grew faint as Stiller closed the store cupboard door behind him and switched on the single light. He raked at the shelves and pulled a jumble of pots and buckets down onto the floor. He stiffened and pushed his ear against the wall. The bare bulb swinging from the ceiling above him threw shadows over the toppled cleaning material. He saw the cracks in the plaster. Just as he steadied the bulb with his bare hand, however, the young officer pushed his way in. "What do you think you're doing?" he shouted. "When I tell you to do something I expect you to-"

Without looking away from the cracks in the plaster, Stiller reached behind him and grabbed the officer's hair. He yanked him down until his head was level with the floor before kneeling on his windpipe. Stiller then bent down until he was inches from the policeman's panic stricken face. "Shut the fuck up," he whispered.

He thought he heard something move behind the wall.

Stiller pushed a finger up each of the policeman's nostrils and covered his mouth while, at the same time, applying more pressure with his knee. The officer struggled, his legs pedalling, his one free arm thrashing helplessly against Stiller's back. Glancing down for a second, he watched as the officer's face turned puce. His eyes bulged out of their sockets. Still trying to pinpoint the sound he'd heard, he dripped a long strand of spit into the young man's eyes as they glazed over. "Night, night," he whispered again, adjusting his uniform as he stood up.

Stiller shook his head. "Fuckin' rats..." He took one more look round the room then leapt up the stairs two at a time. Back in the Hellenic Hall he moved over to the door marked Computer Room. He spent a few moments looking round but it proved equally fruitless. He decided to get out while luck was on his side and before anyone discovered the young policeman's body.

On the street outside, several tell-tale glints of gun metal on the roof opposite signalled his men's positions. He would go back to the canal and search that area instead. Having seen the amount of police in the museum, it was unlikely that anyone could hide in there for any length of time. And besides, they would really go to town on the place once they'd found the body of the young officer. In minutes, he binned the uniform and regrouped with his team. He took Stein with him and told Schmitt and Landenberg to remain behind and cover the museum. "Check out the basement windows."

"Already did," said Stein, "they're tiny and barred."

"Maybe. But if they're in there, and something tells me they still might be, they're about to be rattled."

Stein's eyes narrowed.

"There's another dead policeman to add to today's toll. The Zurich Police won't like the fact that he's been killed under their very noses." Stiller ruffled his hair and then focused on Landenburgh and Schmitt. "Call me when the shit hits the fan."

Schmitt and Landenberg nodded before backing into the shadows.

24

MATT WAS NEAREST to the top of the stairs when the commotion began. He waved Imur over. They waited until the footsteps had disappeared before turning the brass key, but the secret door was jammed. "I need more weight behind this part here!" called Imur, shoving hard with his shoulder.

Kalef and Matt pushed with Imur but only managed to force a gap of about five inches. Imur shone his torch through the opening and a body came into view, wedged against the other side of the hidden door. "We can push it open. We just need more men."

As Kalef signalled to the seraphim to come and help, Matt watched the beads of sweat run down Imur's nose and settle on the tips of his moustache. "Do you think it was Stiller?" he asked.

Imur coughed nervously. "I'm sure it was. This man probably saved us." Imur shone his torch through the opening again.

Matt glimpsed the man's blond hair. "There must be another way out of this place," he said.

"Of course there is," grunted Imur, but we need to get this man into the chamber before he's found. I don't want any unnecessary investigations to unearth our holiest place. Not after six hundred years of peace."

As the seraphim arrived, Imur positioned them against the door and issued his instructions. Steadily, the door moved inward. Matt watched the corpse buckle back under the strain until there was a loud snap.

"His spine," panted Steph.

Matt felt the bile rise in his throat as they grabbed onto the dead man's legs and hauled him in like a rag doll.

Suddenly light filled the store cupboard from above.

Imur's whispering tone became frantic. "Shut the door."

Someone was clattering down the stairs towards them.

Matt and the other men pushed the hidden door shut just as the people reached the store cupboard.

Matt listened.

"What a mess," said a voice.

Matt heard the clatter of falling buckets and mops. "Did you see that?"

"What?"

A second person had joined the first in the cupboard. "The whole place just shook."

Imur and the others remained completely still.

"It's just the Polybahn. We're probably near Karl Schmid Strasse station down here. We won't be far from the gears and stuff."

Matt heard them moving closer to the hidden door. "It's 7:45," said the voice, "the Polybahn stopped running thirty minutes ago."

Matt shoved his ear closer. His years in Zurich had given him a good knowledge of Swiss-German.

"Tests. The Polybahn must be doing safety tests," said the second person. There was another scuffling sound but this time their voices tailed off. Matt heard them arguing over the exact site of the Karl Schmid station and whether Zurich had ever suffered a major earthquake or not.

He moved away from the door as Imur and the others dragged the corpse down into the main chamber and dropped it on the sandy floor.

Jessica stepped away but Linda moved closer. "Look at his eyes," she whispered, her voice full of curiosity.

"No thanks." Jessica moved further away.

"Asphyxiation," said Kalef. He twisted the corpse's head to the side and pointed to the marks on the man's throat. "He will have to share this tomb with..." He motioned towards the carved sarcophagus.

"An honour indeed," said Imur. He threw Kalef a withering glance.

Lucius whispered to Matt while the Seraphim sect deliberated. Matt pulled him closer. "Who do you think is inside their precious tomb?" wondered Lucius.

"Never mind that, I've just worked out our angle." said Matt.

Lucius edged closer.

"Look, as far as we can tell there are no Seeds or even witnesses to the Eden Seed left. No test crop, research farmers, no documents and no museum specimens. Right?"

"Right," said Lucius.

"No job, career, or income, unless we get another specimen. Right?"

"Yes, but..."

"More importantly, I have to assume that Stiller has other ex-KGB in position to kill my family if I don't get him a sample of the Eden Seed first."

"I don't follow you," whispered Lucius.

"That's just the point. You don't follow me; you follow Imur. Or should I say, we follow Imur and, with his protection, we examine these archaeological sites and hope that they're right," said Matt, his heart racing.

"You mean we let them take us to these sites and steal another Seed specimen for Vectan-Brosman."

"And Stiller," added Matt. "I have to let Stiller know that we need more time."

Lucius didn't seem to like the sound of the plan. "Imur and Kalef won't let us take a sample of the Eden Seed. They're not stupid."

"We'll have to find a way round that one later," said Matt.

Imur walked over to Matt and Lucius. "We will bury the policeman here before we leave."

It was almost 9 P.M. when Imur made them close their eyes and face the wall.

"Please face the tomb and keep your eyes shut tight. I cannot stress the seriousness of your failure to do so." His mesmerising voice echoed round the chamber for a moment before a large grating sound shook the floor beneath their feet. The Seraphim followed Imur's commands to the letter, but Matt squinted across at the last second. Imur had just taken his hand away from a black stone on the opposite wall.

"Open your eyes!"

He sounds like a second rate cabaret magician, thought Matt.

There was an audible gasp from the assembled onlookers. Where there had been a solid stone wall, there was now a large opening. It led through the bedrock beneath the University Museum. A massive piece of engineering, the tunnel was a good thirty feet wide and perhaps twenty feet high. Matt looked back at the carved tomb behind him, and realised that this must have been the passageway through which Imur's ancestors had hauled the colossal relic so many years before.

As Kalef and Imur moved forward, ancient electric lighting sprang to life, revealing a polished marble floor. The walls were covered in various ornate carvings and inscriptions.

"Can we stop for a moment, Imur?" asked Jessica. "These hieroglyphs are so unusual. What do they mean? I'm not familiar with the story."

"I'm sorry, Miss Baron, but we just don't have the time." Imur tried to move her on.

Matt saw how animated Jessica had become.

"Do they tell the story of the tomb?" Her question hung unanswered in the dank air as she traced the various outlines with her fingers. "It tells the story of the ones that lie inside the tomb, doesn't it? There are two people in the tomb."

Matt could see the representation of two incredibly tall figures held high above a huge army by what looked like a host of angels. "Whose tomb is it, Imur?"

Still unwilling to engage with Jessica, Imur hurried them along. They walked on past even more intricate glyphs that depicted a series of vanquished armies and the familiar winged tomb they'd just left behind. He recognised chariots, great ziggurat towers and even something that looked like the Ark of the Covenant, held high on the shoulders of outlandish, long-forgotten warriors.

"These warriors don't look like Sumerians or Huns. They're not Egyptian either," mumbled Jessica.

Matt breathed in her heady perfume as she stopped beside him.

"Please, Miss Baron, I must insist that you do not touch the walls." Imur told Kalef to close the doorway behind them and, with another drawn out rumble of stone against stone, the entrance to the chamber that housed the winged tomb sealed tight behind them. It grew darker the further down the tunnel they went, and before long Matt felt a chilling breeze against his face.

"We are near the opening," announced Imur.

Linda steadied herself between Lucius and Matt as the breeze began to ruffle her hair.

Matt felt her tense when another rumbling noise echoed ahead. It was as if a great slab had shifted in the darkness before them.

"Everyone!" Imur addressed them all. "When I give the command, we have exactly thirty seconds to cross the threshold. After that, anyone left in this part of the tunnel will be trapped." He waited a few seconds then shouted, "Move!"

As they ran into the gloom, not really knowing where they were going, Matt heard the sliding and grinding of the mountain rearranging itself behind them. In the confines of the tunnel, it sounded as though the whole city was being swallowed up by the bedrock it had perched upon for so long. Matt almost tripped as struggled against a fresh blast of cold air that made him shiver.

Imur jumped over a small underground stream and urged them on. "Come quickly!"

One by one they stepped over the trickling stream and stood behind Imur. Only Kalef and Jessica were left in the tunnel when the huge sheet of granite began to move down above the stream. His awkward stooping stance made it difficult for Kalef to keep his balance on the slippery tunnel floor. Matt saw the massive sheet of solid stone above the stream sliding downward. It was going to block Kalef in the tunnel.

"Kalef! Jump!" Jessica had just crossed the stream when Kalef dived forward. The wall of stone slid down quickly over Kalef's position. Kalef scrambled to keep his footing, ducking as he threw himself forward. His long legs were going to be crushed.

Linda dived forward and caught Kalef's robe. She heaved with all her might and managed to pull him the inch or so necessary to stop him from being squashed beneath the monstrous block of granite.

It crashed down into the stream, slipping perfectly into the contours of the stepping stones they'd just crossed.

"The water will be forced back into the tunnel behind," gasped Imur. "The tomb is safe for now." He helped Kalef to his feet and watched as the tall Ethiopian brushed himself down. "We need you now more than ever, Kalef. Please try to be more careful."

Kalef bowed toward Imur then took Linda's hand. He kissed it and looked up into her grey eyes. His amazingly white teeth shone from the gloom as he whispered, "I will never forget what you just did for me."

They wandered on down the passageway until they came to a large foundation stone. Above their heads, Matt saw lights through an ancient wrought-iron grate. This was the source of the cold breeze. Snowflakes drifted down onto their heads, and occasional footsteps clattered over the grill.

"Where are we?" said Lucius, in a shaky voice.

"We are at the base of the old university building. Its foundations still lie buried beneath the new campus restaurant," answered Imur.

"That's almost half a mile from the museum."

"Yes, Doctor, but we are still in danger until we can be sure that Stiller has no other lookouts in the area."

They waited until there were no more footsteps before easing the grill up from the walkway above. Steph and two of the seraphim pulled themselves up and then helped the rest of the party out onto the snow-covered path. They placed the grill back in position before following Imur to a mini bus in the campus car park. They climbed inside.

Matt studied Imur as they bunched together in the mini bus; his waxed moustache and lacquered hair shone in the darkness as his penetrating eyes scanned the passengers. Matt sighed and felt a sudden urge to call Peter, but he knew his son was at least a little safer with Stiller in Zurich. Jenny was another matter altogether. He would have to face her at some point, but at least that horrendous moment could be delayed for now. He was a coward and a cheat, so he would face the consequences as and when... It was only now, sitting shivering in that bus, that he realised what he'd had and what he'd now lost.

The rest of Imur's men sat silently awaiting their master's instruction while Kalef mumbled into his mobile.

Matt noticed that Jessica and Linda had sat next to each other. He still found it hard to believe he'd actually made love to Linda. The memory had already slipped into that dream-like space reserved for all his misdemeanours and fantasies. Before all this he'd managed to keep them compartmentalised from his guilt. But now the boundaries in his mind were breaking down and he didn't know what to do.

As sleep began to wash over him, his thoughts drifted back to the Eden Seed. He remembered more clearly than ever the Seed's crimson sheen, its unique shape and the delicate amethyst hooks that dangled from its edges.

He wondered if Imur could read minds as well as lips. The mysterious little man had turned to face Matt that very instant. He issued a small, "Hhhm..." like an old man 'in the know'. Matt could feel his legs jumping with tiredness. His eyes were closing.

"Mr. Malcolm?"

Matt forced his eyes back open.

"I'm not convinced the doctor can remember what the Seed looks like, but you can, can't you?" said Imur.

If only this strange little man knew how different the seed looked, thought Matt. It's outer husk was normal enough, but inside...

The owner of the Café Zimmerman, a man Matt had overheard being called Isaac, started the bus.

Imur's prying tone reminded Matt of an old Latin teacher he used to loathe back in his school days. His name was Mr. Samson. His questions were always selected to cut him down to size. "What do you mean, you can't remember yesterday's passage for Pliny? Perfect or imperfect, what was the tense?" The old bastard knew fine-well that Matt had no idea what the class had been rote reading the day before, never mind the fucking tense. He just wanted to prove to Matt that he had the power.

"Mr. Malcolm?" pressed Imur.

Matt jerked awake again. He felt like smacking him, but he managed to hold back. "Of course I can remember what it looks like, Imur. And, with a bit of luck, you are going to show me where there's more before we're all slaughtered by Stiller, aren't you?"

"I hope so. But first we shall drive to a safe-house."

"I don't think there's such a thing," said Matt, hunching down into his seat and pressing his cheek against the cold glass window of the minibus. He half expected to see Stiller's pale face as they left the car park, but there was no one in sight. Eventually, as the windows steamed up and ran wet, he thought again of Jenny and Peter back in England, he thought of his lack of willpower, his lack of respect for the ones who loved him most, and his complete stupidity.

25

"IT'S FROM GLASGOW," said the desk sergeant.

Inspector Watt read out the fax: "Yesterday morning, at 9.33 A.M., one mile off the Isle of Arran, a passenger on the Ardrossan ferry reported something suspicious floating in the sea. The coast guard was called, and within one hour a body was retrieved. A passport was found in the inside pocket of the man's checked Armani jacket. Although the corpse had no head, nor any fingers or toes, the general description and clothing seemed to match the name on the passport: Mr. Grame Barclay, an executive at Vectan-Brosman Pharmaceuticals. Mr. Barclay had last been seen in the Horseshoe Bar, in the centre of Glasgow, the previous evening. The build and clothing seem to be a perfect fit. Having cross-matched the names in the central database, I found your report about a Mr. Malcolm, another employee of Vectan-Brosman. I've just spoken to the company CEO who informs me that Matt Malcolm worked for the same company until two days ago. It was Barclay who fired him and now, as you know, Matt Malcolm has disappeared along with the company secretary and the head of their Research and Development."

"Get this." Watt turned to face the desk sergeant. "We know that Malcolm's car was found abandoned less than six hundred yards from his girlfriend's house, which, according to the C.I.D., has blood all over the place. We also know that Malcolm's wife killed a female kidnapper, who'd held her son and her hostage."

The desk sergeant nodded.

"Well, the C.I.D. have just informed me that the dead kidnapper was none other than a Miss Sylvie Bern."

The desk sergeant shrugged.

Watt smiled. "Malcolm's mistress, and the owner of Brin Cottage."

"Ah," said the desk sergeant, none the wiser.

"Ah, indeed. It's pretty clear that Mr. Malcolm has got to be in the frame, wouldn't you say?"

"Yes sir." The desk sergeant stopped doodling on his report and asked, "How do you think Mrs. Malcolm's going to feel when she finds out she's killed her husband's lover?"

Watt pushed his fingers through his thinning hair and took a sip of coffee. "Perhaps she knows already." He picked up a spoon and began stirring. "Shit, I was beginning to like her too."

* * *

ALESCORTH WAS TEEMING with police by the time Watt brought Jenny down from the hotel to the station. He'd relayed the news to his team about the discovery of the dismembered body of Barclay had and authorised a full-scale manhunt for Matt Malcolm. The C.I.D. had contacted their colleagues in Europe but he decided that the main search would centre round the Glasgow area, where Matt Malcolm still had some family. After three hours of calls, however, it was becoming pretty obvious that his immediate family had lost contact with the high-flying Matt Malcolm.

The local C.I.D. had also informed him that a dead dog had been found in the kitchen at Brin Cottage. Had Malcolm killed the dog? He reread the report. It had been shot. The upstairs bedroom was covered in gore but there was no body. Had Malcolm killed Barclay there first and then shipped his body up to Scotland? It didn't seem to tie in with the death of Miss Bern. Were Matt and Jenny Malcolm in this together?

Inspector Watt's mobile phone rang, but he saw who it was and ignored it. He was much more interested in the snapshot of Miss Bern that lay on his table. Her face was barely recognisable, smashed in by a heavy iron.

He glanced across at a second piece of paper on his desk. Strathclyde police had analysed Barclay's remains and had reported that he was blood group A, rhesus positive. Watt killed the call from his wife and dialled the local lab. "Any joy with the results on Brin Cottage?" In the long pause that followed, his door creaked opened and Jenny Malcolm was shown into his office.

He cupped the phone and signalled her to sit down.

The voice on the other end of the phone explained that the blood from Brin Cottage was not even human.

"What? Are you sure? All of it?" Watt sighed and hung up.

"I want to go to Brin with you," said Jenny.

Watt studied her. She was much more attractive, now that she'd changed and cleaned herself up. "I had intended you to come with me all along, Mrs. Malcolm, but now that the C.I.D. are in there it's going to be more difficult. They always pull rank on us lot. And, you see..." He studied her soft but determined expression, "things have just got a little more complicated."

* * *

STILLER HAD HIS steely gaze fixed on the harbour below. Cruise liners, container ships and luxury yachts all vied for space in the blue-green bay of Genoa. The warm waters lapped against the limestone cliff walls that edged the coastline while the busy terminals bustled with passenger ferries.

He knew that Matt Malcolm and his Syrian friend, Imur, had somehow hidden in the University Museum the night before. There had been no discovery of the policeman's body in the storage cupboard, which meant that either the Zurich Police were completely incompetent or that Imur's men had found the body first and somehow taken it with them when they'd left. According to his information there were two women and nine men. Schmitt and Landenberg had seen the minibus leave the campus car park at 10:34 P.M. and had called Stiller for instructions.

Now, however, the rules of engagement had been altered. Stiller's paymaster had called once more and explained that he wanted the group followed for the time being; no one was to be killed, not yet.

This had disappointed Stiller immensely, but money was money, and he would do as he was told for now. It seemed that the Syrian was a philanthropist of sorts, having made charitable donations to the museum over the years, sponsoring archaeological digs and even contributing to the upkeep of the University buildings. Stiller's contacts had found out that the African was called Kalef Mandula, an Ethiopian human rights lawyer who dabbled in ancient history and was, at one time, an acquaintance of the younger woman. Her name was Miss Jessica Baron, ex-European Chief Justice.

Stiller panned across the bay and picked out the diminutive white villa seven hundred yards below his position. He adjusted his Zeiss binoculars and focused in on Miss Baron. He watched as she showered and then dried her short, blonde hair. His eyes drifted up over her breasts and settled on her soft, fragile neck. It would snap so easily under his powerful fingers. A shiver of anticipation coursed through him.

"They've booked a ferry to Sardinia," said Schmitt, his thin voice scratchy and irritating.

"Really," said Stiller, without once taking his eyes off of the younger woman. She bent over to pick up her towel. "We'll be waiting for them when they get there.

You never know, our orders might change again and it would be such a shame to miss out on such pleasures." He gave Schmitt a wry grin as he lowered the glasses. "You did well in Zurich. Monitoring every vehicle in the campus paid off."

"It was standard procedure in our department. I knew the minibus would be the most likely escape vehicle." Schmitt smiled smugly to reveal a set of yellow, rodent-like teeth that protruded beyond his thin bottom lip. "It's just a pity we couldn't have intercepted them before Lugano. It would have been so easy last night."

Stiller slipped on his dark glasses and examined his perfectly maintained Heckler. "They'll meet their maker soon enough, but first I want you to get a photograph of everyone down there. I need to know who is expendable and who is not. I want you and Landenberg to compile records on all of them before mid-day: names, jobs, hobbies, indiscretions..."

"But we have most of that already," wheezed Schmitt.

"I want more." Stiller walked back into the villa through a large pair of French windows and sat down on the leather sofa. He stretched out and waved Landenberg over to join him. Landenberg, in his mid-thirties and sporting a noticeable paunch, grunted as he got up.

"Find out what time they are going to reach Sardinia," said Stiller, "and make sure that you and the weasel are there to meet them."

"What about you? Will I book you a flight too?"

Stiller sighed; he was too tired to answer such a ridiculous question. He flicked the Heckler up into mid-air, tapped it with his right shoulder and caught it with his left hand. The safety catch was off and the gun primed by the time it rested under Landenberg's chin. "I'm going to do some macro risk assessment."

"Macro?" enquired Landenberg, his eyes shifting nervously.

"Up close," whispered Stiller. He sat up and smiled, pushing Landenberg back with the barrel of the gun. "You need to lose some weight. Not exactly what I'd call fighter pilot reactions."

Landenberg staggered backwards and cursed Schmitt, who had begun to laugh at him through the French windows.

Stiller pushed his fingers through his dark, greasy hair before picking up a small leather bag from the coffee table. "I need to go."

26

AS THE FRONT DOOR clicked shut, Landenberg and Schmitt bickered amongst a jumble of cases and cameras.

Schmitt had managed to get a shot of them all except the older woman, who seemed to have slept later than the rest. He watched as Landenberg tapped unremittingly on his various keyboards, saving a variety of files and pictures to the remote wireless storage system.

An hour later, there was a knock on the front door. Schmitt lifted a Chinese semi-automatic from the coffee table. "Stiller?"

Unnerved, Landenberg placed his forefinger over his lips and moved forward.

Schmitt heard a key turn in the lock and saw the black metal handle dip towards the floor. He knelt down and aimed.

The door opened and Stein stepped inside.

"For fuck sake, Stein," snapped Schmitt, "I thought you were supposed to wait in Zurich?"

Stein marched in. "Jumpy bastards. Stiller told me to wait a few hours, and then follow you down here. He wanted me to shadow you. Wherever you go, I have to follow, but not until I've waited for two hours. KGB crap, remember!"

They nodded.

Stein kicked his holdall across the marble floor. "Open it. I brought you some breakfast."

Schmitt and Landenberg unzipped the holdall and snatched at the croissants and doughnuts that lay on the top layer. Underneath, Schmitt saw Stein's pistol and his KGB issued sniper rifle. There were also spare passports and about six or seven neat piles of assorted currency.

"The police found the two Arabs that Stiller fucked up in the University flat. They're going bananas, and there's still no sign of their missing officer."

The portly Landenberg licked his fat, sugar-coated lips. "He's over the top."

"He's a grade one fuckin' psycho alright, but he's thorough," said Stein.

Schmitt munched on a fresh croissant, spilling greasy flakes over his shirt and trousers. "I think he could be the best I've ever worked for, but he's got his own agenda, and we are all surplus to requirements. Just remember that." He saw the spark of recognition in his colleague's eyes and sniffed before planting his off-white incisors into another doughnut.

* * *

AS MATT WATCHED Imur wash his face, he studied the deep lines beneath the cleric's eyes. He knew that Imur hadn't slept a wink during the two hundred and seventy mile journey the night before. Never able to sleep properly himself, Matt had counted off the miles before they'd stopped at the villa. He'd overheard Imur instructing Isaac, the café owner, to book some ferry tickets to Sardinia.

"We have to see if we are being followed," Imur said.

Puzzled, Matt couldn't see how booking some tickets would make them any the wiser. He also couldn't believe that they'd managed to lose Stiller quite so easily. Imur had nattered in Swiss-German, thinking Matt asleep, and he'd overheard the name of their destination: the Mura Della Marina. He'd watched the dawn and marvelled at the wonderful views over the Gulf of Genoa. Hopefully, this place would give him some breathing space to get his head straight. He had an incredible urge to beg for someone's phone and call Jenny, so he closed his eyes until it passed.

Ensconced in the safe house, Matt heard Imur walk past his bunk. Isaac joined him, a few yards away beside the bathroom door. Imur spoke in a whisper. "Once Mr. Malcolm has identified the Eden Seed, I will arrange for its safekeeping, away from the pharmaceutical giants and those with the money who would undoubtedly try to buy their own immortality.

Matt squinted across as Imur knelt down and muttered a small prayer to 'Yahweh'. He anointed himself with some kind of oil before kissing the silver seraphim that hung round his neck. Isaac followed his lead, watching as his master waxed his perfectly trimmed moustache. "Your contacts at the ferry terminal, Isaac... any news?"

"You were right, Imur, our contact at the ferry terminal has been asked if there were any last minute bookings for eleven adults. They know we are here."

Matt saw Jessica Baron emerge from the bathroom. He'd seen her earlier, her towelling robe barely clinging to her curves as she passed the open door.

Imur bowed as she walked back to her room then called after her, "Miss Baron, would you please keep the windows closed." He waited until Jessica had returned to her room before speaking again to Isaac. "It can only be Stiller. Don't cancel anything. Instead, book an additional flight for four and then another for seven to Cairo. Kalef has had no answer from Addis about travel passes or permits, so we may have to do the journey illegally after all."

"I don't think we'll be able to get a flight from Genoa to Cairo, not direct," said Isaac, already dialling his contact.

"Try your best," said Imur.

Kalef walked in, glancing down at Matt's bed as he moved across the whitewashed room. "Good morning, Mr. Malcolm," he said loudly, as if issuing a warning to Imur.

Matt tensed and then opened his eyes fully.

Imur hesitated. "Kalef, Stiller knows we are here."

The tall African closed his eyes and muttered a small prayer. "Then we must assume we are being watched right now, my friend."

"We would be dead by now if that were the case," said Imur.

"Not if Stiller's boss has guessed what we are about to do," said Matt. He blinked, and then held his black-framed glasses up to the sunlight. He gave them a quick wipe.

Kalef and Imur were obviously annoyed at his suggestion. Matt saw Kalef give Imur a quick shake of his head, as if to say: don't say too much.

"Your usual Aramaic would have been a better choice if you had intended keeping your conversations more secret." Fearing the amount of time left to satisfy Stiller's demands, Matt had decided to rattle the two clerics.

"So you know who Stiller is working for?" said Imur.

"Stiller is obviously working for a competitor or, perhaps, a rich loner." Matt saw he had their attention and continued, "He has probably guessed that we don't have the Seeds. Either he or, more likely, whoever is paying him, has worked out that you are taking the doctor and me somewhere else."

Imur toyed with his moustache. "Very well thought out, Mr. Malcolm. So what would your next move be?"

"You mean what would I do if I were Stiller?" Matt heard the door behind him swing open. It was Lucius. "I would wait and see what we do next," he finished.

Lucius Schlesinger looked much older than his sixty years, having slept very little on the minibus and no doubt, thought Matt, having been pestered all night by Linda. Matt felt another pang of jealousy as Linda appeared from the bedroom behind Lucius. She clutched a towelling robe around her, which was far too small.

Imur and Kalef both turned away.

As they did, Linda let the robe fall open. She gave her breasts a quick shake for Matt's benefit.

Matt didn't know where to look. He flushed crimson.

Linda closed the robe and winked at him.

He still hadn't worked out how to deal with this out of control, lustful version of his long-time secretary.

"Good morning, Linda," he said.

"Morning boys." Linda walked over to the bathroom, the short robe scarcely concealing her ample buttocks.

Lucius, seemingly oblivious to the whole scene, addressed Imur. "How long are we to remain here, Imur?"

On hearing the bathroom door click shut behind Linda, Imur looked up at Lucius. "We were followed here last night, and we were just discussing what might be our next move. As it stands, I can tell you that we've booked a ferry to Sardinia."

"Your first site is in Sardinia?" said Lucius. "Not at all," said Imur.

Lucius rubbed his wrinkled forehead, "I'm not sure I follow you, Imur."

"Mr. Malcolm is probably right. Stiller has been told to follow us. We know he's watching us because he has already checked the ferry ports and asked for details on any party of eleven travelling in the next few days. Kalef thinks we are being watched right now."

Matt saw Lucius turn pale.

"Don't worry, Doctor Schlesinger," said Imur, "I'm making some alternative travel arrangements." Imur called Isaac over. "Any flights?"

"I can get us on a 4 P.M. flight to Port Said, this afternoon."

"Fine. What time are we supposed to leave on our 'journey' to Sardinia?" asked Imur.

"Tomorrow, Thursday, 10 a.m.," said Isaac.

"Excellent. We may get a sixteen hour advantage if we can just get out of here without being seen in the next five hours."

Matt found the small silver winged pendant in his pocket. His fingers folded round it. "And how, exactly, do you think we're going to manage that?"

27

STILLER MADE HIS way out of the villa garden and down the hillside, passing between the holiday apartments and shops that lined the cobbled streets on the way to the Mura Della Marina. He hoped that Matt Malcolm and his group would still be weary after their midnight drive over the Alps. If he was lucky, there was a good chance that he would be able to get close enough to plant a bug in a holdall or a piece of clothing.

With no sign of anyone outside, Stiller walked down the side of Malcolm's villa and put his back against the whitewashed wall. Above his head, the green shutters of the bathroom window were closed, so he switched on his earpiece and pulled out the Russian issued mini-endoscope. His six-foot-three stance made it easy for him to slide the fibre through the lowest slit in the shutter. The picture that appeared on his watch face a second later showed the inside of the bathroom. There was nobody there at the moment, but the door had been left slightly ajar and he could see and hear several men talking in the hall outside the bathroom door. The small man with his back to him was first to speak. Stiller decided this was Imur.

"We will have to create a diversion if our plan is to be successful. Isaac, I want you to organise lookouts covering all aspects from the villa. Once they're in place, send one of the men outside to walk round the garden. Scan all the overlooking windows for lens reflections or any suspicious movements. Once we've decided where he is we can orchestrate the diversion accordingly. Steph!"

A powerful man with Slav features joined the men in the hallway and produced a piece of paper.

Stiller heard someone approaching from the back of the house so he retracted the endoscope. Before the crunch of small stones grew too loud he reached up and clipped a micro bug onto one of the closed green shutters and slipped away.

A pool boy carrying a small bucket and a hose attachment rounded the corner, but Stiller was already walking up the hill between a row of shops and restaurants. He mingled with the lunchtime shoppers and was soon lost in the crowd. As he climbed, he thought of Sylvie and the careful training he'd given her over the years. He pushed his way up the hill, anger rising in his chest. In his mind's eye, he could still see the Malcolm woman, tied to the radiator, and wondered again how she'd managed to overpower his best agent. The Malcolms will pay. Every last one of them will pay, he decided.

* * *

JENNY MALCOLM FELT the car brake suddenly. She dug her nails into the leatherette seat and then looked up the quartz-chipped driveway at the idyllic white cottage. Her eyes instantly fixed on the cross-cross lattice windows and she wondered what horrors lay inside.

There were five police cars and an incident caravan, all crammed into the driveway.

"What a bloody shambles," snapped Watt, "I mean, they've rutted the lawn, would you look at that."

Jenny saw Watt's face redden.

Distractedly, he continued. "Do you see that man with the white braid round his hat?"

"You mean the Chief Inspector?" said Jenny.

Watt leaned back in genuine surprise. "Well done."

Jenny hated this kind of condescending tone.

"He's flown down here from Glasgow to ask you some questions about..."

"About the girl I killed?" Jenny looked down.

"Yes, but there's more," said Watt.

They shuffled out of the car and continued up the garden path.

"You see," continued Watt, "first there was the matter of your husband's abandoned car, then there was the matter of the break-in and, of course, your intervention." Watt waved a young officer towards him. "Then there was a certain coincidence that has...let's say, muddied the waters slightly."

She watched Watt write several words on his pad. He tore off the sheet and handed it to the young policeman. "Quickly." He nodded back in the direction of the Chief Inspector and the young man mouthed the words, "Okay, sir".

"What muddied the waters?" asked Jenny, feeling her heart quicken.

"The girl you killed last night lived here."

Jenny stopped, digging her heels into the stones. She felt giddy.

Watt continued, "By telling us to look for Mr. Malcolm at Brin," he nodded towards the cottage, "I assumed you knew about your husband's affair."

Jenny could feel a wave of nausea building in her stomach. "You're telling me that I've killed Matt's lover?" She staggered backwards.

Watt steadied her, "People are going to assume you knew what you were doing."

She looked into Watt's tired brown eyes. "I had no idea who she was when I..." She scanned the upper bedroom window. "What was Matt thinking? What has he done?"

"Men are fickle creatures," explained Watt, unhelpfully.

Jenny tried to compose herself. She took in a long, slow breath and then said, "I don't mean the affair. I've half expected as much for years. But how could he get involved with a psychotic bitch like that? How could he let her threaten his family?"

Watt stepped up towards the front door and signalled to a constable. "There's more, Mrs. Malcolm."

"Brilliant!" whispered Jenny. "What now?"

Watt asked the constable to explain the situation inside the cottage.

"Well," he began, "apart from finding Miss Sylvie Bern's dead dog in the kitchen, there's been some kind of scuffle in the bedroom upstairs. Blood, lumps of..." Watt stopped him. The Chief Inspector was walking towards them.

"Inspector Watt, is this the suspect's wife?"

Watt straightened. "Yes sir."

Jenny fought an inexplicable urge to run, but she addressed the Chief Inspector instead, "I still don't understand. What's Matt done?"

"We're not entirely sure yet, Mrs. Malcolm, but it's not looking too good." The Chief Inspector's accent was similar to Matt's when he drank too much - Glaswegian.

Watt addressed the Chief Inspector. "The blood upstairs in the bedroom didn't match your man in the water."

Jenny tensed. "What man? Who was in the water? Was it Matt?"

"Type B?" broached the Chief Inspector, cutting across Jenny's questions.

"Only if 'B' is for Bovine," answered Watt. "It's bull's blood."

The Chief Inspector looked, with incredulity, at Watt then glanced down at Jenny Malcolm. "What can you tell us about your husband's affair, Mrs. Malcolm?"

Jenny could feel her shock and fear turning into frustration and anger. "I asked you if this other man you found was Matt?"

Tight lipped, Watt shook his head. "It wasn't Matt."

"Mrs. Malcolm," pressed the Chief Inspector. "How much did you know about Matt and Miss Bern?"

"Oh, I think you could tell me much more than I could tell you. I only found out on Monday by mistake. An e-mail..."

"I see. And so you decided on revenge?" pressed the Chief Inspector.

"What?" Jenny couldn't believe it. "That screwed up bitch found me, not the other way round. I had no idea, until about five minutes ago, who I'd killed."

"I must warn you, Mrs. Malcolm, Inspector Watt is taking notes and whatever you say will be..."

"Shut up!" Jenny pushed past them, "I want to see inside."

Watt ran ahead and caught Jenny by the arm. "Best not take that kind of attitude, Mrs. Malcolm. If you can just calm down a little, we can all have a look around."

Watt nodded to the constable then opened the front door and ushered them in. The stench of faeces and decay made her gag. There was a dead dog lying in the kitchen. Jaws still agape, its red hair was matted with dried blood and its eyes were clouded.

She covered her mouth.

Watt issued a reluctant sigh. "I did say it might be a bit of a mess..."

"It's not the dog," said Jenny. "It's those." Her eyes were fixed on the montage of pictures that covered the wall. They showed Matt, the dog, and the girl she'd killed on Monday night, all in various happy family poses. She pressed on past the kitchen.

"Mrs. Malcolm?" called Watt. He quickly followed her.

Entering the living room, she pointed at the goatskin rug and began to shake. "I bought Matt that rug two years ago. He said he didn't like it. Said he was going to take it to the dump."

On the mantelpiece, a framed picture showed Matt and Sylvie standing outside an ornate, red stone cathedral. Jenny screwed up her eyes. "Where the hell is that?"

The Chief Inspector peered over her shoulder and answered, "I'm pretty sure that it's Santiago de Compostela, Galicia. It's in Spain."

"Spain!" She began to cry.

She felt Watt's hand clasp her shoulder. "Look, I'm really sorry, but could you just come upstairs?"

The Chief Inspector shuffled in beside them and flashed Watt a cautious frown.

Watt continued, "You really didn't know this Sylvie girl, did you?"

"That is for the courts to decide, Inspector!" corrected the Chief Inspector. He gave Watt a hard stare.

"The first time I laid eyes on her was last night," protested Jenny.

Watt led them to the bedroom upstairs.

"I don't think I can go in there," she said.

"It's a bit of a mess alright but..."

Jenny turned to go back downstairs.

Watt gripped her arm. "It's all for show, Jenny. What you're going to see... It's all animal blood."

Jenny spun round to face them, her fists clenched. "You two just don't get it, do you?"

Watt and the Chief looked bemused. The young constable busied himself with his notebook further down the hall.

"It's not the blood or whatever else there is in there that I can't stand; it's the thought of Matt and her, in there. In this house, living a whole different fucking life! For Chist's sake."

Watt flushed.

The Chief Inspector gave her a condescending nod that made her want to smash his face in.

"Jenny, we've found Matt's boss," said Watt.

"His body," added the Chief.

Jenny, regaining her composure, wiped away the tears. "Who?"

Watt fingered his black notebook, "A Mr. Barclay."

"And you think that Matt and this Sylvie killed him here?"

"Not anymore. But something caused Matt to bolt from here in a hurry and disappear."

Jenny pushed open the bedroom door and stepped inside.

Watt tried to stop her. "Mrs. Malcolm..."

Jenny saw the dried-in blood and the stained underwear scattered over the quilt. She saw the crumpled towels heaped on the floor of the en-suite and she saw the pictures, more pictures, lots of pictures.

Watt asked, "Can you see anything of Matt's in here that might help us? Nothing's been touched. A wallet, a note, a bag, a folder...?"

Jenny stood still for a long moment and then, after scanning the whole room, shook her head.

Jenny saw the Chief Inspector's expression harden.

"Mrs. Malcolm," he continued, "I'm afraid I need you to come back to the station for further questioning."

"But, Sir..." protested Watt.

"This was a bad idea, Watt," said the Chief.

Outside, two young constables led Jenny to a waiting police car. As she slipped into the back seat she heard one of the constables relay a message to Watt.

"Sir, we've just discovered another two bodies." Excitedly, the constable read his notes, "a man in the gamekeeper's cottage, less than half a mile away, and another at the Grantham Services on the A1."

* * *

BACK IN THE Genoese villa Landenberg, Schmitt and Stein played back the video conversation between Imur and one of his men.

Stiller paused the recording. "They know they're being watched." He looked over to Landenberg, "How the fuck is that possible?"

Landenberg looked sick. "I've no idea, all my contacts are still good, and my guy in Genoa is one of the most reliable..."

"I didn't ask you to defend your fuck-up. I just want to hear some theories as to how that Syrian cocksucker is one jump ahead of us."

Schmitt stifled a grin as Landenberg squirmed.

Stiller smacked his fist into Schmitt's left ear.

"Uuuuhh!"

Unmoved, Stiller homed in on Stein. "I thought you said these two were good?"

Stein stared back at Stiller, ignoring Schmitt who'd fallen back onto the tiled floor.

"They must have a source in the same ticket office as we do," he said.

"Ten out of fucking ten!" said Stiller, stepping over Schmitt. "You stand to make two hundred thousand Swiss francs each, but you also stand to lose your balls if any of you compromise my advantage again. Understood?"

All three, including the sprawling Schmitt, nodded back.

Landenberg glanced down over the rooftops and chimneys at the white villa below. "The African is outside."

28

KALEF HAD WALKED round the safe house four times already. A few minutes before, Matt agreed with Imur, Lucius and Kalef on the only possible vantage point. There was no view of their current position from the sea, and the houses on either side obscured their position enough to make things difficult from that angle. Stiller had to be on the hill behind them and, after a few seconds of debate, they agreed that attack was their best defence.

Kalef had asked Linda to put the food mixer onto full, to cover their conversation.

Matt's stomach sank as he listened, as best he could over the racket, to their plan. What's going to happen to Jenny and Peter if Stiller gets hurt or killed? he wondered.

Imur issued his commands. "While Kalef walks round the outside of the villa as a distraction, you..." he pointed to the war hardened Slav, Steph, "...can take Hulut and Matt up the hill, past the shops and restaurants to look for the most likely vantage point."

"But..." Matt protested.

Imur continued, "Hulut is the logical choice, having served with you in the Balkans."

All eyes fell on Matt.

"And Matt?" whispered Steph, his voice full of alarm.

Kalef tapped Imur on the arm. "Imur, we need Mr. Malcolm to stay safe, otherwise we have nobody that can identify the Seeds in..." he cut himself short as the food mixer slowed and then switched to full again.

"God will protect him, Kalef. And besides, I'm sure the Doctor will remember enough about the Seeds should anything untoward befall Mr. Malcolm."

Still terrified at all sorts of prospects, Matt saw Kalef turn away from Imur. The African had a look of bewilderment etched in his normally noble features.

Steph spoke up again, "The Seraphim, yes. But Mr. Malcolm? He's far from ready for any real premeditated violence."

Imur seemed to smile to himself before saying, "Mr. Malcolm hit a man between the eyes with one shot on a moving boat. As I said, the Lord will protect us."

Matt, still too drowsy to function properly, looked Imur in the eye and thought about the mess he'd made of his life. He wanted to be something other than a useless pawn. "Show me what to do, and I'll do it." The thought of Stiller terrified him, but the guilt he felt about Jenny and Peter being drawn into this nightmare because of him was unbearable. That, combined with a blind sense of bravado and growing dislike of Imur, filled him with a determination that superseded logic.

* * *

STILLER PEERED INTO Landenberg's laptop as he pointed through the French windows. "Use the anti-refractive lenses. I don't want them to see any reflections!" He tapped Landenburgh on the shoulder. "What are they saying?"

"It's hard to tell, there's a food mixer going. Listen for yourself."

Stiller punched the wall in frustration and then moved closer. He listened in. He could just make out a woman's voice. "Tell them their lunch is ready. It's couscous and lamb, but no vegetables until someone goes shopping."

Another woman answered. "We're supposed to be looking out for anyone that might be watching us."

The first woman's voice, which sounded more mature, answered. "They're all bloody paranoid, let's eat."

* * *

MATT HAD SUGGESTED that they may have been bugged already and had helped Lucius and Imur write out a script for the women to read through. His idea was to distract Stiller while he, Steph and Hulut checked out the overlooking properties. Matt watched as Imur packed everything they needed for their next move. He needed to get going to wherever Imur was taking them, find the Eden Seed and get back to Jenny and Peter as quickly as possible.

Matt looked over Imur's shoulder out the back door of the villa. The air was warm and he could see the harbour in the distance, jammed with ferries and cargo vessels.

Linda scribbled a note and passed it to him. It read: 'This is madness. Call it off.'

Imur intercepted the note and smiled. He shook his head and wrote: 'It is God's will.'

Linda mouthed the words 'fuck off' before backing off.

Matt's stomach tightened. He looked down at the cumbersome gun Steph had given him. Jessica was next to move forward. She pushed her lips against his ear. "Matt, please, you don't have a clue how to do something like this. Let the

Seraphim do it themselves." Matt smelled the same perfume he had in Munich and sensed her warmth.

Steph tapped his shoulder and pointed up the hill.

It was time to go.

* * *

IT WAS STEPH who noticed the car first. Salt and mud had partially covered the 'CH' sticker but the Audi A4 had a Zurich registration number plate and the odds were high that this was the villa they'd been looking for.

Matt felt his mouth become dry as he followed Steph down the set of red-tiled steps that led through the evergreens to the front door of the slightly shabby villa. It had peeling black window shutters and a mass of dormant creeping fig that sprawled over the off-white walls. Its tendrils as thick as a man's arm, it wound skyward, through the ornate balustrades to the upper floor.

Steph signalled to Matt, as one would to a small child, firstly putting one finger over his lips and then pointing above his head to the overgrown balcony on the first floor using two fingers. Matt had seen this type of signal in a hundred war films but quickly realised that this was for real. He was about to attempt to enter a heavily guarded villa and attack a world-renowned assassin trained by the KGB.

He'd only set eyes on his gun twenty minutes beforehand and he wasn't completely sure he could release the safety catch, let alone aim and fire. It felt so heavy.

Matt gave Steph a plaintive stare and waited for the signal to fall back and hide, but it never came. Instead, Hulut, the tall seraphim selected for the mission, kicked his backside and pointed again at the balcony above. Matt shook with nerves as he climbed up through the scratchy stems, eventually gripping onto the rusting handrail of the balustrade. Flakes of orange rust floated into his left eye and almost caused him to shout out, but Hulut had joined him and was already pulling him over the top rail. Matt flopped down onto the small tiled ledge and let out a small sigh as the air was forced from his lungs.

Below, Steph had already disappeared and, as Matt pulled the automatic free from his coat, he watched Hulut slip the window catch with a small curved blade.

* * *

INSIDE THE SHABBY villa, Stiller continued to listen in to the inane conversation between the two women and grew ever more suspicious. "Stein, check upstairs."

Stein, not looking particularly happy to move from the comfort of his seat, stood up and lifted his pistol from the coffee table. He wandered over to the stairs in the corner.

Stiller heard the thud and turned to see Stein looking back at them with a quizzical stare, his face a ghostly white. Blood ebbed through his fingers and his legs buckled.

"Move!" Stiller rolled twice and fired into the kitchen. Plaster exploded from the wall near to the kitchen door, but now the marble floor around Schmitt and Landenberg cracked and splintered too. Bullets rained down from the upper balcony.

* * *

BEFORE THEY'D FIRED, Matt had seen Steph in the kitchen below. The Slav cracked off the first shot. Matt felt sick but Hulut punched his arm and began to fire.

Matt pressed the trigger, firing indiscriminately down into the living room below. Through his narrowed eyes he saw the man at the foot of the stairs jerk back. A bullet had caught the man in the shoulder, but he'd managed to spin round, aiming a shot from his pistol at Matt.

Matt, the adrenalin rushing through his veins, squeezed his trigger again.

Hit in the forehead, the back of the man's skull shattered, spraying grizzly, light-pink lumps of flesh and bone over the two men who clambered and crawled over the debris in their effort to avoid Hulut's onslaught.

Matt shook with fear as he fired his weapon, his right arm cramping because he pressed the trigger too hard.

A bullet split the small marble pillar to the left of his knee. He threw himself down onto the upper landing.

Hulut moved down the stairs towards the man Matt had just killed. It was then that Matt saw the familiar black mane outside the patio doors and shouted, "Hulut, the French windows!"

Hulut lifted his aim from the two men that now sheltered behind an overturned stone table and cracked off a round in the direction of the French windows.

Glass showered over the floor but Matt saw Hulut jerk back and clutch his throat.

Stiller's bullet had ripped into Hulut's jugular and split his windpipe.

Praying Stiller wouldn't see him, Matt watched as Hulut shook his head, as if trying to shake some stinging wasp from his hair. He dropped his gun.

Matt heard a grotesque gurgling sound as Hulut fell.

Terrified, Matt now edged back towards the upstairs bedroom he'd just come through. He was desperate to reach the safety of the outside balcony.

Steph resumed firing from the kitchen.

Stiller fell back, ducking back out of the French windows.

Matt heard one of the men caught in the living room shout out in a high-pitched voice: "Upstairs. There's one more upstairs!"

A mixture of confusion and fear overwhelmed him. He should have stayed put in the safe house. Fingering a cold brass bedstead, he continued to move back towards the window and out onto the balcony. Someone was coming up the stairs.

Matt reckoned he could fire straight through the door and catch them at the top of the stairs. He pulled on the trigger but it didn't move. His gun had jammed. He clawed at the slippery metal catch as an unstoppable feeling of helplessness seized him. It was the kind of powerlessness that plagued his most terrible nightmares. He banged the gun off the shutters of the window but it still wouldn't work. He edged away from the window.

Someone kicked the bedroom door open and fired.

Perched on the rickety veranda, he flattened himself against the outside wall.

Inches from his head, shards of wood and plaster exploded through a storm of floating feathers, out over the garden below and into the street.

A tattered lace curtain beside his face wavered back into place.

Someone was walking through the rubble in the bedroom towards the balcony. Still his finger strained against the jammed trigger.

Matt didn't know whether to jump or stand still. He'd stopped fumbling with his gun and crouched down as low as he could, in an effort to reduce the immediate target area for his approaching assailant.

A heavy-set man pounced out through the fluttering curtain onto the balcony and fired to his right.

Matt was on the man's left.

The half a second advantage allowed Matt to swing his heavy gun into the man's lower back.

The man groaned and crumpled to his knees.

As Matt lifted his gun for a second strike, a loud crack shook the veranda. It tilted down on one side and fell away from the wall before jerking to a sudden stop.

Held precariously by the thick foliage, the whole balcony began to judder as the tendrils snapped one by one.

Matt had wrapped his arm around the rusting balustrade. He could see that his attacker's excessive weight was proving too much for the rusting pins that supported the balcony. As it moved again, he lost his footing and the whole veranda fell away beneath him. He closed his eyes as it slammed into the concrete walk-way at the back door.

Winded and bleeding, Matt crawled free of the tangled mess.

A muffled Russian curse issued from the back door of the villa beneath him. Matt's attacker, a stocky man in a black leather jacket, lay still, his gun snarled up in the remnants of the creeping fig.

Steph suddenly appeared from the kitchen and pulled Matt up the red-tiled drive, back onto the street. In the confusion, Matt saw the skeletal frame of a second man stagger out from the dusty shadows of the back door. He fired.

Matt and Steph rolled onto the road above, then, giving Stiller's villa a wide berth, scrambled down the steep hill towards the safe house. Pushing past dazed shoppers, excited children and nosy women, Matt ran as fast as he could, trying not to lose sight of Steph.

"What... what about H... Hulut?" spluttered Matt, his eyes stinging with sweat.

"It's no good, he's gone." Steph's voice was still strong as he slowed, glancing back from time to time to check for any sign of the skinny, weasel-faced man who had appeared from the back door of the dilapidated villa. But there was no sign of anyone.

"Did you get Stiller?" panted Matt.

Steph shook his head and caught Matt's arm. "Just keep on walking. Don't look back."

"But..." Matt protested, the sound of sirens already splitting the morning sky. The racket echoed off the rambling buildings that lined the cobble-stoned streets.

While Matt's chest pounded against the unwieldy gun under his coat, Steph assumed a nonchalant gait as they passed the safe house and turned a sharp left towards the seafront.

Struggling to control himself, Matt noticed that the passers-by soon ignored them. All eyes were on the racing police cars that made for the scene of the carnage behind them, high on the hill.

Making a wide circle back to the safe house took another fifteen minutes.

Jessica opened the back door. "Matt!"

Imur appeared at her side. He looked at Steph. "Hulut?"

Steph shook his head.

Jessica turned back into the house. Matt could tell she was crying.

"We've bought ourselves some time, that's all," said Steph.

"We didn't get Stiller," said Matt.

Imur placed a hand on Matt's shoulder. "Even so, I told you God would take care of you."

Matt felt confused. He was still in shock.

"We will be in Egypt by tonight," said Imur.

29

IN MILWAUKEE'S GREEN belt, the pristine Marketing Department of Meldan Industries buzzed with latest estimate targets and forecasts. The regulations department had completed the proof-reading of the data and Ted Burrows had authorised a further two, expensive line extensions to their new leukaemia vaccine.

His last phone call had been with the Federal Drug Administration, who had just pointed out that his objections to Vectan-Brosman's Leukivec could not be upheld as they had now submitted another six sets of trial data that had shown, without doubt, that the human safety index of their cancer vaccine was just as good as his own. In fact, the same Pennsylvanian University had screened both vaccines. This meant that Ted Burrows would have to back off. Any further doubt thrown on Leukivec would have the inevitable knock-on effect of delaying the release of his own, improved version.

Burrows slammed his hand down on the FDA folder and paged security. "Get me Evans, now!"

Evans, head of internal security, had worked for Burrows for ten years. He'd kept him well informed of any internal weaknesses in the company and had dealt with the odd external threat when required. Vectan-Brosman's Seed Project was currently costing them one hundred million U.S. dollars per month. It was time to act.

The square-jawed ex-marine entered Ted Burrow's office and sat in the leather chair as instructed.

"I've had a call from the FDA, who have just informed me that Vectan-Brosman did all their trial work at the same University as we did. Someone screwed up, and it's you, Evans, that's supposed to inform me of that kind of thing, not the fuckin' FDA!"

Burrows felt his anger build. He took a sip of water. "Any news from Barclay?"

Evans twisted in his chair and wondered how to break the news. "Well, there's been a complication on that front, Sir."

There was a pause while Burrows snatched a breath between his clenched teeth. "And what would that be?" He hissed.

"He's dead, sir."

"He's fuckin' what?"

Evans unfolded a shiny piece of fax paper and read, "It is assumed that the remaining torso is that of one Gerard Barclay of Vectan-Brosman Pharmaceuticals, even with the prints and head removed. The passport, general physical description and dress seem to match the remains..."

Burrows snatched the piece of paper out of Evans' hand. "Strathclyde Police. Who the fuck are they?"

"Scottish police force, Sir. I don't know how or why it happened, as yet, but I have a contact in Glasgow who has informed me that it sounds like the work of a local hit-man called Brad Kennedy. He has the pretty unsavoury habit of torching the fingers and toes of his victims while they're still alive."

"Then, why the fuck leave the passport in his fuckin' jacket?" Burrows saw the blank look on Evans' face and carried on. "Do you think Sir John has found out that Barclay's been passing us information?"

"Possible, but..."

"No," Burrows interrupted, standing up. "Sir John isn't that kind of guy."

"Not unless he's in league with the KGB, he's not." Evans allowed himself a semblance of a grin. "Kennedy had strong links with the KGB, back in the seventies. In fact, he did time for distributing extreme, left-wing literature."

"So what are you trying to say?" Burrows hated it when Evans adopted this kind of smug tone.

"My guess is that someone else is aware of the Vectan-Brosman Seed project. Someone's figured out that Barclay was leaking to the wrong side and has put a stop to it. That someone has connections with ex-KGB members and probably knows that we destroyed the test crop in Spain," continued Evans.

Burrows closed his eyes and drew another deep breath as he thought back to Evans' botched job that had left two Almerian farmers dead.

Evans seemed to read his thoughts and whispered, "I didn't want there to be any traceable evidence to Meldan Industries, Mr. Burrows. I wanted to guarantee-"

"Guarantee my ass. Do you think it's Ueshima?"

"Possible. But there is another factor," said Evans.

"And what the fuck is that?" snapped Burrows.

"Matt Malcolm," said Evans.

Burrows thought back to the over-confident marketing manager who'd stitched him up in Munich. "That arsehole who stitched us up in Munich?"

"Yes, and guess who Strathclyde police have as public enemy number one?" Without waiting for a reply Evans continued, "Matt Malcolm's wife. According to my source in Glasgow, Mr. Malcolm's done a runner."

Burrows moved closer, "I thought you said Kennedy killed Barclay?"

"Barclay?" Evans drew back, "I'm sure he did, but one of the last things Barclay did was to fire Matt Malcolm. What if Malcolm authorised the hit?"

"So why are they holding his wife?"

"His wife is said to have killed Matt Malcolm's mistress, a Miss Sylvie Bern. Now she's a definite KGB hook up."

"So you think the Malcolms have a KGB link?" enquired Burrows.

"All I know is that Mrs. Malcolm is being held for killing a known KGB trainee," said Evans, "and that Mr. Malcolm, having had an affair with this girl, is now in Zurich, and his ex-boss is missing a head."

"That bastard's after the Seed for himself. There must be more Seeds somewhere," said Burrows. With more than a hint of his military past he grunted and walked over to his personal library. He pulled a red, leather-bound book from the top shelf and placed it on his reading bureau.

Evans squinted across and asked, "The Bible?"

"No. It's our accounts for this year so far. We are more than one billion dollars behind forecast and the banks are getting jittery." Burrows hadn't told his shareholders or the bank about the hundred million dollars blackmail money they'd been paying out to Vectan-Brosman. He'd simply re-directed some of the pension fund. "I'm going to give you two very simple instructions, Evans. One: cancel the monthly payments to Vectan-Brosman, and two: find Malcolm and kill him."

Evans shifted in his seat and straightened his collar. "Yes, Sir."

Twenty years of Marine indoctrination made him perfect for a job like this.

"Right against left, Mr. Burrows. Just like the old days. The free world against the dregs of communism."

"Mmm..." mumbled Burrows. "I don't think it's quite as simple as that, Evans."

As soon as Evans left the room Ted Burrows put the ledger back on the top shelf and consoled his own surge of guilt with the thought that Malcolm was probably the only man left alive with the secret of the Vectan-Brosman Seed, and that once he was eliminated the world would be set back on its safe, predictable course again. Burrows hated disruption, change, or, for that matter, anyone who got in his way. Malcolm had marked his own card in Munich, and now Evans would punch it. But Burrows was nothing if not thorough, so he buzzed his secretary and said, "Get me the personnel file on Evans."

* * *

STILLER HAD NEVER felt such rage. Pinned tight beneath the fallen balcony he was unhurt but unable to move. He'd only just managed to grab Schmitt's skinny wrist and pull himself free of the jumble of stone and rusting metal when Landenberg stirred beside him, his fat, dust-covered face emerging from the rubble.

"A grenade?" said Landenberg, still stunned.

Stiller eyed him with contempt and ruffled his long hair, dust flying into the portly man's eyes, "There was no grenade, just your big ass, you overweight, fuckin' fat pig."

Schmitt just managed to stifle a grin as he caught sight of Stiller's red eyes. "The balcony can only hold three tons, Landenberg."

"Did you follow them, Schmitt?" Stiller coughed.

Schmitt's mocking smile slipped into a frown. His voice thinned. "I... I thought you were hurt, so I came back to..."

"Get me out of here!" Stiller was completely beside himself and was just about to smack Schmitt with the shoulder grip of his Heckler when the first of four Italian police cars pulled up several yards away from where they stood, sirens screaming. Stiller quickly crawled back through the rubble beneath the collapsed balcony and squeezed his way into the open kitchen door. Schmitt followed. Stiller saw that Landenberg was already caught in the police sights. He'd frozen as a warning shot had ricocheted off the plaster above his head.

Stiller and Schmitt both tore through the shattered French windows and helter-skeltered down through the scrub and cacti until they were a good five hundred yards away from the whistles and shouts above. Bullets flicked the undergrowth around their heads as they made their escape. Stiller pushed on relentlessly, snapping the limbs of small trees as he tried to slow his descent. Soon the firing above them stopped. They huddled at the back of a row of shops lining the cobbled path down to the seafront. Stiller slipped out into the street with Schmitt and mingled with the tourists and lunchtime shoppers.

"In here, Schmitt," he snapped. Ducking into a doorway Stiller pulled himself a chair. They were in a bustling café called La Tornado. He ordered himself an espresso.

Schmitt looked uneasy as he dragged a wooden chair over to join him. "Is this wise?"

Stiller simply glared at Schmitt as if he were a piece of dirt and proceeded to stir a lump of brown sugar into his coffee.

Blood trickled down Schmitt's left cheek. He'd been hit but he seemed oblivious to the fact.

While Schmitt ordered a mineral water and a croissant, Stiller's mobile buzzed in his pocket. Before answering it, he stared at Schmitt, jerking his thumb towards a door marked, 'Singore'. "Go wash what's left of your fuckin' ear off your shirt."

Stiller answered the call.

"Progress report," said the voice.

Stiller waited until Schmitt had disappeared into the toilet. "They have eluded us for the moment." The silence at the other end of the line seemed to last an eternity. He felt compelled to say more. "But they won't get far without me knowing." He knew that back in his KGB days better men than him had been terminated for less.

Still, the silence continued.

Devoid of any emotion, the heavily disguised voice on the other end of the line eventually spoke. "You will no longer lead this operation. You will take your orders from the Vectan-Brosman man when he arrives tonight from Milan. He has been fully briefed and has a good insight into the strengths and weaknesses of Dr. Schlesinger and Matt Malcolm. He has also seen the pictures of the women, whom he also knows, and has been updated on the Seraphim sect, the Syrian and so forth."

Stiller knew then that, no matter what the orders were from his paymaster, he would find and kill Matt Malcolm, whatever it took. He would kill him, slowly, face to face. "We may need to activate two more operatives; the members of this sect are well-trained and well-armed."

"How many casualties have we had so far?"

Stiller spoke in a monotone. "Two."

"Killed by who?" pressed the voice.

"Both by Malcolm, but it was just-"

"He is a philandering marketing manager, not a fuckin' SAS assassin. What's going on?"

"He just took a couple of lucky shots," explained Stiller. There was another long silence.

"I take it we haven't had to pay out so far?" said the voice.

"There has been no actual cost as yet other than a few deposits, but I may need more men to-"

The voice cut him off mid-sentence, "to deal with Malcolm, who is obviously much better than you. Your new controller will decide what is, and what is not necessary, Stiller. Meet him tomorrow morning at the café Zebrine, near to the ferry terminal. He will be there at 10 a.m. He will make himself known to you then." The line went dead just as Schmitt returned from the toilet and the waiter arrived with the croissants.

30

MATT KNEW THE history. Port Said was originally a camp founded to house the men working on the Suez Canal but, by the late eighteen hundreds, it was a major port bustling with trade and newly constructed maritime consulates. Perched on reclaimed land from Lake Manzala, Matt thought it looked like any other Mediterranean resort. He looked out across the beach from one of the many holiday homes that lined the seafront and stared, blankly, at the line of tankers and ferries that took their place in the queue to enter the Suez Canal.

Matt pulled his white plastic chair along the tiles until it rested next to Lucius. "Time is running out. Where has Imur disappeared to now?"

"Kalef says he's gone to see a friend at the National Museum."

"Imshar Khedival is a very good contact for us here in Egypt." It was the high-pitched voice of Kalef. He knelt between them and flashed his dazzling white teeth. "The Shiria Palestine is not far; Imur should return soon and then we can travel onwards to my homeland." He touched Matt's shoulder and whispered, "You did very well in Genoa. Steph said that you fought bravely."

Matt bowed his head as he thought back to the carnage and his bout of panic on the balcony. "I'm not used to guns or killing. It was totally stupid of me to volunteer. Totally insane."

"I agree," said Lucius, unfolding a map of Port Said he'd found in his bedroom and quickly changing the subject. "Did you know that the Statue of Liberty should have stood right there?" He pointed to the edge of the harbour.

Matt and Kalef listened to the doctor as he explained that the sculptor Auguste Bartholdi had originally intended the New York landmark to represent Egypt carrying the light of Asia. Strangely, it was one of the Khedival family that put a stop to it, deciding it too expensive.

Linda and Jessica appeared at the edge of the flower-lined terrace of the villa. They chattered as if nothing much had happened over the last three days, as if the biggest thing they had to worry about was lunch.

"Morning boys." Linda sat opposite and crossed her legs, eyeing Matt for a reaction.

Matt had, however, set his gaze on Jessica Baron. She was wearing the same dark skirt and blouse as she'd worn the day he'd seen her in Zurich, none of them able to acquire any change of clothes in the maelstrom of activity that had followed them here to Egypt.

As if reading Matt's thoughts, Jessica addressed Kalef. "When do you think we can get some new clothes and a decent meal?"

"Imur is attending to this as we speak," said Kalef. He beamed at her and somehow managed to fill the small patio with a wonderful sense of calm. The tall Ethiopian had an amazing aura that made Matt admire him and feel a little jealous at the same time.

Matt could see how Kalef might be attracted to Jessica Baron and her love of antiquities, but he decided that the tall African was much more interested in Linda. Despite being in her early fifties, Linda had at least ten times the sexual magnetism of Jessica.

Seemingly sensing Matt's thoughts, Linda moved behind Kalef and put her arms on his shoulders. "Now this is what I call a real man. What do you think Lucius?" Her firm breasts squeezed against Kalef's shoulder blades.

The gracious big African continued to smile kindly.

Matt couldn't believe her; she was a million times more vivacious than anything he'd ever fantasised about in the office, and so brazen. He realised now that every double-entendre she'd offered up in the office was probably a massively blatant buying signal. He really was pathetic, not because he should have seen the signs but because he was married then and now and he should know better. He was only beginning to appreciate Jenny now that he had most probably lost her for ever.

He glanced at the Professor. What was he all about? Lucius was either totally oblivious to Linda's flirtations or completely at ease with them. Matt couldn't decide.

"What do you need new clothes for, Jessica? Just get a robe and relax," said Linda. She wandered past Jessica and leaned over a whitewashed wall that separated them from the beach. She pointed at one of the huge cargo ships, revealing a good length of leg, and much more.

Visibly shaken, Kalef was the first to stand up and make himself busy, but Matt, easily reverting back to type, had decided to enjoy the view, see if Lucius objected. Jessica, oblivious to Linda's exhibitionism, had caught hold of the fleeing Kalef. "When are we going to get to Axum? I presume that is where we are headed."

Annoyed by Jessica's distraction, Matt listened in.

Kalef put his finger to his lips. "You are a clever girl," he whispered. "Then, you always were, Jessica. Axum is indeed our destination after we have secured safe passage through Eritrean air space. There is still a war in that region, you know."

"I understand." Jessica saw Isaac and three of the seraphim arrive with an array of carrier bags, which they dumped on top of the large kitchen table. Still within earshot, she caught Kalef's arm once more. "What's the site in Axum? There are rumours that the Ark of the Covenant is being guarded there, and that it's even been paraded through the town."

Matt, still watching as Linda moved over to an olive tree, saw her check her angle and then pull her robe open a little further. Only Matt and Lucius had a privy to this blatantly provocative flash.

Linda stared straight into Matt's eyes and smiled.

Lucius continued to sip his coffee.

It took a loud burst of laughter to snap Matt out of his trance.

"That is complete rubbish, Jessica," laughed Kalef, "you should know better."

Distractedly, Matt got up and followed Kalef and Jessica outside.

"And I suppose you know where the Ark really is?" said Jessica, reproachfully.

Kalef lowered his voice to a more conciliatory tone. "I know that we examined everything in Axum, but found nothing of any real consequence."

"Maybe you're just trying to protect it, Kalef," said Matt.

Kalef and Jessica paused.

"There were a few Egyptian relics," said Kalef, "and some wooden tablets dating back to 300 B.C., probably from the Byzantine era, but the true Ark... no."

"So where is it?" Jessica pressed.

Kalef scanned Matt's face and said, "Where it has been since 1308."

"I don't understand," said Matt.

"I think Kalef is referring to The Knights Templar, Matt."

Just then an ebullient Imur stepped onto the sun terrace with a tall, distinguished-looking man.

31

KALEF GREETED THE man who'd just entered with a bow and a kiss on both cheeks. "Imshar, my friend, how are you?"

"Very well, Kalef, very well," he said.

Imshar was just as polished and debonair as Imur. Both had impeccably kept moustaches and extremely expensive looking suits that shone and glinted in the sunlight. Imshar was a good ten inches taller than Imur and had a rich, booming voice to match his bearing. "Such a beautiful woman, Kalef, should not be ignored," he said, eyeing Jessica.

"My apologies, this is Miss Jessica Baron," announced Kalef.

"Enchanted." Imshar kissed the back of Jessica's hand.

Having entered the terrace from the back garden, Imur and Imshar now stepped inside the villa. Linda and Lucius were back in the kitchen, busy making tea.

Lucius is definitely in on Linda's licentiousness, Matt decided.

Imshar spotted Linda. "You have another beautiful woman with you, Imur."

Imur cleared his throat and narrowed his eyes. Linda and Lucius were giggling and whispering as they searched the fridge.

"Quite." He immediately turned to face Matt. "This is Mr. Malcolm."

Imshar drew his gaze away from Linda and smiled politely at Matt. "Pleased to meet you Mr. Malcolm."

"You must be another of Imur's 'angels'," said Linda.

Imshar's eyes flashed back over Linda. He gave her a wry smile. "Yes, I am also a member of the Seraphim."

"Good for you," said Linda, in a very sensuous tone.

Imshar began to unpack the various carrier bags he'd brought with him and continued to speak. "You should be safe here for a few hours, but it's only a matter of time before our adversaries put two and two together and trace your flight to Port Said." He lifted a basket from the various bags on the ground. "I can recommend the pineapples and the figs; they have come from my own garden." His face split into a toothy smile.

Matt felt embarrassed by Linda's initial taunt. As he helped open more of the bags he decided that Linda was a sexual control freak. She wanted to be the centre of attention.

"Linda, Lucius, look, we have new clothes!" said Jessica.

Lucius pulled a pair of trousers free from the nearest plastic bag and held them against his leg.

To Matt's further embarrassment he watched as Linda poked at the clothes inside the bag. She looked as if she was prodding a dead body.

"Where did you get these?" she asked.

Imshar said nothing and eventually Linda found something she liked. She held a white blouse up to the light.

"Regretfully," mused Imshar, "better designed for travel in the desert than some of the grand hotels and restaurants I could have shown you, had we the time."

Matt decided that Imshar was a gentleman and a diplomat to have ignored Linda's disparaging behaviour. And his tack was obviously working, as Linda soon changed her tune.

"Oh, I'm sure we could take some time out, Imur, couldn't we?" said Linda, sizing up Imshar.

"I think not," said Imur, curtly.

"Ah well, God willing, I can show you my wonderful country some other time." Imshar now addressed the whole room, which now included the rest of the seraphim. "In three hours you will travel by bus to Cairo, then from there I can fly you across Sudan and Eritrea. I have my own private jet." He bowed again to the ladies, as if expecting some extra special regard for being such a resourceful man. Jessica smiled politely, but Linda continued to busy herself, sorting through the fresh smelling clothes that now covered the kitchen table.

Matt saw Imur become distracted before the small, manicured Syrian ushered a protesting Linda into an adjoining bedroom along with a large pile of clothes. "Were you frightened that she was going try them on right here?" asked Matt.

"Quite so, Mr. Malcolm," said Imur.

"What?" Jessica laughed and followed her into the bedroom.

Imshar continued, "We cannot wait any longer than three hours as it is far from certain that all of the fighting factions on the ground will obey the clearance signal."

Matt felt his chest tighten as he concentrated his mind on Jenny and Peter. "Look, where exactly are we going, and when can I expect to get back to England?"

Jessica returned in a white linen outfit and spoke. "Matt, we have to go to Axum, in Ethiopia. Imur and Kalef want to show you a site where they hope you can identify another sample of the Eden Seed."

"And then you'll just burn them, I presume?" said Matt. Jessica looked over to Kalef.

"I mean," continued Matt, "why don't you just burn every damn seed in the site and then you can be sure you've destroyed the right ones?" Matt was trying his best to stay calm. It was Thursday, 10 a.m., and he knew that he was running out of time. However, this was a question that he'd longed to ask ever since Zurich.

"We must know exactly what the Eden Seed looks like," explained Imur. "There may be other sites, other chance finds..." Imur turned to Lucius. "I am also wondering whether Dr. Schlesinger here has a unique method of screening? For all we know, he may have stumbled on the exact fermentation technique that unlocks the life-giving powers of the Eden Seed."

"You mean you can't just pop one in your mouth and crunch it up?" asked Matt.

Imur answered. "I doubt it, Mr. Malcolm."

This was the first time that Imur had admitted that he needed Lucius and himself; both were key to Imur being able to identify and, presumably, protect the secret.

Matt was beginning to feel anxious and trapped.

Linda stepped into the kitchen, dressed in white. She'd obviously been listening in. "So you're just like all the other greedy bastards? You want to keep the secrets of the Seed for yourselves."

Matt saw Imshar and Imur tense.

Lucius spoke up, "Linda, Imur says he wants to prevent the power of the Eden Seed from being used as a weapon. He and his sect are the only ones, as far as I can see, that don't want to make a financial gain from all this, he-"

"He's no better than the rest!" Linda blustered.

Imshar produced his silver winged pendant. "We promise you this, Miss Linda, Mr. Malcolm: we are all bound by our very lives to keep the Eden Seed from the human race until such times as God decrees."

"There you go again, talking about God as if he's a personal friend of yours," snapped Linda, "and only you have a direct line. Every stupid sect on this Godforsaken planet thinks the same thing."

"I agree," said Matt. "I don't believe in God, Imur. So let's talk about the practicalities." A bead of sweat ran down Matt's forehead. He could feel himself losing control. Tiredness and stress were eating into him.

Imshar sat down at the kitchen table. "I can assure you, Mr. Malcolm, that this planet is not Godforsaken. But if you wish to talk in simple terms, so be it. Vectan-Brosman and the two other companies you blackmailed are all after the Eden Seed so they can control the global pharmaceutical industry. You got lucky first and so, to you... the spoils. However, that will never be enough for any company or any individual who has the money and the resources to get hold of the Seed for themselves. Greed will out!"

"What? You want this for your own ends the same as everyone else. Linda's right," said Matt.

Imshar stood up and pointed straight at Matt. "Sit down and shut up! I'm not as polite as Imur, and I've had just about enough of your questions. Get ready to go in three hours; otherwise I'll leave you here as bait for Mr. Stiller."

Matt's Sunday deadline burned inside him and quashed his desire to floor this pompous git. He caught Lucius's eye. He didn't see much point in keeping the deadline secret now.

Imshar resumed his polite smile and made for the door with Imur. Lucius followed them.

Matt picked up his gun from the sideboard and asked Steph to show him how it worked again.

Steph smiled. Gladly taking on the role of instructor, he asked, "Can you remember, Matt, what this weapon is called?"

Matt stared blankly until he produced the word "Beretta" from somewhere in his confused mind; what with anger, fear and guilt all vying for space in his head, he found it difficult to remember what Steph had told him in the brief twenty minutes before the assault on Stiller's hideout.

"It's a 93R Beretta; the 'R' stands for 'Raffica' which means burst - firing, in Italian, while the '93' tells you that it uses 9mm bullets and indicates that this is the 3rd model to be developed. Got it?"

"But it jammed when I was on the balcony," Matt protested, noticing the door close behind Imshar. He could still hear him jabbering in Arabic or perhaps Aramaic, he wasn't quite sure.

"It didn't jam, Matt. It can fire 20 rounds in rapid succession and, in my estimation, you rattled off twenty rounds in the first few minutes. You have to aim, give it a small burst fire, stop, re-aim and repeat. It's a powerful weapon; don't waste it."

"But this bit?" Matt indicated a piece of metal that protruded from the trigger guard.

Steph held the gun up to the window and flicked the movable piece forward. "This is the front grip, which can be unfolded and, in conjunction with the shoulder stock, gives you a really stable and accurate firing position."

"So it's not a safety catch?"

Steph smiled. "No." He led Matt away from the kitchen and told him they would spend the next hour practising the quick change of the magazine.

After about an hour, Lucius relayed Imshar's instructions to Matt. "They spoke in Aramaic," explained Lucius. "Imshar explained to Imur that his plane would be waiting at the old military runway, six miles south of Cairo, fully fuelled and with a pilot. He's arranged a minibus for Kalef, Imur, Isaac, Steph, and all of us. One of the Seraphim called Vichy, along with Hulut's brother who's apparently called Malek, will remain here. Imshar explained that eight would have to be the maximum number for the remainder of the trip. It must be to do with the size of Imshar's private jet."

Matt nodded. He'd never known the names of all the Seraphim. "Imshar is going to remain here with Vichy and Malek, to check for any further parties who might pick up on our trail. They'd debated keeping Linda and Jessica in Port Said, but decided that Kalef may need Jessica's help with some of the artefacts and that Linda..." Lucius flushed, "would keep you and me more manageable."

"Yeah. We need to talk about that sometime," mumbled Matt. Matt saw Malek, the brother of Hulut, checking their guns.

32

THURSDAY MORNING, 10 a.m., Stiller felt the tap on his shoulder in the café Zebrine. He turned round to see a tall, broad-shouldered man he'd seen before. "Stiller, we've found out where they're going," he said.

Immediately, Stiller felt anger rise up within him. "Well if it isn't Gerald Barclay; I thought you were supposed to be dead."

Stiller and the scrawny Schmitt checked for prying eyes, but the café had been chosen well. A plethora of ferry workers chattered and moaned in Italian, Indonesian and French. The din created the perfect cover.

Barclay ignored Stiller's comment and continued, "They're heading for Ethiopia, North Ethiopia, to be fairly vague, but that's as good as I can do just now. And, yes, I am dead, officially. Please remember that."

Stiller thought Barclay looked tired. Dark bags hung under his sunken eyes and his leathery jowls jerked and quivered every time he spoke. His freckled face was deeply lined and his slightly curled, dark brown hair looked as though it had been recently stained as he could pick out the faint spots of henna on the collar of his shirt.

"How many of them are there?" asked Schmitt, dully.

Barclay seemed to struggle with Schmitt's thick Swiss-German accent, "It's a bit of a movable feast. But the last time I received a contact there were ten: an African named Kalef Meduka; a Syrian called Imur Falsath; Miss Jessica Baron; Matt Malcolm; Dr. Schlesinger; another four from their weird sect and..." Barclay suddenly sounded doleful, "my one time secretary, Linda Parfait."

Stiller teased his long black hair and leaned in. "Who's your contact? You said 'the last time I received a contact'."

"Sorry, that's classified," snapped Barclay.

Stiller pulled Barclay's chair forward under the table with his right foot until the American's face was inches from his own. "There's no such fuckin' thing as 'classified'."

Barclay looked shaken. "I... I don't really know who the contact is myself. Okay?"

Stiller held him there for a few seconds, trying to sense whether Barclay was telling the truth or not, inhaling his naked fear. He could almost taste the sweet adrenalin that pumped through the big American's cholesterol-clogged veins.

Barclay eased back. "I was told that you might need more men."

"Or women," corrected Stiller. "The best operative I ever worked with was a woman."

Barclay sighed. "Yeah, tough break, the way that last girl of yours was killed: bludgeoned to death by an iron."

Stiller stiffened. He'd never known exactly how Jenny Malcolm had managed to dispatch Sylvie. He made a mental note to make her death particularly slow. "Unprofessional," he muttered, feigning indifference. "Even the best can become too complacent. And yes, we will need another two operatives."

"Go ahead, hire them. I mean, you'll be able to call on some ex-agents, won't you?"

"Yes, of course," answered Schmitt.

The fact that Schmitt had bypassed him and answered the American first was unforgivable in Stiller's eyes. This Swiss weasel would suffer too, when the time was right.

"We are still on an observation exercise, not a hunting foray, understood?" said Barclay.

Stiller dug his nails into his left knee and gave a tight-lipped nod.

"I have a private plane which will take us on to Cairo. How soon can you get the other operatives?"

Schmitt reached for his phone but Stiller caught his wrist. While watching Barclay, he sipped his espresso then opened his mobile phone. "Cairo, you say? The last we heard they were heading for Sardinia. Still, you'll know best." Stiller dialled and waited a few seconds, "Yes, it's me. Who do we have in Cairo that may still be interested in some work?" There was a pause while Stiller scribbled a quick note. He snapped the phone shut. Stiller studied the names on the beer mat. "This one, Hassan Khan, I've worked with in Afghanistan. He's one of the best."

"When do we fly, Barclay?" said Schmitt, pocketing his mobile.

Stiller's devilish eyes darted across the table. Schmitt lowered his gaze and said no more.

Barclay addressed Stiller. "We fly in one hour."

Stiller examined the American's face. "You switched sides then?" he asked.

Barclay shifted in his seat. "I'm not at liberty to..."

"My paymaster had you 'killed off' so you could safely come over. Didn't he?" pressed Stiller.

Barclay opened his mouth to speak but Stiller pushed on. "You'd better hope that your ex-boss buys your murder."

Barclay's face turned grey.

Stiller smiled and added, "I bet you don't even know who your new boss is. Do you?"

"Look Stiller, I don't have to tell you everything, okay?"

"I thought as much. And I suppose you're experienced in combat scenarios and surveillance?"

Barclay stiffened. "You're the expert in that department. I expect you to run the ground operations."

Stiller knew the American would be a coward when it came to the bit. "Good, just as long as we understand each other. The Seraphim sect is very well-armed, and although you say we are to observe and not maim, they are out to kill anyone who might threaten them. Your understudy, Malcolm, has killed two ex-KGB so far."

"Matt Malcolm?" Barclay scowled disbelievingly. "No way."

"I will have to settle that score eventually, Barclay," said Stiller.

"Eventually," said Barclay, "and Stiller..?"

"Yes, Sir." Stiller sipped his espresso and raised an   eyebrow.

"I want to be there when you settle that score too. But not until the little shit goes wherever these religious fanatics are taking him and does his bit...ok?"

Stiller wasn't going to be threatened by this jerk. He eyed the waitress behind the American and thought back to the younger woman in the shower. "Who are the women again?"

He saw Barclay scan the café, suspiciously, but everyone was too wrapped up in their own conversations. "As I said earlier, the older one is Linda Parfait, a secretary of mine who is apparently having an affair with the old professor. Wrong place, wrong time."

"And the younger blonde?"

"She used to be the European Chief Justice. Her name's Jessica Baron. She's as sharp as a tack, so how she got caught up with this Seraphim sect, I'm not sure. She was at the original meeting in Munich, so she knows the full potential of the product."

Schmitt's thin neck strained forward. Tentatively, he asked, "What exactly is the product?"

Barclay shook his head. "Sorry, I can't say at this point."

"But it's obviously worth a lot of money." Schmitt grinned.

Barclay stood up and walked over to the crowded doorway.

Stiller took a final sip of his drink before standing up too.

Schmitt whispered in Stiller's ear as they pushed past the people in the doorway, "What do you think, Stiller?"

Stiller ignored him, his eyes fixed venomously on the broad expanse of Armani jacket in front of him. He followed Barclay over to a black VW people carrier. He felt the warmth of the Italian springtime sunshine on his face and closed his eyes. He paused to slip on his sunglasses. The air was rich with a mixture of freshly made bread and burning diesel. He had to focus on the money for the time being. Revenge and his need to kill would have to wait for now.

33

BY THURSDAY LUNCHTIME, Jenny Malcolm had been reunited with her son, Peter. The C.I.D had given her the benefit of the doubt, and good lawyer, recommended by Inspector Watt, had meant bail had been granted by 9 a.m. Her mother's house was tiny and twee, but due to the ongoing forensic investigations at her own place, and the conditions of her bail, this would have to be home for now. She wasn't sure if she could ever go back to their house again anyway. It harboured too many phantoms.

Lying on her mother's bed, she sniffed in the reassuring dampness of the candlewick cover. As a small girl, she used to pluck out the little tufts while her mother and father listened to the radio on Saturday mornings. The thread-bare patches were still there. She felt their smoothness as she traced the bumpy texture of the cover with her fingertips.

Inspector Watt was due to visit them at 12:30 P.M. He wanted to interview Peter, alone. She'd made quite a fuss at the station when the inspector first suggested it, especially since the Scottish Chief Inspector had already spoken to Peter the night before. She wasn't sure why, but something about Watt made her feel safe.

She was confused by the fatherly yet sexual aura that emanated from Watt. She gripped the pink cover and wiped a tear away from her swollen eyes. What am I doing? Why am I attracted to this man? He must have been twenty years older than her but he was tall and in control. She needed someone to be in control just now. She also had an illogical need for revenge - sexual revenge.

"Mum?" asked Peter, "when's Dad going to come back home? I mean, he sounded different when he called the other day, kind of scared."

"I'm not sure, son."

"What's going on, mum? I mean, why did that woman want to hurt us?"

Jenny sat up on the bed and looked straight into Peter's copper-coloured eyes. "Look, Inspector Watt's coming over to ask you some questions. He'll be here in about ten minutes and I want you to tell him the truth."

"What will he ask me?" Peter took another bite out of his chocolate egg. There were Easter eggs in the shops already.

"Oh, just things like: did your dad and I fight much? Or: have you ever seen that woman who tried to hurt us before? I don't really know for sure."

"Did you kill her, Mum?"

Jenny felt her chest tighten. "I was trying to stop her hurting us. I had to do something. That woman was evil, son...in so many ways," she added, distractedly. Jenny saw Watt's car pull into the drive. She fixed her hair and went downstairs to open the door.

"Hello, Jenny. May I come in?"

"Of course, it's freezing out there."

In a hushed tone, Watt told her about a body being found off the west coast of Scotland. He told her that they had suspected that it was Gerard Barclay, Matt's boss. But how Barclay's ex-wife had, just that morning, ruled it out. "She said it wasn't him."

"What do you mean 'she said it wasn't him'? How could she be sure?"

Jenny heard Peter moving on the stairs.

Watt led her into the kitchen as he explained: "You might expect it to be difficult enough, what with his head, fingers and toes missing, but she just took one look at the torso and said, 'It's not him.'" Watt smirked.

"I don't really think it's a laughing matter," said Jenny.

"No, of course not. I'm sorry. Apparently he was circumcised and fairly well..."

"Yes?" prompted Jenny, knowing fine well she didn't need to.

"...proportioned," added Watt, suddenly interested in his fingernails.

"I see," said Jenny, flushing at the thought of Barclay being on the large side. "So it's not him?"

"Well, not according to his wife."

"But why would someone try to fake his death?" said Jenny.

"Presumably to cover up the fact that he is involved in the whole damn thing," said Watt.

She began to make Peter a peanut butter sandwich while she thought about Barclay, and said, "He's switched sides."

Watt smiled. "That's what I say too. But what side was he on and which side is he on now?"

Jenny touched Watt's hand and asked, "Do you have to quiz Peter again? He's still totally freaked out by the whole thing."

"Look Jenny, rightly or wrongly, I decided you weren't in the frame on Monday night, but it's procedure. A female counsellor is on her way. We'll make it as quick as we can."

Jenny realised that she hadn't moved her hand away from Watt's.

"I shouldn't even be telling you this stuff about Barclay but..." Watt stared into her eyes as she squeezed her fingers tight round his.

"Mum, is this the man that's going to ask me the questions about dad?" asked Peter. He'd marched into the kitchen and begun rummaging around in the bread tin.

Jenny pulled her hand away. "Eh, yes, in a minute. Another lady is going to help him."

"It's okay, mum," said Peter. He hadn't even looked at her. In seconds he'd returned to the TV and settled back down on his gran's sofa with a packet of crisps.

Watt's mobile purred.

Jenny watched him cup the phone and take the call. His expression was solemn as he nodded and muttered quietly.

He closed his mobile and ushered her back into the small kitchen. "Matt's been traced to Genoa."

Jenny flinched at his name, then sighed and asked, "Is he okay?"

"We think so, but there's a trail of dead people almost everywhere he's been. He's mixed up in something big and it's out of my hands."

"Have they taken you off the case?" she asked.

Watt shrugged. "I'm certainly way down the list. There's four dead in the U.K., that we know of, and another seven, so far, in Europe. I'm supposed to interview the head of Vectan-Brosman today. Sir John James, no less. One of his staff seems to pop into the frame every five minutes on this one. It might be some kind of industry vendetta."

"For Christ's sake." Jenny took a shaky breath.

Watt put a comforting hand on her shoulder. "I'm not sure there's anything you can do. Just tell me if he phones you. You've got my card."

Jenny felt a strange sensation build inside her. She didn't want Watt to leave. "Will I still see you?" she blurted, suddenly feeling stupid.

"I'll recommend that we monitor your safety for another couple of weeks, at least." He smiled. "I'll still have to pester you now and again, if that's alright."

Jenny felt her face flush red. "Any time."

* * *

EVANS HAD NEVER lost touch with his CIA connections. As soon as Burrows had given him the green light he'd made the calls. They checked and cross-checked flights and credit card transactions but nothing showed up on Matt Malcolm. It was only when he hacked into the Vectan-Brosman secure e-mails that he noticed the tickets. Linda Parfait had taken a flight to Zurich on the night of Malcolm's disappearance. She'd worked for both Matt Malcolm and Barclay. His contacts in the CIA discovered that there had been five murders in Zurich that week, all on the same day: Tuesday. A taxi driver found shot beside a wrecked boat that had smashed into a canal embankment; two policemen shot in cold blood in a university museum; and two young Arab emigrants found tortured and killed in the University residence of Dr. Lucius Schlesinger, the head of R & D for Vectan-Brosman. There was also a police officer missing, last seen in the University and presumed dead. The trail went cold in Zurich but after looking for any similar incidents within a three hundred mile radius of Zurich, Evans discovered that two more men had been shot dead on the Wednesday. One of these was Andy Stein, ex-KGB, while the other was, as yet, unidentified. A further ex-KGB operative, a Pascal Landenberg had been arrested near to the scene in Genoa.

Evans couldn't wait to tell Burrows, so he phoned, via satellite, from the Meldan Industries company jet. Burrows had been impressed, but then asked Evans where Malcolm was now.

Evans smiled smugly to himself, as he looked out the small circular window of the Lear jet at the three slightly offset pyramids below.

"I'm in Egypt, sir, and my contacts say that Linda Parfait made the trip here from Genoa. Not alone, mind you; she had another three guys with her. I've seen the CCTV footage from Genoa airport. Matt Malcolm arrived separately with a party of seven."

"Who's backing him?" pressed Burrows.

"The CIA should get me that information fairly soon, Sir, but I can tell you there's a real mixture... a real mixed bag."

"Do you think Malcolm's got the product with him?" asked Burrows.

"Could have, but there's no way to be sure."

Burrow's voice became ominous. "Just make sure you're thorough."

"Yes sir." Evans eased back into his leather chair as the jet landed. His friends in the CIA had given him three days' grace before they picked up Malcolm themselves. Interpol and the British Police hadn't quite caught up, but it wouldn't be long before they did. Evans had to eliminate Malcolm and disappear undetected.

Evans had hand-picked three old buddies from the Marines, all more than able, even in their fifties, and all well-armed. He knew Linda Parfait and her entourage had landed in Port Said at the same time as Malcolm. He knew roughly where they were now, and he'd decided to cover the last part of the journey by road.

A couple of hours north would take him to the beach homes of the Port Said rich, and hopefully by that time the CIA would have contacted him with an exact location.

* * *

AS MATT TOYED with his Beretta and sucked hard on his recently jammed thumb, he saw Imshar open the door that overlooked the beach. To the left of their villa, fishermen were busy hauling their long nets up the beach. Gulls fluttered in the warm breeze over their catch. To the right of the villa, Sunni Arab women stood, fully clothed and ankle deep in water, paddling serenely in their own, reserved, section of beach.

Imshar spoke quietly. "We have to go, Mr. Malcolm. I'm sorry if I was a little abrupt earlier but, as you know, time is not on our side. The forces of evil are closing in and, although I've done all I can to get you this far, it will, eventually, be up to you to set things right, my friend."

Mournfully, Matt shrugged his narrow shoulders; "I wish I'd never set eyes on the damn Seeds." He slipped the Beretta back into its holster and picked up a small, but heavy, leatherette bag before making his way onto the green minibus outside.

As they drove off, Matt noticed a cluster of duty-free shops and cafés. Rickety tables spilled out over the pavements where wiry, old men played backgammon and drank coffee. Above them, like a thousand war-torn flags, rows of washing fluttered in the warm Mediterranean breeze.

Matt squeezed in beside Jessica. She wore a clean white shirt and pair of khaki shorts that would have looked stupid on most, but not her. If she'd been waring a hemp sack, she'd have looked great to Matt. He was pathetic, totally unsuited to marriage and a complete failure, he decided.

In minutes they were on the chaotic Ismailia highway, where cars, horses and buses literally jostled for poll position. They clipped a camel as they overtook a taxi on the inside lane of a dual carriage way. The beast bellowed loudly, but they didn't stop. It was bedlam.

Further out of Port Said, they passed miles of lush reed beds, where black cattle waded, knee-high, through the flood plain of the Nile amongst pied kingfishers and buff coloured Egyptian plovers. A mishmash of orange-sellers were interspersed between the mud-caked villages and, more ominously, various black-shirted army personnel posed beside their jeeps and lorries as they travelled south.

By the time the minibus reached Ismailia, Jessica had fallen asleep on Matt's arm. The pins and needles had become unbearable so, reluctantly, he pulled his arm free.

She opened her eyes for a second, mumbled, and then fell back to sleep.

For a further ten minutes his arm throbbed until the blood reinvaded his veins and arteries. He looked across the aisle at Imur and asked, "How far now?"

Imur flashed a reluctant smile and explained: "A further seventy-five miles to Cairo then three more to the airfield. A couple of hours or so."

Matt looked round the bus and realised that he was the one of the few still awake, so he nestled down in his seat and drifted off.

34

THE C.I.A. CALLED Evans on the northbound Ismailia highway. "We think we have a location. 133 Beach Boulevard. The holiday home belongs to Imshar Khedival, a very wealthy entrepreneur who runs the local museum and most of the customs officials. He wanted clothes for eleven people, two of which were women."

"You mean you're not certain of the location or the target?" said Evans.

The contact became agitated. "Don't push your fuckin' luck, Evans. You've got two days' grace, that's it! Understood?"

"You said three days." Evans cupped the mobile and typed the address into his laptop route planner. "And..."

"Forty seven hours and fifty nine minutes, then we take over," said the voice. The line went dead.

Evans told their driver to hang a right as they left Palestine Street.

They soon found number 133. It faced directly onto the beach and two silver Mercedes cars sat in the driveway at the back.

"Perfect. Stop at the end of the road," instructed Evans. "Yes, Mr. Evans," said the driver.

The three old comrades who had joined Evans for the mission scanned the villa. Bill O'Hare, Evan's old drill officer spoke up, "There could be more than a dozen of them in there. Our best chance is the 'treble S'." This stood for surprise, stun and select. A tried and tested method the old war buddies had used in Hanoi. It allowed them to pick off some targets and leave others.

Murdo Matheson had always preferred to kill first and ask questions later. "Fuck off; we'll just wipe the whole fuckin' place off the map."

Both O'Hare and Evans had been forced to cover for the big Irish-man's wartime atrocities in the past, but he'd never lost them a fight and had saved both their lives on more than one occasion.

"I think the CIA might get a little twitchy if we blew half the street into the sea," said Evans. "We'll go in with stun grenades and rapid fire. We needn't be too selective, Murdo."

Bill O'Hare unpacked four stun canisters. "What about the women?" he asked.

"Wrong place, wrong time; we do the lot then fuck off back home. Okay?" said Evans.

"Fine by me," said Matheson, the growing smile on his face giving him the look of a deranged, redheaded ape. Matheson gave them each a 5.56mm M249.

"It's been a while since we've used the SAWs," said Evans. 'SAW' stood for Squad Automatic Weapon. The M249 had always been their unit's weapon of choice.

Matheson dished out the ammunition. "We'll use a four-and-one mix; M855s with a M856 tracer."

O'Hare couldn't see the sense in using such a powerful weapon at such close range. "This machine can kill at 800 yards, so what in fuck's name..?"

"Look," Evans agreed with Matheson, "we're used to the gun and the ammo mix so let's not fuck around with it."

After kitting out, they primed the gas cylinders and moved in. Evans decided to approach from the beach while O'Hare and Matheson closed in from the adjoining properties. The driver, a quiet but reliable Korean called Kuhn Sung, parked the car and prepared to place motion-sensing explosives under each of the two Mercedes parked outside the villa.

The door facing the beach was open and Evans spotted two targets immediately; he saw that Matheson and O'Hare were in position and already aiming at the side windows. He held up two fingers. Matheson held up one, while O'Hare signalled that he could see no one.

Evans watched as the man nearest to the beach terrace chattered into his mobile.

He signalled to O'Hare and Matheson. He was close enough to hear the clatter of metal on the marble floor before the canisters filled the air with acrid white smoke. The tall man who'd been speaking on the phone fumbled for his gun before crumpling, to the ground.

Evans aimed at a smaller man, who'd covered his mouth with a handkerchief, and cracked off a round. The smaller man buckled, his right leg ripped off below the knee.

It was Matheson who entered the beach house first. He leapt inside the smoke-filled kitchen and fired. Plates and cupboards exploded as he moved on through to the hallway. O'Hare drew alongside him and followed.

By the time Evans stepped onto the terrace it was becoming clear that they'd missed the main group. Through a narrow window, he saw a man race out of the front door towards the nearest silver Mercedes. The vibration caused by him jumping inside and slamming the door was more than enough to send a surge of current through the Semtex stuck to the back wheel suspension bracket. The car lifted a good four feet off the ground with the sheer violence of the explosion.

In the seconds that followed, all three ex-marines searched through the rooms. The place was practically empty. Panic began to grip Evans.

"Enough!" Evans signalled his men to ease off and assess. The man who'd been hit in the legs had stopped screaming and was now whimpering in the middle of an ever-growing pool of blood.

Matheson pulled an eight-inch serrated knife from his belt and cut the wounded man's throat. The dark-skinned man convulsed for about fifteen seconds then slumped against the floor.

"Check the tall fucker; I think he's the local contact," said Evans. Thankfully, Matheson hadn't reached him yet.

Evans dragged him out of the front door. "Help me get him into the car, now!" He boiled with rage. The CIA hadn't told him that there were only three targets at the address, none of which was Matt Malcolm.

Still trembling with excess adrenaline, Evans stared down at the tall figure in the foot well of the BMW X5. "Let's get some distance between that fire and us before the whole fuckin' Egyptian army turns up."

Neighbours and passers-by ducked back into their houses or crouched down behind parked cars as the X5 screeched past.

It wasn't long before Kuhn Sung reached the outskirts of Port Said. The stench on the back road used by the port's refuse lorries caused Imshar to stir and regain consciousness. Evans turned round in time to see Matheson put his foot on their captive's neck. "Keep him out of sight."

Sprawled beneath the back seats, the man looked like a tattered tramp, certainly not the refined gentleman he'd seen on the phone before. Evans had decided that this was Imshar Khedival, the owner of the villa.

Evans spat out of his window then leaned over. "Mr. Khedival, where are the others?"

Blood trickled from Imshar's ears.

"We'll give you one last chance, pal," said Matheson, "where are your fuckin' friends, before I slit your slimy throat?" Matheson had drawn his commando knife and the cold blade now drew a fresh line of blood from Imshar's neck.

Imshar's eyes blazed with defiance.

Evans pulled Matheson away. "You're the local contact, aren't you? So speak up!"

Imshar began muttering a strange prayer but stopped when Matheson's foot pushed down on his throat.

Evans leaned in closer to Imshar. "You have three seconds to tell us where Matt Malcolm is headed. We know where you work and..." Evans moved in closer,

"...where your family is spending their holiday, Mr. Khedival." This was wild conjecture on Evan's part but it seemed to strike home.

Imshar's eyes bulged in terror.

Evans squinted up at Matheson. "My friend, here, likes to do women and kids in the most disgusting ways you could imagine, don't you, Matheson?"

A tear rolled down Imshar's face before his left hand flashed upward catching the blade of Matheson's knife. Twisting it upwards, Imshar forced the serrated edge through the tendons behind Matheson's knee.

Matheson screamed, as his foot flopped off the Egyptian's windpipe.

A stream of warm blood poured down over Imshar's face but he still managed to draw the pistol from his leg holster and place it against the back of Kuhn Sung's seat.

"Stop him!" yelled Evans

Ishmar fired.

Fragments of rib and lung tissue spattered over the windscreen.

Evans raised his gun as Kuhn jerked forward but the X5 clipped the dirt bank and flipped over on its side. The noise was deafening as it slid along the concrete road, crashing through several big boulders before finally coming to rest against the side of a giant metal skip.

During the chaos, Imshar had fired another shot, which found Matheson's groin. Evans, still holding his M249, emptied a burst up into the foot well catching Imshar, Matheson and Kuhn, but the vehicle was rolling. There were a series of grunts then all went quiet as the two bodies in the back flopped down on top of Evans. He could hardly breathe; blood streamed over his face, flooding his nostrils and mouth.

Thinking he was drowning in his own blood, Evans gagged and coughed, trying to swallow the hot, salty fluid. It was O'Hare who caught his leg and heaved him out of the carnage.

His hands burned on the hot tarmac as he pulled himself further away from the wreckage. Evans wiped the blood from his face and sat up. The first thing he saw was the expression of bewilderment on O'Hare's face. "What the fuck...?"

"Shut up, O'Hare!" Panic and anger had sapped his patience. He spat on the sand and leaned back against the huge metal skip. "We underestimated that fucker. He was well trained."

"Well trained! A secured, wounded man has just killed half our number and wrote off a bullet-proof vehicle. Well trained?" O'Hare punched the steel skip and threw his M249 to the ground.

"Listen!" said Evans, still too weak to stand up. "Cool it."

"Cool it? Fuckin' cool it? Now what the fuck are we going to do, eh?"

"Shut up and listen!" Evans knelt up and stared at the overturned car. "I can hear a mobile phone."

A burring sound was coming from the wreckage.

"It must be the Egyptian's. Quick, get it out of there."

O'Hare looked at Evans in complete disbelief. "You get it out of there. Smell those fuckin' petrol fumes. We need to back off."

Evans snorted out more blood, threw down his gun and crawled towards the wreckage. He lifted himself up onto the side of the X5 and reached in with both arms. Matheson's body was lying on top but he could see the Egyptian's blood-stained jacket pocket.

Flies, drawn to the gore, buzzed and pestered him while he struggled to free the ringing mobile. The stink of petrol made him cough but still he forced his fingers past Matheson's twisted leg until they slipped inside Imshar's warm silk pocket. He grabbed the vibrating mobile and tried to pull himself out again, but he was stuck. "O'Hare!"

He felt O'Hare grip his shirt. He heard it rip.

"Get out of there you stupid fuck!" yelled O'Hare.

Matheson's grasping fingers had wrapped round Evans' belt. O'Hare heaved again and he fell back onto the road.

"Uh!" Evans hit the road hard. "He's still alive. Matheson is still alive." But O'Hare got Evans by the collar and dragged him away.

As Matheson shifted, the X5 tilted back towards the road, but jammed at an angle on a boulder. Matheson's face was covered in blood, but they could tell he was mouthing the word 'help' through the cracked glass.

Unsure what to do, Evans sprawled to his knees.

A flame flickered out from the exhaust.

"Get behind the bin!" yelled Evans.

They both dived for the steel skip but the fuel tank blew in the same second, throwing them sideways against the rocks and rubbish.

As Evans opened his eyes, he saw the thick black smoke rise up into the sky. The smell of burning flesh filled the air and there was a sickening crackling sound as fat dripped free of the carcasses into the flames. "O'Hare?" Evans shook O'Hare's shoulder then turned him round to face him. His eyes were wide open. Blood dripped from the side of his mouth. "O'Hare!" Evans noticed the jagged, metal fragment lodged in the side of O'Hare's head. He pushed O'Hare's lifeless body away from him and lay back amongst the spillings and grime.

Two Egyptian vultures circled above him like a pair of white-winged angels. They sailed the currents, patiently waiting.

35

STILLER DUCKED OUT of the Boeing 757 and instantly felt the heat of the Egyptian sun on his face. His dark glasses shielded his pale eyes and he cursed Matt Malcolm for bringing him to the place he hated most of all. Africa didn't suit him. It never had. Even back in his operational days he had opted for the colder climes rather than suffer the discomfort of the Dark Continent. He looked at the scrawny, weasel-like figure of Schmitt, scampering ahead to help Barclay with his bags. They'd jettisoned all their weapons in Italy and now the plan was to meet Hassan Khan, a man with whom Stiller had spent a very long winter in Afghanistan. They'd assisted the Russian army in extracting information from the Taliban tribal leaders and helped rescue a few high-ranking, captured Soviet soldiers.

Out in the airport car park, Hassan Khan beamed at Stiller as he pulled up in the Mercedes van. He looked much older than Stiller remembered, but it was at least twenty years since he'd seen him last. His greying beard and slightly hunched stance made Stiller wonder if he was still up to the action that might be required.

Hassan Khan nodded briefly at Barclay and Schmitt then turned to his old comrade. "Stiller, how are you, my old friend?"

"I am well, but we need to move," said Stiller.

Khan's expression changed to one of puzzlement. He laughed and patted Stiller on the shoulder as he climbed into the silver van. "There's no threat to us here, my friend; this is not Afghanistan."

Once in the passenger seat Stiller explained. "We're following a group of people who have already killed two Swiss operatives and caused the death of another in England." Again, he thought back to Sylvie and felt a renewed surge of hatred towards the Malcolms. "They have contacts everywhere and..."

"So do I. So do I, my friend." Hassan beamed. He pointed to a bag on the floor. "And I have your gun of choice. I presume you still favour the Heckler?"

Stiller nodded his approval.

Barclay leaned over from the back seat and asked, "Where is the other operative?" He eyed Stiller. "I thought you said you needed two more to help you."

Hassan answered. "The other operative is finishing some work next to the mosque."

Barclay continued. "We have to find out if they've already moved on to Ethiopia."

Hassan shook his head and gave Stiller a sly look. "You never said anything about working in Ethiopia. I had some business at the Eritrean border a few years ago and there may be a few people who still hold a grudge." Hassan looked for a reaction on Stiller's face, but found him nonplussed. "Like half the Ethiopian Army," Hassan added.

Stiller ignored Hassan's remark and addressed Barclay. "Why don't you call your classified contact and find out where Matt Malcolm is now?"

Barclay's mobile buzzed in his pocket.

He covered the screen and read the message before switching it off.

"Nice timing," said Schmitt, sarcastically.

"They're flying from Cairo to somewhere called Gond tonight." Barclay tapped Hassan on the shoulder. "Are there any flights from Cairo to Ethiopia tonight?"

"No, not on a Thursday. They fly Saturday and Tuesday and that's to Addis Ababa. Where did you say they were flying to?"

"Gond," said Barclay, a puzzled expression forming on his sweating face.

"No such place, unless they mean Gondar, but there are no flights from Cairo to Gondar unless..."

"Unless what?" pressed Stiller.

"Unless they're using a private runway." Hassan pulled to a stop in front of a tall minaret and got out. Just as he did, a diminutive figure in a yashmak stepped out from the shadows and waved at the Mercedes van.

Stiller studied the girl.

She bowed towards Hassan and opened the side door of the Mercedes. No more than five feet high, she nodded at the three men in the van and settled in the back seat.

Stiller was annoyed at Hassan's apparent lack of professionalism. "Your wife?" he asked.

"Your second operative." Hassan beamed, throwing the van into gear.

Stiller drew his fingers back through his straight black hair. "Hassan, I have already stated that this mission may be very demanding and..."

"And you should have no fear," said the girl, removing her veil. She looked directly into his eyes. "I am more than a little familiar with the dangers of working with you, Mr. Stiller," she said.

Stiller had not seen such a beautiful woman for a long time. She had addressed him in flawless Russian.

The weasel, Schmitt, turned round and gave her a greasy grin, which widened as she pulled off her silk trousers. Now sitting in no more than a white gstring, she threw her bundle of clothes onto the floor of the van and opened a small bag. Shaking her hair free, she slipped into a set of western clothes and sighed.

"This is Solana," said Hassan. "I trained her myself. Found her in a Taliban village near the Turkestan border. She was only twelve when they killed her mother for disobeying the tribe elders. She'd given Solana a book to read. They were about to take Solana's sight away, as a little added punishment, when I interrupted the proceedings." Hassan toyed with his beard as he turned left, straight across a rocky field, before joining a faint track that seemed to lead out into the desert. "Solana has spent eight years with me now, and I can promise you that she's more than capable." Hassan eyed Solana in the rear view mirror and asked her in Arabic, "Did you get the number of the Mullah's henchman?"

Solana produced a small Eriksson mobile from her bag and threw it over Barclay's head. "The Mullah's," she declared.

Without looking back Hassan snatched it before it hit the windscreen and smiled. "We've being doing a little work for the British government."

Stiller could just make out the tail-fin of a small plane in the distance. As the dust cleared, he began to see a runway and the semblance of a control tower. "How many planes use this strip?"

Hassan stopped the van at the perimeter fence and eyed Stiller in the mirror. "There are usually six planes here. I can only see four." He threw Solana a pair of rubberised, Zeiss binoculars and jumped down from the driver's seat. "Check the tower for any activity. I'll go in through the fence with him." He pointed to Schmitt.

Stiller climbed down from the van and watched as Hassan and Schmitt pushed through a breach in the wire fence. They made for a corrugated hut, which lay between them and the nearest plane.

A small ten-seater with a blue tail-fin burred into action. As it moved forward, a cloud of dust rose up from the runway.

Stiller noticed Barclay fiddling with his mobile. He punched the American on the shoulder and pointed to the plane in the distance. "Leave it. If that's Malcolm, I'll be really pissed off."

* * *

ON THE SMALL twin engine Fokker, Matt watched as Jessica rummaged around in her bag. She saw him staring at it and asked: "Do you want to phone home?"

"What?"

Jessica waved the small Ericsson mobile under his nose.

"Why didn't you say you had a mobile earlier?" said Matt.

Jessica shrugged. "I don't know."

Matt looked out of the small porthole of a window and wondered when the madness would end. He'd lost the will to call home. He was afraid of Jenny's reaction, afraid of what she might say about his affair. He was certainly far too ashamed to speak to his son. It was then, amidst the dust and his own guilt-laden daydreams that he saw something that made his blood run cold. "Jessica, look."

Jessica handed him the mobile.

"No, not that. There, out the window." Matt leaned back in his seat so Jessica could take a look.

"At the fence. There, do you see him?" he said.

But the small twin-engine plane had gathered speed and the desert dust now hid what Matt had seen from the window.

"It was him!" Matt unbuckled and tried to stand up.

Behind him, Imur caught hold of his shoulder and pushed Matt back down into his seat. "Stay safe, my friend."

Matt stared hard at Jessica. "It was Stiller. He was standing at the edge of the airfield. There were two, maybe three others."

Jessica shrugged. "I didn't see anyone. There's no way he could have caught up with us."

Matt turned and peered through the gap in the seats at Imur and Steph. "I saw Stiller!" he shouted. But the racket of the take-off stifled his voice. They circled the runway and climbed. "There," Matt persisted.

Imur followed his gaze. Far below Matt could see a silver van parked at the side of the airfield. Imur stroked his waxed moustache and signalled to Steph.

Steph peered down into the sand below and nodded. They had all seen the familiar raven-haired assassin. Stiller had found them.

"How?" hissed Imur.

Steph sighed and produced a notepad. He jotted down a sentence and showed it to Imur.

Imur closed his eyes and sighed. "We will follow this up later. He may not know where we are bound."

Steph gave Imur a doubtful expression that made Matt's heart sink even deeper.

Depression spread through the cabin as they soared higher into the Egyptian sky. Only Kalef seemed to be calm. He was holding court, with Linda and Lucius listening intently. Matt sat behind Kalef and listened in.

Kalef had decided to give them a lesson on Ethiopia as a distraction. He explained that his homeland was the only country in the whole of Africa never to be colonised. It had retained its culture and its treasures. He explained that its capital, Addis Ababa, was the third largest city in Africa, with over five million inhabitants, and that there were wonderful museums there where the very beginnings of mankind were on display. "We will soon fly over the cradle of humanity," he said, beaming with an inner pride that could not be stifled, even by Linda's yawns or the thought of Stiller. He told them how Addis Ababa meant 'New Flower' and how it had been founded by the wife of the Emperor Menelik II in the 1880s.

"But we're not going to Addis, are we Kalef?" said Linda, closing her eyes.

Kalef smiled and said, "Who can say?"

Although Kalef was obviously well educated, his English, Matt noted, was stilted. He accentuated his vowels and had a high-pitched, child-like tone that you would expect to be annoying. As it happened, it wasn't; it was actually quite soothing. Matt decided that he must be at least three inches taller than Lucius, which would make him six foot-four.

"We will land at Gondar then travel for one day, by bus, until we reach Axum," Kalef said.

"We don't know if it was Stiller, Matt, not for sure," said Jessica. She'd plumped down in the empty seat next to him.

"What, there's going to be another giant, hippy-haired Russian watching us take off from a runway in the middle of the bloody Egyptian Desert?" snapped Linda. "I thought you were supposed to be clever or something?"

Jessica pushed herself back into her seat and stared into the middle distance.

Matt adjusted his black-rimmed glasses and peered out of his window again before saying, "Not always very diplomatic, our Linda."

"Not diplomatic..." replied Jessica, "she's an obnoxious old slut!"

Matt sank deeper into his seat as Linda's face appeared in the gap between the seats in front. "At least I'm honest with myself. I like being a slut. You're just jealous, Miss high and bloody mighty Baron."

Jessica pushed her face forward. "Jealous of what?"

"Now, come on." Matt patted Jessica's bare arm but she pulled it away. He decided it was probably safer to gaze out of the window instead of playing peacemaker.

Nothing more was said and he soon concentrated on the landscape below. It had become more mountainous, and there were patches of green and white that signified a more temperate climate than he'd imagined.

* * *

STILLER CAUGHT UP with Hassan just as the blue-tailed Fokker took off. "That's got to be them."

Hassan nodded and pointed to the control tower at the southern edge of the runway.

They all raced back into the silver van and Hassan put his foot to the floor, smashing through the flimsy perimeter fence.

As they rocked and bounced over the rough terrain Solana clicked a fresh magazine into her Kalashnikov and strapped a Soviet NR 43 Combat Knife onto her left thigh. Barclay and Schmitt held onto their leather hand grips as the Mercedes gained speed and veered south. Solana's smooth brown thighs pushed against the back of Stiller's hand as she adjusted her various holsters.

As they slowed, Stiller looked across at the three remaining planes that nestled beneath the observation tower. They were locked tight, with canvas sheets covering their windows against the dust and sand. "I'll go ask some questions," he said.

Barclay made to open his door but Solana gripped his arm. "You stay over there." She pointed to a rusting windbreak that lay beneath the flight-control tower. "Take this!" She threw Barclay a pistol. "The safety is off. If anyone comes out of the tower, other than us, use it."

Barclay, somewhat hesitantly, slipped down from the van and edged toward his position in the shade of the tower. An overwhelming wall of stifling heat slammed into the big American as he left the comfort of the Mercedes and sweat instantly filled his eyes.

Stiller smiled to himself, pleased at the American's discomfort. "Never shot a gun in your fuckin' life, have you?"

"It's not in my remit," panted Barclay.

Stiller circled the big American. "Just do what Solana says. We might be dealing with more of these sect fuckers and they'll kill you if you don't kill them first."

Hassan, Schmitt and Solana followed Stiller into the tower. Stiller drew his gun and raced up the stairwell. He kicked the door in and grabbed the first person he saw.

"Please!" screamed the man.

Stiller held a dark-suited gentleman in a vice-like grip. He pointed his pistol at a second, more agitated, man who cowered in the corner. He was dressed in a white, full-length kandura. "Who was in that plane, and where were they going?"

"A private party of travellers who paid us well for giving them the use of our runway," said the man in the dark suit.

"Look, I'll give you a starter for ten. I know they were going to Gondar, in Ethiopia. Correct?"

The Arab in the kandura took a step back. His eyes widened with fear.

"Fine, I'll take that as a yes," said Stiller.

Solana slipped the NR 43 from the holster on her thigh and moved behind the Arab.

Hassan and Schmitt lifted a grey file from the large desk in front of Stiller and examined it. "They are due to arrive in Gondar at 5 P.M., local time," said Hassan.

Stiller tightened his grip and whispered into the dark-suited man's ear, "Which one of these planes is fuelled up and ready to go?" He turned the man's face toward the remaining planes parked below.

The Arab in the kandura answered. "That one." He pointed down from the sloping tower window at a Lear jet with a green canvas cover and the number GF45 printed on its tail fin.

"But you can't just take it." The man in the suit pleaded.

"You." Stiller pointed to the Arab in white. "You're coming with us." The Arab shook his head and tried to break free, but Hassan gripped him by his tunic and pulled his arm up behind his back until he shrieked.

"You," Stiller whispered into the ear of the man in the dark suit. "My guess would be that you are one of these Angels, the seraphim." He winked at Schmitt. "That's what Barclay called them, isn't it?"

Schmitt revealed his dirty teeth in a vicious grin.

Stiller whispered into the man's ear, "So you should be good at flying, right?"

Without waiting for a reply, Stiller launched the dark-suited man into the air. He flew past Solana and slammed onto the thick tinted glass of the flight tower.

The man screamed, suspended above the desert, thirty feet below. "How many of your weird little sect members are on the plane?" The man whimpered as the glass creaked.

"Sorry, didn't quite catch that." Stiller raised his pistol and aimed. The man in the dark suit spat at Stiller. "I will never tell you."

Stiller laughed. "Impressive."

Stiller nodded towards Solana and she instantly understood. The Russian issue commando knife flicked free of her slender fingers in a blur of steel and sunk into the man's side.

"ARGHHH!"

"Very good Solana, you've found his colon and, unless I'm mistaken," Stiller sniffed in the hot air and picked up a faint hint of ammonia, "his left kidney?"

The man clawed at the glass then reached back at the hilt of the knife. His tailored suit dripped with blood and urine spilled down over the glass slope back onto the floor.

Below the tower, Stiller saw Barclay move out from the windbreak until he stood under the suspended man.

"Time to use your wings!" said Stiller. He shot a neat hole in the glass above the little man's head.

The suited man panted with relief in the sudden realization that the shot had missed him, but then held his breath as the glass around his head crackled. The weight of his body and the hole made by Stiller's bullet caused a thousand hairline fractures to spread out around him like a spider's web. He screamed one last time as the pane shattered beneath him.

Below, Barclay retreated as the man plunged down towards him in a shower of green-tinted glass.

Stiller edged over the hole and stared down at Barclay. The twisted body twitched next to the American. He grinned as Barclay scrambled back under the rusting windbreak.

In moments, Stiller and the rest of his team appeared below the tower. "Hassan, drive us over to that jet. We should be able to outrun Malcolm as long as this useless fucker is telling the truth." He jabbed his Arab captive in the ribs.

Solana pulled her dagger free of the suited man's side, gripped his hair and slit his throat. He thrashed for a second or two and then lay still.

"For God's sake," moaned Barclay. "Was that really necessary?"

They piled into the van and dragged the Arab, screaming, with them.

Schmitt stepped back out onto the sand and pulled Barclay inside. "Just get in the van." Schmitt laughed as he slammed the heavy Mercedes door shut.

Hassan started the engine and drove out towards the Lear Jet.

Stiller guessed that Barclay had never seen anyone killed before. Schmitt turned round to whisper to Stiller, "Hassan's trained the girl well. She's a little vixen, a real ruthless bitch." He eyed Barclay. "Just like my ex-wife." Barclay glanced back out of his window at the dead man in the sand. Hassan passed a piece of paper over to Stiller. "We've got the flight-plan and the landing times. We'll catch up soon and get Mr. Barclay a little more acclimatised to our methods."

"Look," said Barclay, "I've got strict instructions to keep them alive and in our sights until they find the Seed."

Hassan braked beside the Lear jet. "What is this Seed you speak of, Mr. Barclay?"

"Nice one, Barclay," snapped Stiller. "Now three more people know what we're after."

Barclay nervously toyed with his mobile as the rest of them walked round the Lear jet.

Stiller and Hassan pulled off its green covers.

Schmitt eyed Solana as she bent over to untie a rope. Stiller smacked him on the back of the head with the back of his hand. "Keep your mind on the job."

Schmitt's weasel-like grin faded into a frown. He pulled the weapons and supplies out of the van and loaded them into the jet.

After a dig in the ribs the Arab produced a key. He was still shaking with fear. "I... I can pilot the plane if you like. I can help."

Barclay shook his head. "We don't need anyone else on this trip, Stiller. But there is no need to kill anyone else."

"I'll decide what personnel we need." He checked over his Heckler and said, "As for who is expendable and who is not... that, in a tactical battle situation, is my call. Got that?" He pointed to the open door that led onto the jet, and Hassan and Solana climbed inside along with Schmitt.

Stiller stood under the wings of the jet with Barclay. He heard the engines turn and waited for the signal from Hassan that they had enough fuel. He made the Arab kneel.

"Please," shouted Barclay. He made to move away, but Stiller pulled him back.

"This man will die because of you. Because you mentioned the Seed."

The Arab was saying a prayer, his head bowed towards Barclay.

"He doesn't have to die. I am in charge of this overall operation. And-"

A crack of fire from the Heckler scattered fragments of the Arab's skull and brains across Barclay's shoes.

"What was that?" asked Stiller. "I didn't quite catch what you said."

Stiller shoved Barclay up the steps of the plane and followed him inside.

Schmitt pulled him down into a seat. "The angel of death is always thorough," he said, revelling in the big American's discomfort.

36

ENJOYING THE FIRST real break of their journey since arriving in Ethiopia and relieved that there was no sign of Stiller, Matt, Linda and Lucius listened to Jessica Baron's rendition of country's history. "Ethiopia has two histories: the first is factual; the second is the perceived truth. The biblical account of King Solomon points out that he was visited by the Queen of Sheba, who returned to Axum and bore him a son called Menelek."

They sat in a blue-painted café, halfway between Gondar and the ancient capital of Ethiopia, Axum. At over 8,000 feet above sea level, the air was cool and dry. A fire danced in the hearth, the yellow light flickering across Kalef's smile every time Jessica hit on some pearl of wisdom that concerned his homeland. Matt felt a twinge of jealousy.

Jessica paused to take a sip of coffee. "You should tell the story, Kalef. It's your country."

"No, no," said Kalef. "Please continue, Jessica. Please…" He flashed another smile. Matt thought that his brilliant white teeth appeared ghostlike, unreal against his ebony skin in the gloom of the café.

"Well," continued Jessica, "although most European archaeologists place the kingdom of Sheba in Yemen, I will persevere with the Ethiopian version of history - The Queen of Sheba's son, Menelek, eventually journeyed back to Judea to visit his father and pay homage, but when he was ready to return to his mother, King Solomon instructed his nobles to send their first-born sons back to Ethiopia to serve Menelek. It is thought that the nobles wanted to punish Solomon for such a despicable demand, so they decided to help Menelek steal the Ark of the Covenant. If they were to lose their sons, Solomon would lose his precious Ark. They instructed a carpenter to build a raft, just in case their boat happened to sink during the voyage across the Red Sea. With the aid of an angel…"

Matt saw Linda sneer.

"…they bore it to Ethiopia. They are said to have housed it in a temple in Axum. This temple was in the general vicinity of the church of St. Mary of Zion."

Matt turned to Kalef. "You're taking me to look inside the Ark of the Covenant for the Eden Seed?" he said, incredulously.

Kalef laughed raucously until he wheezed with delight. "But the Ark is no longer here, Mr. Malcolm. I told you already."

Matt turned to Jessica. "But I thought you said that the Ark of the Covenant was in Axum?"

"I said no such thing," said Jessica. "I just told you a story."

Imur was now standing behind Kalef. "Tell me again, Mr. Malcolm, where are you from? Where is your homeland?"

"Scotland. I was born near Loch Lomond."

Kalef and Imur looked at each other and nodded in a conspiratorial manner that annoyed Matt. Imur spoke softly and earnestly. "You probably grew up within a few miles of where the Ark lies now."

Matt looked totally bemused, as did Jessica. "Roslyn?" said Jessica.

"No," said Imur, dismissively. "But that is enough storytelling for now. We must move again before Mr. Stiller gets us in his sights."

Imur suddenly looked very solemn. "I've just found out that Imshar has been killed in Port Said, and I am almost sure that Matt was right. Stiller was at the airport in Cairo. He is back on our trail once more."

"How, in God's name, does that freak of nature keep finding us?" said Linda.

"That is a very good question, Miss Parfait." Imur flattened his moustache then eyed the Europeans.

Matt heard the bus rattle out on the road.

"I think we may have a mole in our midst," said Imur.

"What?" Lucius looked across at Jessica.

Imur followed his gaze. "Which of you has a mobile phone?"

Linda stared down at Jessica's small canvas bag. "You do. Don't you, Jessica?"

Matt saw Imur finger his Beretta.

Jessica narrowed her eyes at Linda. "Don't be so stupid! Why would I tell that psychopath where we are? I want to find the Seed as much as anyone else here." She stared at Kalef, willing him to speak up for her.

Kalef assumed a serious tone. "I'm sure Imur is only trying to ensure our safety, Jessica. But it does seem strange that Mr. Stiller is able to find us every time we move on."

Jessica reached inside her bag and produced the Eriksson T2. "Here, take it!" She threw it across to Imur and stormed outside.

Matt stared at Imur. "All of your followers have mobiles, Imur. Isaac, Steph, even you Kalef. I suggest you confiscate theirs too."

"I mean no one any offence, but I must rule things out for the greater good," explained Imur.

"There is a lot at stake here, Mr. Malcolm," said Kalef.

"You're telling me," snapped Matt.

Imur paid the Ethiopian café owner and then boarded the bus behind Matt. The rest of the sect members were already aboard. Isaac and Steph had kept a look out for Stiller. They rechecked their weapons meticulously. Kalef was to be the driver for the last fifty miles into Axum.

On the bus, the mood darkened. Linda sat herself down on the back seat once she saw that Jessica was sitting at the front.

Matt decided to try and placate Jessica. "I've told Imur that it's unlikely."

"What, that I'm in cahoots with a murdering Russian?"

"Yes… no… I mean… You're not, are you?" Matt floundered.

"Fuck off, Matt!"

Matt grimaced, but stayed put. "Is there any particular way you'd like me to fuck off? I could jump out of the window or just slither off my seat onto the floor…"

Jessica closed her eyes. "Why do you always think you're in with a chance, Matt?"

Matt put on a 'little boy caught' expression and shrugged.

"I mean, ever since Munich you've flirted and stared."

"Shit, do I stare?" said Matt, shifting nervously in his seat.

"Yes, you stare," said Jessica.

"I can't believe I'm that obvious, I mean, do I drool too?"

She smiled. "I'm pretty sure you drool."

"Don't tell me I scratch myself too, and grunt. Do I grunt?" said Matt, a smile forming at the side of his mouth.

"Shut up, Matt." She turned her head to look out of the window. "I was so excited about coming to Axum, and now Imur's spoiled the whole damn thing."

"I enjoyed your history lesson, but you never finished it." He moved in a little closer.

Jessica nodded towards a stone statue that looked very modern. "That's the other history."

"That looked like Lenin."

"It was. The Communists deposed Heilie Selassie, a direct descendant of King Solomon, in 1974. That was the end of the lineage."

"Surely you don't believe the King Solomon bit, do you?" said Matt.

"Who knows? The idea of that lineage and its continuity certainly kept the country united on many occasions. The Italians got as far as Axum but were pushed back and eventually defeated by the Ethiopian Army at Adwa in 1896. Long before that, Ethiopia encompassed Yemen. At that time Axum was well positioned as a trading city between East and West and even traded with the southern parts of the continent."

"You know a lot about this place, don't you?" said Matt, his eyes settling on a group of houses in the distance.

"You don't think that I'm some kind of 'mole', do you?" asked Jessica.

Matt shook his head. "I don't know what's going on." It was almost 4 P.M., and he noticed that the bus had slowed down. Outside, he noticed a group of women carrying water on their heads. They wore their hair in braids that trailed over their scalps and formed a semi-circle at the back of their necks. Matt thought the braids would probably pad the heavy water jars. "Whatever's happened over the centuries, the people look as though time's stood still for a thousand years," he said.

"They're Tigray women. They often wear those green and white robes."

Matt watched the group for as long as he could, strangely jealous of their lives and its pure simplicity.

Traffic was light on the mountain road; a few motorbikes and cars interspersed with the odd camel or mule. The Ethiopians they'd seen so far looked happy, always smiling and willing to help. They waved at the bus with a real sense of wonder and the children would run alongside for as long as they could when they passed through the villages and towns.

Set high up on the hill to his left, Matt noticed a monastery adorned with strange, double-bisected crosses and narrow-slit windows. On the roadside below it he glimpsed an ominous stone that hung down from a tree on a length of rope.

"It's a kind of bell," said Jessica. "After Armenia, Ethiopia was the first country to declare Christianity as their official religion, around 330AD. The Ethiopian Orthodox church was left to evolve on its own. Free, in the main, from Roman influences or outside doctrines, it encompassed many Jewish and pagan traditions as well as Christian. At one time an Egyptian bishop sent a Coptic Bible into the land as a kind of guidebook on Christianity, but no one was sent with it to interpret it, or impose any church customs. Ethiopian Christianity is truly unique."

Matt feigned interest, but was actually staring at Jessica's breasts through her blouse.

"You're drooling again," she reminded him.

"No, go on. Tell me more," said Matt, trying to be less obvious. He couldn't help himself. Mesmerised by her soft curvaceous mouth and her deep blue eyes he found himself drawn to her sheer intelligence. She was electrifying. He'd spent his life falling in love with complete strangers: in shops; in bars; or simply with girls that passed by on the street. He was a hopeless case and he knew it.

"You're married, Matt, aren't you?" asked Jessica.

The question caught him by surprise. "Yes... But..."

"So you're one those men who doesn't really care if they're married or not. Let me think... Life is too short, just take it while you still can. Am I close?" she pressed.

"You make it sound horrible," said Matt. He still loved Jenny and Peter, but he'd never been truly faithful to anyone. He suddenly thought of Linda and how she just took whatever she wanted. She'd never made any official commitment to anyone.

"You see, as much as I can't stand Linda, I do respect her honesty," said Jessica.

Matt paused and then asked, "Are you reading my mind?"

Jessica laughed. "No, Matt, I'm reading you face. I can actually see the part of you that wants to hold back. You probably have a trace of decency about you."

Before Jessica could say any more, the bus jolted to a halt.

Imur stood up and waved a hand for silence. "We are in Axum. Steph, Isaac, Matt, Lucius and Jessica - could you please go with Kalef. Linda, there is a small inn just here."

Linda protested but was soon calmed by Lucius. "We won't be long, dear. It's probably safer here."

Kalef spoke to Linda, "I know the man who owns this place. You can rest. We won't be long."

Matt could see that Linda was exhausted.

"Fine," bleated Linda.

Lucius turned to Matt and whispered, "I presume we are to follow our original plan? We're going to identify the Seeds then procure some for ourselves."

Matt eyed Imur and Kalef. "If we can. But I have to admit, if it wasn't for Jenny and Peter, I think it might be best if the damn Seeds were destroyed forever, just as the Seraphim want..." He noticed Kalef, turning to face them.

"What do you think of Axum, Matt?"

He shrugged in a kind of non-committal way that was cordial enough. For the centre of such a mysterious and glorified empire, Axum was, to Matt's mind, a bit of a disappointment. The stone buildings had corrugated iron roofs and the streets were littered with old fragments of pottery and rubbish. He could see a few brightly painted, glossy, blue houses and there was a plentiful array of ancient stelae set at various angles but, apart from that, Axum could hardly be described as awe-inspiring.

Matt could see that Kalef was just about to endow him with some great nugget of knowledge when a uniformed man caught the African's attention. Kalef quickly engaged the man in conversation and then bowed before passing him some money. He turned back to face Matt. "He will take our payment to the National Museum. We can explore as we wish now."

"You mean we are free to wander round the ruins?" said Jessica.

"Yes, but first we must visit the 'Holy of Holies'."

"I thought the Ark story was fictitious?" said Matt.

Kalef shook his head and laughed before marching up a small grassy slope towards what could only be described as an ugly collection of buildings. It actually looked to Matt as if there had been at least three attempts at the one building.

There was a very old set of foundations to one side; a well-proportioned chapel, and a new monstrosity of a building. It was bigger in size than the other two attempts, but that was about it. Matt couldn't believe that the Ethiopians would have built such a thing. St. Mary of Zion, if that's what it was, reminded him of a slightly dilapidated funeral parlour. It was big and dull, and the two huge stained glass windows set on either side of its doorway looked completely out of place. Even its bell tower looked like something you might find garnishing a tacky Indian restaurant in deepest Bradford.

As they approached, Matt asked Kalef, "Where's the security?"

Kalef murmured something in a strange tongue and then explained, "No Ethiopian would ever dare to enter the chapel without the permission of the priest, let alone enter the 'Holy of Holies'." Kalef's voice died down to a whisper as he walked through a simple gate.

A wizen old man dressed in black seemed to appear from nowhere.

"The priest," whispered Jessica.

Kalef bowed low and issued a respectful greeting in some strange language. "Please, come in Kalef," said the priest in English.

"I thought Kalef said he wasn't going to take us to the Ark?" said Lucius.

"It's not even here, according to him," reminded Matt.

Their feet pattered loudly as they shuffled into the echoey, stark interior.

Matt peered into the gloom. The chapel was very roomy but dull. There were a few decorative murals on the walls that almost saved it from utter blandness, but other than that it could have been any one of a thousand dreary churches.

Jessica nudged him. "The altar was donated by the Soviet Union."

"Really," he replied, trying his best to seem interested.

After some more whispering between the old priest and Kalef, Matt was waved across to join them.

Jessica made to follow him, but Kalef shook his head in warning.

Suddenly nervous, Matt moved toward a red velvet curtain that marked some other chamber, but stopped short of going in. The priest disappeared for a moment, then reappeared with a scrap of parchment. He gave it to Kalef, who bowed once more and led Matt back to the rest of the party.

"We now have the location of the tomb," said Kalef.

"Are we going where I think we are?" asked Jessica.

Kalef smiled and folded the parchment away.

Matt had seen the six-winged pendant of the Seraphim hanging round the old priest's neck. "You people are everywhere, aren't you?" he said.

Steph gave him a knowing wink.

Outside, they made their way through a helter-skelter array of stone stelae until they reached the main road again.

37

HIDDEN BEHIND A massive stele adorned with false doors and windows, Stiller adjusted his binoculars. He was determined, this time, to finish the job properly. Matt Malcolm and his entourage had just reappeared from the chapel. He undid the safety catch on the rifle and focused in on Malcolm's head. It bobbed in and out of target as Matt walked between a mishmash of concrete plinths.

"Wait!" said Barclay. The big American's voice grated in his head. "We need to observe and follow. Nothing more."

Stiller lowered his aim and spat into the sand. "We need to intercept and extract information."

"They're getting back on the bus," said Hassan.

"Barclay!" spat Stiller, "you'd better be right. We could have taken them."

* * *

MATT AND HIS group, led by Kalef, retook their seats on the bus. Isaac drove while Kalef gave the directions. It was beginning to get dark as they drove the few miles out of Axum, eventually stopping beside a stony gully that appeared no different to tens of others they'd passed already.

This time everyone, bar the portly Isaac, got out of the bus and began the climb through the rocks and debris that littered the lonely valley. As they gained height, a small village came into view. Lights flickered and goats bleated in the half-light of the Ethiopian dusk.

"This is the village of Gobedura," said Kalef. Matt marvelled at the tall Ethiopian as he strode ahead through the rocks and scrub. Nimbly, and with child-like excitement, he covered the rough terrain until he reached the edge of the village.

Kalef clicked on a torch and pointed it at the outline of a life-sized lioness carved on the flat side of an enormous stone. Although it appeared to be very ancient, the detailed chisel marks had formed an amazingly realistic creature. Matt had never seen anything quite like it. It was incredible.

Lucius, slightly out of breath, caught up with Imur. "I would say that this has been etched by the same gifted artist who made your tomb in Zurich, Imur."

Matt saw Imur's eyes flash up at the doctor menacingly.

"You half expect her to move. Don't you?" said Jessica.

"Indeed," whispered Kalef. "The lioness's soul has been hammered into the very rock." His voice was ethereal and lower pitched than usual. He studied the piece of parchment that the priest had given him then looked up and pointed his torch at an old weathered tree. Matt watched as a small flock of siskins alighted on its branches and then drifted off into the cool night air. They reminded Matt of the birds that had scattered, like so many leaves, above Brin Cottage only a few nights before. That moment seemed distant to him now. So much had changed since then.

Kalef waved them across to the weathered tree.

Matt thought he recognised the object hanging down below its twisted branches. It was one of the Ethiopian stone bells Jessica had shown him earlier.

Kalef turned to Imur. "Imur, may I have your pendant?" He took Imur's silver, six-winged pendant and, still holding the scrap of parchment, explained. "The ancient text is written in Geez, a language that is never spoken."

Everyone gathered round to see.

"The parchment says we must place three seraphim pendants inside the bell." He placed his and Imur's pendants inside a tiny hole set in the stone bell, then turned to Steph. "I need yours also, my friend."

Steph handed the tall Ethiopian his pendant and stepped back as Kalef placed it in the stone bell with the other two. They sat neatly in three indentations, each an exact, three-dimensional match.

Matt looked at Jessica incredulously and whispered, "Are they for real?"

Jessica looked just as confused as him. "Shhh... Let's see what happens next."

Kalef struck the hanging stone bell with another stone. They looked around them as the eerie chime echoed off high cliffs and filled the gully. Then, as they all stood round the twisted tree, a deep rumble grew steadily until the rock beneath their feet shifted.

"Stand back!" said Kalef.

There was another crack and they all focused on the lioness.

Matt watched the huge, carved slab of rock shift, smoothly, into some hidden recess and then disappear. In the faint light, they could just make out a set of polished marble stairs disappearing down into the darkness.

Kalef spoke as he put his foot on the top step. "Let us see what wonders the true Queen of Sheba has kept secret for so long."

Jessica could hardly contain herself as she fell in behind the tall Ethiopian. Tugging at his sleeve with one hand she traced the wall next to her. "Kalef, these are the same type of glyphs we saw in Zurich. The same as the ones we saw when we walked from the winged tomb. Are they Sumerian?"

Matt pushed in beside Jessica as Kalef explained. "No, my friend, if you had time you would see that they are a blend of Hebrew and Egyptian."

"And the lion?" she pressed.

"The lioness is the mark of one of Solomon's chieftains, a man called Arbranim." Kalef moved further down the steps and halted at a huge granite door. "His first born son left with Menelek and the Ark. It is said that he took many of the ancient seeds and grains from the Holy of Holies to cultivate here in Ethiopia." He traced a relief on the wall that depicted fields full of crops. "My hope is that these seeds and grains were sealed up in this tomb along with Sheba's remains, just in case she needed them in the afterlife."

"And the parchment?" pressed Jessica.

"Written in the same ancient Semitic text: Fangurian." "Fang...what?" asked Matt. But even he could see that the marks were similar to those he'd seen in Zurich.

"In essence," explained Kalef, "they are a mixture of very old first dynasty Egyptian hieroglyphs and actual written text."

They all came to a halt in front of a huge door. Matt noticed a beautiful angel carved on the lintel, its wings   outspread as if to protect the one inside. It was a six-winged Seraph.

"Now what?" said Matt, suddenly feeling claustrophobic as the rest of the group gathered round him and shuffled closer to the door.

Kalef glanced again at the fragment of parchment he'd been given by the priest in Axum then lifted his gaze to the mix of beautifully carved animals on the stone gate. The beasts were intertwined in a complex helix.

Matt thought that they bore a striking resemblance to the Celtic carvings sometimes found in northern Britain.

Imur held his oil lamp close to the parchment.

Kalef read it out. "The inscription says - 'the mother's eyes, already seen, forever seal the tomb.'" Sweating profusely and obviously struggling to see the meaning of the text, Kalef turned to Jessica and handed her the parchment.

Jessica traced the strange text with her fingertips and then looked again at the intricate door carvings. "The mother's eyes, already seen," she repeated. Jessica looked to Imur and then to Lucius, but neither was able to offer any interpretation. Then Jessica tapped a replica of the sphinx-like carving they'd seen outside. "The lioness," she whispered. "The lioness is the mother we've already seen." Matt could hear the excitement building in her voice.

"Yes," said Kalef, "and the eyes?"

"The eyes must be the eyes of the lioness. She's looking up towards the angel."

Matt saw that the eyes of the lioness on the lintel were too high for her to reach.

"We have to cover her eyes, Kalef," said Jessica. "Her eyes must seal the tomb? You have to put your fingers over her eyes."

Kalef looked puzzled for a second or two, and then laughed. "You crazy lady, I think you might be right." Kalef reached up and forced his fingers into the hollowed-out eyes of the lioness.

To Matt's amazement, the huge, wonderfully carved granite door groaned then swung inwards. A rush of stale air whisked over them in the dark stairwell, ruffling their hair and momentarily dousing their lamps. There was also a musty stench that made him catch his breath and sent a shiver down his spine. It felt as if some long dead god or goddess had just passed right through him. He took off his glasses and wiped them clean with his shirt.

The size of the cavern, now revealed, was truly astounding. It stretched back from the doorway for what seemed like miles. It was even high enough to accommodate a wonderfully decorated stele, bigger than anything they'd seen in Axum and more magnificent. It was adorned with bright paintings and plated, in parts, with pure gold. The false doors and windows on the stele were, again, covered in animals and birds.

"Please do not touch anything here, unless Imur or I say it is safe. You can be sure that there will be many traps set for thieves and looters," said Kalef. "One false move and we could all be locked inside the tomb forever."

"Brilliant," said Matt.

"Steph, stay outside the doorway in case we become trapped. If we do you will have to cover the eyes of the lioness for the door to reopen."

Steph nodded and retraced his steps back into the stairwell. The rest of the group moved further inside, staring in utter amazement at the piles of gold and rubies that lay at the base of the central stele.

"Look at these statuettes," said Jessica.

"Look at the diamonds," whispered Matt. There were heaps of diamonds dotted over the floor. Massive walls of pink stone rose through a symmetrical set of vaults and apses to a huge cupola, bedecked with more seraphim. There was a massive mural of a lioness and even a representation of the Ark of the Covenant. The tip of the shining stele protruded upwards where, like a needle, it seemed poised to puncture the dome above.

Imur took a deep, unfaltering breath and then turned to Matt. "It's time for you to get to work, Mr. Malcolm." He nodded towards Lucius. "You too, Dr. Schlesinger. This area here is the Queen of Sheba's granary." He pointed to a set of recesses in the wall behind them. "Supplies for the afterlife. Please feel free to examine the jars."

Jessica rushed about like a child let loose in a sweet shop, while Kalef tried to calm her down and make sure she didn't stumble on any traps.

Matt and Lucius got to work on the different jars of grain. Matt's pulse raced as he thought of Jenny and Peter.

Imur shone his torch over the various caskets and boxes, and as they began filtering through the grains and seeds it became very apparent that everything was perfectly preserved.

Matt pushed his fingers into the various lots of grain until he cried out in pain. He examined his thumb. Blood trickled down over his palm. He knelt down and eased some more grain from the sack, a little more carefully this time. The Seeds were decagonal and covered in fine purple hooks . "Lucius!"

Kalef and Imur pushed in beside him. Imur could hardly believe it. He was sweating. "Are you sure?"

"I... I..." said Matt, studying a handful of crimson, decagonal seeds. "They're the right shape but..."

"I think I'll take those, if you don't mind, Mr. Malcolm!" The thick accent sounded Russian.

Matt spun round.

Imur pulled his Beretta from its holster.

"I wouldn't do that if I were you, Mr. Falsath." Stiller stepped through the intricately decorated door of the tomb, his finger already twitching on the trigger of his Heckler. He held his left hand behind his back.

Matt watched in horror as the unusually tall Russian walked across the great hall that formed the tomb, the flickering shadow of the Queen of Sheba's stele passing over his face in the torchlight.

Matt felt for his gun, but remembered that he'd left it on the bus outside. Then it began to dawn on him. This could be perfect. He could hand the Seeds over to Stiller right here. The threat to his family would be over.

Kalef shouted out, "Steph!"

Stiller smiled sardonically and then mimicked the Ethiopian's high pitched voice, "Steph, Steph..." He laughed. "You mean this one?" From behind his back he produced a grizzly severed head. He lifted the head to his face and asked, "Are you called Steph?" He laughed again. "I think he's gone a little deaf." Still dripping blood, Matt half-expected the lips to twitch a reply, but there was nothing, only a pair of startled eyes bulging out from a pale, lifeless face.

Jessica screamed and dug her fingers into Lucius's arm.

Stiller lifted the head to his ear and nodded, as if hearing some mystic words of wisdom from the blooded lips.

They all watched in complete horror as Stiller sighed and whispered, "Yes, they will all join you soon."

Stiller tossed the head against the beautifully painted stele and turned to face Matt.

Matt knew that it wasn't Steph's head. It was Isaac's severed head that Stiller had thrown against the stele. How has Stiller managed to miss Steph? There is still a chance that we can get out of this if Steph has managed to hide. He might even have his gun trained on the psychopath right now, thought Matt. He'd never seen the Russian so close before. His long greasy hair was pulled back into a ponytail and his skin was a ghostly white. Stiller narrowed his cold eyes and continued to walk towards Matt.

Behind him, a girl and a man came into view. They had their semi-automatics trained on the group. "Everyone get down beside Mr. Malcolm. Quickly!" said the girl. She was around five foot with black hair and sallow skin. She handled the gun easily, as if it was an extension of her arm.

Jessica moved away from the piles of rubies and gold until she reached Matt, Lucius and Kalef. Imur, too, shuffled across the floor of the tomb until he stood a little closer the rows of jars that filled the recess in the wall.

"I need you to drop your weapons on the floor. Now!" said Stiller, lifting his aim until the barrel of his Heckler was level with Imur's head.

Imur and Kalef placed their weapons on the floor of the tomb.

"Thank you. Now..." He turned to face Matt Malcolm. "We meet at last, Mr. Malcolm. I wonder if you'll be as forthcoming as your wife."

Matt flinched, letting the crimson seeds trickle through his fingers before he clenched his fists. "I hear that she was more than able to take care of herself."

Stiller, still staring into Matt's eyes, lunged out and gripped Jessica by the throat. "If I'd been there myself, Mr. Malcolm, I would have made her and your son suffer. But then, there's still plenty of time for that. I've got a very thorough and professional countryman of yours ready and waiting for that particular job. Like me, he takes great pride in his work." Stiller grinned and increased the pressure on Jessica's throat.

Beads of sweat ran down Imur's face. "Stop! You've got what you wanted." He took a step forward.

Stiller pushed the barrel of his gun against Imur's smooth cheek, stopping him in his tracks. As he released Jessica, he traced her wet skin with his long, pale fingers, down from her throat until they came to rest on the bare patch of skin on her chest. Her blouse was open and, as he turned back to face Matt, he slipped his hand inside the white cotton and squeezed her left breast. Jessica's eyes widened and she tried to pull back, but Stiller gripped even harder.

"Your nails... Please stop..." Jessica tensed, a tear rolling down her cheek.

38

"OPEN YOUR HAND," whispered Stiller.

Matt showed Stiller his empty palm.

Stiller glanced down at the crimson seeds that lay around Matt's shoes. "Is that the real Seed, Mr. Malcolm?" Stiller looked into Matt's eyes. "Because..." he glanced back at Jessica, "you're a lying, cheating bastard, aren't you, Mr. Malcolm? Couldn't give a shit about your wife, not really."

"I love my wife." Matt felt his throat become dry.

Stiller shook his head scornfully. "Love the one you're with, would be more accurate. You see, I'm pretty sure you like Miss Baron. I can tell. Have a nose for this kind of thing. And, as I don't have your wife here to test your resolve, I will have to make do with the girl you'd like to fuck."

Jessica's eyes widened as Stiller increased his grip. "Where is our great leader, Hassan?" he barked over his shoulder.

The bearded man behind Stiller answered. "He's back at the bus with Schmitt."

"You see," continued Stiller, "our new head of operations isn't too keen on the nitty-gritty, down and dirty stuff. Is this the Seed or not?" Blood began to seep through Jessica's blouse as Stiller dug his nails into her flesh. She trembled with pain, her knees already buckling.

Matt didn't know what to say. He was fairly sure it was the right seed but he wasn't convinced that Stiller wouldn't just kill them all once he got what he wanted. He glanced at Lucius, who seemed to read his thoughts and announced, "These are not the same, Matt. They are the right colour but they are not the right shape or size."

Without releasing his grip on Jessica, Stiller turned on Lucius. "Dr. Schlesinger, I presume?"

Lucius nodded. "There's no need to be so cruel. Leave the girl alone."

Stiller pushed the barrel of his gun under the doctor's chin and let go his grip on Jessica. She slumped to the ground in a cascade of sobs and tears.

"Are you telling me that Mr. Malcolm is expendable?" Stiller's black eyes glinted in the half light, a trace of excitement curling his thin lips into a malevolent smile. He trained the gun on Matt.

Lucius was totally thrown by the question. "No... No, of course not. He is the only one who can really tell what the Seeds look like."

"Well then, that means you are expendable, Dr. Lucius. Right now would be a good time to say your goodbyes." Stiller pushed the old doctor to his knees and placed the tip of his Heckler to Lucius's temple. Lucius looked up at Imur who was shaking his head.

"Stop this now," he yelled.

Stiller widened his smile and placed his forefinger over the trigger.

Crack! The noise was deafening.

All hell broke loose. Stiller fell back on top of a large pile of rubies, his arm oozing dark blood. Hassan and Solana began shooting up into the vaulted roof above the stele. They rolled behind an assortment of statuettes and aimed upward. Another succession of rounds ripped across the floor of the tomb, scattering scarlet rubies and pulverising the ornate carvings and jars.

In the confusion, Matt pulled Jessica into the recess that contained the jars of grain and crouched down as low as he could.

Kalef quickly scooped up his gun and immediately opened fire.

Stiller rolled off the pile of rubies in a hail of bullets. He lay behind a small stele, about seven feet high. Matt could hear him panting. But as Kalef moved forward to finish him off, a burst of fire sent the tall Ethiopian reeling back beside Imur.

Lucius was still in the open, frozen to the spot.

As Hassan and Solana fired up at the cupola, pieces of priceless treasure showered down on them all below. An ornate Seraph wing crashed onto the floor just feet from Lucius. A golden statue smashed down onto the rubies below and scattered them, like shrapnel, across the chamber. Several fragments caught Stiller's henchman in the throat and he fell to his knees, a torrent of blood dripping through his fingers.

Matt couldn't believe the carnage. He could only guess that it was Steph, but why would he fire on Kalef and Imur? Why would he destroy the tomb... the artefacts?

Stiller had been pulled to safety by Solana, who ducked and weaved between the bullets as they rained down from above. She knelt and aimed up at a balustrade that circled the base of the cupola. But the more she fired upwards the more they were all showered with heavy fragments and further firepower. She managed to get Stiller to his feet, but Matt could see that the tall Russian's neck was bleeding badly and his arm was completely limp. With a scream of frustration Stiller ran with her, back towards the entrance of the tomb.

As soon as they began running, however, there was a whoosh and an explosion that sent rock showering down everywhere. The towering stele jerked to one side. Free of its plinth it shuddered before crashing onto the ground. The sound was incredible. The whole hundred and twenty foot column then split in three places as it fell and then disappeared in an impenetrable cloud of dust.

There was a scream from the recess next to where Matt and Jessica lay. Matt shouted out, "Kalef? Imur?" Dust and debris covered his face. His ears were still ringing with the noise of the collapse. Every breath was a struggle. He couldn't find Lucius.

Everything went very quiet, and then he heard Imur's voice, "Matt, keep hold of the jar that contains the Eden Seed." The sect leader's face was grey with dust while his normally exquisite moustache was thick with a hoary powder that made him seem like one of the statues, honed from the rock of the tomb.

"They're gone." Matt pointed to a huge pile of rubble. "Who fired down on us?" he asked, still worried about where Stiller might be.

"It must have been Steph," said Imur, "But I don't understand why he kept firing, why he's destroyed such a holy site. It's against every code he's ever known. I can't believe..."

A terrible gurgling groan caused Imur to pause.

"Help me."

As the dust settled, Matt and Jessica could see one of Lucius's legs protruding from a piece of the fallen stele. Imur knelt down and climbed under the great stone. Miraculously, the huge lump of granite had saved the doctor; it had wedged itself against the side of the cavern as it fell, leaving a space of a yard, or so. Lucius pulled himself free, shaken and in a state of shock, but completely unharmed. "Who fired down on us?" he asked, between coughs.

"I'm not sure," said Imur turning back into the recess to check on Kalef. But Kalef wasn't there. Part of the small vault where they'd hidden had collapsed.

"Kalef! Kalef!" Matt and Jessica soon joined Imur, hauling and scraping at the rubble with their bare hands. Linda and Lucius joined them too until, at last, they saw a hand; Kalef's long, black fingers flicked and grasped at the dusty air.

"Quickly, dig faster. Dig faster!" Imur, for all his size, worked like a Trojan, shifting boulders and scooping dust away until Kalef came into view. His eyes blinked open but his mouth was full blood.

Although the rocks had left a space for Kalef's legs and head, a huge piece of stone lay, immovable, on his stomach. Jessica looked away. Matt knelt down beside him. Kalef was dying. He could see how the heavy stone had pushed Kalef's intestines up under his ribs. His upper torso bulged, irregularly, beneath his torn clothes.

Kalef whispered, "I... I feel very cold..."

"Don't speak Kalef; you must save your strength," said Imur. The seraphim leader's eyes filled with tears as he handed Matt Kalef's Beretta. "Cover the main doorway in case Stiller returns."

Terrified, Matt felt the weight of the gun in his hands. He hovered over Kalef, unsure whether to stay or go.

Kalef pulled Imur close to his dying lips and whispered, "Do not let this disaster keep you from going on..." Kalef coughed up more blood. "Go back to the Holy of Holies and give the priest back this parchment. I have told him to give you a second route to the Seed, should I not retu..." Before he could finish, Kalef's eyes glazed. He lay perfectly still, his left hand still clutching the piece of parchment that had led them to the Queen of Sheba's tomb.

Imur took the ancient sheet of text and closed Kalef's eyes.

Jessica sobbed.

Lucius was already walking towards Matt and the doorway they'd come through earlier.

"What are they doing?" Imur had seen Lucius staggering past Matt towards the door. "Lucius!"

Matt, seeing Lucius move past him stepped, awkwardly, over the piles of rubble after him. "It's not safe, Stiller could be..."

A noise cut Matt's words short. It hadn't been a shot or a shout; it was the unmistakeable noise of stone slipping over stone.

"The lintel!" Jessica had seen it first.

Inadvertently, Lucius had tripped on a slightly raised stone slab. He'd triggered something and now the lioness gate was beginning to close.

Pulling on Imur, Jessica scrambled towards Matt and the doorway. "Kalef told us to watch out for traps, though God knows how this mess hasn't set off more before now." Her words were shaky as she struggled across the uneven floor. A deep crimson stain covered her blouse.

The lintel had already moved halfway down the pillars of the lioness doorway.

Lucius ducked under the descending lintel.

Matt, Imur and Jessica were trying their best to slip and stumble forward.

"Quickly!" shouted Lucius. He peered under the descending lintel, waving them towards him. He found a large piece of granite and slid it into the grooves that guided the lintel to the ground.

The sound of the splitting stone echoed round the chamber.

Matt stooped through the ever-narrowing gap just as the lump of granite disintegrated under the pressure of the lintel. He spun himself round on the dusty floor and grabbed Jessica's arm. She just made it through as Imur rolled under the lintel beside her. Kalef's piece of parchment fell from Imur's grasp. He turned to go back.

"Leave it!" screamed Jessica.

A second before the lintel smashed into the floor, Matt thrust his hand under the falling stone and snatched the fragment of parchment.

Crash! The lioness doorway that had led to the incredible wonders of Sheba's tomb was sealed tight. Imur reached up and pushed his fingers into the eyes of the lioness but nothing happened, nothing at all.

In the dim light thrown by an abandoned torch, they could see the headless body of Isaac lying awkwardly under a thick film of dust. Behind him, three sets of footprints led upwards. There was a small set of prints that must have been left by the woman assailant, beside them, Stiller's own. It was the third set that puzzled them. These weaved in a zigzag fashion up the stairs towards the night sky above them.

"Why would Steph sneak out before coming to see if we were alright?" asked Matt, handing the scrap of parchment to Imur.

"It's not Steph," said Imur.

Matt had seen Stiller's bearded accomplice fall in the firefight. So who was it? Who had left the footprints in the dust? Matt tried to think back to Stiller's exact words but he was too mixed up, he couldn't focus.

"There were another two people mentioned by Stiller," said Lucius, "someone called Schmitt and someone else he referred to as his 'new head of operations'."

"Yes," said Jessica. "And he said they were waiting at the bus. Our bus, I presume." Jessica clutched her chest and gasped.

"Are you alright?" asked Matt.

Jessica closed her eyes and steadied herself on the wall.

Matt felt awkward. He remembered Stiller's taunts.

"Of course I'm not alright." She forced herself further up the steps.

"Matt." Imur grabbed Matt's arm. "The Seeds. Did you...?"

"No, I dropped them. The jar got buried beneath the rubble." Matt had forgotten all about the Eden Seeds. He tried to put his arm round Jessica but she shrugged him away.

"We can't afford to wait here a moment longer," said Imur. He glanced down at the Beretta in Matt's hand. "Be prepared for more trouble."

Matt undid the safety catch and climbed the smooth alabaster stairs. Matt's head was full of screams, gunfire and betrayal. As he moved on, he tried to keep his head clear but fear was biting into him. He felt sure that Stiller and the rest of his henchmen would be waiting for them, ready to pick them off, one by one, as they raised their heads above the stairwell.

Imur climbed up beside him. "Be ready, my friend. A quick death is better than being buried alive. They might lock us in, close the upper door. Better to fight our way out than die like rats."

As Matt got closer to the top of the stairs he could see the branches of the old weathered tree flickering in the moonlight. The stone bell hung down from its branches like a corpse on an executioner's rope. He braced and then, with a nod from Imur, bolted up the last of the stairs. Matt threw himself over the rim of the stairwell, screwed up his eyes and fired.

He braced and waited.

There was nothing. No hail of bullets. No single shot between the eyes.

Matt continued forward and knelt in the dust beneath the swinging stone bell, scanning the black horizon.

Their bus was gone.

As Matt signalled the others to come up the stairs, Imur reached up and put his hand into the small hole in the stone bell.

Lucius supported Jessica, both of them shivering in the night air.

Pulling his hand free, Imur held up the three seraphim pendants and said a small prayer to Yahweh, his god. As he did so, the stone slab that had hidden Sheba's tomb for three millennia slid back into place. A deep rumble below their feet seemed to signal another rock fall in the tomb. All trace of the riches and carnage below sealed forever, thought Matt. What have we done? How will I save Jenny and Peter now? Once the ground stopped shaking, Matt heard a groan. Breathing heavily, he braced himself against the tree and aimed his gun into the darkness. "Who's there?"

Again, there was a faint groan.

Imur turned to Lucius, who had lifted a torch from the ground. "Bring the light over here, Lucius."

As Lucius walked closer to the lump on the ground, Imur and Matt kept their aim steady.

"Mmm... Imur?" The voice was faint.

"Steph!" Imur ran over to his friend and lifted him into a sitting position. There was a deep cut in the back of Steph's head that stuck his matted brown hair to his scalp. Steph looked up at Matt. His eyes were dull, his complexion ghostly.

"Stiller?" Matt prompted.

"Who? No. Well, I don't think so." Steph was still struggling to form a sentence.

"This wasn't Stiller," sad Matt. "He wouldn't have left Steph in one piece."

Jessica tore a fragment of cloth from her blood-spattered blouse and spat on it. She dabbed the back of Steph's head.

Steph edged up onto his elbows and asked, "Where's Isaac and the bus?"

Imur rolled his eyes and said another prayer. "Here Steph, wear your pendant close to your heart." He turned to Matt. "I'm sure Kalef would have wanted you to have this."

"Kalef?" Steph rolled into a kneeling position and stood up. "Where is Kalef?"

Imur handed Matt the silver six-winged seraphim. "Without your bravery we would not be able to continue our search." Imur held up the parchment. They all watched as it fluttered in the breeze.

"Reaching back like that, for the parchment... You could have lost an arm, Matt," said Jessica, reproachfully.

Matt studied the little pendant before placing it round his neck. "Without your help I would be lying dead in a service station off the A1, or..." Matt thought back to Zurich and Genoa. "This whole thing's been my fault," he said.

"I guess," said Jessica.

"I'm sorry, Jessica, are you okay?" said Matt.

"I'm just relieved to be out of there. I'll survive," she whispered.

Still looking dazed, Steph was about to ask another question when Imur said, "I'm afraid Isaac and Kalef are both dead."

Matt saw the pained expression on Steph's face. "Kalef said that the priest would give us another map if we failed here at the tomb."

"This is all my fault," moaned Steph.

"Hardly," said Matt, mopishly. "Someone saved our skin in that tomb."

Imur gave him a reproachful glance.

"I know Kalef was unfortunate, but we would all be dead by now if that gunman hadn't shot down when he did."

"Or gun-woman," added Jessica, "it could just as easily have been a woman."

"Of course," said Matt, in a placatory tone.

Jessica turned to Imur, obviously still in pain, "And you said that Sheba was buried here three thousand years ago. That's well before Axum even existed."

"Before Axum was named, to be exact," said Imur, defensively. "It wasn't called Axum then, Jessica. It was called Sheba."

"Getting back to the present," said Matt, interrupting their discussion, "where do you suppose Stiller is now? Where is the bus? And who the hell fired down on us from that balcony? It obviously wasn't Steph."

Imur gazed out across the gully into the night sky. "We can only assume that Stiller has our bus, as he intercepted Isaac. As far as our mystery assailant is concerned, It seems as though there is a third party involved in the hunt for the Eden Seed. Whoever they are, they obviously knew where we were going, which means that they either followed us or Stiller."

"Or they have someone on the inside who is still passing on our location," said Steph, steadying himself on a boulder as he began his descent down the hillside towards the road.

"We all came under fire. Why would you say such a thing?" said Jessica. Matt could hear the anger escalating in her voice. She was obviously still annoyed about the mobile phone incident in the café earlier that day.

"You should never rule out any possibility, no matter how improbable," said Imur. He turned to face Matt. "Should you, Matt?"

* * *

HIGH ABOVE THEM on a hidden ridge, Evans pulled a heavy pack out from under a cluster of gorse. The dark-haired girl had grazed his shoulder just after he'd taken out the Arab with the beard. It stung like mad. He'd call Burrows tomorrow, tell him that he was back on their trail. The last thing he wanted was some other party killing Malcolm before him. There was more to it now than just doing Burrow's bidding. This Seraphim sect had killed his best buddies. If anyone was going to get hold of this Seed now it would be him, no one else. He scrambled down the ridge at a safe distance until, eventually, he saw the lights of Axum.

39

"HOW MANY OF your people have been killed now, Stiller?"

Stiller pushed Solana away from his wounded arm and rounded on the bulky American. "Your fuckin' insider didn't say anything about a mystery sniper up in the gods. Your insider said it would be straightforward." Stiller spat as Solana reached over to tighten his bandage.

"I would have thought that a man of your persuasion would be prepared for all eventualities," said Barclay. "I'm used to getting results."

Stiller raised the barrel of the Heckler until it rested on Barclay's chest. "Don't push your fucking luck, Barclay. Don't forget, you're dead already. Your headless, fat corpse was found floating in the fucking sea. Just remember that, my friend."

Solana eased Stiller back into his chair. "Don't move your arm just yet. It needs rest." She poured some boiling water into a blue-rimmed enamel bowl. "Whoever the sniper was, it's most likely he was American," she said, pouring disinfectant into the boiling water. "He used an M249 and he also fired off an RPG. It was an M-72; the flare from the exhaust is a give-away."

"Very good, Solana." Stiller was becoming more impressed by her all the time. He may have found a good replacement for Sylvie, he decided, especially now that Solana's mentor, Hassan, was dead. "So you see, Barclay, you better be telling us the whole fuckin' truth because it's all starting to look very suspicious."

"What do you mean!" said Barclay.

"Well, firstly you decide to stay out of trouble in the bus, then, the man in the roof..."

Solana grunted. "Man or woman."

"Or woman," Stiller corrected himself, "is using the American Marine, standard weapon of choice - the M249."

Solana dabbed the hot disinfectant onto Stiller's cuts. She prised four rubies out of his cheek and a sliver of gold from his neck.

Stiller didn't even wince. He just continued to berate Barclay. "We never had a third player until you turned up."

Barclay's face flushed with rage but Stiller continued. "What has your contact said? The one that sends text messages to you, but doesn't tell you who they are."

Stiller saw Schmitt trying his best to stifle a grin.

"There's someone else on the trail, alright, but I'm not sure who they are yet. Nobody is," said Barclay.

Stiller could see the fear in Barclay's eyes. "And you're shittin' yourself."

Barclay shifted nervously.

Stiller unclipped his ponytail. "You hope that your death is believed. Because if it's not..."

"It would be a fuckin' mess, yes." Barclay closed his eyes.

"That's why you stayed on the bus, made us leave the scene so quickly. You didn't want to be seen, did you?" Stiller tossed a ruby to Schmitt, who quickly shoved it into his pocket. "So what now, Mr. Barclay?"

Barclay sighed. "We wait."

"We should never have left the contact site before performing a proper assessment." said Solana.

Annoyed by her logic, Barclay pressed on. "Our paymaster told us to eliminate any other parties and to watch Malcolm until he finds the Seed. It was as simple as that."

Schmitt and Stiller rose from the small bed they were sitting on and looked out of their window into the night sky above Axum. "Solana's right, I think we should go back now," said Stiller. "It's better to hunt than be hunted."

"Wait!" Barclay stood up and groped for his mobile. He looked at the text message. "It's from our paymaster," he muttered. He read the message. "It says: 'Last chance. Will come myself if you fail again.' "

"Well?" asked Stiller.

Barclay walked to the window. "My contact must still be alive."

Stiller spat on the concrete floor, picked up his coat and signalled Schmitt to follow him.

A dog barked a single hole in the silence until a cock crowed far off in the distance. It would soon be dawn.

* * *

BY THE TIME they'd reached the outskirts of Axum, there was a faint glow in the western sky. Steph, still concussed, had walked in a kind of daze while Lucius had sighed and panted with every step.

Jessica walked to his left, her hair still thick with dust from the tomb. Matt and Imur had speculated about who might have fired down on them all from the high balcony and what might have become of Stiller.

Imur raised his hand. "It will soon be light. We should go back down to the inn."

"Linda?" gasped Lucius. "Oh, my God."

They'd forgotten all about Linda.

They all quickened their pace until they reached the inn where they'd left Linda.

A shutter squeaked open above their heads and Linda peered out. A second later a slightly dishevelled looking inn keeper pushed the shutters fully open.

"Surely not," whispered Jessica.

Imur cleared his throat. "Eh... we should wash, freshen up a little."

Inside the small hotel, Matt closed his eyes. He longed for sleep.

Linda, having extricated her 'guest' and listened to their story of events, pulled Matt against her chest. "This poor boy looks exhausted. I think he should stay with me and Lucius."

"I think he'd be safer with Stiller," said Jessica.

Imur cleared his throat and continued. "I will go with Matt to St. Mary's of Zion Church to see the priest who knew Kalef. We will see if he can give us the location of the second site, while Steph..." Imur glanced across at the tall Slav, "...you can organise some proper transport. Wait for us here with the women and Lucius."

Imur toyed with his moustache. "Matt and I should be no more than two hours. That should give us enough time to find the priest and get back with the information we need." Imur took Matt's arm and walked a distance away from Steph and the women before saying, "I don't want to discuss what we will do next or where we will go in front of anyone else again, just you."

"But..." Matt protested. "You don't still think we've got a mole?"

"I don't know what to think. All I know is that we cannot take any more risks," said Imur.

"Fine." Matt wanted to say 'go find the priest yourself, I'm too tired, leave me', but he couldn't.

As daylight threatened, Matt and Imur found their way back to the toppled stones that littered the open space in front of the new Church of St. Mary of Zion. Its large, green-painted windows loomed above them as they tried to open the rusting gate, but it was shut tight.

"We'll have to find another way in," said Imur

"Just climb over and knock on the door," said Matt, scanning the doorway for some sign of a bell.

Imur shook his head. "If we start banging on the door, half of Axum will hear us, not to mention Stiller and whoever else is on our trail."

"I suppose," said Matt, hesitantly. "So where should we start?"

"At the back, of course. Let's try and find out where the priest might be sleeping," said Imur.

"Kalef told me that the priest sleeps down beside the Ark of the Covenant?" said Matt.

"Beside the replica of the Ark," Imur corrected.

"Of course," mumbled Matt, dully, following Imur to a hole in the perimeter fence. "You'd think they'd repair this kind of damage, wouldn't you?"

Imur slipped through the hole easily, followed by Matt. They put their backs against the rendered wall and crouched beneath an unbarred stained-glass window as Imur explained: "It's not the replica of the Ark that the old priest guards; the other artefacts that came to Axum with the true Ark are his main concern." Imur's face shone in the first rays of the sun.

Matt still thought Imur was a crackpot of the highest order but, having seen the tomb of Sheba, he stifled the urge to be sarcastic and, instead, issued a tight-lipped nod.

Imur stood on a lump of concrete that lay beneath the window. He found the biggest section of the leaded window, a sheet of stained glass almost a yard square, and began to trace round the join where the glass met the lead with his knife. After completing this motion several times, he tapped the pane inward at the base until it gave way. Reaching inside, he gripped the pane then twisted it out through the space at an angle.

Matt was impressed. The whole process had taken less than two minutes and now they were climbing into one of the most holy places on the planet.

Inside, the dark church echoed to their footsteps. Their eyes soon adjusted to the gloom and Matt picked out the thick red curtain in the far corner. "Right there. That's where Kalef went inside to talk to the priest."

The curtain hung on polished brass hooks that made no noise when Imur slid the screen open. Matt's heart raced as they walked behind the curtain into the Holy of Holies. They passed through two dark archways before they finally reached the inner sanctum. There, on a stone plinth, a large irregular object lay covered by a thick, black velvet shroud. The priest was nowhere to be seen. Imur searched the room behind, leaving Matt with the mysterious object. Was this the false Ark? Unable to contain his curiosity, he edged forward. He glanced about the room one more time, lest Imur or the priest should appear, and then gingerly lifted up the edge of the black shroud. It weighed a ton.

Matt noticed it had a solid consistency, like the leaded gowns worn by radiographers, but it felt soft to the touch. As he pushed the shroud upwards, he glimpsed the gold beneath. It seemed to be luminescent, to have a light of its own. The dim candle that shone in the corner flickered. His heart sank as he heard the footsteps He backed away from the Ark. Imur was trying to becalm the little priest who was completely apoplectic.

As soon as Imur held up his hand and said a certain word, however, the priest suddenly stopped shouting and bowed. Matt couldn't believe the change in the small man. Imur produced his pendant and glanced at Matt who did the same.

As Imur showed the priest the parchment, Matt felt a pang of guilt for daring to look upon the Ark. Strangely, his head had started to thump loudly and he felt quite dizzy. His over tired, paranoid mind told him that he had looked upon the real Ark and that he would soon die a horrible death. It was then, as Matt felt a second wave of anxiety wash over him, that the priest began shouting again. He was pointing at him. The priest rounded on Matt, reaching out with his thin, delicate fingers until he brushed Matt's face.

Matt froze, his mouth suddenly dry.

The priest seemed to calm down. He looked Matt in the eye. Then, without warning, spun round and stared at the shroud that covered the Ark. Matt felt another tinge of paranoia and began to sweat profusely. The priest touched Matt's face for a second time and shook his head reproachfully.

He led them across to an old wooden box that looked as though it was about to fall to pieces. The priest opened the ancient lid and produced another sheet of parchment that matched the one Imur was holding.

"Thank you," said Imur, backing away. He caught Matt's sleeve as he went.

They both shuffled through the two archways and out through the velvet curtain. In the silence of the church they eyed each other for a second before Imur said, "You looked at the Ark, didn't you, Matt?"

"No," Matt lied. He didn't know why he'd lied; he just felt it would be easier.

Imur moved closer to Matt and gripped his wrist.

"I didn't. I..." Matt protested.

Imur grimaced, pulling Matt sharply round a plain stone pillar. "Never mind that. Look. Outside."

Matt followed his gaze across the pews to the window they'd come through earlier. Someone was outside, and it was still only seven in the morning.

"Now what?" said Matt, panicking.

Imur drew a silver PP6 pistol from his jacket. Matt knew what it was, because Steph had drummed everything there was to know about the Seraphim's weaponry into him ever since Genoa.

"We will leave by the front door," said Imur.

Matt saw the priest appear from the curtain and nod his approval.

Imur slipped open a simple metal bolt at the bottom of the heavy door.

"But that's crazy," Matt complained. "It might be Stiller."

"Trust me, Matt. Come!" Imur eased the door open.

The sun had climbed a little higher and there was an easy, amber light building in the west. There was no sign of anyone else at the front of the Church, so they opened the door a little wider and pushed through.

As the cold air hit them, they moved quickly towards the cover of the toppled stones to the front of the church. Imur dragged Matt behind a biggish stele and ducked down. "Let's see who's been following us." They waited for about three minutes before a figure edged round the wall. Both Imur and Matt gasped in amazement.

"It's Jessica," whispered Matt, about to stand up and wave, but Imur pulled him down. "Don't be too hasty Matt," he whispered. "We may have found our mole."

40

EVANS HAD SEEN everything. He'd watched Matt and Imur race out of the Church of St. Mary of Zion then hide amongst the maze of toppled stones. He'd seen Jessica Baron edge round the side of the church and then peer inside the open front door. He was surprised when the small Middle Eastern man held Matt Malcolm back. Mistrust within the ranks, he thought. A lack of solidarity was always useful in an enemy. He'd also seen how close Malcolm and the Middle Eastern man had come to bumping into the Russian and his skinny KGB henchman. Evans smiled. He'd kept one step ahead of the Russian, identified as Vlan Stiller. The Arab's phone he'd taken in Cairo had given him the last numbers dialled. He'd relayed these to the CIA and had received flight destinations and even call transcripts. He'd been waiting for them all.

Evans had decided that Matt Malcolm must still be on the trail of the Seed. What had he and the sect leader taken from the Church of St. Mary of Zion? Was Malcolm on some kind of quest to find another source of the seed that Evans had destroyed in Spain? What he couldn't figure out was who exactly was pulling the strings. Was Malcolm still working for Vectan-Brosman, even though he'd been publicly sacked or was he working for these religious sect members – the Seraphim? And who was Barclay working for? He'd spotted the American at the bus outside the tomb. He couldn't wait to tell Burrows that the treacherous fucker was still alive. Evans figured Barclay might be working for himself.

He would have to find out where Matt Malcolm's next site was going to be, then watch and wait until the idiot found the right seed this time. He would kill them all and receive the plaudits from Burrows. He knew now that he may have blown it back at the tomb. He should have waited until Malcolm had identified his precious seeds and then attacked. But Stiller was too close. The Russian might have got away with a sample. His dilemma now was whether he should break off from Burrows and the CIA now, go it alone like Barclay, or stay in the Burrows camp. Sitting on his rooftop vantage point he decided to keep Burrows in the loop a little longer. He dialled the private number.

"Sir?"

"Yes, Evans. Have you brought The Seed Project to a satisfactory conclusion yet?" Burrows didn't sound like himself. He was talking as if someone might be listening in to their conversation.

"There are other complications, Sir. We have another party involved, apart from the sect."

"What difference should that make, Evans? Your instructions are clear. They couldn't be simpler. No more Seed, no more payments."

Evans decided to play his hand. "Barclay is still alive."

"Where is the son of a bitch?" Burrows raised his voice.

"He's here in Ethiopia. He's onto Malcolm and he's employed some help, Russian help."

There was a pause before Burrows spoke again. "All the more reason to tidy up."

Evans heard Burrows excuse himself from some meeting or other. "Sir, I've closed down the source of the Seed here in Ethiopia. They tried to get some from a tomb but I shut it down. If there were any Seeds there, they're under a million tons of rock now. I'm still observing because I think this weirdo sect might know about another site. Another location for the Seed."

"I'm coming out there, Evans."

"But Sir..."

"But nothing. Just watch them and get as much information as you can. Let me know where you're going to be in eighteen hours."

The line went dead.

"Fuck." Evans felt like throwing his mobile against the nearest wall. This was the last thing he needed.

* * *

THE SUN WAS up, and there was still no sign of Matt Malcolm and his entourage. The morphine injections had tempered the pain in his shoulder and now, as he waited back at the doorway of their hotel, Stiller took in the view. The morning sun had given Axum an amber glow and the surrounding hills seemed to blend in with the houses and stelae that littered the valley. Evergreens and thorny, grey shrubs lined the steep valley walls and Stiller wondered if perhaps Matt Malcolm and the sect had been crushed or trapped in the tomb after the collapse of the giant obelisk. He fingered the three rubies that Solana had dug out from his neck and face. He felt their cold, sticky smoothness and wondered if the American who fired down from the roof of the tomb was still here in Axum. Had he been trapped or even killed in the tomb?

At precisely 10.45 a.m., Barclay received another text message from his contact. It said: 'To Addis then north to new site.'

"Was that all they said?" pressed Stiller. "Where are they now?"

Barclay, his big face flushing, explained. "Look, Stiller, the contact is alive so I can only presume that some of them made it out of the tomb. We took their transport, which means that they either walked back to Axum or they had other help."

"You mean the American?" said Solana, still looking very crestfallen. "He killed Hassan."

"Yes, well... I don't know." Barclay peered out of a grimy window with its flaking green paint onto the street below.

"Let's get going then," snapped Stiller.

Schmitt filled the commandeered bus with diesel. "How do I get to Addis Ababa?"

"It's south of here," explained Barclay. He stabbed his finger into a dirty map and tossed it across to the weasel-faced Schmitt. Stiller saw the hate in Schmitt's eyes as he plucked the crumpled map from the footwell. They would have no idea where Malcolm's group was until Barclay's contact made another call. He closed his eyes and made a silent wish that the next site after Addis would be in much cooler climes.

Barclay's mobile buzzed into life.

Stiller snatched it from the American and listened in. Solana shook her head in warning when Barclay tried to get up and take it back. She had her gun trained on his groin.

Stiller smiled at Barclay and waited.

"How are things progressing, Barclay?"

As before, the paymaster's voice was disguised. It was clear enough, but there was no hint of an accent, age or gender. Stiller grunted and handed the mobile back to Barclay.

Shaking with anger, the American snatched it back.

"Barclay!"

"Yes, I'm here... Sorry," said Barclay.

"I hope you're going to give me a favourable update," said the voice.

"We're still in pursuit, but it's not too clear where they're going next and..." Barclay winced as Solana's finger wavered over the trigger. He lowered his head to the phone as Stiller and Solana closed in. "...there seems to be another interested party. They've gained knowledge of Malcolm's whereabouts."

"And how could that be possible?" said the voice.

"I'm not exactly sure," said Barclay.

"Put Stiller on, now!"

Barclay winced then handed Stiller the mobile. "He wants to speak to you."

"I fuckin' bet he does," said Stiller. "Yes?" He adopted a sweet but menacing tone.

"Mr. Stiller, when are you going to get a sample of the Seed I require from Mr. Malcolm?" said the voice.

"We are dealing with a well-trained, well-armed sect. And there looks to be an American concern on the trail." Stiller gave Barclay a disdainful look. "I wouldn't be surprised if the CIA is involved."

"What makes you say that?" said the voice.

"The firepower used by our last contact was confirmed to be standard U.S. Marine issue."

"There will be a two million dollar bonus if you can collect a viable sample of the Seed we seek and then dispose of all evidence. Understand?" Stiller looked at Solana and felt a surge of regret. "Understood," he said.

* * *

IN ADDIS ABABA, Matt and Imur were in discussions with the hotel receptionist.

"We need four single rooms and..." Matt glanced across at Lucius and Linda, "you'd better make one of them a double."

The receptionist shook her head and announced, regretfully, that they only had three rooms left, none of which were doubles. Matt sighed. "Fine, we'll sort out the sleeping arrangement later." He signed the register as James Kaminski and pointed to Imur in the hope that the little Syrian had enough money to pay for the deposit.

Matt and Imur had agreed to say nothing about their sighting of Jessica outside the Holy of Holies. They wanted to see if she offered any explanation but, so far, she had not. When Jessica had finally reappeared, about half an hour after Imur and Matt had returned to the inn, she'd been holding an armful of fresh bread. When she was reminded how dangerous it had been to go in search of food at six in the morning when there was every likelihood that Stiller or one of his psychopaths were still looking for them, she simply made her apologies and proceeded to share out the warm, unleavened bread.

This had left Matt very confused. He felt himself falling for the vivacious, intelligent ex-Chief Justice but he was now becoming just as suspicious as Imur. Why had she followed them to the church, and why then fail to come up with a better excuse, unless, of course, she was telling the truth.

"Matt?" Linda walked over the marble floor of the reception hall, smiling at him. "When can we go home?"

He immediately thought of Jenny and Peter. A wave of foreboding invaded his thoughts. He shrugged. "You'll have to ask Imur."

"Fine." Linda grabbed hold of the leader of the Seraphim. "Is that it then? Job done? All sources of the Seed destroyed?"

Imur was in no real mood to discuss his next step with anyone other than Matt, but he would have to tell the rest something. "We'd better meet in..." he eyed the room keys, "105."

Linda had provided Imur with an agenda, which she'd scribbled on a sheet of hotel paper. Matt eventually got hold of the sheet and laughed when he saw that the hotel was on Eden Street. "Now is that synchronicity or is that synchronicity?" he said.

Jessica was the only one who smiled back. "I need to speak to you, Matt," she said, quietly.

"About time too," said Matt, hoping she was going to, at last, explain her reasons for following them to the Holy of Holies.

Jessica led Matt to a dark corner of the lounge bar. Huge mirrors and intricately carved wooden statues lined the walls.

"This country is full of surprises," said Matt. "I mean, this hotel doesn't exactly fit into the 'feed the world' scenario, does it?"

Jessica winced as she tried to sit down.

"Are you okay?" Matt recalled Stiller's expression of sheer delight when he'd dug his nails into her breast.

"It still hurts like hell, but it's only superficial." She cupped her left breast as she shuffled back into the deep sofa.

"You should get someone to look at that," said Matt, not for one minute intending any innuendo.

Jessica smiled and said in a hushed tone, "It's not a pretty sight."

"Oh, I didn't mean I wanted to..." Matt flushed. "No, it was terrible..."

"I know what you meant. Thanks." She looked out from the lounge bar, across towards the reception area where Imur and Steph still lingered. "I wanted to ask you something."

Matt leaned forward.

"I..." she hesitated. "Do you think Lucius is the one who's passing information onto Stiller."

The suggestion took Matt by surprise.

Jessica saw the look of disbelief in his eyes and rephrased. "I mean, that's what Kalef thought before..." Her voice tailed off, tears filling her light blue eyes.

"Kalef said that Lucius was the informer?" Matt couldn't believe it.

"Not in so many words, but he told me to be very careful what I said in front of the doctor. He said he'd heard the burr of a mobile coming from the doctor's room the night we were in Port Said."

"But why say now? Why didn't you tell us this when you were practically accused of betraying us in the café north of Axum?"

"Kalef told me not to." Jessica wiped a tear from her cheek.

"He did what?" Why is she telling him this now? His eyes drifted across to the window behind her and to the silhouettes of the Entoto Mountains. Their ghostly shapes merged into the hazy skyline high above the city. "What are you trying to say? It's Friday, and I've got very little time left before..."

"Before what, Matt?"

Matt fidgeted; he had to tell someone else about Jenny and Peter. He had to take the chance that she wouldn't tell Imur. Besides, if she was the mole, she'd know already. "My wife and kid have been threatened," he blurted.

Matt looked into Jessica's eyes for any sign of recognition, any sign that she already knew. But there was none, only a genuine expression of sadness and concern. He knew how to read people. "I've been told by Stiller that they will both die if I don't acquire a sample of the Seed by Sunday, 4 P.M."

"The tomb," said Jessica. "Stiller said that he had someone... So you're telling me that he was referring to your family? I was in pain, no one was listening properly." Jessica looked Matt straight in the eye. "I'm sorry, Matt; you must be totally wound up."

"Like a spring," Matt whispered back.

"But you promised Imur that you'd identify any remaining Eden Seeds then let him destroy them."

"So now you're going to tell Imur," sighed Matt, suddenly doubting his judgement.

"No, no. I don't know what to do. But Stiller is here..."

"And if you'd been able to listen..." Matt corrected himself, "concentrate... you would know that he has a killer waiting to do his dirty work back home."

Jessica sighed deeply. "I never heard..."

"Anyway," continued Matt, "you didn't seem to be too worried about Stiller this morning when you vanished for an hour."

41

JESSICA SCREWED UP her face into an expression of disbelief. "You think I'm the mole, don't you? You all think it."

"Not after what Stiller did to you..." Matt knew, instantly, that he shouldn't have mentioned her disappearance; he'd promised Imur.

"Total and utter crap," she hissed. Jessica was incensed. "I'll tell you what... Let me confess."

"I'm all ears," said Matt. He noticed a group of African businessmen at the bar. One or two of them had seen Jessica and had begun to leer.

Ignoring their licentious stares, Jessica continued, "On our first day in Axum, I was quite jealous when Kalef took you, and not me, inside the church of St. Mary of Zion. I've always wanted to see where the Holy of Holies is kept."

"Allegedly kept," Matt corrected.

"Quite. But to go inside and actually talk to the priest is unheard of."

"So you thought you'd take a look for yourself?" asked Matt.

The Africans in the corner bellowed with laughter.

"Don't mind them," said Matt. "They've probably been away from home for too long."

Jessica pulled the hem of her shorts down and took a step back. "So you were spying on me?"

"It didn't look too good, Jessica, you following us there and then sneaking in after we'd left."

"I didn't follow you there. I went there myself. I thought it might be the last chance I'd get to see the place they kept the Ark."

"And did you?" said Matt.

Still flustered, Jessica replied, "Did I what?"

"See the Ark of the Covenant?"

"Don't be so bloody stupid. Nobody has ever seen the damn thing apart from the priest."

Matt stared into her penetrating blue eyes. "After this morning, Imur suspects you. He thinks it's you who's been passing information on to Stiller."

"Look Matt, I know I shouldn't have gone there on my own without telling anyone, and I realise that I should have admitted where I'd been at breakfast, but how can you sit there and accuse me of spying for Stiller? Especially after what he did to me in the tomb." She glanced down.

Matt felt a mixture of shame and desire. "What did you do in the church?"

"I... I had a look round. But as soon as I approached a red velvet curtain in the corner the little priest appeared and ushered me away. He threatened to call the police unless I left immediately. But I'd been inside. Seen inside the church where the Ark is supposed to be kept."

"You risked your life for a look round a crappy church?"

"I suppose I did, yes," said Jessica.

Matt laughed. "You're off your rocker." He looked at her pale face and saw Jenny for a moment. Her expression was identical to his wife's when they had one of their superficial arguments. Doleful and child-like. It was a face that could dissolve any argument in seconds. The look, its familiarity, was like a kick in the balls and he felt sick.

Jessica put her hands on her hips. "What's wrong?"

Matt switched his gaze to the raucous Africans behind her, who'd been mimicking thrusting movements and other sexual taunts behind her back.

Jessica flicked her hand, waving away the unwanted onlookers "Fuck them."

"I think they've got the wrong end of the stick," said Matt. He took Jessica's hand. "Let's go before they offer you a good price."

"A good price for what?" Her eyes narrowed as she stared over at them. She pulled away and marched over to the Africans at the bar.

Matt whispered as loudly as he could after her, "Jessica, the last thing we need is to draw attention to..."

"Jessica?"

It was Imur.

Jessica stopped a few yards short of the businessmen who were suddenly very preoccupied with their drinks and papers.

"We need to talk, Jessica," said Imur. He'd left Steph in the reception area. "You too, Matt."

Imur led them back from the bar area towards the front door of the hotel and lowered his voice. "Let's not attract unnecessary attention, please." He toyed with his moustache nervously and continued speaking in a whisper. "I've made contact with the Seraphim in Addis. They say that there's been an incident at Axum."

Matt and Jessica both strained to hear the little man.

"It's the priest who guarded the Holy of Holies," he continued, "he's been found lying in St. Mary's of Zion with his throat cut."

"What?" Matt glanced at Jessica then back to Imur.

"Did they take the Ark?" said Jessica.

"No, Jessica. Everything is in place, but it seems that the priest had been tortured. Someone extracted, or at least tried to extract, information from him before slitting the old man's throat. The locals are in an uproar, and they are blaming us."

"What do you mean they're blaming us?" said Matt, suddenly uncomfortable at the stares of the passers-by.

"It happened this morning, early," said Imur looking at Jessica. Jessica shook her head in disbelief. "For God's sake, Imur, you don't think it was me."

"It sounds more like Stiller's handiwork to me," said Matt.

"I agree, but we saw you, Jessica. There, at the church, this morning, and you haven't even admitted it yet."

"She has," said Matt, cautiously. "To me, just a moment ago."

Imur looked at Jessica a held an accusing stare as he said, "We must presume the worst. We must presume that someone has managed to get the truth out of the priest before they killed him."

Jessica was close to tears. "How dare you, Imur? You are the one who begged me to come on this God forsaken rollercoaster ride. How dare you!"

"But you know where our next site is, don't you?" said Imur, his eyes still fixed on her.

Jessica tried to contain herself. "Let's get one thing straight. I have never, unlike both of you, killed anyone in my life. And, yes, I think I know where the next most obvious site might be, but not because I tortured some little priest to get the information. I used my common sense, my brain, and my intuition." She gave Imur a derisory stare. "That's one of the reasons you invited me to come with you in the first place."

"You were at the business meeting in Munich, Jessica; you knew Kalef and he admired your intelligence, your knowledge of archaeology and..." Imur paused, "I thought you were honest, and that your heart was in the right place."

"It was stupid to go to the church alone, I know that now, but as I've told Matt, I only wanted to have one last look before we left."

They walked towards the hotel lifts, passed extravagant displays of lilies and begonias, before Imur produced the piece of parchment that he and Matt had been given by the priest that morning. As the doors of the elevator closed, he handed it to her. "I had to be sure, Jessica. I had to accuse you then look into your soul."

"So, I presume that by giving me this," she flashed the parchment in front of them both, "that my soul passed the test?"

"I need you to translate it for me, Jessica. Although I pray to the Lord for guidance every day, I am no expert at the really ancient texts. Kalef told me that you were his equal in these matters and..." Imur seemed to sadden at the mention of Kalef's name. "He told me that you alone could unravel the ancient text should anything befall him."

As the elevator halted, they slipped out and made for room 105. Before they could knock on the door, however, Steph opened it and ushered them in.

Lucius and Linda were sitting on the bed drinking coffee. The tall Slav pointed to the bags in the corner. "We still have plenty of fire-power; I just need to arrange the flights."

"Good," said Imur. "Let's pray to God that we can go to our next destination undiscovered this time." He looked suspiciously at Linda and Lucius before turning on the lamp at the desk. "Jessica, place the parchment here and tell me what you can."

As Imur, Steph and Jessica gathered round the ancient parchment, Lucius caught Matt's elbow and pulled him down onto the bed. "Matt," he whispered, "I've had enough of this now. We both have."

Linda nodded.

"We have to find a way of contacting Vectan-Brosman. They have to help us. We want no further part in this madness." Lucius clasped Linda's hand. He looked weary and frightened, as though he was about to collapse.

"Of course, Lucius, I agree but you know why I-"

"Matt," Jessica interrupted. "Come and see this, it's absolutely fascinating."

Hesitating for the briefest of moments, Matt got up and walked over from the bed. He bent over the little scrap of yellowed papyrus.

"This text is exactly the same as an ancient type of Assyrian cuneiform text found near Mosul," said Jessica, her left hand pinning the parchment while she scribbled on the hotel notepaper.

"I'm sorry, but I don't follow," said Matt.

Still agitated, Lucius wandered over to join them. Then, with a sigh of resignation, he looked down at the parchment. "Mosul, in Iraq?" he asked.

"Yes," said Jessica. "These glyphs were first unearthed and translated by people like Rawlinson, Agassiz, Layard and Smith in the nineteenth century. The site near Mosul turned out to be the ancient Biblical city of Nineveh. It was there that they unearthed the twelve clay tablets that formed an ancient Babylonian poem that told the story of creation. They were called the Tablets of Gilgamesh."

"You are very well read, Miss Baron," said Lucius, moving a little closer.

Matt eyed Jessica with some suspicion. "How do you know all this stuff? I mean, it's impressive enough being a Chief Justice by the age of..." Matt hesitated, realising that he didn't actually know her age.

"Twenty nine," Jessica muttered, still poring over the text.

Matt flushed. He thought she looked a little older and was now relieved he hadn't guessed.

"I've always studied 'this kind of stuff', as you call it, Matt. My father was Head of Antiquities at the British Museum, which meant that we made the odd trip here and there. And I've been there." She pointed back down at the parchment.

"Where?" said Matt, sheepishly.

Jessica traced her finger over a set of glyphs on the parchment. "Nineveh." Jessica began scribbling even more frantically on the hotel notepaper. "But this is different from anything I've seen in London," she said. "The interesting part is right here." She pointed to a series of scratches on the parchment that meant nothing to Matt or the others. "This relates to the ancient city of Ur." She saw the look of incomprehension on their faces and tried to explain: "Look, a man called Charles Leonard Woolley, and his wife Katherine, went to southern Iraq, to a place called Tell al-Muqayyar. There, they excavated a city called Ur of the Chaldees. Their estimates put it at over 4,800 years old."

"Abraham was born in Ur," interrupted Imur.

Jessica adjusted the desk lamp. "Yes, according to Genesis, the biblical Abraham came from Ur, but this parchment is very strange. It seems to be complimentary to the story of creation, it mentions Gilgamesh and," she closed her eyes and whispered and took a deep breath, "it seems to confirm the existence of the king lists."

Matt could see the excitement building in Imur's eyes.

Linda lay on the bed, her eyes fixed on the ceiling. "Just get to the point."

Jessica threw her a withering glance and continued. "Scholars have never given much credibility to the king lists, both before and after the flood, due to the vast life spans attributed to the earlier rulers. But since the rediscovery of the Eden Seed and the possibility of its effects..."

"Not a possibility, a fact," said Lucius, suddenly more animated.

"...it seems that the written chronology might actually be fact," Jessica finished.

Linda crossed her arms and bounced her left leg on the bed. An annoying squeak filled the room.

Jessica held up the parchment. "It's incredibly specific. It says that the Man of Shuruppak came to rest 2,840 years before the tale of Gilgamesh was written. There is also a detailed picture of a boat and a mountain." She held the delicate sheet in her outstretched hand.

There, on the yellowed papyrus, Matt could now make out the shape of a mountain and an elongated boat.

"Who is the Man of Shuruppak?" asked Lucius.

"You might know him by his other name," said Imur, "Noah."

"So, to sum up, your honour," Linda moaned, "this parchment shows us where Noah's Ark came to rest and..." Linda issued a long yawn, "it even gives us a date?"

"Precisely," snapped Jessica.

"Well, if the Gilgamesh story came from Ur, about 4,800 years ago?" Lucius eyed Jessica, who nodded. "According to my calculations the Ark hit ground just over 7,640 years ago."

"But where is the mountain?" pressed Linda. "Where are we going next?"

All eyes fell on the shapely Linda as she slid off the bed and bent down to open the mini bar.

"I mean, that's what you're eventually going to get to, isn't it Jessica?" Linda snatched a handful of miniatures and dropped them onto the bed.

Jessica closed her eyes, trying to calm herself, and pointed to a set of scratches below the drawing of the mountain. "These are the letters 'rrt'; they usually refer to Urartu or the mountain of Ararat."

Imur nodded to Steph, who slipped out of the room to make the set of calls necessary to facilitate their journey. But as the Slav closed the door behind him, Imur stared at the remaining group members and sat down beside the desk and the parchment. His eyes seemed to glow in the dim light thrown by the desk lamp. Imperiously, he scanned them one by one until his gaze fell on the floor behind them. "I know there is still someone in this group who is passing on information. After the disaster in the tomb and now the death of the priest in Axum, I am convinced that one of you is passing on information. Why you would do this, and for what precise motive... I can only speculate, but I've decided to tighten up security."

42

Everyone glanced at each other suspiciously before refocusing their attention on the demure little man. Imur's voice had gained a sweet but threatening tone. "While you've been getting settled, Steph has removed all your belongings."

There was a murmur of disgruntlement as they noticed that their bags were missing.

"Instead of picking on one particular person," his pupils dilated as he focused on Jessica, "I have taken the liberty of purging all." He began to stand up, but Linda got to her feet first.

"What have you done with my things?" she said, her tone suddenly dark and foreboding.

"We have," Imur hesitated, "made them safe."

Linda looked fit to burst with rage. "How dare you; I had personal jewellery in there that belonged to my mother. Money and..."

"And an Ericsson mobile, which you failed to declare when Miss Baron was accused of spying just north of Axum," he finished.

All eyes now fixed on the teetering Linda Parfait. Even Lucius shook his head in disbelief.

"You bitch," said Jessica, her blue eyes blazing.

Linda paused, momentarily thrown by their looks of loathing. "How... how dare you!" She stormed over to the window and squinted down into the street below. "What have you done with my stuff?"

Imur motioned for calm. "There's no need to panic. All your possessions are quite safe and will be returned to you on the completion of our quest, which, I may remind you, is the positive identification and destruction of the Eden Seed."

"Why do you always call it the bloody Eden Seed?" Linda snapped.

Her sudden interest in the Seed itself seemed to catch Imur by surprise. "It was first grown in the garden of Eden, Miss Parfait," said Imur, his eyes narrowing.

"So you say," hissed Linda.

Matt saw how Linda's temples pulsed, and asked, "Was it you, Linda? Have you been passing information back to Stiller?"

Linda rounded on him until she moved to within an inch of his face. "No, Matthew, I have not."

Matt stepped back and sat down on the bed with a bounce sending Linda's miniatures flying into the air before they landed with a series of clinks on the floor.

Linda made to leave the room but Imur held the key aloft and continued, "Whether or not you are upset by the removal of your personal items, or the fact that suspicion has now fallen on you, Miss Parfait, I care not. My one driving aim is to bring this bloody episode to a conclusion as quickly as possible." Imur's tone quieted. "We've lost too many good men already."

Linda's voice quavered. "If any of you think I would risk Lucius or put you in the kind of danger we've witnessed so far, you must be crazy. Neither Lucius nor I want to be here at all. Just remember, Imur, it was you and your bloody angels that kidnapped Lucius in the first place!" Shaking, she knelt down and scooped up a miniature bottle of brandy, then unscrewed its lid.

The brass handle of the bedroom door clicked as Steph came back in from the hallway. Smiling and holding his mobile tightly in his right hand he nodded at Imur. "I've managed to get us on a flight."

"Good," said Imur.

The tensions of the last few minutes eased a little as Steph explained that it was the only flight going to Yerevan from Addis that whole week and that one of the sect here in the capital had secured them the last six seats.

"Excuse my ignorance," said Linda, "but where exactly is Yerevan?"

"In the circumstances, it might be safer for us all if you just tagged along," said Jessica, a small smile of satisfaction forming on her lips. "Don't get caught up in the details."

Linda ignored her and turned to Lucius. "Well?"

"It's in Armenia, dear. And it's probably the nearest airport to Mount Ararat. That would be right, wouldn't it, Imur?"

"It would," said Imur, moving over to the window to close the curtains. "I would like you all to stay in this room until we leave tomorrow at..." he looked to Steph.

"It's an 8.45 a.m. departure," said Steph, "so let's call it 5 a.m."

"Fine," said Imur. "We should stay put for our own safety. Steph and I will be next door." Imur paused beside Jessica and whispered, "When we get there, no sightseeing this time, Miss Baron."

Jessica formed a disgruntled expression which was almost instantly obliterated by an involuntary yawn. Then after a slow stretch, she resumed her examination of the parchment.

As the door closed shut behind Imur, Matt stood up and walked over to the green crinoline curtains that edged the window. Outside, he saw that the light was fading. Although it had been warm during the day, Jessica said that they could expect frost during the night. Jessica moved away from her notes and opened the curtain a little more. "I spent three days here in 1999," she said. "I was addressing the OAU."

"And what's the OAU when it's at home?" asked Matt, suddenly brightened by the fact that Jessica had moved so close.

"Addis is the headquarters for the Organisation of African Unity. It's the unofficial capital of Africa." She saw that Matt was more interested in the streets below. "That," she pointed beyond a series of red-tiled houses, "is the Mercato. It's the largest open marketplace in Africa. You can buy just about anything from anywhere there."

Matt saw what looked to him like a yellow-painted railway station with an oval garden to the fore. The patch of garden had a statue of the Ethiopian lion in the middle, set high on a stone plinth, and the marketplace teemed with Volkswagen beetles, blue and white minivans and donkey trains.

"So, let me get this straight," he said. "You did a presentation here when you worked for the European Justice Department."

She moved closer. "Yes, that's right. There are more than five million people here and, as I've told you already, this city is packed with history and culture. It will, one day, be the true capital of Africa, in some form or other. I spoke at the University, in the Ethnological Museum. I used Lucy in my presentation."

"'Lucy?' broached Matt.

Jessica smirked. "I know you prefer your ladies to be on the mature side, Matt, but Lucy is..."

"Hardy har, har," said Matt, suddenly remembering a TV article about 'Lucy', a little 3 million-year-old woman unearthed in Ethiopia a good few years before. He noticed that Linda was well into her third brandy and had sprawled back onto the bed beside Lucius. The old doctor seemed to have swallowed quite a few himself, judging by the little pile of whisky bottles on the bedside cabinet.

"So is it just the older type you go for Matt, or will anything do?" said Jessica.

Matt was taken aback by her brashness and smiled as he continued to look across the darkening city. "Look, I could tell you a pile of lies but..."

"Why spoil the habit of a lifetime. Just let them flow..." said Jessica.

Matt flushed, but saw that Jessica had become distracted by Linda picking up the phone beside the bed.

Jessica bristled. "Linda?"

Linda had developed a stupid grin. She shushed Jessica with a heavily ringed finger. "Could I have a bottle of brandy, please?" There was a pause. "Room 105," she said. "Oh," Lucius had nudged her while holding up an empty whisky bottle, "and a bottle of whisky too, please."

Jessica shook her head disdainfully before turning back to face Matt. "Tell me then, Matt Malcolm, what's your angle?"

Matt had never met someone so astute for a long time. She was like a younger version of Jenny, but more confrontational. "Well," he started, "I like women."

"So I was right. If she has a pulse and her own teeth..." She glanced across the room at Linda and corrected herself. "Forget the teeth bit. If she has a pulse, she will do; is that it?"

"The pulse isn't necessary, Jessica. But a rounded figure and a sharp, sexy wit are a definite." He ran his eyes over her and smiled. He had a captive audience and he wanted to see what she would say next.

She said nothing. Instead, to Matt's utter surprise, she touched the back of his wrist and traced her fingers along the back of his hand, until she reached his wedding ring.

"And this?" she whispered.

"This..." Matt looked down at the band of gold that Jenny had bought him in Cancun. "This is a reminder that I'm not perfect."

"You're certainly far from perfect, Matt, but..." Jessica paused for what seemed like five minutes but was probably only five seconds, "I find you interesting."

Matt's heart almost leapt free of his chest. He was completely at a loss. And then something quite unexpected happened... a dark wave of guilt grew inside him. Unbidden, it had come from nowhere and he was beginning to sweat. "I..."

The sound of breaking glass shattered the moment.

"Damn!" Linda clawed at her chest for a second then stood up to go to the bathroom. The aroma of brandy spread over the room as Linda pulled off her jumper.

"I can't quite compete with those," whispered Jessica.

The guilt subsided as Matt watched Linda's breasts bounce as she walked into the bathroom.

"But at least I have my own teeth," she added.

Matt decided to take advantage of Linda's departure by moving his arm round Jessica's slender back and then, still not completely sure she wasn't just teasing him, he dared to pull her in closer. She didn't resist. He looked straight into her eyes. "117 is free."

Jessica opened her mouth a little and gave him a quizzical look, as if she hadn't heard him properly. "We've been told to stay put."

"Ah, I get it," said Matt. "You're only leading me on because you know we can't do anything about it?"

She winked. "I should get back to my parchment. There's a piece missing."

"But..." Matt felt cheated, deflated, frustrated. He didn't know what he felt. Where had that horrible feeling of guilt come from? He'd never really experienced that before. Was it a good thing? Did it mean that Jessica was special, or was it just because Peter and Jenny were in so much danger?

"Where the hell's that porter with the booze?" said Linda, waltzing back into the bedroom wearing no more than a straining white bra and a pair of lace knickers.

Lucius giggled like a child. "Linda..."

"Oh shut up, you know you like it when other men see me in my glory." She winked at Matt and audaciously lowered the left cup of her bra.

"For God's sake, Linda, have some sense of shame," said Jessica.

Her rebuke, however, was lost in a further fit of giggles as Lucius pulled her down onto the bed.

Just then, there was a knock on the door and everyone froze.

"It'll just be the porter," said Linda, hoisting her bra back into place.

Matt felt for the handle of his Beretta. "We don't know that for certain." He moved into the bathroom and, drawing the gun, signalled Linda to open the door.

Jessica slipped the parchment into the drawer of the desk and moved back to the window.

Linda turned the handle and eased the door open.

43

JENNY MALCOLM WATCHED Inspector Watt as he strolled up the driveway. He looked nervous and flustered as he adjusted his tie and flattened his grey hair.

She opened the door. "Inspector."

"Ah, Mrs. Malcolm, I hope you don't mind me just appearing like this but I thought I'd come and give you an update."

"Come in, it's freezing out there." Jenny had hoped he'd come. It had been two days since she'd seen the inspector and she was unsure whether it was the lack of updates or the inspector himself that she'd missed the most. She marched ahead, unplugging the Hoover and winding back the flex. "What's happened now?"

"Well, I've been to Vectan-Brosman's head office and had a chat with a few people in the marketing department. Matt was well liked, although they say he was completely disorganised. Not a detail man." Watt paused. "I'm sad to say, that no one was particularly surprised that Matt was having an affair."

What an odd thing to say, thought Jenny. An ember of rage still glowed inside her, ready to ignite whenever she was reminded of Matt. "So you're telling me, quite undiplomatically, if I may say so, that Matt was a serial shagger," she snapped.

"I'm sorry, I..." Watt was floundering, his mouth half open.

"No... It's me. I'm sorry." Jenny drew in a long breath. "I shouldn't have bitten your face off. Tea?"

Watt shrugged. "Yes, that would be nice, thanks."

She knew Watt was staring at her as she stretched up to lift the kettle down from the cupboard. Her mohair jumper rode up to reveal her midriff.

"I..." Watt cleared his throat. "I didn't get to meet Sir John James." The pitch of his voice lifted a little as she reached back up to get the tea bags.

"Ah, well, not many people get to see the big cheese these days. He's always been hard to pin down. Matt always says that..." She hesitated. She got moments like that, where she totally forgot what had happened that week. For a second or two it was nice to be back where she'd been ignorant and comfortable. But it was only for a second, as inevitably, a dark cloud of depression, like an unwelcome shadow she couldn't shake off, would pour over her and completely douse out any trace of happiness. "Here." Jenny handed Watt his cup.

Their fingers touched.

Watt flushed. "We've found out that Matt's been to Egypt," he continued, almost burning his lips.

"Sounds like fun," said Jenny, facetiously.

"Not exactly. There have been more casualties," said Watt.

Jenny's heart sank as she waited for Watt to explain. *Is he going to tell me that Matt is dead?*

Watt read her expression. "No, not Matt, but his prints were found on one of the weapons."

Jenny was speechless.

"Did he know how to use a gun?" asked Watt.

"You must be joking. Apart from a few company jollies: clay pigeon shooting and..."

"No, no, I just wondered. I told the Chief Inspector that I would ask."

"So who's been killed this time?" said Jenny.

"Three ex-marines and five Egyptians, so far." Watt paused.

Jenny put down her cup and closed her eyes.

"I'm only telling you all this in the hope that it might help," he said.

"Help you or help me?" Jenny had regained her composure. *Watt knew she had no clue about Matt's whereabouts or motives. He just wanted to find a way to see her again,* she decided. *Why should she even consider him? An old inspector, who'd probably never strayed in his life.* She saw him fidget with his notebook nervously. It made her smile. She decided that it was the contrast between Matt and Watt she liked the most.

"I asked you if the updates were for your benefit or mine?" Jenny had seen a blankness fall, like a curtain, over the inspector's features.

Watt put his cup down. "The updates are to help you... help you remember something that might give us a clue to Matt's next move. It might help us both. I get my killer and you get your husband back."

"What? My philandering, disorganised, arsehole of a husband. Why would I want him back?"

Peter walked into the kitchen, his eyes darting between his mother and the inspector.

"Are you okay, son?" said Watt.

"Yes, I suppose. Do you know where my dad is?"

"We're getting there, but no, not exactly. Has he tried to phone you again?"

"I wouldn't know if he had" said Peter, kneeling down to rummage at the back of a cupboard. "The policeman took my phone off me."

"He did what?" said Watt.

Jenny nodded. "That's right; he said it would be easier to get a fix on a possible position if they had it at the station."

Watt looked confused, as if he knew nothing of this at all.

"Is he here now? Can you see the policeman who took your phone?" Watt moved over to the kitchen window. They could just see the nose of the police Mondeo poking across the driveway outside.

"What's wrong?" said Jenny.

"Nothing really."

She knew he was lying.

"I just want to know who took Peter's mobile away; he should have filled out a D11 and given you a receipt." He flicked the net curtain to the side and pointed to the two policemen in the car. "Which one was it?"

Peter peered into the street outside.

Jenny had noticed that the Ford Mondeo had been there for most of the morning. Peter struggled to open a packet of crisps and then stared out of the window. "Neither of those two. This one was thin. You know mum; it was the one with the blonde hair. The one that stinks of smoke."

"Yes, I remember him," said Jenny. She thought it was very unprofessional to reek of tobacco on duty.

Watt's face paled. "Thanks son, I think I know who you mean."

He's lying again, thought Jenny.

"When did he take it?" Watt continued.

"Just this morning, about eleven," said Peter.

"Don't worry, I'll get it back." He began to play with his keys. "Look, Jenny, I mean Mrs. Malcolm, I'd better go."

"But you're hardly in the door." Jenny flushed, almost matching Watt's complexion.

"Sorry, I'll be back soon. I need to get to the station, that's all. I'll phone if I find out anything else."

He has no idea who took Peter's phone. He's trying to cover it up, she decided. Disappointment rose in Jenny's chest. She'd felt safe until now.

As Watt moved over to the patrol car, Jenny could see that he was already speaking into his intercom. She turned to Peter. "Don't worry, your dad is okay."

"You mean the disorganised arsehole?" he whispered.

"Ah," sighed Jenny.

* * *

AS THE BEDROOM door opened, Linda literally squawked with surprise. "Imur?"

Imur, blushing through his sallow skin, looked beyond the half-naked Linda and motioned to Jessica.

Steph, on the other hand, smiled and surveyed Linda with obvious delight.

"Oh don't be so prudish, Imur." Linda beamed. "I was expecting the porter."

"Yes, two men were never going to be enough for Linda, so she ordered a third," said Jessica.

"Don't knock it till you try it, darling," said Linda, arranging herself on the bed like some Rubenesque model.

Matt put the Barretta back into its holster and shook his head. "All these years, Linda, and I thought you were beyond reproach, one of the untouchables."

"I was," she said, slurring slightly.

Imur held up a hand for silence. "There are more pressing matters to address. I think I've found our spy."

Everyone waited to see what Imur would say next. Matt glanced round the room to see who appeared the most uncomfortable.

"Well?" said Linda, impatiently.

Imur put his hand on Matt's shoulders. "It's been Matt all along." "What?" said Matt, speechless for the second time in so many minutes.

"When Steph went through all the bags a second time, he came across your mobile, Matt."

"He couldn't have. I left it in Zurich, under the cushion of a leather sofa in the Café Zusse."

"That's correct. But the two sect members who followed you into the bank across the street from the café retrieved the two phones you placed there: yours and our sadly missed Jimmy Kaminski's. They were packed on the minibus with the luggage the night we fled to the safe house in Genoa."

A darkness threatened to engulf him as he remembered his last conversation he'd had with his son in the Café Zusse. "Well, I didn't know you still had my phone," said Matt.

Imur's forefinger came to rest on his moustache. "Where did you get the phone? Your own, not Jimmy Kaminski's."

"I... it's a company phone." Matt wondered where this was going. "So, Vectan-Brosman issued this phone?" Imur flicked the phone across to Matt who caught it and tried to switch it on. "Yes, but look. It's been dead since Monday night."

"But it's not dead, is it Steph?" said Imur.

Steph edged round Linda's bed and took the phone from Matt. He began to remove the battery.

"As you can see," he held the phone up to the dim bedroom light. "If you remove the battery and then the sticker underneath," he peeled back a white sticker that had several bar codes and numbers on it, "there is a little spy within. Even though your battery is dead, Matt, this..." he picked out a tiny black circular object, "...is always on."

"What is it?" said Jessica.

"It's a bug," said Linda.

"But..." Matt watched intently as Linda sat up on the bed and drained the last of the brandy bottles. "How do you know that, Linda?"

Imur, his gaze fixed on the floor, gestured to Steph. "Please, Miss Parfait."

Steph threw her a towel. "Please, take this, Linda. Imur is uncomfortable with your nakedness."

"Tough!" Linda sat upright so that the towel fell to the ground.

"You knew that Matt's phone was bugged?" said Steph.

Linda looked straight into Steph's dark eyes. "No, Mr. Bashful, Matt is not a Rep."

Matt was now beginning to boil with rage. He remembered how, in Zurich, Linda had told him that the company had known about his affair. He knelt down beside her. "What do you mean by 'not a Rep', Linda?"

"All the Sales Representatives have a tracking device in their phones so we can see exactly where they are at any given time." Linda shrugged at Matt then smiled. "But you should have had a new phone when you were promoted two years ago, Matt."

"How..." Matt was struggling to come to terms with the revelation that Vectan-Brosman would do such a thing. "My phone went on the blink two months ago; this is a Rep's phone."

"Ah, and you forgot to tell me?" said Linda.

"I didn't know I had to," said Matt.

"I would say that every Sales Rep has got an excellent case against the Company. It's a blatant infringement of human rights," said Jessica.

Linda reached down to the floor for a miniature of vodka. "All the multinationals do it, dear. Grow up!"

Matt took his phone from Steph. "If only your two Arab friends had left it where it bloody was, we might not have lost Kalef or..." Matt paused. "Wait a minute. Are you saying that Vectan-Brosman is in league with Stiller?"

Steph had the circular bug on the end of his finger. "This little device has relayed our location back to somebody for the last week.

"How accurate is it?" asked Lucius.

"It gives out a GPS signal to the nearest ten feet," said Steph.

"Jesus." Matt closed his eyes. This had changed everything. Linda stood up. "Let me see it."

Steph, his eyes fixed on her straining bra, reluctantly handed her the bug.

Linda blinked then held it under the desk lamp beside Jessica and Imur. "It's not one of ours."

"And you would know, wouldn't you Linda?" asked Matt, still annoyed at the company's intrusive tactics.

"Yes I would, my dear. Every bug has a code beginning with CV followed by four numbers. This bug has nothing written on it at all."

"Jesus," said Matt.

"Whoever placed it inside Matt's phone will know where we are by now. We will have to move quickly."

"Oh, piss off," said Linda. "Can't we relax for one night?"

"Not unless you want to relax for eternity, Miss Parfait." Imur gave the map to Jessica. "Put this with the parchment. When we get to our next site it would be best if you work with Steph on the exact co-ordinates of the Ark."

Jessica glanced across to Linda. "Better cancel your booze."

Linda clinked the remaining empties off the bed in her direction. "I'm tired," moaned Linda.

"Get dressed, Linda," said Jessica, "we're going."

"What about the bug?" asked Matt.

"Don't worry, it's been deactivated. If any of your Reps want to know how to kill their bug, just tell them to leave it beside a magnet for an hour."

"A magnet?" said Matt.

Deftly, Steph unclipped the front of the television and pulled a small speaker free of its housing. "Most speakers have a magnet powerful enough to degauss this kind of bug."

"Thanks Steph. The first thing I'm going to do when I get back, if I get back, is to send a worldwide e-mail to every bloody Rep on the planet."

Steph opened the bedroom door and ushered everyone out into the lobby. "Follow me."

44

STILLER SMILED AS he drove past the rusting Russian signs on the way to the Addis airport. Toppled in 1991, the old communist regime left its stamp in the form of these fading symbols. 'Workers of the World Unite', the nearest one read. He issued a low growl as he thought of home, his real home where, even now, buildings and statues lay in a similar state of ruin. The 'perfect way' had turned out to be the 'big mistake', and Stiller had become one of its casualties. Yet, he thought, there were still opportunities in the new world. Still a good chance he could use his skills to ensure a wealthy retirement.

Distractedly, he watched as mules, goats and cars all vied for space on the busy highway. It was then, as they swerved round a filthy red bus, that Stiller's eyes narrowed behind his glasses. They were slowing to a halt. Four police cars and a troop carrier were blocking the highway ahead. "Is this normal, Solana?" he asked.

"Sometimes, but it's not good. We should try to find another way round."

He scanned the highway for a side road or a turning place.

"Schmitt, arm yourself." Stiller drew his PP3 pistol.

There was the clicking sound of weapons being primed and magazines being pushed home as Stiller spied a sharp turn to his left. "Hold on."

Barclay slumped down into his seat. "I hope you're as good as you say you are, Stiller. We better not end up in a stinking Ethiopian prison."

Solana spoke. "There's another patrol on this road too. We will have to find a different way."

"There is no other way", said Stiller, his voice deep and threatening.

At a distance of fifteen yards from the block, Solana, Schmitt and Stiller were all ready.

Two men stepped out of the single police car. Dressed in dark green jackets and khaki fatigues, they held their weapons awkwardly.

Stiller tapped Solana on her shoulder. "Use your knife. Schmitt, get the key for the patrol car. I'll begin the contact." As he issued his instructions, Stiller maintained a calm resonance to his voice. The ability to remain focused was imperative.

"We don't have to kill them, Stiller," Barclay whispered, anxiously. But as the policemen waved them to a halt, Stiller positioned his PP3 under his left leg. The end of the barrel sat snugly against the inside panel of the door. He released the safety catch and raised his thigh; just enough to ensure that when he snapped his knee down, the gun would fire.

"Stiller, please!" said Barclay in an urgent whisper.

They came to a halt.

"Where have you come from?" asked the first policeman, no more than eighteen.

Stiller eyed him through his dark glasses, never once taking his hands off of the top of the steering wheel. The last thing he wanted to do was panic them.

"We're on our way to our hotel," he replied. "What seems to be the trouble?"

The older officer ignored Stiller and scanned the Lada. "My colleague asked where you came from, not where you were going." The older officer's voice had gained an imperious tone. He spoke to Stiller in the same way he would have spoken to a small child who'd stopped paying attention in class.

Barclay had received a text one hour before that said: the Imperial Hotel, Eden Street. They had to check it out before reaching the airport.

"Please step out of the car." The younger policeman lifted the tip of his semi-automatic level with Stiller's chest and winked at his older colleague.

Just then the intercom sprang into life inside the patrol car.

Solana listened carefully to the message. "Axum has faxed descriptions of four Europeans for the killing of the priest."

Unaware that anyone in the car could translate, the two policemen undid their safety catches and moved a few feet back from their Lada.

Solana gave Stiller a small nod in the rear mirror just before he checked the trajectory and prepared to fire. With a downward flick of his thigh, the bullet slammed through the door panel and hit the older man in the groin. One second later he pulled the PP3 free and fired his second shot, shattering the younger man's elbow. His gun dropped to the ground at the same moment the older man began to scream.

Solana stepped out of the rear door and threw her knife, a serrated NR 43, which caught the older man in the windpipe and stifled his cry. The younger policeman had urinated in shock, and now stood screaming, clutching his shattered elbow.

Schmitt stepped out of the back door of the Lada, his weasel-faced grin the last thing the young policeman saw before receiving a vicious crack to the face with the butt of Schmitt's AK47. It caved in his left eye and he dropped.

"No point wasting bullets," Schmitt wheezed. He side stepped the fallen rookie and stood on the older policeman's throat to retrieve Solana's knife.

"I don't like loose ends, Schmitt," said Stiller, already dragging the twitching bodies back to their car. "Get the keys."

Schmitt followed Stiller's eyes to the bundle of keys on the sand.

Feeling a slight pulse from the younger policeman, Stiller gripped a tuft of wiry hair, jerking his head forward then to the side. The resulting crack was louder than any of the two shots fired from the PP3. The built in silencer made it no louder than a child's pellet gun.

Barclay retched as the young policeman's deformed head dropped forward onto his uniformed chest at a grotesque angle.

Solana stood guard at the back of the Lada.

"Any witnesses?" asked Stiller.

"A beggar, I'll take care of it," she said, completely unmoved by the two killings.

Stiller smiled and raked his fingers through his long, black hair. "Well trained, Hassan. Well trained, my old friend," he said to himself. His smile flattened, however, as he looked down on the shaking bulk of Barclay hunched in the passenger seat of the Lada.

"Pathetic," mouthed Stiller.

Schmitt grinned.

Stiller checked on Solana, who had almost reached the beggar.

Balanced between a twisted old stick and his undernourished mule, the beggar looked vacantly in the general direction of her footsteps. "Hello? Friend, hello."

Solana drew a second knife from her shirt and stabbed it towards his gaunt, withered face.

But there was no reaction, not even a flinch. She held the tip of the blade a few inches from his eyes, turning it, watching for any sign of fear. Her shoulders dropped and she put her knife back into its sheath. The beggar's hand stretched out towards her and she placed a couple of coins in his trembling hand. "Here, for your mule."

The beggar gave her a toothless grin in reply then gnawed each of the coins in turn, pirate style, before slipping them into his pocket. "God be with you, my dear. And your friends..." He blank stare, unfaltering, remained fixed on some distant, nondescript part of the sky.

Solana stopped dead in her tracks and redrew her knife. "But I am alone, old man," she said, her voice notably more sinister than before.

The old man looked puzzled. "But a woman with such a young voice would not walk these streets alone... surely."

Stiller glanced back at Schmitt. He'd parked the police car at the side of the road and propped the corpses up in their seats. He moved closer to Solana.

She re-sheathed her knife and walked back over to the Lada.

Stiller caught her shoulder as she neared. "Are you sure he's blind?"

"Certain. I checked," she said.

Convinced, Stiller turned back to the Lada. "Barclay? Where are we in relation to their hotel?"

Barclay, still shaking, folded the street map over until he found Eden Street. "Straight ahead, then first left. Why..." His voice was thin. "Why do you enjoy killing so much?"

"It's my job, Barclay, and I like to be the best at what I do, unlike you."

"What do you mean?" said Barclay.

"I mean, you must have fucked up big time to be here in the first place. You never exactly made it to the top of the tree in Vectan-Brosman."

"You don't know the first thing about my job or my life." Barclay's fear still clawed at him. "You're just a hired hand. I have the knowledge that..."

"Knowledge, my ass, Barclay. Malcolm has the knowledge, you're just a fuckin' greedy bastard, the same as me." Stiller made sure everyone was in the car and accelerated.

"Malcolm..." continued Barclay, "Malcolm's just a fast-track fuck up, an embarrassment from day one. He and Schlesinger stumbled on the Seed by mistake and milked it dry." Barclay had turned a deep shade of puce.

"Malcolm's the key," wheezed Schmitt. "In the tomb, the old Arab with the moustache said he didn't know what the Seed looked like. It was to the younger one, Malcolm, that he turned to for confirmation."

Stiller beamed. "So you see, my fat American friend, we know that Malcolm is more crucial than you in this hunt. You're pretty fuckin' useless as far as I can see."

"I know the players," snapped Barclay. "I've just told you where they are now. You know nothing about my life or my expertise in this industry. I know how Malcolm thinks, how they all think. You know nothing except how to kill."

"I arranged your disappearance in Scotland. I had to know everything about your life in order to construct your death. I thought it was particularly self-centred of you to sacrifice your old life for mere money. Your wife, Sandra, was forced to look at that bloated torso and-"

"SHUT UP!" screamed Barclay, sweat glistening on his cheeks.

"We're here," said Solana, peering up at the multi-storey Imperial Hotel.

Stiller followed her gaze. It stood proud against the backdrop of the Mountains. The communist-built hotel seemed shabby and much less grandiose than the four illuminated red stars on its roof implied.

Solana leaned over from the back seat. "Mr. Stiller, the radio in the police car said that someone killed a priest in Axum."

"Mmm..." Stiller stared blankly ahead. "There's every possibility that our mystery American did it. I can't see Malcolm's lot killing a priest unless..." He checked that his PP3 was in place then punched Barclay on the arm. "Come with me."

Barclay flinched.

Stiller turned to face the two in the back seat of the Lada. "Schmitt, cover any other exits that might be to the rear. Solana, stay with the car."

Hauling Barclay out of the passenger seat, he climbed up the ten concrete steps that led to the hotel reception.

Self-consciously, Barclay trundled after him.

Stiller dragged him through the hotel door and pushed him forward towards a startled-looking receptionist. "Describe Malcolm and ask them what rooms they're in. There's no way you're going to get all the easy jobs from now on, Barclay. Now that I've been assigned leader again, I'm going to make sure you have your fair share of shit too."

Barclay turned slowly to face the waiting receptionist.

"Yes, sir?" she prompted. The ebony-skinned receptionist held her smile and straightened the pens on the desk.

"I'm looking for a friend of mine," began Barclay, "a Mr. Matt Malcolm. He would have been with several other people, two women and..."

"Yes Sir, I think they checked out."

Stiller moved in closer and eyed the receptionist. "What were their room numbers?"

The receptionist squinted back at Stiller. "That's not really company policy, sir."

Stiller lowered his dark glasses. "Now, look, you stupid fuck..."

Barclay edged in and slid a hundred dollar bill towards the startled receptionist. "Sorry, it's been a long day."

"Eh, 105, 117 and 119, sir, but they've..."

"Gone?" finished Stiller. "Where have they gone?"

"I don't know," the girl chirped, a more belligerent tone filtering into her voice, "but they didn't even use their rooms. None of the beds were slept in."

"Thanks for your help," said Barclay.

As they moved away from the reception Stiller caught Barclay by the elbow and led him towards the hotel elevators. "Not bad, Barclay."

"See, you don't actually have to kill everyone who pisses you off. There are other ways to get what you want."

Stiller issued a small grunt. "You stick to your ways and I'll stick to mine." He saw that the old brass clock above the doors showed 5:17 P.M. "Let's take a look at their rooms. There might be some clue as to where they were heading next."

After searching 119 and 117 they eventually reached 105. Stiller slipped his credit card between the door and the lock until it clicked open. As the door swung inwards they saw that the desk light was still on. There were indentations in the bed. The curtains were drawn shut and there was a hotel note pad lying on the desk. Stiller held it up to the lamp. "Someone has had the sense to realise that anything they'd written would show. They've torn out a good ten or twelve pages."

It was in the bathroom that Stiller finally hissed a little 'yes' of joy. There, imprinted on the soft toilet paper, someone had left them a message. Stiller unclipped the roll from the holder and took it across to the desk lamp. Carefully, he pulled the paper open and held it up to the light. Barclay watched uneasily, still worried that they might be caught trespassing in the room or that the Seraphim sect had laid a trap.

"Write this down, Barclay," said Stiller.

Listening intently, Barclay scribbled down the letters and numbers. "Yerevan, 8:15."

"Armenia," said Stiller, "and 8:15 must be the time of the flight, though it doesn't say whether that's tonight or tomorrow."

"Let's ask the receptionist again, get her to phone the airport," said Barclay.

As they travelled down in the lift, Stiller eyed the bulky American. "Who's your contact Barclay, the old doctor? His old whore? Or is it the younger one with the firm breasts?" Stiller's thin lips curved sadistically as he thought back to the woman's light blue eyes. He'd enjoyed the way they had widened as he'd dug his nails into her warm flesh.

Barclay shook his head. "I was told I'd get text messages, not notes," he mumbled. "I can't believe it's anyone from Vectan-Brosman. It must be one of the sect."

"Perhaps," said Stiller. "I hope it's Miss Baron. She could come in very useful. Ever killed a woman, Barclay?"

"You're a sick son of a bitch, Stiller," hissed Barclay. "Schmitt told me what you did in the tomb." He sighed and strolled purposely over to the reception once again. "Can you phone the airport for me...?"

On rejoining the Lada, Barclay relayed his findings. He explained that the flight to Yerevan was due to leave on Saturday at 8:15 a.m. Solana suggested that they go to the airport and intercept them there but Barclay reminded them all that there would be no point in intercepting them before Matt Malcolm had identified the Seeds at their next location.

"So who killed the priest in Axum?" she asked.

"I bet the old fuck gave whoever did it the next location," said Schmitt.

"As I said, my money's on the mystery American," said Stiller.

"Pity you didn't think of chatting to the priest," said Barclay, obviously insinuating that the American was more resourceful than him.

Stiller dug his nails into the steering wheel and continued along the main airport road. "Old tombs, churches... Armenia is full of them. I worked there in eighty-two, but I think we're missing something."

"You're missing the significance of Axum," said Solana.

Stiller glanced at his old friend's prodigy for a moment before accelerating. "And what would that be?"

In the back seat, Schmitt's grin grew even wider. He tapped his forehead with his forefinger. "She's good."

"Shut up, weasel," snapped Stiller.

Solana continued. "The old priest guarded the Ark of the Covenant."

"I read about that," said Schmitt.

"Don't tell lies, you can't fuckin' read." Stiller grinned at Schmitt in the rear view mirror, then turned hard left. He could see the flight tower of Addis Ababa airport.

"The point is" continued Solana, "the Ark of the Covenant is probably one of the two most sought-after religious relics in the world."

"So where is the second site?" Barclay enquired.

"Well if they are looking for some ancient variety of Seed and they are going to Armenia, my guess would be the other Ark," said Solana.

"You're telling me that there are two Arks of the Covenant?" said Stiller.

"No Stiller, she's telling you that they are going to the other biblical Ark - Noah's Ark," said Barclay.

Stiller almost veered off the road as he laughed and cursed at Barclay. "The Turkish and Soviet air force have been flying over that area for more than forty years. Don't you think they would have seen a huge lump of wood sticking out of the mountain by now?"

Solana, busy rechecking her ammunition, answered quietly. "Well, the tomb existed. And an Ark of sorts is reputed to lie in the Church of St. Mary of Zion. Who's to say that this Seraphim sect hasn't found the real resting place for Noah's Ark?"

Stiller brought the car to a halt beside a row of dilapidated tenements. He'd parked directly beneath a blinking neon sign that said: The Bliss Bar. As the light flashed red on their faces his mood became sombre. "Do you know where this Ark is, Solana?"

Solana's face looked beautiful in the strange light. "Even in Afghanistan, when I was a child, there were stories told of an Ark on the mountain called Ararat."

"You can see Mount Ararat from Yerevan," said Stiller, "I remember people talking about it now. But it's in Turkey, not Armenia."

"If we could get a flight to Turkey, before they leave for Armenia, and wait near to Ararat, we could follow them then strike once they have found the Seed," said Barclay.

Stiller pushed his fingers through his black hair. "One, they are going to have problems crossing from Armenia into Turkey; two, the Turkish government doesn't just allow anyone to go to Ararat and we are only guessing where they are going. We have no proof."

"Let's take a chance," said Barclay, passing his mobile to Solana. "As you say, Stiller, I'm no longer leader of the group, but it might make some sense to check out the available flights to Northern Turkey tonight. We can't exactly sneak on the same flight as Malcolm and his entourage, unseen."

Reluctantly, Stiller decided that it was probably their best option. "Schmitt, find out if there are any ex-KGB in the region. Solana, forget the airport. We need to hire a private jet, preferably from a private runway. Money is not a concern."

"I wonder where the American is?" said Solana.

Barclay had opened the window of the Lada in the hope of getting better mobile reception. "With any luck, he's already in an Ethiopian jail. I would think the death penalty would be a cert for killing the guardian of the fuckin' Ark of the Covenant."

In Addis, the night air was bitterly cold. Barclay eyed his phone and read out the text. "'No vocal contact, nothing. Do not lose them.' What do you think it means?"

Stiller stretched. "As I said, someone has had the sense to ditch the mobiles. We'll stick with the message left for us in the hotel. Turkey, then Ararat."

45

EVANS HAD JUST eaten two tins of chicken curry and was now busy studying the Russian's face through his binoculars. The red neon light gave Stiller a surreal, ghoulish appearance that caused Evans to retreat a little further into the shadows. He'd followed them all the way to Addis and watched them park outside the Imperial Hotel. It was there that he'd managed to attach the S11b to the side of their Lada. No bigger than a dime, the bug had a range of over two miles and a battery life of a month. It gave him their position on a GPS to within a yard, and its microphone was super-sensitive. This made it useless when the car was moving due to the background noise, but now that they'd parked up, it was as clear as a bell. A small FM radio had been tuned into the bug's frequency.

The girl called Solana spoke again: "Schmitt's got us a plane and it can leave tonight."

"When?" said Stiller.

Schmitt cupped his mobile. "For $30,000 it can have us in Yerevan by 3 a.m."

Evans smiled then called his CIA contact, a man called Briggs. He'd tidied up the mess he'd made in Port Said and supplied him with the weapons and surveillance equipment he'd needed for Ethiopia. Evans would have to ask him for yet another favour.

"Yeah," said Briggs. He sounded less than happy to hear Evans.

"They're going to Armenia and then, I think, on to a mountain in Turkey called Ararat. I'll need transport and new equipment when I get there." Briggs said nothing. "Briggs, can you hear me?"

"What are they after, Evans? What's so important?" Evans said nothing.

"And who killed the priest in Axum?" pressed Briggs. "They're going fucking bugs about that one."

Evans didn't think they'd known about the priest. "I think Malcolm's group is after something like..." Evans paused. He would have to be very careful what he said. "I think it's some kind of document."

"Yeah, right. Look Evans, I don't have authorisation to protect you much longer. The only reason I'm doing this is because you saved my ass thirty years ago and..." now Briggs paused, "we might just get the chance to lock up a cluster of ex-KGB."

Evans knew Burrows would be livid if he revealed anything about the Seed to the CIA, so he phrased the next part carefully. "If I'm right, Briggs, it could be in the U.S. interest to find out what they're really after. Here's the rub. They keep going on about Noah's Ark."

"What?"

"You know - 'the animals went in two by two...'" Evans was embarrassed by the suggestion of the Ark, but he thought it might deflect the CIA from asking any more questions. He wanted the Seed for himself but he also knew that Burrows was on his way and that time was against him.

"Never mind the Ark, who killed the priest?" said Briggs.

"The psycho Russian would be my guess," Evans lied.

"Look, Evans, we know about the Syrian, Imur Falsath, and his little group of weirdos. I want the names of all the other players. You give me something and I'll give you something," said Briggs.

Evans explained that there were four in the group he'd followed: Barclay, an American who'd once worked for Burrows and had recently faked his own death; Stiller, who he presumed to be ex-KGB, an evil son of a bitch; a girl named Solana, seemingly from Afghanistan; and a thin weasel of a man, in his fifties, called Schmitt."

"I have Ark co-ordinates here as: N39 degrees 41' to N39 degrees 44' E44 degrees 15'30" to E44 19'30"; we've had them for some time," Briggs added, indifferently.

Totally dumbfounded, Evans jotted down the information. "You know where Noah's fuckin' Ark is?"

"That's what's on file," said the nonplussed Briggs, "We've been after Stiller for some time so I'm gonna take a chance and get you to the co-ordinates I've just given you, so listen up."

Evans, still keeping an eye and ear on the blue and white Lada across the street, took down all the information before phoning Burrows. He couldn't afford to alienate Burrows yet. There was still a chance that this whole thing was just one big goose chase which meant that he might yet need his job and pension. He cursed himself for not hiving off some of the Seeds he'd destroyed in Spain, or at least thinking of himself before now. But he didn't even know the significance of the crop at the time. He would give the location of the Ark to Burrows and meet him there.

The Lada pulled away from the Bliss Bar, but this time Evans didn't follow; he had the information he needed to get one step ahead. He abandoned the Russian-made motorbike and walked off. Behind him, a pair of tattered curtains swished and flayed pathetically in the bitter breeze.

* * *

THE OLD BEGGAR edged his head above the broken balcony, chipped and strafed with bullet holes. His pock-marked face merged with the run down exterior of the building. He'd heard everything that the American had told his boss, a man called Burrows, but he was extra cautious this time. He'd shadowed the American since he'd left the Church of St. Mary of Zion. He'd watched him cut the old priest down when he hadn't received the information he'd wanted. He'd witnessed the carnage at the roadblock, and had seen how Evans had beamed with a kind of twisted respect as he'd watched the big Russian dispatch the policemen. It was there that the young, beautiful agent they called Solana had almost caught him out. A small silver pendant slipped free from his rags as he leapt down onto the deserted street below. The six-winged seraphim sparkled in the blue shadows.

* * *

MATT WATCHED AS Imur shook hands with the old beggar. He gave Imur a sheet of notes and, to Matt's surprise, a set of co-ordinates. Steph spread out a tired-looking map of North Eastern Turkey. Its edges worn with age, it curled up against Steph's forearm as he held it down for Jessica.

As Imur thanked the old beggar for the use of his house, Matt watched the old man peel off a latex face to reveal a handsome, younger version of Kalef. "This is Sanjef, brother of our dear departed friend, Kalef."

"Welcome to my home, such as it is," said Sanjef, in perfect English, and with the same high-pitched voice as his brother. "I have watched out for you ever since Imur called me to Axum. I just wish he'd called me sooner."

"Yes, I am truly sorry about Kalef," said Imur.

Sanjef bowed his head and sighed. "I can only guess that Kalef would have liked the idea of spending eternity in the true tomb of Sheba. His soul is, without question, at peace with God." Sanjef slipped off his rags and hung them neatly over a tallboy that sat in the corner of his small living room. He glanced through a narrow doorway at Linda and Lucius lying fast asleep on top of his bed and chuckled to himself.

Matt could still smell the sweet scent of stale brandy.

Imur followed Sanjef's gaze. "They are all very tired."

"Indeed," whispered Sanjef, a trace of a smile fading from his lips as he moved over to the desk and the map of Turkey. "As far as I can understand," he explained, "the American works for someone called Burrows, and is in communication with someone who has given him the co-ordinates I've just given to Steph."

"Burrows?" Matt felt his pulse quicken as he thought back to the meeting in Munich.

Imur nodded. "Good work. It will be interesting to see where the co-ordinates lead us."

Sanjef's teeth shone out from his ebony skin and Matt felt a tingle ripple down his spine. The resemblance to Kalef was unnerving. The Ethiopian pressed his fingers together in an arch and said, "Evans mentioned something about Noah's Ark."

"What?" Imur became very agitated for a few moments but then said a small prayer that seemed to calm him down.

Matt pushed forward. "Who is Stiller working for, Sanjef?"

"Sorry, I couldn't get close enough to say."

"No matter... you have done well, Sanjef," said Imur.

Sanjef bowed, retreated a few steps and bit on a smile. "Evans has been listening in on Stiller. He bugged their car when Stiller searched your room at the Imperial Hotel and from what I can gather; he listened in and discovered your next destination."

"How?" said Jessica, suddenly crestfallen. "You took the bugs out of the mobiles."

Imur waved his finger at her and motioned Sanjef to continue.

She gave Imur a withering stare.

"Stiller found something in your hotel room," said Sanjef. "As a result Evans is flying to Northern Turkey."

Jessica reread the co-ordinates. "But how in God's name...?" For a second time, Imur shushed Jessica. "What did he find?"

Seeing Jessica's rage build, Matt touched the back of her hand. "I knew Burrows had to be involved, he had too much to lose."

Jessica eased her hand away from Matt's. "You do realise that by setting your monthly ransom you've probably caused at least a dozen people to be killed so far?"

This wasn't the response Matt had hoped for. She'd turned her anger onto him.

"We've matched the co-ordinates," said Steph. This time Imur stared down at the map.

"They correspond to a region on Mount Ararat." Imur closed his eyes.

"It's a region known as the Black Glacier," continued Steph. "Do you think the Ark is buried there?" said Matt.

"I know it's buried there," he said, becoming more agitated than Matt had ever seen him. "How? Who has this information?"

"The Americans know everything," said Matt, with a laugh in his voice. But his attempt at humour fell on deaf ears. Everyone just stared at him as if he'd just farted at a funeral.

Imur began nodding to himself while tapping the map. "The Ark is still safe."

Matt gazed at the little man and wondered how, if the Americans had the exact co-ordinates.

Imur addressed Jessica, "We've always known it was there, my dear. I believe someone may have guessed its location. It even tells us in the bible that it came to rest on Ararat. What people don't know is why it has never been found."

"Okay..." began Jessica, "Explain. Why has it never been found?"

"It lies under an ancient overhang of granite which in turn is buried beneath a moving glacier that is three hundred feet thick. It is only now, after receiving the second parchment from the priest at Axum, that I think we may have the answer." Imur peered down at the piece of papyrus that lay at the side of the tattered map. The map was of Greater Ararat and Little Ararat, two separate parts of the mountain. "It's all very well guessing the location of the Ark; the real trick is to gain access. That's why we needed the priest's parchment. There is, however, one more problem to overcome."

"What?" asked Matt. He knew the clock was ticking on his family and he didn't want to think that there might be any further delays.

"I can see that the parchment is incomplete but what do you mean, Imur?" pressed Jessica, holding the yellowed paper up to the desk lamp.

Imur let his eyes close in contemplation. "This is only one half of the parchment. To gain access to the Ark, we need to marry this piece to its other half."

"Which is where?" said Matt, sounding more much more desperate than he intended. He could see now, the small serrations on the edge of the parchment that showed where it had been torn in two.

"In Yerevan, of course." Imur opened his eyes and tapped the side of his nose with a wrinkled forefinger. "We are still one step ahead of our enemies."

Jessica rubbed her tired eyes and sat down. "So what you're saying is, that even if Stiller and Burrows get there first, they will be scratching the surface of a three hundred foot glacier without any hope of getting near the Ark itself?"

"Precisely, Miss Baron... precisely. Tomorrow, after we are suitably rested, we will go to Yerevan, as planned, and meet an old friend of mine." Imur traced the contours of his waxed moustache before bowing politely and retiring to a bedroom across the hall from Linda and Lucius.

"Well, that seems straightforward enough," said Matt, with more than a hint of sarcasm. "He hasn't said how we're going to get from Yerevan to Mount Ararat without Stiller or Burrows' henchman intercepting us first; or how, if we even manage to find any samples of the Eden Seed, we can escape the site without being compromised."

"Have faith, my friend," said Steph, "Imur will find a way."

Matt looked up at the clock on the wall. It was five past ten. He wondered how long it would take them to get to Yerevan, find the other part of the parchment and then get to the Ark. How could he possibly save Jenny and Peter? "Steph, have you still got the mobiles? I need to phone home. I need to try."

Steph gave Matt his own mobile. "I need to stay close, check who you are phoning. I'm sorry."

Matt felt awkward. If he let Steph overhear, the sect might realise his full situation. "Look, you dial. My son is called Peter. Here is the number'."

Steph pressed the keys as instructed and then handed Matt the mobile.

It rang three times.

"Hello?" said a voice.

It wasn't Peter. "Who is this?"

In a deep growl, the voice with a thick Glaswegian accent, replied. "This is the man who is going to kill your family when you fail, pal."

Matt felt an emptiness wash over him. He slumped to the floor. "You know something..." the voice continued, "I'm actually looking forward to it." The line went dead.

Matt could see that Steph was concerned about him. He let the mobile fall to the floor. He hadn't been prepared for this. He felt claustrophobic, trapped... It was as if he was in a dark coffin, buried deep beneath the earth and running out of air.

"You okay?"

Matt tired his best to maintain some semblance of control. His vision was blurred, his head was pounding. "Yes, yes," he lied, beads of sweat forming on his brow. Steph glanced at Matt as if to say, 'you don't look it'.

Matt took a deep breath and waved his hands dismissively saying, "It's just marital problems."

Steph looked suspicious, but he nodded, only half convinced, and walked into Imur's room.

Matt glanced up at the clock and did the calculation. He had about fifty hours to get Stiller a sample of the Seed. He should have given the Russian the Seeds from the tomb. The thing that stopped him was Stiller's threat to kill his family no matter what. He had to think of something else, some other way of protecting them. He needed to speak to Lucius.

Jessica's voice made him jump. "If the Ark is safe, the Seeds are safe. Why lead anyone else to a second potential site?" Jessica opened her hands, expecting an answer of some kind.

"Wait a minute, Jessica. He has to get another sample."

"But..." Jessica's look softened.

"My family will be killed if he doesn't. Remember?"

"I'm sorry, Matt. What are you going to do?"

"I don't know yet. I don't know." Like a lead weight, exhaustion gripped him. He had to rest. He had to be ready for tomorrow. He was far too tired to come up with any clever answers for Jessica.

He bedded down in the living room while Jessica, with some reluctance, crawled into a camp bed in the narrow hallway. Imur and Sanjef shared the second bedroom, leaving Linda and Lucius to sleep in what Matt assumed was Sanjef's own double bed.

They were due to rise at 5:30 a.m., but it was still only 3:15 when Matt felt the cover slide off his back. He froze for a second, caught between sleep and consciousness. It was the scent that he recognised first of all. "Linda?"

"Shush, unless you want to get Steph up as well." She put her fore finger to his lips and crawled in beside him, pushing her naked breasts against his bare back.

Matt shuffled away from her. "For God's sake, Linda, what...?"

But she had worked her way down his back and her warm hands were already cupping his genitals. Softly, she caressed and teased him before easing herself down his back. She pulled him over and slipped her warm, moist mouth over his. Sleepily, he gasped as quietly as he could, trying to ease himself away from her wet, persistent grip. I shouldn't be doing this when Jenny and Peter are in danger... He waited for the black cloud of guilt to suffocate his desire, but it never did. All notion of resistance faded, and as his fears ebbed away, Matt was soon drawn into her warm body. As they kissed, he eased himself deeper into her, half-sleeping, yet still on the very brink of abandonment. He began a steady rhythm that soon became his sole purpose, his reason for being.

As her nails dug harder into his back, pain merged with a building sensation of ecstasy. Opening his eyes in an effort to focus on something, anything else, to prolong the absolute pleasure, he gasped.

Matt had to look twice to be sure.

Steph was lying fully awake on his mattress, watching them.

Matt ceased all movement for a second then, as Steph smiled and turned away, he slowly began to move in rhythm again, to get his head back to where it had been moments before. Linda's eyes were closed. She was lying on her back facing the opposite direction of Steph's bed, yet she seemed to sense his hesitation.

Doing his best to ignore the unwanted voyeur, Matt turned her face towards him and kissed her deeply.

She pulled back and giggled, biting down hard on his shoulder. The pain was so intense that he tried to withdraw but she kept him there, deep within her, until he too gasped and relaxed.

Without a word, she rolled free of his bedding and crawled, naked and on all fours, across to Steph.

Flushing with embarrassment Matt watched with a mixture of disgust and excitement as she turned Steph round to face her. Her large breasts hung down, soft and milky white in the dim light. Matt lifted the material of his sleeping bag to his face but he couldn't take his eyes off her. As she bent over to kiss Steph on the lips, his heart raced. He watched her move over Steph's hard, athletic frame, gripping him with her knees before she began to rock. Watching Matt, not Steph, she stared into his eyes, her rhythm steady and forceful until her new mate let out a muffled gasp. Steph closed his eyes and slumped back onto his bedding a wide smile splitting his face.

Matt tensed as she stepped away and then bent down to pick up her robe. She knelt down beside him and whispered, "Enjoy that, Matt?" He felt her warm breasts brush against his skin for a moment, and then she drew back. His eyes grew heavy. Confused, unsure if it had all been a dream, he drifted off into a deep sleep.

46

AT 12 P.M. LOCAL time Matt and the rest of the group arrived at the deserted Erebuni Airport. No words passed between Steph and Matt about the previous night's visitation by Linda. Matt, far too worried, confused, and full of guilt, felt it would be best left that way. Brazenly, Linda had offered them coffee before they'd left for the airport and then, during the flight, had flirted outrageously with Lucius. They'd seen the twin peaks of Mount Ararat as they made their descent onto the Armenian plateau. On the ground, the 17,000 foot mountain completely dominated the horizon. He'd seen the glaciers that had supposedly kept the Ark safe over the millennia and had hoped, prayed that he could still find a way to save his family.

In their Jeep on the way to Yerevan, Sanjef put forward his own ideas about the biblical flood. He gave Matt and Jessica a date for the flood of about five thousand six hundred years B.C. and explained that it had been caused by seismic shifts in the Earth's crust. The Atlantic had apparently poured into the Mediterranean basin between Morocco and present-day Portugal. Sanjef explained that the Mediterranean had been a huge desert at one time and that it had suddenly been drenched by thousands of feet of seawater.

"But I thought God had a hand in all this?" said Linda, more than a hint of sarcasm in her voice.

"Of course he did," said Sanjef, with a wry smile. "I am only explaining the effect, not the cause."

Still trying to imagine the deluge of the Atlantic pouring through the gates of Gibraltar, Matt felt their Jeep surge forward and saw, for the first time, the tower blocks of Yerevan. Covered in winter snow, the rose coloured brick of the Soviet tenements gave the city an unnatural hue.

"They used 'tuf' stone to build these houses," said Imur, suddenly less morose. "The pink rock is quarried close by."

They had left all their arms and possessions behind in Sanjef's flat and were now totally unprotected as they drove into the heart of Yerevan. Matt noticed a sign that said 'Alex Manoogian St' and asked Imur where they were going.

"I know this city well." said Imur. "We will go into the downtown Getron Area, through Republic Square, and then south, into Mashots. It is there that Jessica can help us once more." Imur turned round in his seat to look at Jessica in the back.

"The Matenadaran?" asked Jessica.

"Indeed." Imur flicked some melting snow from his jacket. "The Matenadaran Museum holds some of the worlds' most ancient manuscripts."

"But surely this city isn't very old, Imur," said Lucius.

Matt had been surprised how much Linda had suppressed the old man. He'd hardly said a word to Matt since they'd left Zurich.

Imur answered Lucius politely. "There were only two thousand people living here in 1827, nothing but a collection of mud huts. Now there are over 1.2 million residents. The new city continues to grow as its tourist industry flourishes.

"And before 1827?" Matt enquired, taking in the view.

"Well, there was a much older city here before that. There has been some kind of settlement on this spot since the days of King Argistis, in 782 B.C. The airport where we arrived still carries the name of his fortress, Erebuni."

There was a bump as their Jeep hit a pothole.

Linda knocked her head against the window and lashed out at Imur. "Do we have to listen to all your crap?"

Everyone stared at her for a moment until Matt said, "Do I detect the traces of a hangover, Linda?"

Linda gave Matt a withering glance before snuggling back into Lucius's coat.

Jessica was the first to speak after the outburst. It was more of a whisper directed at Imur, "The wooden tomb you keep under the University Museum in Zurich. Did it come from here?"

Imur smiled to himself but avoided an answer by changing the subject. "I deposited certain parchments here in 1997. It was only then that this city's great library became 'safe'."

Matt wondered if they'd ever get an explanation for the tomb at the Seraphim's headquarters. Imur never failed to avoid any proper discussion on it.

As their Jeep slowed down to accommodate the heavy traffic and another series of potholes, they passed a small coffee house called the Skvoznyachok Café. Briefly, a delicious aroma permeated the Jeep. Imur breathed in deeply. "They make excellent Eastern coffee in there."

It was Saturday morning, and Matt's heart began to race again as he thought of Jenny and Peter. "How long is this going to take, Imur? How long before we get what we need and then reach the Ark?"

Imur saw the concern on Matt's face. "Why do you ask?" Matt hesitated for a second then said, "I miss my family."

The deadline had been set at Sunday, 4 P.M., and Matt couldn't get it out of his mind.

Lucius gave Matt a pat on the shoulder.

Jessica caught Matt's eye and shook her head, mouthing the words, 'they'll be okay'. But Matt remembered the call from the night before and felt his chest tighten. Stiller had someone in place to do his dirty work and Matt had to find a way of stopping him even though he was more than three thousand miles away.

Ahead of them the tree-lined avenue seemed to run into a sheer cliff-face. As they got closer, however, Matt noticed a set of massive doors set into the hillside.

"Why are the doors so big?" asked Lucius. "Are they plated in copper?"

Steph answered, pulling his collar up around his neck, "The whole building is recessed into the hillside and the doors you see are double steel blast doors, designed to protect the collections inside in the event of a nuclear holocaust."

"How ridiculous," said Linda.

Steph shook his head. "It's true, Linda."

"Yeah, right..." she laughed even louder.

"Let's go inside before we run out of luck," said Imur. His voice was full of pent up anger. "Just remember... Stiller may have arrived before us. As for the American..."

"Hopefully he's freezing his ass off on the side of a glacier," said Matt.

"Hopefully," said Imur, his voice brightening. He slid free of the vehicle and continued up the snow-covered steps that led to the main doors. He told Sanjef to stay near the jeep, then continued his commentary. "This place was built between 1945 and 1957. It's one of the more useful Soviet repositories. Many European cities store their valuables and manuscripts here: Vienna, Beirut, Paris and London... They all use the Matenadaran.

Walking through the grand entrance of the Matenadaran they looked in awe at the mosaic of a fierce battle and then at a succession of colourful frescos that lined the stairs.

Their footsteps echoed around the vaulted ceiling but they slowed now and again to examine a carefully-lit manuscript or a beautifully laid out book fixed behind the ubiquitous bullet-proof glass.

Steph let Imur walk ahead before turning to speak to Matt and Jessica. "The true wonders of this great museum lie deep in its armoured cellars."

Jessica told Matt that she'd never visited Armenia before, but explained that she knew of the Matenadaran. "They have the Gospel of Lazarus here," she said, a look of child-like excitement on her face. "It dates back to 887AD. Isn't it amazing to think that we have something much, much older than that here in my pocket?" She traced her moleskin coat with her long, elegant fingers. "I can't wait to see the other half of the parchment."

"Jessica?" It was Imur. He was standing beside a wizened old man who wore a dark uniform. "Please come with me."

"What about the rest of us?" said Matt, all too aware that time was running out.

Seeming to understand Matt's question, the old man, who Matt decided must be some kind of curator, muttered something to Imur.

Imur, his eyes fixed on Matt, called them all forward to another copper-covered door. "The curator has said that we can all go through."

Once inside the door, they wandered through a melee of display cabinets and plinths. Jessica hovered over one of the glass cabinets for a few seconds. A strange manuscript, written on palm leaves in the shape of a fan, had caught her attention. "Ancient Indian?" she suggested. Jessica was obviously frustrated that she was being rushed past such an array of treasures.

Imur let her question go unanswered as he continued to lead them down a long marble hall. This time the door at the end was locked. Stooping, the curator fumbled with a large set of keys that jingled and rattled until he found the right one. With a single click, he pushed open the door and they walked into a circular room with a dull, metal cabinet in the centre. This time it was Imur who removed a key from his inside pocket and counted along a row of small, numbered drawers until he reached the one marked 'twenty-three'. He inserted his key and turned it to the left.

The drawer slid open.

Linda, Lucius, Steph and Matt all gathered round as Imur lifted the parchment free. Jessica produced the other half and laid it beside the new piece. It matched perfectly. While the tension increased and Jessica got to work trying to decipher the ancient text, the old museum attendant backed off into the shadows of the room and made himself scarce. He had been trained to respect the privacy of the paying elite who could afford to store their treasures here.

"It's here," said Jessica. "There's a set of directions on the other parchment that only make sense when the two halves are side by side."

"What does it say," said Imur tentatively.

Matt worried that someone in the room might yet pass any information onto to their enemies. Could one them actually be the 'mole'?

"It says: 'enter the mountain of pain from the green tree'." She looked to Imur for some sign of recognition.

He closed his eyes. "The Turks still call Mount Ararat, Agri Dagi, 'mountain of pain,' but..."

"Then it says: 'the lioness will kiss the doorway to heaven's store'."

"There's the green tree on the other half of the parchment," said Matt. "It's on the mountain. Well, I think it's supposed to be the mountain."

Steph and Jessica moved in closer and agreed that it might be a tree, but then Imur asked where the lioness might be. They studied the other half of the parchment, but could only assume that there would be a carving of a lioness, as there had been in Ethiopia, to mark the way once they got there.

Steph pulled out his modern map and pointed at a village. "Ahora. The village of Ahora is exactly at the spot marked by the green tree," he said.

"Is there anything else, Jessica?" asked Imur.

"There is one more line," said Jessica, ominously. "Under the shield of stone you will remain until time itself stands still." She scribbled every bit of detail into her notebook.

"Is that it?" said Linda, impatiently.

"It seems a little vague," said Lucius.

Matt, still pestered by guilt from the night before, was unable to meet his old friend's stare. "Imur, you said that the Ark is trapped under a wall of granite?"

"That is the story passed down through the legends of India and the Far East. But I'm not sure whether the 'you' in the quote refers to the Ark or the persons who would disturb it."

"Let's hope it's the Ark," said Matt.

Imur thanked the curator and asked him to store the piece of parchment, given to them by the murdered priest, in a different metal cabinet to its matching half. He nodded and afterwards placed his and Imur's key back in his inside pocket.

After leaving the Matenadaran they were all relieved to see Sanjef still waiting for them at the base of the steps. They boarded their dilapidated green Jeep and drove into the centre of Yerevan, past the Opera House and on towards the Republic square. They drove by the Mellat Bank and down into the pre-Soviet area with its wooden balconied mansions until they stopped at a particularly uninspiring mud hovel.

"What now Imur; can't we just travel on to Ararat?" said Linda, sounding more embittered every time she spoke. She gave no hint or sign of the events of the night before, but continued instead to grow more impatient with the whole group. She even snapped at Lucius when he snuggled in too close or moaned about being tired.

Imur said nothing; he simply told Steph to pick up three bags from the mud house. Steph jumped down from the passenger seat next to Sanjef and wandered over to the dwelling. As soon as Steph approached the front door, three bags were placed at the side of the house. Matt watched as an old grey-bearded man slipped back inside and shut the door. Steph shrugged and heaved the heavy canvas bags onto the minibus.

Imur signalled Sanjef to drive on. "Steph, the weapons... make sure that they all work properly. There should also be flares and thermal clothing. Please check."

After rummaging about, Steph answered. "It's all here, Imur. Matt can help me check the weapons." He threw Matt a Beretta with a shoulder rest and told him to practise reloading the magazines.

With Imur's contacts, they soon passed through the area south of Yerevan without any problem and with no sign of anyone following them. They had been told to wait until nightfall before crossing into Turkey, and had been directed to an old farm that straddled the Armenian and Turkish border. They bounced and jolted down a series of muddy tracks that laced an expanse of vineyards. The soil was as black as coal and strewn with ash.

St. Hripsime's Vinery produced some of the best wine in the region and the owner, another seraphim, gave them a meal of freshly baked rosemary bread, olives and some very strong cheese. They drank some of the best red Merlot Matt had ever tasted. He couldn't help thinking about the hours slipping away from him as he ate. It felt, very much, like the last supper, apart from the fact that there were only eight of them at the table, not thirteen. The analogy made even more sense as Matt thought about the Judas in their midst. Had one of them passed on everything to Stiller? Restless, Matt eventually drifted off to sleep wrapped in an old army blanket. He dreamt of Jenny and Peter, and of being attacked by a white dove that pecked and flapped relentlessly around his face.

47

HE WOKE WITH a start, before the rest of them. It was still dark, but there was a hint of dawn in the eastern sky. Linda had supped more than her fair share of wine that night too, and Matt had wondered if he or Steph would get another visitation. But they were all in the same room and even Linda, he decided, wasn't quite that brash. The visitation in Sanjef's flat had puzzled him. Not only did he question Linda's motives, he questioned his own. Was he mad? Did he have to say yes to any female that offered herself to him? But even Steph, Imur's right-hand man, had succumbed.

He also pondered, as he looked round the room, on the whole religious aspect of their journey. He had never given the slightest thought to Noah's Ark or the Ark of the Covenant before this. Apart from the presentation in Munich, where he'd used the odd biblical reference to add a little dramatic effect, he hadn't so much as looked at a prayer book since Sunday School, twenty-seven years before. He saw Imur stir.

What was the strange old cleric up to, he wondered? Jessica was right. Imur was, to all intents and purposes, leading Stiller and Burrows directly to the Eden Seed, yet he had said he was trying to keep them safe.

"We need to move," said Imur.

Steph and the owner of the farm, a man named Molak, were already on their feet by the time Matt slid out from under his covers. He watched as Imur combed his dark hair and checked his moustache in the mirror. Pressing a little wax between his thumb and forefinger, Imur pulled the tips of his moustache down until they were, once more, two perfect, glistening points.

Tracing his own face, Matt felt his rough skin tighten in the cold air. His last shave had been in Port Said.

Imur tapped Jessica on the shoulder. "Time to go, Jessica."

Her blonde hair was untidy and her eyes were still heavy. "Fine, fine. I'm awake," she mumbled.

Matt liked the way she looked first thing in the morning. The confident intelligence that normally exuded from her was toned down, lost in a few confusing minutes while she searched for who she was supposed to be. For those few moments she seemed vulnerable, delicate, even child-like. He caught her eye as she ruffled her hair. He opened his mouth to speak but Imur interrupted. "This door is made from the same type of wood as the Ark - Cyprus Fir." He knocked it loudly with his knuckles. "Let us hope that the Ark is still intact and strong. Matt, you have to identify the Eden Seeds as quickly as you can, then..." Imur turned to see what the commotion was to his left. "Now what?"

Linda and Lucius had sat down to breakfast at the same wooden table they'd eaten from the night before. Dirty dishes and wine bottles littered the tabletop and Linda was moaning about the mess.

Imur raised his hands and addressed the whole room. Steph and Molak stood beside Sanjef. Matt and Jessica sat at the cluttered table beside Linda and Lucius. "God will look after his own today. So have faith. Be sure that no matter what or who may stand in our way, we will succeed."

Matt thought Imur would have made a great CEO. He had a nice blend of charisma and quirkiness. He had presence.

"It's essential that we leave right away," Imur continued. "According to Molak, our host, there are only two hours when the border is unguarded." He checked his watch. "We have 119 minutes to get as close to Ararat as possible before the Turkish Army tries to stop us."

Leaving their battered green Jeep behind, they boarded Molak's black Hummer, already loaded with their bags, and set off down a heavily rutted, snowy track. Now and again they caught a glimpse of Ararat's twin peaks - the highest of which, Greater Ararat, stood out like a pale ghost against the early morning sky.

They journeyed on, without incident, for at least sixty miles before the track split into two beneath the towering peaks. One led east and the other west.

Steph tapped Sanjef on the arm. "Here, Molak said we should take the eastern track. He said that, although the Black Glacier is on the west side of the mountain, we should head towards the village of Ahora on the east."

"That's what the parchment indicated," reminded Jessica, nodding her approval.

Matt, on seeing the sheer mass of the mountain, felt a pang of hopelessness. Even if there was a way through the mountain, it would be a good two miles in length, and, after centuries of earthquakes and glacial shift, he wondered if they would ever find a way through to the Ark.

Jessica seemed to read Matt's thoughts. "It looks a bit daunting from here, but if others, sometime in the future, try and succeed, or merely find the Seeds by mistake, after locating the Ark, our whole struggle so far has been in vain. We have to make sure they are made safe."

"Precisely," said Imur. "I have every confidence that we will make it through."

"I still can't understand how the Americans could know the exact co-ordinates of the Ark," said Matt, almost slipping off his seat as they hit a particularly deep rut in the road. They had begun to climb up the side of the mountain.

Imur spoke to Matt. "We have to assume that they don't know the way through the mountain. There have been expeditions in the past that have returned without any sign of the Ark. By ruling out these areas of the mountain they probably pinpointed the glacier as the most likely spot."

"How are you going to ensure that the Eden Seeds are destroyed if we find any?" said Matt, his stomach tightening as he tried to think of a way of getting a sample out of the mountain, unnoticed by Imur. He saw Lucius's expression, which seemed to say, 'Be careful.' Imur, on the other hand, offered no explanation. Instead, he busied himself chatting to Sanjef in Aramaic.

As they progressed further up the mountain, they could see the glow of fires and lamps flickering in the early morning light. A cluster of shacks littered the hillside in the distance.

Matt wondered if Stiller was already there, waiting for them.

Again, Lucius seemed to sense his concern. "If they're there before us they will either wait out of sight and see what we do, or they will pounce straight away and torture us until we reveal the route to the Ark."

"You really know how to cheer someone up, don't you, Lucius?" moaned Matt.

Imur stopped chatting to Sanjef but had obviously been listening in. "Lucius is right, but we must bear in mind that they may have been delayed or stopped completely from coming any closer to the mountain by the army patrols. This is a sensitive military zone."

"Do you honestly think Stiller would let the Turkish army get in his way?" said Matt, nervously toying with his Beretta.

A disconsolate Lucius slumped back into his leather seat next to Linda.

As the blue dawn edged over the horizon, they parked the Hummer in the village of Ahora and pulled on their rucksacks. Sanjef was going to remain with the vehicle, so he threw the packs to Steph who handed them out. Everyone, even Linda, was expected to carry something.

Their thick, thermal clothing seemed cumbersome as they left the warmth of the Hummer but they soon felt the benefit as the freezing air bit into their faces and dried their nostrils.

A dog barked as they made their way up the main street. No more than a snowy track, it was lined with faded wooden shacks. Smoke wisped upward from the rusting chimneys and yellow lights flickered through the cracks of the shuttered windows.

As the snow crunched beneath their feet, Matt moved closer to Jessica and whispered, "Where are we going? Do you really know what you're looking for?"

Jessica pulled her scarf down a little and said, "We're looking for a green tree."

Matt stared disbelievingly at the sea of snow-dusted conifers that stretched away from them on all sides. "Well, that narrows it down."

"You haven't got a bloody clue, Jessica, have you?" said Linda who, despite her thick clothing, seemed to have overheard Matt's questions.

Ahead of them, Imur and Steph came to a halt. An old woman staggered across the street. She struggled under the weight of a bundle of firewood. On seeing the group, she hesitated, only for the briefest of moments before trundling onward. Her breath seeped up in clouds, into the cold, morning air.

Imur smiled at her and addressed her in Turkish: "Good morning." The old lady stopped this time, tilted her head to one side and said, "Are you looking for the Ark?"

Her reply was in English and blasé, as if she saw a different set of adventurers every week.

"Yes, as a matter of fact we are," said Imur. His moustache had already turned white and the breath escaped from his mouth like a succession of fleeting phantoms.

Matt, slightly embarrassed, hoped he wasn't going to ask her where they might find a green tree.

Imur took the logs from the old woman and helped her across the street. "Have there been any others seeking the Ark? Anyone recently?" The old woman laughed, revealing a set of blackened teeth and shook her head. "It's usually summertime before anyone comes this way. You seek in vain. The Ark is a myth, my friend." She smiled at them one last time before busying herself stacking her logs.

Imur turned back to the rest of the party. "At least we don't seem to have company this time." He scanned the village for a sign, some kind of clue.

Jessica brushed past Matt. "What do you think we should look for, Imur?"

"In the Bible, in the Book of Kings, there is a green tree mentioned, a green bay tree."

"It's an Assyrian reference. I wondered about that," said Jessica. "But it's unlikely you'd get a bay tree growing here and it would never survive all this time. You said that you thought the ark was over seven thousand years old."

"I did not say 'I thought'," Imur clarified, "I said 'I knew'."

Matt rubbed his gloved hands together. "Why don't we look for a tree that could survive over seven thousand years?"

Imur and Jessica looked at him with more than a sense of lassitude.

"Matt's right," said Lucius. "There are examples of Yew trees growing to incredible ages. There's one in Scotland at..." He'd lost the name. His memory was waning.

"Fortingall," said Matt. "My mother took me there once. She said that the tree was over five thousand years old. It was sixteen yards in diameter. She said it was ancient even at the time of Christ's crucifixion."

"Well, if we are to pursue that line, there's one place we could try first." Jessica pointed at the old lady, who'd just finished stacking her logs. "Imur, ask her where the graveyard is."

"The graveyard?" said Matt.

"Yes, even before Christianity there were special burial sites which were marked with Yews. They were supposed to ward off evil." Jessica waved at the old lady and pushed Imur forward.

Imur chatted quietly with the old lady who pointed up the street towards a snow-covered grove on the left. It had a wooden gate with a strange arch, which looked overly elaborate compared to the rest of the village. It had begun to snow again and large clumpy fakes spiralled downwards through the first rays of the morning sun.

Lucius took hold of Linda's hand but she dropped it and folded her arms. "Now where?" she panted, impatiently.

Matt saw the wounded look on his old friend's face and felt another pang of guilt.

"Come on Linda, you can do it," said Lucius, his voice full of encouragement.

"You can always wait with Sanjef in the car if you think you're too old for the climb," said Jessica.

Linda bristled. "Yes, you'd like that, wouldn't you? The last person who waited in the vehicle ended up missing a head!" Linda's voice echoed round the gravestones.

"Shhh, Linda... keep it down," said Jessica.

"Across there, are those Yew trees, Lucius?" asked Matt.

At the far end of the graveyard a group of trees no more than twenty feet high stood out from the rest of the conifers in the clearing. With a darker hue than the other trees their long, fine needles looked familiar.

"Yes, yes..." Lucius trundled towards them.

"What tree do you think we should look at first?" asked Matt.

"It's a single Yew, not a group," said Lucius. "Look how the lower branches have rooted over the years and see how the centre of the trunk has decayed while the outer rim is still intact." Lucius paced across from one side of the trunk to the other. "At least twenty-two yards in diameter."

"Which means?" prompted Linda.

"Which means, my love, that this tree could be the right age." Lucius beamed at Imur.

"Rubbish," said Linda.

Everyone stared at her but Matt knew that she might be right.

Lucius tried to explain. "If the Fortingall tree is sixteen yards in diameter and five thousand years old, this one could be as much as seven thousand years old."

"It's possible," said Imur, his amber eyes wide with excitement. "What was the next part of the text, Jessica?"

Standing just outside the rim of the main trunk, Jessica glanced round the graveyard for a stone slab or a carving that resembled a lioness. "It went on to say," she fumbled with her notebook, "the lioness will kiss the doorway to heaven's store."

Imur told Steph to scour the grove for the shape of a lioness. "It may be carved on a gravestone or..."

"You're looking for a seven thousand year-old gravestone?" Linda's tone was scathing.

As much as Linda's taunts were annoying, there was always a ring of truth to them, thought Matt. Also, Imur seemed to be getting more nervous by the second. He was probably wondering how long they had before Stiller showed up. Matt helped clear snow from the gravestones while Jessica tried to translate the lines another way. But after twenty minutes of searching and further examination of the text, they found nothing that got them any further than a deserted, snow-covered graveyard.

Lucius stepped back into the centre of the collapsed tree trunk and called on Imur. "Come here. Everyone, step inside the old rim of the trunk. Stand beside me and look up the mountain."

Bemused by Lucius's request, Imur then Jessica stepped over the withered bark rim and joined Lucius in the trampled centre.

One at a time, a smile lit up their faces.

"What is it?" said Matt, edging into the circle beside them.

"The lioness is right there." Lucius turned Matt round until he faced the right way.

Formed from the ancient rock of the mountain, the shape of the lioness was unmistakable. Reclining on all fours, in a sphinx-like fashion, the lioness looked exactly like the one they'd seen carved into the rock at the entrance to the tomb of the Queen of Sheba. It was about fifty yards in length and almost a quarter of a mile further up the mountain.

"Where do you think we should go now?" asked Linda, now in awe of the enormous form that loomed before them.

Jessica was whispering the word 'kiss' to herself over and over. "Surely the word kiss must refer to the lion's mouth?" said Matt.

"Let's go and see what we can find." Imur wiped more snow from his eyes and moustache. "It's getting heavier. We should climb up as Matt suggested."

"You know it's amazing; when you move back out from the centre of the Yew it doesn't look like a lioness at all." Lucius pulled Linda in and out of the circle to stress his point.

"Okay, okay, I get it," she snapped at him. Linda had lost her bubbly sense of humour and Steph, normally focused, had taken to peering down towards the village, as if he was expecting someone.

"You've got to stand right in the middle," Lucius repeated.

"Yes, Lucius, we get it," said Linda, impatiently.

"Can you lead us up to the lioness's mouth, Steph?" asked Imur.

"Lucius is right about the formation merging into the side of the mountain when we step out of the centre. It's not going to be easy."

Matt watched as Steph re-entered the circle and trained his binoculars on a dead tree, which looked to be close to the apparent mouth of the lioness.

"It will be better if we ignore the lioness altogether and simply aim for that dead tree." Steph took one last look down into the village of Ahora before setting the pace up the mountain.

* * *

JENNY REMEMBERED the car. A dark, metallic-blue Audi with a large man at the wheel who doodled and chain-smoked each time he parked up. Was this the man who'd taken Peter's mobile? If it was, he'd been in police uniform before and in a police car. She wanted to call Inspector Watt, just to hear his voice more than anything else, but she also wanted to check whether the man in the Audi was one of his officers.

After lunch she looked out again but the car and the big doodler had gone. A sense of growing paranoia and a need for some kind of revenge for Matt's affair pestered her. She knew that her mother would be back from her cruise that night, and, with Peter at the Sunday school trip until half past three, she had the house to herself. She'd fantasised about making love to Watt and part of her knew that she would give him every opportunity to do just that if they were in the house alone together. Her finger hovered over the phone for a few seconds, but then she made a fist with her hand and turned away. I can't, she thought. Peter might come back early and she was delusional if she thought Watt would drop everything and race over to be by her side. He had a wife of his own. She was just as bad as Matt.

Part of her wanted to be.

* * *

AT TWENTY-FIVE minutes past three he would park at the bottom of Willow Terrace. There were several hours before he had to be in position so he checked his watch and then, with his fat nicotine stained fingers, he placed a small satellite messenger device on the dash. It blinked the words: 'ready to receive'. Beside him, on the passenger seat, there was a silver, metal case. He called it 'his box of delights'. He smiled and lit another cigarette.

48

ONCE THEY'D REACHED the dead tree, Steph dropped his pack and walked over to the outcrop of granite that had formed the face and mouth of the lioness. Matt noticed that Jessica had produced her notebook again and was busy poring over the words of the parchment. "A 'kiss'," she muttered, as her eyes met Matt's.

"If you think it will help," said Matt, trying to stifle a smirk.

"Matt, shut up. What's another word for 'kiss'?" she said.

He turned to Lucius, "Why do women do that thing?" Lucius looked bemused.

"You know, when they tell you to shut up then ask you a question."

Lucius was too much out of breath to answer at first, but he smiled and eventually said, "The word 'kiss' can also mean to 'touch lightly'."

"What?" Matt was confused.

Lucius cleared his throat and turned to Jessica. "Perhaps we have to tap something gently."

Imur moved over beside Steph and began searching the rock face for a cave, a hole or a mark of some kind, but there was nothing.

A loud crack of gunfire made them all stop in their tracks and look back down towards the village.

"Stiller?" said Matt, a nervous sweat suddenly causing him to feel uncomfortable.

"It could have been a villager hunting for all we know," said Linda, but no one really took her explanation seriously.

Steph redoubled his efforts and whispered, "All they have to do is follow our footprints. They'll have no need to find a tree or see any lioness."

"Great," sighed Matt. "Here, behind this bush. He flicked the snow from a crooked fir that obscured the rock. "There's a set of three holes here."

"Just like the ones we found in Axum," added Jessica with a smile.

As they gathered round to look, Imur knelt down and took his silver pendant from its chain. The six-winged seraphim sparkled in the morning light as he asked Steph and Matt to remove theirs. Imur carefully placed each of the three figurines into the matching holes and gasped. "They fit perfectly."

Lucius shook his head. "I don't understand how this works. There are only a few grams of silver and..."

"A gentle touch. A kiss..." said Jessica, dreamily. "You said it." Jessica's words were cut short as the sound of stone sliding over stone filled their ears. A huge part of the rock face, which had looked perfectly seamless before, eased apart. Slowly and smoothly, it moved, until an amazing archway covered in letters revealed itself.

"The doorway to heaven's store," said Jessica.

Matt watched as she took a step at a time. She stopped to trace the wedge-shaped text. "It's cuneiform text. It says: 'The Man of Shuruppak has sealed the door to heaven's store', and..." she stopped short.

"What?" said Linda.

"Nothing, I'm not sure what this says." Jessica flushed and gave Imur a withering glance.

He pulled her through the arch.

"Not so quickly!" she protested. Why does everyone always prise me away from this kind of thing? It was the same in the tunnel under Zurich."

"Look Jessica, it's not that we don't want you to have fun, it's just that there's probably a psychopath in hot pursuit," said Matt.

Steph came to Matt's aid. "Jessica, it sounded like a semi-automatic in the village a moment ago. We can't afford to hang around."

Reluctantly, Jessica moved away from the archway and followed the rest. Matt waited for her. "Back at the archway, what did the last part of the text say?"

"I'm not sure but it might have been a curse." "Nice," said Matt. "A nasty one or...?"

"There's not much point in having a curse if it isn't nasty," said Jessica. "We need to get out of here as soon as we can, or we might never get out."

"Suits me, I've only got until four o'clock before Stiller, or whoever's paying him, calls my bluff."

As they wandered further into the smooth-walled tunnel, they left daylight behind them and followed the bright sulphurous fares held by Steph and Imur.

Jessica moved closer to Matt and whispered, "I thought you said the police were protecting your family now?"

"They are, I think," Matt whispered back, suddenly becoming more morose.

"How, in God's name, are they going to know if you've got the Seed today or not? Your mobile's gone and we're inside one of the biggest mountains on the planet." Jessica caught hold of Matt's shoulder and slowed him down. "You want them to catch up with us, don't you? Stiller will kill us."

"No. I... I don't know what I bloody want. All I know is that I don't want my wife and kid to be killed because of me." Matt jerked his shoulder away and continued after the rest of them. Imur and Steph were a good thirty feet ahead by now and the light from their flares wasn't bright enough to see properly. "Let's just see if your Man of Shup..."

"Shuruppak," corrected Jessica.

"Whatever. Let's just see if he's parked his boat in here somewhere." Matt looked back into the blackness from where they'd come. There was no sign of anyone following them. The conversation with Jessica had started his head pounding. She was right. It was probably too late already. A thousand doubts began stabbing into him, each one a hook that caught his flesh and tried to pull him back into the light. He should have phoned the police and told them everything, he should have given the Seed to Stiller straight away back in Sheba's tomb...

The tunnel was quite substantial, roughly ten feet high by about fifteen feet wide, and each step led them deeper into the mountain, further away from any communication with the rest of the world.

They'd walked for about an hour before the tunnel began to widen. Jessica stopped abruptly. "Look." She pointed at another set of markings. Matt saw more of the ancient cuneiform writing and noticed that there were drawings this time too. The outlines of goats, cattle, hens, oxen, donkeys and geese adorned the walls.

"I don't see any elephants or mice," said Linda, trying, as usual, to bait Imur.

"No, but considering there are two million species of coleoptera alone, I don't think you should take the story of Noah's ark quite so literally, my dear." Imur's tone was condescending.

"Beetles, Linda," explained Lucius. "Imur's quite right; it would be nigh impossible to gather an example of every single living creature. There are still millions of species as yet unnamed. Not to mention..."

Lucius fell silent as they turned the next corner. Ahead of them, the tunnel had widened even more. Daylight began to creep along the ochre-painted walls. The more they moved forward, the brighter it became, and soon there was no longer any need for the yellow flares. As the roof space opened up, a blue-green hue began to permeate the tunnel. The strange light dappled the granite floor with circles of emerald and sapphire. It was as if they were standing in the aisle of a giant cathedral, bathed in the light thrown down by a thousand stained-glass windows. It became incredibly cold again and Matt removed his glasses to wipe off the condensation. The pictures that had depicted a huge exodus of creatures disappeared from the cave walls as they moved forward and...

Matt felt his mouth fall open.

It was there.

Resting under a massive overhang of granite and surrounded by a curtain of ice, the structure was completely intact.

Their shrieks of amazement began to fill the enormous cavern. The size of a current-day oil tanker, a huge wooden vessel lay before them. Protected from the elements and the outside world for millennia, it was unmistakably the biblical Ark.

Imur knelt down and prayed to Yahweh, his lord. Steph too, now shaking, joined Imur on the cold granite floor of the cavern.

It was Lucius who spoke first, with reverence, and in a whisper. "450 feet long, 75 feet wide and 45 feet high with three interior decks and," he pointed up at the sloping wooden roof, "there's the window, built into the roof."

Matt turned to his old friend: "How...?"

"You need to read the Bible one day, my friend: Genesis, chapter six, gives a pretty accurate description." The old man was trembling. "I can't believe it's real."

"This has to be the find of the century," said Matt. "It's totally intact. Look at it. It's Noah's Ark!"

Lucius pointed up to the huge overhang of granite. "That's why no ground penetrating radar managed to pick it out. The rock has kept it safe from the glacier as well. Absolutely fantastic!"

Linda had said nothing so far, still mesmerized by the immense structure.

Matt felt a chill of fear slither down his spine as he remembered Jessica's mention of a curse.

As if reading his mind she whispered, "Under the shield of stone you will remain until time itself stands still."

"What?" said Matt.

"The third line of the parchment matched the line at the entrance of the tunnel."

"Yes, well, it was right," said Matt. "It's under a shield of stone."

"It's us," said Jessica.

"Don't get all freaky on us now, Jessica." Matt couldn't understand why Jessica was speaking like some kind of harbinger of doom when the most amazing wonder of the ancient world lay before them.

"The third line says that we will remain here until time itself stands still. Now that we've seen this, I don't think we're going to get out of here. No one is meant to see this. No one." Her face turned grey and she looked close to fainting.

Matt put his arm round her. "It probably doesn't mean that..."

There was a clatter of falling rock behind them in the tunnel. "Quickly!" said Imur. "Let's get inside."

Matt could hear voices now, echoing out from the tunnel behind.

The Ark was flat bottomed but had come to rest at a slight angle, which meant the doorway on the port side was higher off the ground than it should have been. A ramp still hung at a precarious angle from the lip of the door, but the first section was four or five feet away from the ground. They all ran the two hundred yards or so until they reached the ramp in the middle of the Ark.

Steph ushered Linda and Lucius up onto the wooden boards first. It was Imur and Jessica who climbed up next, leaving Matt to scramble up just in front of Steph. Matt turned to help Steph but he was heavier than Matt imagined and he had to ask Imur to come back down the ramp to help him. They heaved Steph and the bags up before clambering through the high open door of the Ark.

As they pulled the bags through the door, two men appeared at the entrance to the cavern.

The first man aimed his gun and fired. The shot splintered the wooden lintel of the door, inches from Matt's head. "Jesus!"

"This is nothing to do with Jesus. Get in!" barked Imur.

Matt knelt down inside the doorway and slipped the Beretta from his pack. Pulling the shoulder-rest free, he aimed and fired. The men, who'd entered the cavern behind them, ducked down behind a rock.

"Who are they?" said Imur. "I don't recognise either of them."

"I couldn't quite see," said Matt, still shaking with the shock of the exchange. He'd managed to crack his glasses, as he'd jumped inside the Ark. "I don't believe it; just when I need them most."

Imur signalled to Steph, "Hold them off. We need to see if there's anything left inside." Lying flat inside the fifteen-foot high door, Steph trained his sights on the rocks at the entrance to the cavern.

Someone tugged Matt's sleeve and led him down another shorter ramp to the thick wooden floor of the Ark.

"Matt, look at this." Lucius beamed. He followed the old doctor and Linda down a flight of stairs to a small balcony that overlooked the deck below. "We're just beneath the main floor. Look, you can see the lower deck from here." Lucius rested his hands on a simple, wooden balustrade, about three feet wide. Able to see fore and aft, there were four rows of enclosures, each stretching the entire four hundred and fifty foot length of the Ark. "Matt, there are more than a hundred enclosures per row. And look at the storage banks." Set into the walls of the lower deck, he could see a myriad of perfectly uniform boxes. Rows and rows of them, perhaps thirty boxes high and as much as two thousand long.

"Maybe he did have insects in here too," said Lucius. "There are tens of thousands of boxes on the lower deck alone. Matt, this is unbelievable."

There was another blast of gunfire.

Imur signalled that they should climb back up the steps to the middle deck. There they saw yet more animal enclosures. These were smaller than the ones on the lower floor and, instead of boxes set into the walls, there were wooden trays stacked all the way along the walls.

"Egg trays?" suggested Matt.

"Could have been for birds or..." Lucius steadied himself. "They must have filled the troughs with rain water from the roof."

Matt looked up and saw the wooden guttering.

Matt saw Linda turn Lucius to face her. "There are people outside firing guns. We need to find the Eden Seed now."

"Yes, yes, but..."

"No Lucius, there's no time," she pressed.

Imur shouted back at them. "Did you check if there are any Seed stores down there?"

"I... I'll go back down and look," said Lucius, a dreamy expression fixed on his face. "Do you realise that this represents the world's first ever gene bank?"

"Matt," pleaded Imur. "Get the professor to focus."

Matt ran back down to the lower floor and gripped his old friend's arm. "Lucius, you need to stay with it. I don't have much time left before..."

Lucius flicked Matt's hand off of his shoulder. "I think they would have kept any seeds or grain on the middle deck. Away from leaks in the hull and away from leaks in the roof. It would also make it easier to feed the bigger animals below."

"Well, what are we waiting for? Let's go and look," said Linda, her teeth beginning to chatter.

Matt flinched. A bullet had splintered through the hull just above his head.

Jessica pushed her hand into the crack revealed by the bullet hole. She licked her fingertips. "You can still taste the bitumen."

"Fascinating," said Linda, sarcastically. "Get looking!"

The trays, the storage vaults, the hatches... they looked everywhere they could think of, but there was nothing.

Dejected, Matt climbed his way back to the balcony that overlooked the lower deck. "The Seeds could be in any one of those boxes down there."

Linda kicked over a small barrel. "We could be here for months looking through all these."

Matt felt an anxiety attack building. His skin burned as a wave of panic swept over him. He gripped onto Jessica. "I'm running out of time. Think, where would you have kept the Seeds?"

There was another burst of gunfire.

"Please," said Imur, his pistol drawn, "We should check as many boxes as we can." He turned to find Steph, who'd now moved further back inside the doorway of the Ark. "Where are they now, Steph?"

Reluctantly, Steph moved forward and squinted out from the doorway. "I'm not too sure. They moved after that last burst of fire."

A horrible knot twisted in Matt's stomach as he watched Linda and Lucius walking along the deck searching for storage cupboards or hatches. "This is no good." He was beginning to lose it.

"Come on, Matt. Help us!" Jessica used a set of ancient sliding ladders that ran on rails for the full length of the ship to look in as many boxes as she could.

"This is pointless," said Matt, peering inside another empty box.

"They might be somewhere else," said Jessica. She moved the ladder on to the next vertical row, pulling open the lower boxes.

"Stop!" said Imur, sweat dripping from his face. "We've lost sight of whoever was firing outside and we're running out of ammunition. I suggest we climb up to the top deck."

"That's it!" said Jessica.

"What's it?" said Linda, her head still stuck inside a hatch in the floor.

"The top deck must have been their living quarters. There's bound to be some kind of galley or kitchen, more storage. Perhaps even some jars or pots..."

Steph appeared beside them. "Imur, I'd rather face them in here. We would only be pinned down if we found the Seed. You get up to the top deck and I'll hit them as soon as they come inside the Ark." Leading the way, Imur slipped on the steep stairway that led upwards.

"Be careful, Imur," said Jessica, her unkempt blonde hair strewn across her face. She caught Matt's hand as, once more, the gunfire erupted from outside. He was beginning to regain his composure.

On the top deck they slumped against the wall to catch their breath and looked around. There were even more animal enclosures but there was also a series of grand cabins, their doors still ajar. Towards the stern of the ship lay the most impressive cabin of them all. There were living rooms, bedrooms and a main hall where tables and chairs littered the floor. A woven crimson rug hung from the wall behind the main chair. Like a throne, it was ornately carved, with double helixes weaving up its legs and over the backrest. The faces of people and animals peeked through the snake-like helixes that wound over the chair, and there was something that looked like a pod or a long decagonal seed, set into the backrest.

"Wait," said Matt. "That shape..."

"It looks very much like a representation of the Eden Seed," said Lucius, moving closer to examine the carving. He traced it with his long fingers and smiled. "I've only seen such craftsmanship in one other place." He looked across at Imur. "I would almost say that this chair was carved by the same master carpenter that carved the seraphim's wings on your mysterious tomb.

Jessica quickly agreed.

They moved closer to the strange throne, their shadows stretching over its surface. A long horizontal window above their heads bathed them in the eerie light that emanated from the glacier outside.

"This ship has been perfectly preserved," said Jessica.

"It's been hermetically sealed inside the mountain," said Lucius, walking over to a large chest that lay behind the throne. He lifted the lid and picked out a small hemp sack, no more than five inches in length, and carefully placed it on the seat of the throne. "This looks promising." Undoing the braid that sealed the sack he put his hand inside and sprinkled the crimson-black seeds over the seat. They matched the shape carved on the backrest exactly.

Matt leaned over, adjusted his glasses, and squinted through the single intact lens. He picked up one of the seeds and held it close. It was shiny and deep red with black lines that ran along its edges. Decagonal in shape, the pod had a row of dark lilac hooks running along each corner. The hooks were still amazingly soft to the touch. Matt remembered the shape and texture of the Seed from before. He looked up at Imur, "This is it." He placed the intricate Seed in Imur's shaking hand. "These are the same as the ones I took from the University Museum. This is-"

"The Eden Seed," whispered Imur, his voice full of wonder.

Behind them, a shout erupted from the doorway of the cabin. "Imur!"

49

THEY ALL TURNED to see Steph standing in the doorway, blood trickling down over his eyes.

"They're on the Ark. I had to pull back."

"How many are there?" Imur snatched the hemp sack from the throne.

"There are two of them, but they're heavily armed and they've got explosives."

* * *

AS EVANS GAINED ground he soon worked out that there was only one man defending the Ark.

"Just blow it," shouted Burrows, reloading. "It will burn and that will be that. No more Seed, no more blackmail!"

Evans, however, wanted the Seed for himself. He wasn't going to burn the only thing that might be his salvation. "We should make sure that they don't have some already. This ship is fuckin' enormous. There might even be another way out."

"Burn it, and bring that overhang down on the bastards. I say what goes down, Evans, not..."

"Shit!" yelled Burrows. A shot had grazed his arm.

"Behind us," snapped Evans, "it's the Russian." Evans pulled Burrows to his feet and ran straight for the cover of the Ark, firing behind him as he went.

* * *

SOLANA KNELT TO take a better shot at the fleeing Americans but as the Ark came into view, her mouth fell open in awe.

"That's the first mistake I've seen you make yet," said Stiller. "Your report card's going to read: 'could do better!'" Stiller pushed her to one side and fired, but the rocks that littered the floor of the cavern sheltered Burrows and Evans.

"I bet that's the American that killed Hassan," said Schmitt, panting as he moved in beside them. "They've made it up the ramp."

Oblivious to the mind-blowing sight of Noah's Ark, Stiller spat out his commands: "Move! Make for the ramp and don't stop firing until I say so!"

Schmitt, Barclay and Solana followed Stiller across the rocky terrain pulverizing the ancient wood that surrounded the main entrance of the Ark.

Stiller was first to reach the ramp. He leapt up and braced, his gun trained on the open door.

* * *

HIGH ON THE top deck, Matt could hear the gunfire below.

Imur steadied Steph and wiped some blood from his face with the edge of his sleeve.

Steph winced, smiled dully, and said, "I would say that all interested parties are now present and correct, sir."

"Indeed." Imur slipped the hemp bag into his inside pocket and followed Steph out of the main cabin. "Everyone, come this way."

As gunfire raged below, they made their way along the top deck.

Linda shouted after Imur. "How are we going to get out of here?"

Imur shouted back at her. "God will show us a way, Miss Parfait. God will show us a way!"

A hatch leading down appeared to their left.

* * *

RACING DOWN TO the bottom deck with its row-upon-row of empty animal pens and endless banks of depositaries, Stiller spied the Americans scrambling up a wall ladder and then through a hatch further along towards the stern. He placed a forefinger over his thin lips then aimed at the roof above his head. As the footsteps grew louder above his head, Stiller nodded sourly, narrowed his hooded eyes and fired.

There was a series of shouts and thumps from the deck above culminating in a blast of return fire.

Below, they all pressed themselves flat against the various pens and waited. There was a scuffling sound, then the clip clop of someone climbing a ladder.

"They must have climbed to the top deck," said Stiller.

Solana went first leaving Stiller, Schmitt and Barclay to follow. But as Solana's head appeared through the opening to the top floor, there was a blast of fire.

Limp and lifeless, her body fell on top of Stiller. He twisted and let her slip down, watching in disbelief as she thumped down at Barclay's feet.

Blood sprayed over the American's shoes.

"For Christ's sake!" screamed Barclay.

Stiller fired upward again, his bullets sending a flurry of timber shards into the upper deck.

Barclay, still staring down at Solana, was frozen to the spot. "She's still alive," he murmured.

"Leave her," whispered Schmitt. He tried to squeeze past. "She's as good as dead, and so are we if we don't move."

"Barclay!" snapped Stiller.

Stiller saw Schmitt shake his head in disgust as urine splashed down the steps at Barclay's feet. "You dirty bastard, Barclay."

Barclay's knuckles whitened as he gripped onto the fifth rung of the ladder. He was shaking violently.

Another burst of fire caused Stiller to slide back down the ladder. He banged into Barclay, knocking him flat on his back. Stooping down, his ghost-like fingers closed round the American's throat. "I'll be back for you, Yankee." Stiller tugged on Schmitt's jacket. "Leave them. Let's find another way up."

* * *

ONCE EVANS HEARD Stiller and Schmitt's footsteps fade below them, he edged over to the stairwell with Burrows to see the damage. He was just about to fire another round when Burrows shouted. "Stop!"

Below him, Barclay, his one-time informant, was trying to pull himself to his feet.

"Well, if it isn't Mr. Barclay... deceased," said Burrows.

Barclay tried to move but he couldn't.

Evans and Burrows both reached down and caught hold of Barclay's chequered collar, heaving him up onto the top deck.

Barclay fell forward onto the cold wooden floor with a sickening thud.

"You've pissed all over the place, Barclay," said Evans, glancing down behind him. "Not a very nice way to treat the Lord's own Ark now, is it?"

Barclay didn't reply.

Evans knew that the shock of conflict combined with seeing Burrows right here in the Ark would be too much for Barclay. Burrows would be the last person on Earth Barclay wanted to meet.

"I guess my sizable payments for spying on Vectan-Brosman weren't enough for you," said Burrows, nervously glancing between the treacherous

American and the dimly lit deck below for any sign of the Russian. "Decide to change sides, did you?"

Barclay was shaking. "I... I thought you wanted to destroy the Seed."

"We thought we had when we burned the crop in Armenia. But just to make sure, in about ten minutes, this whole place is going to blow to smithereens. The Seed, along with anyone left inside, will be history." Burrows laughed at his own joke. "Do you think I want you or any other fucker ever holding me to ransom again?"

Burrows knelt down and pressed the barrel of his gun against Barclay's temple. "You even had your new paymaster stage your death. Now that was impressive."

Evans saw Burrows increase the pressure of the barrel against Barclay's temple.

Barclay began to sob. "That... that..."

"That would have been me," said a familiar voice.

Burrows almost choked with surprise when he realised who it was.

Emerging slowly from the gloom, a tall, stooped figure walked into the light. The Russian, Stiller, and a skinny, weasel-faced accomplice, stood either side of him, their weapons trained and primed.

Evans hesitated, unsure what to do.

Barclay opened his eyes and gasped, "Sir John? Oh, thank God," he panted, obviously panic-stricken. I... I don't understand."

Sir John James, the CEO of Vectan-Brosman, the man who launched Barclay's career in global pharmaceuticals, tapped his dry lips with a long, wrinkled forefinger.

Barclay fell silent.

As Sir John stepped forward, Stiller, without once taking his eyes off Evans, handed the old man a small Luger pistol.

Sir John's sallow skin seemed ghost-like, almost translucent in the dappled gloom. "So, after spying on me for all those years, you got a better offer, Barclay."

Barclay tried to speak: "I never... but-"

"But your new, mystery paymaster paid twice as much, didn't he Barclay? And he was very careful to conceal his identity. Who did you think I was?"

Barclay tried to speak again but Sir John brought the barrel of the Luger to his lips. "Shhh... It doesn't matter now." He shook his head, dolefully. "So, without even knowing who I was, you accepted my offer, had a man killed on your behalf, put your family through hell... and then joined up with my associate here, Mr. Stiller?"

Stiller smiled at Barclay; it was obvious to Evans that the Russian was relishing every minute of the American's discomfort.

At least they had something in common.

Schmitt issued a weasel-like wheeze of laughter, and Sir John adjusted his aim.

"Wait, I can explain," pleaded Barclay, his eyes wide with fear.

With a derisory shake of his head, however, Sir John pulled the trigger, his bullet ripping through Barclay's groin and burying itself in the deck below.

Evans grinned as Barclay screamed and pulled his knees together. Blood poured over his knuckles and seeped out across the dapped deck. Whimpering, pleading helplessly, the big American looked up at his old boss and wailed, "Please, I beg you..."

Sir John lifted his aim. This time the Luger was trained between Barclay's eyes. His forefinger traced the curve of the trigger and tensed. Evans saw Sir John mouth the word 'traitor' before the deck around them seemed to explode.

Bullets cracked into the beams above their heads and tore into the ancient timbers at their feet. Evans dived for cover, pulling Burrows to the floor. "We need to get out of here," he urged, 'before our own explosives catch us out!"

50

HAVING USHERED EVERYONE down from the deck above, Steph and Imur
fired as they moved, pausing every few seconds to locate their targets.

Spying Stiller, Matt fired but missed as, instinctively, the Russian hit the
floor and rolled behind a wooden support.

A tracer bullet whizzed past Matt's head and he too fell flat on the deck,
scrambling for cover.

Stiller's weasel-faced accomplice stepped out of the shadows, his gun
trained on Matt, but Imur fired and caught him in the throat before he could fire.

He staggered back and fell through the open hatch, catching hold of the
body that lay prostrate beside the opening.

There was a scream as the man, obviously still alive, was dragged down
after him. There was a heavy thump below.

"Was that..." Matt's mind was racing. It was very dark but he could have
sworn he recognised the wounded man.

Deciding that Stiller and the others must have found another way down,
Imur dropped through the stairwell, after the wounded man, to the deck below.

Steph and Matt followed.

"Wait!" Sidestepping the bodies that lay at the bottom of the steps, Matt
screwed up his eyes. "Barclay?"

Barclay called out. "Matt... It's you... please..."

The corpse of Stiller's weasel-faced accomplice lay, open-eyed and lifeless,
beneath Matt's old boss.

Another burst of fire made him pull back, away from the stairs. If that had
been Stiller firing, he would have been dead, they all would have been. No, this was
someone else, an older man. Again, there was another flash of recognition, but Matt
discounted it.

Still too exposed, Matt sprinted away from his position and ducked, with
Imur and Steph, behind a wooden support.

Matt was suddenly too frightened to fire, afraid that one of these distant
figures held the key to his family's survival.

"Stop firing!" said a voice full of authority.

Matt recognised the voice instantly.

Matt signaled Imur and Steph to lower their guns.

Through the smoke, like some undead phantom, Sir John James, the CEO of Vectan-Brosman, came into view. Barclay lay in the carnage halfway between them, whimpering like a child.

Matt had to steady himself.

"Matt!" It was Lucius.

The professor, Jessica and Linda must have found another way down. They were somewhere in the darkness behind him and the seraphim. Steph reached back and pulled them out of the line of fire.

Without taking his eyes off of Sir John, Matt reached back and caught hold of Lucius's sleeve. "They're all here. Barclay, Burrows and now..."

"Sir John?" Lucius whispered.

Still too afraid to come out into the open, Matt and the seraphim waited.

"What about the Americans?" shouted Imur.

"They have run off," answered Stiller, "back through the doorway."

Matt didn't like the sound of that. Why would they bolt now?

Imur shouted across the deck, "We will hold our fire as long as you do."

* * *

"MATT!" SIR JOHN'S distinctive voice echoed out over the freezing deck.

All manner of thoughts and theories raced through his mind as he watched Sir John move closer.

He glanced at Imur and saw the outline of the hemp sack beneath his coat. He still had the Eden Seed. Tentatively, he answered, "Sir John?"

Sir John's voice was steady and emotionless. "You did well, Matt. You brought us to the very source of the Seed. Well done. Now all you have to do is hand it over."

Matt stepped out into view, nervously eyeing Stiller. "The Ark is empty, there's nothing left," he lied.

Sir John smiled and shook his head. "I don't believe you, Matt, and I'm willing to make you a bet to prove it."

Matt's heart raced as he tried to figure out who was working for whom and, more importantly, if Jenny and Peter were still safe. He had no idea what time it was.

Sir John carried on talking as the long-haired Stiller fingered the trigger of his Heckler. "Your wife, Jenny, is very disappointed in you, Matt."

Matt couldn't believe it. How could his boss, Sir John, Vectan-Brosman, do this to him?

A sardonic smile had fixed itself on Sir John's face. "Are you willing to risk your family for a few dried out Seeds?"

Matt felt his heart quicken.

Sir John continued, "Your son, Peter, is surely too young to die at the hands of one of Mr. Stiller's associates." He patted Stiller on the back. "You see, there's a certain Scottish gentleman, a man who is very proud of his work - a detail man." Briefly, Sir John looked down at the crumpled, snivelling heap that was Barclay and shook his head. "A loyal man, who will do exactly as he has been instructed." Sir John glanced at his watch.

Matt tensed, his chest almost bursting with frustration and rage.

"Matt, I bet that you can give me a sample of the Seed in the few remaining minutes before I send this GPS signal up through the ice and down to Mr. Kennedy's mobile. He's parked outside your mother-in-law's house right now and it's..." he glanced down at his watch, "almost 3.34 P.M. If he gets no signal from me to say stop, he will happily carry out his instructions." Sir John's tone darkened. "Your time is almost up."

"What is he talking about?" snapped Imur.

Matt looked back and eyed Imur. His left hand was resting protectively on the hemp sack that lay beneath his jacket. "Give it to him, Imur!"

Imur reached inside his coat. "They have your family hostage?"

Steph stayed Imur's hand.

"Steph, no!" Matt was beginning to panic. "They will die if I don't give him the Eden Seed."

Steph, still holding his gun, moved his free hand from Imur to Matt. "Matt, we're under an overhang of granite that must be a hundred feet thick. There's no way he can send any signal, GPS or otherwise, from the Ark."

Sir John cocked his head to one side. "Very well deduced. I'm sorry but I didn't quite get the name?"

"Steph. His name is Steph," said Linda, stepping out from the shadows. She stopped briefly beside Matt, fixed her hair, and then and made her way across the glistening deck towards Sir John.

Matt whispered sharply, "Linda, be careful!"

But Linda, as brazen as ever, kissed the paper-thin skin of Sir John's cheek and took her place beside him.

"I think we may have found our mole," said Imur.

"Linda!" yelled Matt. "What are you doing?" His voice moved from anger to apathy halfway through his question.

"You're quite right about the granite, Steph. That's why I have to send the signal through the glacier," said Sir John. "The signal that tells Kennedy not to kill Matt's family." He sent Linda back across the deck towards Imur. "Bring the sack to me, Linda, and then I can give Matt the GPS device."

Slowly, Stiller raised his aim as Matt urged Steph and Imur to drop theirs. "Give it to her, Imur!" said Matt.

Jessica stepped into the blue light that seeped down from deck above and blocked Linda's path. "You lying, treacherous bitch!"

"It's all about picking the right side," explained Linda, pushing her aside before snatching the hemp bag from Imur with a sharp tug. She hovered, briefly, in-between Steph and Matt. "And..." Linda smiled seductively, her eyes flashing between Matt and Steph, "it's all about having a little fun along the way."

Suddenly incensed, Jessica caught hold of Linda's hair and twisted it round her hand.

Linda screamed as Jessica pulled her round, then down until her back arched.

"Leave her alone!" said Lucius, a look of complete disbelief on his tired face. "Please, there's been enough violence."

Jessica saw the old man's confusion, his pain. She released her grip then pushed Linda away towards Stiller and Sir John. "You're better off without her, Lucius," said Jessica, still shaking.

Unconcerned, Sir John took the hemp sack from the whimpering Linda and tapped it with the GPS device. He looked into Matt's eyes and bit his bottom lip. "I'll just keep this a little longer. My insurance that you'll let us leave in peace."

Matt stepped forward. "You said..."

The whole Ark shook, taking their feet away, as an enormous explosion tore through the hull below them. An intense heat seared their faces as flames licked up from a hole in the floor. The whole structure was ablaze. The ancient crossbeams and supports buckled as smoke poured up from the lower decks.

Matt coughed then opened his eyes to see that Stiller had been caught fast. He was pinned to the deck by a broken beam. The same, massive piece of cedar had fallen directly onto Barclay too, crushing his pelvis flat. Matt could see Barclay's fingers tensing as he screamed in agony.

Matt watched, dreamily as Stiller, trapped fast, twisted in vain in an attempt to escape. Matt tried to remain focused. Barclay had stopped screaming. He lay still. Matt felt a soft hand touch his. "Jessica?" He knelt down and caught hold of her arm. "I think you're okay. Try to stand."

As Jessica got to her feet, there was a deafening creak. The whole Ark pitched several feet to starboard.

"My glasses!" Matt scanned the deck as best he could.

"Here they are." It was Steph.

Lucius and Imur were also beginning to get to their feet. There was no trace of Linda or Sir John and the smoke was getting blacker by the second. They could feel the heat building.

Steph pointed along into the darkness behind them. "There's another way out, down here." Matt could see that Lucius was struggling. "Come on Lucius, you can do it!" As they turned to run, Matt stopped short. He saw it lying on the ground beside Stiller. Sir John had dropped the GPS device. Ignoring the acrid smoke, he darted back and bent over to pick it up.

"Not so fast, Malcolm!" wheezed Stiller, his face drenched in blood.

Only inches away from the Russian, Matt saw that his skin was incredibly pale; his dark eyes, the soulless orbs of a heartless killer, burned into him.

Matt reached down, but Stiller snatched up the GPS with his left hand. "Push this beam off me now!" he ordered. "Or your child will die a painful death. I guarantee it."

Matt brought his foot down hard onto Stiller's wrist and bent down. The Russian's cruel eyes narrowed in pain as he dropped the GPS, but he brought his right hand up in a fist that caught Matt on the side of the head.

Matt saw flashes before his eyes. He staggered back, vomit reaching the back of his throat before he coughed and rolled away from Stiller. Through the pain he felt it in his hand. He had the GPS and something inside him willed him to stay conscious.

Stiller tried to bring his right leg up in a kick, but the weight of the beam kept him at bay so he changed tack. "I'll get the Seeds back for you!"

Matt hesitated for a second then turned back, kneeling down, just out of the Russian's reach. His head was still pounding but he saw the desperation in Stiller's eyes and felt a strange sense of release. "Imur was right, Stiller. He might be a complete nut, but he was right. In the few months since its rediscovery, the Eden Seed has caused nothing but trouble, death and destruction." Matt looked up at the shattered roof of the Ark. "No wonder he wanted to make a fresh start."

"I can save your kid, I..." Stiller's voice was soft, laced with false concern.

"You don't give a fuck about my kid, or anyone else for that matter," said Matt. He moved as close to Stiller as he dared and said, "That's why, considering you're probably just as dangerous as the Eden Seed itself, I think it's best if I just leave you here to burn."

"Malcolm! I'll find you and kill you! I promise!" Stiller screamed and cursed as Matt walked away. Matt only glanced back one more time. The ancient pitch had ignited in the roof above Stiller's head. Bright, burning droplets of fire rained down from the ceiling. Schmitt's body was already burning, silent as the flames began to engulf it.

Matt turned and ran. He had to catch up with the others, escape from the flames.

51

BURROWS AND EVANS had barely cleared the Ark when the explosion ripped through the port side. Showered with debris, Burrows had taken a large splinter through his lower back. It protruded from his abdomen like a bloody red spike. Evans doubled back to support him but he could tell, by the stink of ammonia, that the shard had pierced the old man's bladder and kidneys on its way through. Burrows had turned very white and his voice was becoming weaker. "Get me out of here. Get me to the helicopt..."

"Sure thing, Mr. Burrows. Try not to speak. I've seen worse," Evans lied.

Behind them, the cedar and bitumen that had formed the wondrous structure of the Ark burned furiously. Huge sparks shot across the icy floor of the cavern and soared upward, ricocheting off of the granite overhang. Yellow flames licked the upper windows and had already covered a good portion of the roof. Burrows screamed in agony as Evans tried to move him back towards the tunnel. The old American's face was twisted in pain but his eyes were fixed on the Ark. Evans turned to see what Burrows was looking at. Vectan-Brosman's Sir John James and a white-haired woman staggered down the ramp of the burning Ark. They dropped the four feet onto the floor of the cavern just as a second explosion ripped through the aft section. Barrels of bitumen, stored deep in the hold, crackled in the inferno.

Evans saw the hemp sack in Sir John's hand and dropped Burrows, roughly, onto the ground.

"Evans!" Burrows screamed out. "Come back here right now." But as Burrows tried to kneel up by himself he convulsed in agony and coughed, a mixture of air and blood rushing up his trachea and spattering out through his lips. For a brief moment, he clawed helplessly at the icy floor of the giant cavern and then fell still.

His eyes fixed forward, Evans now walked back towards the Ark and Sir John, his semi-automatic primed. "Drop the sack now!" He had to shout to be heard over the roar of the flames.

Sir John gripped the hemp sack tighter and pulled Linda back. They ran away from Evans and the mouth of the tunnel in the direction of the glacier.

Evans tried to fire but his gun had taken a knock in the blast and it failed. "Fuck!" He saw his abandoned rucksack lying nearer to the Ark; his M-72 rocket launcher was within reach. He threw the launcher over his shoulder and rummaged in the rucksack as he walked on after them.

Linda and Sir John made it past the Ark and were close to the edge of a deep crevasse.

Evans gathered his thoughts. He dug deep into his kit bag. "Yes!" He found his pistol. Kissing the gun, he held it in front of him. Still carrying the heavy M-72 on his back, he moved to the aft of the burning boat.

* * *

MATT WATCHED STEPH take aim with his Beretta but Evans was more than two hundred yards away. If he missed, they might not get a second chance. "I'll go after him," said Steph. "We need to make sure that the Seed is destroyed."

"I'll come too," said Matt, desperation in his voice. "Steph, you need to help me fire this GPS off. My wife and kid-"

"Why didn't you tell us about your family?" snapped Imur.

"Give it to me," growled Steph. He glanced down at the GPS messenger. "There's still no signal. You have to get out from this overhang, get right under the glacier. Come on."

Jessica took Lucius's hand and made to go back towards the tunnel but Lucius pulled free. "I can't believe she's really that bad, Jessica. Not Linda. She's wild, even stubborn, but..."

"Don't be so bloody stupid! She was ready to let us all burn. She doesn't give a shit."

"Jessica's right, Lucius. Please go back to the tunnel with her," pleaded Matt.

Jessica hauled on his arm but Lucius pulled free and, in a daze, wandered after Imur, Matt and Steph.

"Lucius!" Jessica shouted again and again but, still in a state of shock, Lucius made his way alongside the burning hull of the Ark as debris fell all around him.

Matt and Steph began to run and they immediately saw that Imur was struggling. Matt noticed blood on Imur's leg.

"It's nothing," said Imur. "One of Stiller's bullets nicked me, that's all." Impatiently, he waved them on. "Just destroy the Eden Seed and fire the GPS. I'll go with Jessica."

Ahead, Matt could see Evans rounding on Sir John and Linda. Still a hundred yards in front of him, it was becoming obvious that Linda and Sir John had nowhere to go. Behind them, a huge crack in the ice barred their way. The blue-green light that streamed down through the Black Glacier of Mount Ararat was caught in the smoke of the burning Ark. It formed momentary rainbows that flickered then died as acrid black smoke belched through the white mist that was forming in the heat.

Evans knelt to take aim.

"Wait! We can still cut a deal!" shouted Sir John.

"You sound just like Burrows," bellowed Evans. "An egotistical, manipulating bastard who would do anything to save himself. Just give me the Seed or I'll kill you both. That's my deal."

"Look," said Linda, "there are billions of dollars here, in this little bag." She'd taken the hemp sack from Sir John and now held it up for Evans to see. "We know how to get the most out of it. We'll process it and make you a billionaire."

Sir John beamed. "She's right. I know how to extract the substrate. It's useless without us."

"You don't know, do you?" said Sir John, homing in on the opportunity. "Burrows didn't tell you what it does, did he?"

"Tell me what?" snapped Evans.

"These," Linda put her hand inside the hemp sack and pulled out a handful of crimson seeds, "will let you live for a thousand years. No disease, no old age, nothing except time to blow your fortune on whatever you like."

Sir John cut in. "My chemists can take this seed and make it into an elixir of life. You need me, Evans."

* * *

EVEN FROM THIS distance, Matt could tell that Evans was confused. He looked down at the GPS messenger. It had a signal, only two bars, but it might still get through. "Steph," whispered Matt. "The GPS is on!"

"The number's pre-programmed, just hit the send button," Steph whispered back, retraining his Beretta on Evans.

Matt hit the button just as Steph fired.

Evans jerked forward as Steph's bullet ripped through his shoulder. "Arghh!" He tumbled across the icy floor and smacked his face on the launcher as it slid off his back.

Sir John raised his hands in surrender, then hesitated. Linda had crumpled, the crimson seeds spilling from her hand. Steph's shot had passed through the soft tissue of Evans' arm and hit her in the chest. She rolled her grey eyes as she toppled backwards.

Sir John spun in an instant and caught her arm. Linda was dead, but her hand still clutched the hemp bag. She began to slip into the void.

Matt ran forward, adrenalin pumping through his veins. He fired repeatedly at Evans and Sir John, but his aim was wild and most of his bullets just tore holes in the ice. Matt saw Evans lying motionless on top of the ice, blood dripping from his head.

Steph stood over Sir John. He watched the old man struggle, panting as he tried, in vain, to pull Linda's dead weight out of the abyss. "Let her go. She's dead," he panted.

Sir John twisted round enough to look up at Steph. "She has the Seeds. Help me back up!"

Steph reached down and caught hold of Sir John's jacket.

Matt glanced back on hearing Lucius, of all people, shouting out behind him. The whole Ark was ablaze now and clouds of steam and smoke made it difficult to see. Matt pressed the green send button on the GPS once more, just to be sure, then turned to check on Evans. He'd moved, stretched forward.

"Get away from the launcher," screamed Matt.

But before Matt could pull the trigger, Evans swung his good arm up in a fist and caught Matt in the groin. Then he rolled and picked up his launcher.

Lucius, deranged by grief, ran past Matt and Evans in an effort to grab onto Linda's arm.

Steph protested, but as he did, Evans hit him hard with the launcher and kicked the Beretta out of his hand. Matt couldn't believe how quickly it had all gone wrong. Lucius was hauling Linda's body back onto the ice with Sir John and Steph was lying unconscious beside them.

Matt dazed and almost sick with the pain, managed to stand.

Evans and Sir John had rounded on him. "Put the gun down, Matt," said Sir John, resuming his normal dictatorial style.

Just then Lucius caught hold of Sir John's leg.

"Get off me!" Sir John kicked hard but Lucius didn't seem to sense the pain.

With a yell and a jerk of his arm Lucius heaved Sir John back towards the edge of the abyss, causing him to lose his footing.

In a daze, Matt watched as his boss, still clutching the Eden Seeds, flayed backwards into the darkness. Matt heard Sir John scream for several seconds before there was a distant, muffled grunt and then silence.

Evans turned on Matt but Matt fired his Beretta and watched as the American staggered back, past Lucius, into the abyss. He managed to pull the trigger of the M-72 as he fell and the grenade roared over Matt's head.

It zigzagged upwards at an incredible speed, missing the Ark and crashing into the granite overhang that had sheltered the Ark over the millennia.

Lucius, tears streaming down his face, watched with Matt as the whole formation shuddered with the impact. Loud groans and creaking sounds echoed over the blazing Ark. Ear-splitting explosions, that sounded as if the world itself was coming to an end, filled the cavern and caused the edge of the crevasse to collapse in a thunderous torrent that took Lucius and Steph down with it. The old man neither screamed nor protested as the ground beneath him gave way. Kneeling next to the unconscious Steph and still holding Linda's hand Lucius smiled, resigned to his fate, as they all slipped into the darkness.

A crack in the ice saved Matt. He was only feet away from the edge.

Huge boulders were breaking free from the overhang above. They rained on the Ark as Matt dodged and weaved his way back towards the tunnel.

Like a giant dinosaur, its skeletal ribcage revealed, the Ark's main beams, charred and buckling under the intense heat, were now pelted by a torrent of rubble. Three great fissures cut across the overhang as Matt pushed on through the deluge of stone and fire. On and on he ran through what felt like hell itself until he saw the outlines of Imur and Jessica. He ran past Burrows' body, twisted and broken, onwards to the mouth of the tunnel.

He could just make them out through the smoke at the entrance of the tunnel. Jessica was screaming out for him to run faster, but then a massive boulder smashed onto the floor in front of him and exploded like a mortar shell, showering him with fragments, lacerating his hands and his face. With only twenty yards to go the whole overhang split into three huge chunks of rock and collapsed behind him.

Matt staggered forward. He felt as if his heart would burst at any moment. He was choking in the filth and heat. The whole mountain seemed to be crashing down around him. Rolling amongst the clouds of dust and rock, he forced himself into the tunnel, and then curled into a ball. Matt covered his ears until the roar of the mountain subsided.

An eerie silence enveloped him like a shroud. The sheer volume of the destruction must have deafened him.

"Jessica... Imur... are you there?" He could only hear his own voice, muffled and detached inside his head. He was pinned down, his chest burned.

Matt could just see an outline through a crack in the rock.

Jessica's face appeared above his. Tears were streaming down her dust-covered cheeks. Her hands trembled as she wiped her eyes and scanned the floor of the tunnel. "Matt!" Jessica's voice was faint. She dropped to her knees and dug.

He still clutched the small GPS messenger, his thumb squeezed tightly over the send button.

"Matt!" Jessica pulled the rubble away from his arm then heaved the rock away from his chest. With a final effort, he pushed himself out of his shallow grave. His mouth was dry and clogged with dirt. "Jess..." He coughed and felt Imur move beside him. Holding a pen torch, the little man looked like a ghoul as he emerged from the carnage. Matt and Jessica were ok, apart from a few cuts and bruises, but

Imur had lost a lot of blood. His moustache was grey and drooping, his dapper clothes ripped to shreds and covered in grime.

"Let's get out of here," said Matt, glancing down at Imur's watch. It had stopped at 4:05 P.M.

"London time," croaked Imur.

"Please, God, make Jenny and Peter safe."

As they neared the end of the tunnel, above the village of Ahora, daylight streamed along the passage. There was someone waiting at the entranceway. Matt felt for his gun but he'd dropped it during his race across the cavern.

"Imur?" The voice that called out was familiar.

Matt tried to focus, wincing in the bright light. "Sanjef?"

Sanjef ran into the tunnel to help them. "Steady Imur, you've been hit." Sanjef carried Imur the last few yards. The sun was shining over the forest below and the dry, cold air tasted as sweet as wine. "There were a couple of helicopters here until a few moments ago but they've gone now. The locals say that the Turkish Army is on its way."

"Sanjef, do you have a working mobile?" said Matt, panic clawing at his chest.

"I found one in the Hummer, but there's not much power left." He handed it to Matt who dialled his mother-in-law's number. It rang seven times before someone answered, "Hello?"

Matt recognised the voice straight away. "Peter! It's Dad. Are you both okay?"

There was a slight pause before Peter said, "Yeah, of course. When are you coming back?"

"Soon," said Matt, tears rolling down his face. "Soon," he repeated.

"Mum says not to bother bringing any presents back."

"Ah," said Matt.

"You're in trouble," whispered Peter.

"I expect," said Matt again, feeling a mixture of relief and anxiety.

"Dad..." The phone clicked off, the battery dead.

* * *

AT THE END of Willow Terrace, Kennedy snapped shut his box of delights and pulled away in his blue Audi TT. He'd received the depressing message that had said his services would no longer be required at 3.59 P.M.

* * *

"ARE THEY OKAY?" asked Jessica.

"Yeah, thank God," said Matt, touching Jessica's arm.

"We'd better be quick." She walked out into the snow.

Matt followed, glancing at the rock face on his way out. He noticed the three holes in the rock that still held the seraphim pendants. Matt lifted them out one by one; the last had been Steph's. "Imur, we have one spare."

Supported by Sanjef, Imur turned his head back to look at Matt; he was barely conscious. "Jessica has earned it. The Eden Seed is safe now." He coughed.

"Under the shield of stone you will remain until time itself stands still," said Jessica.

Matt handed her the silver seraphim.

Imur smiled at Jessica as the tunnel entrance disappeared. The slab of stone that hid the passageway into the Ark rolled back into place.

As Sanjef lumbered down the snow-strewn track with Imur, Jessica turned to Matt, "What will you do now?" she asked.

"I've got a lot of tidying up to do when I get back," he said, bursting to tell her how he really felt about her.

"And..." she hesitated, catching his sleeve, "and is there anything you would like to tidy up here?"

Covered in dust and soot, they stood above the snow-covered forest. Beyond that, a great plain stretched out before them like a never-ending patchwork quilt of greens and browns, its russet hue eventually merging into the hazy horizon in the distance.

Matt moved closer and felt the warmth of her body against his. "I've been a liar to myself for too long," he said.

She wrapped her arms around him and kissed him on the lips. She looked up into his eyes but there was nothing definite, no clarity. Matt knew she sensed his confusion, his vague uncertainty. He still didn't know what he wanted. It was obvious and she understood.

"Go home and sort yourself out." She sighed. "I'll be in Zurich if you ever need to tidy up some other time."

Matt formed a smile and nodded.

* * *

IN ZURICH, AT the University Museum, a young student had just completed his first exhibit. It showed an Asiatic Python, weaving down the trunk of a twisted acacia tree. Leaves and grasses had been placed strategically to give the appearance of an ancient forest floor.

Deep in amongst the tangled foliage, a few strange, crimson-tinged, decagonal seeds, tipped with violet hooks, hung down through the grasses and ferns.

Referring to the snake in his text as the germ of all evil, the young student had named his exhibit: 'The Eden Seed'.

ABOUT THE AUTHOR

Damian Peck is a pseudonym. The author hails from Loch Lomond where he still lives and writes in various genres. He's toured in rock bands in America and Europe and has worked in the Pharma industry for over twenty five years. He never fails to be intrigued by the hidden weaknesses and strengths in people, the spirit of creation, and the many mysteries of antiquity.

damianpeck@hushmail.com

www.ingramcontent.com/pod-product-compliance
Lightning Source LLC
Chambersburg PA
CBHW020817260626
47169CB00003B/704